THE FIRST OMNI BOOK
OF SCIENCE FICTION

Here are fourteen amazing works of finely crafted science fiction. For an imaginative grasp of man's future—and the kinds of men and women who will live in that future—experience some of the most highly acclaimed science fiction writers of our time, including Isaac Asimov, Greg Bear, Dean Ing, Robert Silverberg, and many others. They'll take you to new dimensions of time and space as they describe both the beauty and terror of all our tomorrows . . . .

THE FIRST
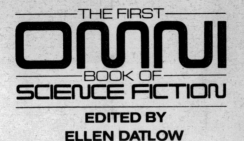
BOOK OF
SCIENCE FICTION

**EDITED BY
ELLEN DATLOW**

**ZEBRA BOOKS
KENSINGTON PUBLISHING CORP.**

ZEBRA BOOKS

are published by

KENSINGTON PUBLISHING CORP.

Omni is a registered trademark of Omni Publications International, Ltd.

THE FIRST
OMNI
BOOK OF
SCIENCE FICTION

CONTENTS

FOREWORD

Omni, first introduced in 1978, is the first magazine that provides science fiction with the forum and the format it deserves. Since its premier issue, OMNI has showcased some of the most entertaining and well-crafted science fiction stories of our times. Just as important, OMNI has brought science fiction to readers who have never read it before. The circulation of OMNI is larger than all the traditional science fiction markets combined, and this anthology is the first time OMNI's fiction has been collected in book form.

All magazines reflect the tastes of their editors. OMNI has had three fiction editors in its first five years of publication, and its fiction has changed over time to mirror those different tastes. Ben Bova, already a noted science fiction writer and the distinguished editor of *Analog* when he joined Bob Guccione's newly-born OMNI, shaped the fiction in the magazine's infancy. Bova's firm grounding in the hard sciences resulted in many stories of a technical nature. Among the best of these is "Found!," written by the inimitable Dr. Asimov, which leads off the anthology. It's a "first contact" story—of a sort. Another, "Sam and the Sudden Blizzard Machine," by Dean Ing, is fast, furious and funny. But Bova's sweep was not limited to hard science, for he also published George R.R. Martin's "Sandkings," a chilling horror story that won top honors in its field in 1979.

When Robert Sheckley took over as fiction editor, he was widely known and loved for his short, compact gems of short stories. His editorial abilities soon took precedent as OMNI moved away from nuts-and-bolts fiction towards the exploration of how technology would affect the future. Epitomizing this more humanistic trend is Orson Scott Card's "St. Amy's Tale," the powerful and moving story of a new religion born out of Earth's ruins, and Tsutsui Tasutaka's "Standing Woman," a tale of technological and political repression.

As fiction editor for over two years, I strive for a balanced variety to OMNI's fiction, but I admit to a penchant for the bizarre. Stories like "Petra" by Greg Bear, about the gargoyles of

Notre Dame coming alive after the death of God, William Gibson's "Burning Chrome," a depiction of a future Los Angels not unlike that visualized in the film *Bladerunner* (although "Burning Chrome" came out first), and Howard Waldrop's lovely, alternate time reverie "Ike At The Mike" all reflect my tastes effectively.

This first OMNI science fiction anthology combines some of the best stories published by each editor. The result is an exciting, thought-provoking introduction to the science fiction of OMNI magazine.

Ellen Datlow
Fiction Editor

THE FIRST
OMNI
BOOK OF
SCIENCE FICTION

FOUND!

By Isaac Asimov

Computer-Two, like the other three that chased each other's tails in orbit round the Earth, was much larger than it had to be.

It might have been one-tenth its diameter and still contained all the volume it needed to store the accumulated and accumulating data to control all space flight.

They needed the extra space, however, so that Joe and I could get inside, if we had to. And we had to.

Computer-Two was perfectly capable of taking care of itself. Ordinarily, that is. It was redundant. It worked everything out three times in parallel and all three programs had to mesh perfectly; all three answers had to match. If they did not, the answer was delayed for nano-seconds while Computer-Two checked itself, found the mal-functioning part and replaced it.

There was no sure way in which ordinary people would know how many times it caught itself. Perhaps never. Perhaps twice a day. Only Computer-Central could measure the time-delay induced by error and only Computer Central knew how many of the component spares had been used as replacements. And Computer-Central never talked about it. The only good public image is perfection.

And it's *been* perfection. Until now, there was never any call for Joe and me.

We're the troubleshooters. We go up there when something really goes wrong; when Computer-Two or one of the others can't correct itself. It's never happened in the five years we've been on the job. It did happen now and again in the early days, but that was before our time.

We keep in practice. Don't get me wrong. There isn't a computer made that Joe and I can't diagnose. Show us the error and we'll show you the malfunction. Or Joe will, anyway. I'm not the kind who sings one's own praises. The record speaks for itself.

Anyway, this time, neither of us could make the diagnosis.

The first thing that happened was that Computer-Two lost internal pressure. That's not unprecedented and it's certainly not fatal. Computer-Two can work in a vacuum after all. An internal atmosphere was established in the old days when it was expected there would be a steady flow of repairmen fiddling with it. And its been kept up out of tradition. Who told you scientists aren't chained by tradition? In their spare time from being scientists, they're human, too.

From the rate of pressure loss, it was deduced that a gravel-sized meteoroid had hit Computer-Two. Its exact radius, mass, and energy were reported by Computer-Two itself, using the rate of pressure loss, and a few other irregularities, as data.

The second thing that happened was the break was not sealed and the atmosphere was not regenerated. After that came errors and they called us in.

It made no sense. Joe let a look of pain cross his homely face and said, "There must be a dozen things out of whack."

Someone at Computer-Central said, "The hunk of gravel ricocheted very likely."

Joe said, "With that energy of entry, it would have passed right through the other side. No ricochets. Besides even with ricochets, I figure it would have had to take some very unlikely strikes."

"Well, then, what do we do?"

Joe looked uncomfortable. I think it was at this point he realized what was coming. He had made it sound peculiar enough to require the trouble-shooters on the spot—and Joe had never been up in space. If he had told me once that his chief reason for taking the job was because it meant he would never have to go up in space, he had told it to me 2^4 times, with $\times$ a pretty high number.

So I said it for him. I said, "We'll have to go

up there."

Joe's only way out would have been to say he didn't think he could handle the job, and I watched his pride slowly come out ahead of his cowardice. Not by much, you understand—by a nose, let's say.

To those of you who haven't been on a spaceship in the last 15 years—and I suppose Joe can't be the only one—let me emphasize that initial acceleration is the only troublesome thing. You can't get away from it, of course.

After that it's nothing, unless you want to count possible boredom. You're just a spectator. The whole thing is automated and computerized. The old romantic days of space pilots are gone totally. I imagine they'll return briefly when our space settlements make the shift to the asteroid belt as they constantly threaten to do—but then only until additional computers are placed in orbit to set up the necessary additional capacity.

Joe held his breath through acceleration, or at least he seemed to. (I must admit I wasn't very comfortable myself. It was only my third trip. I've taken a couple of vacations on Settlement-Rho with my husband, but I'm not exactly a seasoned hand.) After that, he was relieved for a while, but only for a while. He got despondent.

"I hope this thing knows where it's going," he said, pettishly.

I extended my arms forward, palms up, and felt the rest of me sway backward a bit in the zero-gravity field. "You," I said, "are a com-

18

puter specialist. Don't you *know* it knows?''

"Sure, but Computer-Two is off."

"We're not hooked into Computer-Two," I said. "There are three others. And even if only one were left functional, it could handle all the space flights undertaken on an average day."

"All four might go off. If Computer-Two is wrong, what's to stop the rest."

"Then we'll run this thing manually."

"You'll do it, I suppose? You know how—I think not?"

"So they'll talk me in."

"For the love of Eniac," he groaned.

There was no problem, actually. We moved out to Computer-Two as smooth as vacuum and less than two days after take-off, we were placed into a parking orbit not ten meters behind it.

What was not so smooth was that, about 20 hours out, we got the news from Earth that Computer-Three was losing internal pressure. Whatever had hit Computer-Two was going to get the rest, and when all four were out, space flight would grind to a halt. It could be re-organized on a manual basis, surely, but that would take months at a minimum, possibly years, and there would be serious economic dislocation on Earth. Worse yet, several thousand people now out in space would surely die.

It wouldn't bear thinking of and neither Joe nor I talked about it, but it didn't make Joe's disposition sweeter and, let's face it, it didn't make me any happier.

Earth hung over 200,000 kilometers below us,

but Joe wasn't bothered by that. He was concentrating on his tether and checking the cartridge in his reaction-gun. He wanted to make sure he could get to Computer-Two and back again.

You'd been surprised—if you've never tried it—how you can get your space-legs if you absolutely have to. I wouldn't say there was nothing to it and we did waste half the fuel we used, but we finally reached Computer-Two. We hardly made any bump at all, when we struck Computer-Two. (You hear it, of course, even in vacuum, because the vibration travels through the metalloid fabric of your spacesuits—but there was hardly any bump, just a whisper.)

Of course, our contact and the addition of our momentum, altered the orbit of Computer-Two slightly, but tiny expenditures of fuel compensated for that and we didn't have to worry about it. Computer-Two took care of it, for nothing had gone wrong with it, as far as we could tell, that affected any of its external workings.

We went over the outside first, naturally. The chances were pretty overwhelming that a small piece of gravel had whizzed through Computer-Two and left an unmistakable hole. Two of them in all probability; one going in and one coming out.

The chances of that happening are one in two million on any given day—even money that it will happen at least once in six thousand years. It's not likely, but it can, you know. The chances are one in not more than ten billion that, on any one day, it will be struck by a meteoroid large enough to demolish it.

I didn't mention that because Joe might realize that we were exposed to similar odds ourselves. In fact, any given strike on us would do far more damage to our soft and tender bodies than to the stoical and much-enduring machinery of the computer, and I didn't want Joe more nervous than he was.

The thing is, though, it wasn't a meteoroid.

"What's this?" said Joe, finally.

It was a small cylinder stuck to the outer wall of Computer-Two, the first abnormality we had found in its outward appearance. It was about half a centimeter in diameter and perhaps six centimeters long. Just about cigarette-size for any of you who've been caught up in the antique fad of smoking.

We brought out our small flashlights.

I said, "That's not one of the external components."

"It sure isn't," muttered Joe.

There was a faint spiral marking running round the cylinder from one end to the other. Nothing else. For the rest, it was clearly metal, but of an odd, grainy texture—at least to the eye.

Joe said, "It's not tight."

He touched it gently with a fat and gauntleted finger and it gave. Where it had made contact with the surface of Computer-Two it lifted, and our flashes shone down on a visible gap.

"There's the reason gas pressure inside

21

declined to zero,'' I said.

Joe grunted. He pushed a little harder and the cylinder popped away and began to drift. We managed to snare it after a little trouble. Left behind was a perfectly round hole in the skin of Computer-Two, half a centimeter across.

Joe said, ''This thing, whatever it is, isn't much more than foil.''

It gave easily under his fingers, thin but springy. A little extra pressure and it dented. He put it inside his pouch, which he snapped shut and said, ''Go over the outside and see if there are any other items like that on it. I'll go inside.''

It didn't take me very long. Then I went in. ''It's clean,'' I said. ''That's the only thing there is. The only hole.''

''One is enough,'' said Joe, gloomily. He looked at the smooth aluminum of the wall and, in the light of the flash, the perfect circle of black was beautifully evident.

It wasn't difficult to place a seal over the hole. It was a little more difficult to reconstitute the atmosphere. Computer-Two's reserve gas-forming supplies were low and the controls required manual adjustment. The solar generator was limping but we managed to get the lights on.

Eventually, we removed our gauntlets and helmet, but Joe carefully placed the gauntlets inside his helmet and secured them both to one of his suit-loops.

''I want these handy if the air-pressure begins to drop,'' he said, sourly.

So I did the same.

There was a mark on the wall just next to the hole. I had noted in the light of my flash when I was adjusting the seal. When the lights came on, it was obvious.

"You notice that, Joe?" I said.

"I notice."

There was a slight, narrow depression in the wall, not very noticeable at all, but there beyond a doubt if you ran your finger over it. It could be noticed for nearly a meter. It was as though someone had scooped out a very shallow sampling of the metal so that the surface was distinctly less smooth than elsewhere.

I said, "We'd better call Computer-Central downstairs."

"If you mean back on Earth, say so," said Joe. "I hate the phony space-talk. In fact, I hate everything about space. That's why I took an Earth-side job—I mean a job on Earth—or what was supposed to be one."

I said patiently, "We'd better call Computer-Central back on Earth."

"What for?"

"To tell them we've found the trouble."

"Oh? What did we find?"

"The hole. Remember?"

"Oddly enough, I do. And what caused the hole? It wasn't a meteoroid. I never saw one that would leave a perfectly circular hole with no signs of buckling or melting. And I never saw one that left a cylinder behind." He took the cylinder out of his suit pocket and smoothed the dent out of its thin metal, thoughtfully.

"Well, what caused the hole?"

I didn't hesitate. I said, "I don't know."

"If we report to Computer-Central, they'll ask the question and we'll say we don't know and what will we have gained? Except hassle?"

"They'll call us, Joe, if we don't call them."

"Sure. And we won't answer, will we?"

"They'll assume something killed us, Joe, and they'll send up a relief party."

"You know Computer-Central. It will take them two days to decide on that. We'll have something before then and once we have something, we'll call them."

The internal structure of Computer-Two was not *really* designed for human occupancy. What was foreseen was the occasional and temporary presence of trouble-shooters. That meant there needed to be room for maneuvering, and there were tools and supplies.

There weren't any armchairs, though. For that matter, there was no gravitational field, either, or any centrifugal imitation of one.

We both floated in mid-air, drifting slowly this way or that. Occasionally, one of us touched the wall and gently rebounded. Or else part of one of us overlapped part of the other.

"Keep your foot out of my mouth," said Joe, and pushed it away violently. It was a mistake because we both began to turn. Of course, that's not how it looked to us. To us, it was the interior of Computer-Two that was turning, which was most unpleasant, and it took us a while to get relatively motionless again.

We had the theory perfectly worked out in

our planetside training, but we were short on practice. A lot short.

By the time we had steadied ourselves, I felt unpleasantly nauseated. You can call it nausea, or astronausea, or space-sickness, but whatever you call it, it's the heaves and it's worse in space than anywhere else, because there's nothing to pull the stuff down. It floats around in a cloud of globules and you don't want to be floating around with it. So I held it back; so did Joe.

I said, "Joe, it's clearly the computer that's at fault. Let's get at its insides." Anything to get my mind off *my* insides and let them quiet down. Besides, things weren't moving fast enough. I kept thinking of Computer-Three on its way down the tube; maybe Computer-One and Four by now, too; and thousands of people in space with their lives hanging on what we did.

Joe looked a little greenish, too, but he said, "First I've got to think. Something got in. It wasn't a meteoroid, because whatever it was chewed a neat hole out of the hull. It wasn't cut out because I didn't find a circle of metal anywhere inside. Did you?"

"No. But I hadn't thought to look."

"*I* looked, and it's nowhere in here."

"It may have fallen outside."

"With the cylinder covering the hole till I pulled it away? A likely thing. Did you see anything come flying out?"

"No."

Joe said, "We may still find it in here, of course, but I doubt it. It was somehow dissolved and something got in.''

''What something? Whose is it?''

Joe's grin was remarkably ill-natured. ''Why do you bother asking questions to which there are no answers? If this was last century, I'd say the Russians had somehow stuck that device onto the outside of Computer-Two—no offense. If it was last century, you'd say it was the Americans.''

I decided to be offended. I said, coldly, ''We're trying to say something that makes sense *this* century, Iosif'' giving it an exaggerated Russian pronunciation.

''We'll have to assume some dissident group.''

''If so,'' I said, ''we'll have to assume one with a capacity for space flight and with the ability to come up with an unusual device.''

Joe said, ''Space-flight presents no difficulties, if you can tap into the orbiting Computers illegally—which has been done. As for the cylinder, that may make more sense when it is analyzed back on Earth—downstairs, as you space-buffs would say.''

''It doesn't make sense,'' I said. ''Where's the point in trying to disable Computer-Two?''

''As part of a program to cripple space flight.''

''Then everyone suffers. The dissidents, too.''

''But it get's everyone's attention, doesn't it, and suddenly the cause of whatever-it-is makes news. Or the plan is to just knock out Computer-Two and then threaten to knock out the other three. No real damage, but lots of potential, and lots of publicity."

He was studying all parts of the interior closely, edging over it square centimeter by square centimeter. "I *might* suppose the thing was of nonhuman origin."

"Don't be silly."

"You want me to make the case? The cylinder made contact, after which something inside ate away a circle of metal and entered Computer-Two. It crawled over the inside wall eating away a thin layer of metal for some reason. Does that sound like anything of human construction."

"Not that I know of, but I don't know everything. Even you don't know everything."

Joe ignored that. "So the question is, how did it—whatever it is—get into the computer, which is, after all, reasonably well sealed. It did so quickly, since it knocked out the resealing and air-regeneration capacities almost at once."

"Is *that* what you're looking for?" I said, pointing.

He tried to stop too quickly and somersaulted backward, crying, "That's it!"

In his excitement, he was thrashing his arms and legs which got him nowhere, of course. I grabbed him and, for a while, we were both trying to exert pushes in uncoordinated directions, which got us nowhere either. Joe called me a few names, but I called him some back and there I had the advantage. I understand English perfectly, better than he does in fact; but his knowledge of Russian is—well, fragmentary would be a kind way of putting it.

Bad language in an ununderstood language always sounds very dramatic.

"Here it is," he said, when we finally had sorted ourselves out.

"Where the computer-shielding met the wall, a small circular hole appeared when Joe brushed aside a small cylinder. It was just like the one on the outer hull, but it seemed even thinner. In fact, it seemed to disintegrate when Joe touched it.

"We'd better get into the computer," said Joe.

The computer was a shambles.

Not obviously. I don't mean to say it was like a beam of wood that had been riddled by termites.

In fact, if you looked at the computer casually, you might swear it was intact.

Look closely, though, and some of the chips would be gone. The more closely you looked, the more you realized were gone. Worse, the stores that Computer-Two used in self-repair had dwindled to almost nothing. We kept looking and would discover something else missing.

Joe took the cylinder out of his pouch again and turned it end for end. He said, "I suspect it's after high-grade silicon in particular. I can't say for sure, of course, but my guess is that the sides are mostly aluminum and the flat end is mostly silicon."

I said, "Do you mean the thing is a solar battery?"

"Part of it is. That's how it gets it energy in

space; energy to get to Computer-Two, energy to eat a hole into it, energy to—to—I don't know how else to put it. Energy to stay alive."

"You call it alive?"

"Why not? Look, Computer-Two can repair itself. It can reject faulty bits of equipment and replace it with working ones, but it needs a supply of spares to work with. Given enough spares of all kinds, it could build a Computer just like itself, when properly programmed—but it needs the supply, so we don't think of it as alive. This object that entered Computer-Two is apparently collecting its own supplies. That's suspiciously lifelike."

"What you're saying," I said, "is that we have here a micro-computer advanced enough to be considered alive."

"I don't honestly know what I'm saying."

"Who on Earth could make such a thing?"

"Who on *Earth?*"

I made the next discovery. It looked like a stubby pen drifting through the air. I just caught it out of the corner of my eye and it registered as a pen.

In zero-gravity, things will drift out of pockets and float off. There's no way of keeping anything in place unless it is physically confined. You expect pens and coins and anything else that finds an opening to drift wherever the air currents and inertia lead it.

So my mind registered "Pen" and I groped for it absently and, of course, my fingers didn't close on it. Just reaching for something sets up an air current that pushes it away. You have to reach over and sneak behind it with one hand, and then reach for it with the other. Picking up any small object in mid-air is a two-hand operation.

I turned to look at the object and pay a little more attention to retrieval, then realized that my pen was safely in its pouch. I felt for it and it was there.

"Did you lose a pen, Joe?" I called out.

"No."

"Anything like that? Key? Cigarette?"

"I don't smoke. You know that."

A stupid answer. "Anything?" I said in exasperation. "I'm seeing things here."

"No one ever said you were stable."

"Look, Joe. Over there. Over there."

He lunged for it. I could have told him it would do no good.

By now, though, our poking around in the computer seemed to have stirred things up. We were seeing them wherever we looked. They were floating in the air-currents.

I stopped one at last. Or, rather, it stopped itself for it was on the elbow of Joe's suit. I snatched it off and shouted. Joe jumped in terror and nearly knocked it out of my hand.

I said, "Look!"

There was a shiny circle on Joe's suit, where I had taken the thing off. It had begun to eat its way through.

"Give it to me," said Joe. He took it gingerly and put it against the wall to hold it steady. Then he shelled it, gently lifting the paper-thin metal.

There was something inside that looked like a line of cigarette ash. It caught the light and glinted, though, like lightly woven metal.

There was a moistness about it, too. It wriggled slowly, one end seeming to seek blindly.

The end made contact with the wall and stuck. Joe's finger pushed it away. It seemed to require a small effort to do so. Joe rubbed his finger and thumb and said, "Feels oily."

The metal worm—I don't know what else to call it—seemed limp now after Joe had touched it. It didn't move again.

I was twisting and turning, trying to look at myself.

"Joe," I said, "for Heaven's sake, have I got one of them on me anywhere?"

"I don't see one," he said.

"Well, *look* at me. You've got to watch me, Joe, and I'll watch you. If our suits are wrecked we might not be able to get back to the ship."

Joe said, "Keep moving, then."

It was a grisly feeling, being surrounded by things hungry to dissolve your suit wherever they could touch it. When any showed up, we tried to catch them and stay out of their way at the same time, which made things almost impossible. A rather long one drifted close to my leg and I kicked at it, which was stupid, for if I had hit it, it might have stuck. As it was, the air-current I set up brought it against the wall, where it stayed.

Joe reached hastily for it—too hastily. The rest of his body rebounded as he somersaulted, one booted foot struck the wall near the cylinder lightly. When he finally righted himself, it was still there.

"I didn't smash it, did I?"

"No, you didn't," I said. "You missed it by a decimeter. It won't get away."

I had a hand on either side of it. It was twice as long as the other cylinder had been. In fact, it was like two cylinders stuck together long-ways, with a construction at the point of joining.

"Act of reproducing," said Joe as he peeled away the metal. This time what was inside was a line of dust. Two lines. One on either side of the constriction.

"It doesn't take much to kill them," said Joe. He relaxed visiby. "I think we're safe."

"They do seem alive," I said reluctantly.

"I think they seem more than that. They're viruses—or the equivalent."

"What are you talking about?"

Joe said, "Granted I'm a computer-technologist and not a virologist—but it's my understanding that viruses on Earth, or 'downstairs' as you would say, consist of a nucleic acid molecule coated in a protein shell.

"When a virus invades a cell, it manages to dissolve a hole in the cell wall or membrane by the use of some appropriate enzyme and the nucleic acid slips inside, leaving the protein coat outside. Inside the cell it finds the material to make a new protein coat for itself. In fact, it manages to form replicas of itself and produces a new protein coat for each replica. Once it has stripped the cell of all it has, the cell dissolves and in place of the one invading virus there are several hundred daughter-viruses. Sound familiar?''

''Yes. Very familiar. It's what's happening here. But where did it come from, Joe?''

''Not from Earth, obviously, or any Earth settlement. From somewhere else, I suppose. They drift through space till they find something appropriate in which they can multiply. They look for sizable objects ready-made of metal. I don't imagine they can smelt ores.''

''But large metal objects with pure silicon components and a few other succulent matters like that are the products of intelligent life only,'' I said.

''Right,'' said Joe, ''which means we have the best evidence yet that intelligent life is common in the universe, since objects like the one we're on must be quite common or it couldn't support these viruses. And it means that intelligent life is old, too, perhaps ten billion years old—long enough for a kind of metal evolution, forming a metal/silicon/oil life as we have formed a nucleic/protein/water life. Time to evolve a parasite on space-age artifacts.''

I said, ''You make it sound that every time some intelligent life-form develops a space-culture, it is subjected before long to parasitic infestation.''

''Right. And it must be controlled. Fortunately, these things are easy to kill, especially now when they're forming. Later on, when ready to burrow out of Computer-Two, I suppose they will grow, thicken their shells, stabilize their interior and prepare, as the equivalent of spores, to drift a million years before they find another home. They might not be so easy to kill then."

"How are you going to kill them?"

"I already have. I just touched that first one when it instinctively sought out metal to begin manufacturing a new shell after I had broken open the first one—and that touch finished it. I didn't touch the second, but I kicked the wall near it and the sound vibration in the metal shook its interior apart into metal dust. So they can't get us—or any more of the computer—if we just shake them apart, now!"

He didn't have to explain further—or as much. He put on his gauntlets slowly, and banged at the wall with one. It pushed him away and he kicked at the wall where he next approached it.

"You do the same," he shouted.

I tried to, and for a while we both kept at it. You don't know how hard it is to hit a wall at zero-gravity; at least on purpose; and do it hard enough to make it clang. We missed as often as not or just struck a glancing blow that sent us whirling but made virtually no sound. We were panting with effort and aggravation in no time.

But we had acclimated ourselves. We kept it up and eventually gathered up more of the viruses. There was nothing inside but dust in every case. They were clearly adapted to empty, automated space objects which, like modern computers, were vibration-free. That's what made it possible, I suppose, to build up the exceedingly rickety-complex metallic structures that possessed sufficient instability to produce the properties of simple life.

I said, "Do you think we got them all?"

"How can I say? If there's one left, it will cannibalize the others for metal supplies and start all over. Let's bang around some more."

We did until we were sufficiently worn out not to care whether one was still left alive.

"Of course," I said, panting, "the Planetary Association for the Advancement of Science isn't going to be pleased with our killing them all."

Joe's suggestion as to what the P.A.A.A. could do with itself was forceful, but impractical. He said, "Look, our mission is to save Computer-Two, a few thousand lives and, as it turned out, our own lives, too. Now they can decide whether to renovate this computer or rebuild it from scratch. It's their baby.

"The P.A.A.S. can get what they can out of these dead objects and that should be something. If they want live ones, I suspect they'll find them floating about in these regions."

I said, "All right. My suggestion is we tell Computer Central we're going to jerry-rig this Computer and get it doing some work anyway, and we'll stay till a relief is up for main repairs or whatever in order to prevent any reinfestation. Meanwhile, they'd better get to each of the other Computers and set up a system that can set it to vibrating strongly as soon as the internal atmosphere shows a pressure drop."

"Simple enough," said Joe, sardonically.

"It's lucky we found them when we did."

"Wait a while," said Joe, and the look in his eye was one of deep trouble. We didn't find them. *They* found *us*. If metal-life has developed, do you suppose it's likely that this is the only form it takes?

"What if such life-forms communicate somehow and, across the vastness of space, others are now converging on us for the picking. Other species, too; all of them after the lush new fodder of an as-yet untouched space culture. *Other* species! Some that are sturdy enough to withstand vibration. Some that are large enough to be more versatile in their reactions to danger. Some that are equipped to invade our settlements in orbit. Some, for the sake of Univac, that may be able to invade the Earth for the metals of its cities.

"What I'm going to report, what I must report, is that we've been *found!*"

STANDING WOMAN

By Tsutsui Yasutaka
Translated from the Japanese
by David Lewis

I stayed up all night and finally finished a forty-page short story. It was a trivial entertainment piece, capable of neither harm nor good.

"These days you can't write stories that might do harm or good; it can't be helped." That's what I told myself while I fastened the manuscript with a paper clip and put it into an envelope.

As to whether I have it in me to write stories that might do harm or good, I do my best not to think about that. If I were to go around thinking about it, I might want to try.

The morning sunlight hurt my eyes as I slipped on my wooden clogs and left the house with the envelope. Since there was still time before the first mail truck would come, I turned

my feet toward the park. In the morning no
children come to this park, a mere eighty square
meters in the middle of a cramped residential
district. It's quiet here. So I always include the
park in my morning walk. Nowadays even the
scanty green provided by the ten or so trees is
priceless in the megalopolis.

I should have brought some bread, I thought.
My favorite dogpillar stands next to the park
bench. It's an affable dogpillar with buff-
colored fur, quite large for a mongrel.

The liquid-fertilizer truck had just left when I
reached the park; the ground was damp and
there was a faint smell of chlorine. The elderly
gentleman I often saw there was sitting on the
bench next to the dogpillar, feeding the buff
post what seemed to be meat dumplings.
Dogpillars usually have excellent appetites.
Maybe the liquid fertilizer, absorbed by the
roots sunk deep in the ground and passed on up
through the legs, leaves something to be
desired.

They'll eat just about anything you give
them.

"You brought him something? I slipped up
today. I forgot to bring my bread," I said to the
elderly man.

He turned gentle eyes on me and smiled
softly.

"Ah, you like this fellow, too?"

"Yes," I replied, sitting down beside him.
"He looks exactly like the dog I used to have."

The dogpillar looked up at me with large,
black eyes and wagged its tail.

"Actually, I kept a dog like this fellow myself," the man said scratching the ruff of the dogpillar's neck. "He was made into a dogpillar when he was three. Haven't you seen him? Between the haberdashery and the film shop on the coast road. Isn't there a dogpillar there that looks like this fellow?"

I nodded, adding, "Then that one was yours?"

"Yes, he was our pet. His name was Hachi. Now he's completely vegetized. A beautiful dogtree."

"Now that you mention it, he does look a lot like this fellow. Maybe they came from the same stock."

"And the dog you kept?" the elderly man asked. "Where is he planted?"

"Our dog was named Buff," I answered, shaking my head. "He was planted beside the entrance to the cemetery on the edge of town when he was four. Poor thing, he died right after he was planted. The fertilizer trucks don't get out that way very often, and it was so far I couldn't take him food every day. Maybe they planted him badly. He died before becoming a tree."

"Then he was removed?"

"No. Fortunately, it didn't much matter there if he smelled or not, and so he was left there and dried. Now he's a bonepillar. He makes fine material for the neighborhood elementary-school science classes, I hear."

"That's wonderful."

The elderly man stroked the dogpillar's head.

"This fellow here, I wonder what he was called before he became a dogpillar."

"No calling a dogpillar by its original name," I said. "Isn't that a strange law?"

The man looked at me sharply, then replied casually, "Didn't they just extend the laws concerning people to dogs? That's why they lose their names when they become dogpillars." He nodded while scratching the dogpillar's jaw. "Not only the old names, but you can't give them new names, either. That's because there are no proper nouns for plants."

Why, of course, I thought.

He looked at my envelope with MANUSCRIPT ENCLOSED written on it.

"Excuse me," he said. "Are you a writer?"

I was a little embarrassed.

"Well, yes. Just trivial little things."

After looking at me closely, the man returned to stroking the dogpillar's head. "I also used to write things."

He managed to supress a smile.

"How many years is it now since I stopped writing? It feels like a long time."

I stared at the man's profile. Now that he said so, it was a face I seemed to have seen somewhere before. I started to ask his name, hesitated, and fell silent.

The elderly man said abruptly, "It's become a hard world to write in."

I lowered my eyes, ashamed of myself, who still continued to write in such a world.

The man apologized flurriedly at my sudden depression.

"That was rude. I'm not criticizing you. I'm the one who should feel ashamed."

"No," I told him, after looking quickly around us, "I can't give up writing, because I haven't the courage. Giving up writing! Why, after all, that would be a gesture against society."

The elderly man continued stroking the dog-pillar. After a long while he spoke.

"It's painful, suddenly giving up writing. Now that it's come to this, I would have been better off if I'd gone on boldly writing social criticism and had been arrested. There are even times when I think that. But I was just a dilettante, never knowing poverty, craving peaceful dreams. I wanted to live a comfortable life. As a person strong in self-respect. I couldn't endure being exposed to the eyes of the world, ridiculed. So I quit writing. A sorry tale."

He smiled and shook his head. "No, no, let's not talk about it. You never know who might be listening, even here on the street."

I changed the subject. "Do you live near here?"

"Do you know the beauty parlor on the main street? You turn in there. My name is Hiyama." He nodded at me. "Come over sometime. I'm married, but . . ."

"Thank you very much."

I gave him my own name.

I didn't remember any writer named Hiyama. No doubt he wrote under a pen name. I had no intention of visiting his house. This is a world

41

where even two or three writers getting together is considered illegal assembly.

"It's time for the mail truck to come."

Taking pains to look at my watch, I stood.

"I'm afraid I'd better go," I said.

He turned a sadly smiling face toward me and bowed slightly. After stroking the dogpillar's head a little, I left the park.

I came out on the main street, but there was only a ridiculous number of passing cars: pedestrians were few. A cattree, about thirty to forty centimeters high, was planted next to the sidewalk.

Sometimes I come across a catpillar that has just been planted and still hasn't become a cattree. New catpillars look at my face and meow or cry, but the ones where all four limbs planted in the ground have vegetized, with their greenish faces stiffly set and eyes shut tight, only move their ears now and then. Then there are catpillars that grow branches from their bodies and put out handfuls of leaves. The mental condition of these seems to be completely vegetized, they don't even move their ears. Even if a cat's face can still be made out, it may be better to call these cattrees.

Maybe, I thought, *it's better to make dogs into dogpillars. When their food runs out, they get vicious and even turn on people. But why did they have to turn cats into catpillars? Too many strays? To improve the food situation by even a little? Or perhaps for the greening of the city. . . .*

Next to the big hospital on the corner where

the highways intersect are two mantrees, and ranged alongside these trees is a manpillar. This manpillar wears a postman's uniform, and you can't tell how far its legs have vegetized because of its trousers. It is male, thirty-five or thirty-six years old, tall, with a bit of a stoop.

I approached him and held out my envelope as always.

"Registered mail, special delivery, please."

The manpillar, nodding silently, accepted the envelope and took stamps and a registered-mail slip from his pocket.

I looked around quickly after paying the postage. There was no one else there. I decided to try speaking to him. I gave him mail every three days, but I still hadn't had a chance for a leisurely talk.

"What did you do?" I asked in a low voice.

The manpillar looked at me in surprise. Then, after running his eyes around the area, he answered with a sour look. "Won't do to go saying unnecessary things to me. Even me, I'm not supposed to answer."

"I know that," I said, looking into his eyes.

"When I wouldn't leave, he took a deep breath. "I just said the pay's low. What's more, I got heard by my boss. Because a postman's pay really *is* low." With a dark look, he jerked his jaw at the two mantrees next to him. "These guys were the same. Just for letting slip some complaints about low pay. Do you know them?" he asked me.

I pointed at one of the mantrees. "I remember this one, because I gave him a lot of mail. I don't know the other one. He was already a mantree when we moved here."

"That one was my friend," he said.

"Wasn't the other one a chief clerk or section head?"

He nodded. "That's right. Chief clerk."

"Don't you get hungry or cold?"

"You don't feel it that much," he replied, still expressionless. Anyone who's made into a manpillar soon becomes expressionless. "Even I think I've gotten pretty plantlike. Not only in how I feel things, but in the way I think, too. At first, I was sad, but now it doesn't matter. I used to get really hungry, but they say the vegetizing goes faster when you don't eat."

He stared at me with lightless eyes. He was probably hoping he could become a mantree soon.

"Talk says they give people with radical ideas a lobotomy before making them into manpillars, but I didn't get that done, either. Even so a month after I was planted here I didn't get angry anymore.

He glanced at my wristwatch. "Well, you better go now. It's almost time for the mail truck to come."

"Yes." But still I couldn't leave, and I hesitated uneasily.

"You," the manpillar said. "Someone you know didn't recently get done into a manpillar, did they?"

Cut to the quick, I stared at his face for a moment, then nodded slowly.

"Actually, my wife."

"Hmm, your wife, is it?" For a few moments he regarded me with deep interest. "I wondered whether it wasn't something like that. Otherwise nobody ever bothers to talk to me. Then what did she do, your wife?"

"She complained that prices were high at a house-wives' get-together. Had that been all, fine, but she criticized the government, too. I'm starting to make it big as a writer, and I think that the eagerness of being that writer's wife made her say it. One of the women there informed on her. She was planted on the left side of the road looking from the station toward the assembly hall and next to that hardware store."

"Ah, that place." He closed his eyes a little, as if recollecting the appearance of the buildings and the stores in that area. "It's a fairly peaceful street. Isn't that for the better?" He opened his eyes and looked at me searchingly. "You aren't going to see her, are you? It's better not to see her too often. Both for her and for you. That way you can both forget faster."

"I know that."

I hung my head.

"Your wife?" he asked, his voice turning slightly sympathetic. "Has anyone done anything to her?"

"No. So far nothing. She's just standing, but even so—"

"Hey." The manpillar serving as a postbox raised his jaw to attract my attention. "It's come. The mail truck. You'd better go."

"You're right."

Taking a few wavering steps, as if pushed by his voice, I stopped and looked back. "Isn't there anything you want done?"

He brought a hard smile to his cheeks and shook his head.

The red mail truck stopped beside him.

I moved on past the hospital.

Thinking I'd check in on my favorite bookstore, I entered a street of crowded shops. My new book was supposed to be out any day now, but that kind of thing no longer made me the slightest bit happy.

A little before the bookstore in the same row is a small, cheap candy store, and on the edge of the road in front of it is a manpillar on the verge of becoming a mantree. A young male, it is already a year since it was planted. The face has become a brownish color tinged with green, and the eyes are tightly shut. Tall back slightly bent, the posture slouching a little forward. The legs, torso, and arms, visible through clothes reduced to rags by exposure to wind and rain, are already vegetized, and here and there branches sprout. Young leaves bud from the ends of the arms, raised above the shoulders like beating wings. The body, which has become a tree, and even the face no longer move at all. The heart has sunk into the tranquil world of plants.

I imagined the day when my wife would reach this state, and again my heart winced with pain, trying to forget. It was the anguish of trying to forget.

If I turn the corner at this candy store and go straight, I thought, *I can go to where my wife is standing. I can meet my wife. I can see my wife. But it won't do to go,* I told myself. *There's no telling who might see you; if the woman who informed on her questioned you, you'd really be in trouble.* I came to a halt in front of the candy store and peered down the road. Pedestrian traffic was the same as always. *It's all right. Anyone would overlook it if you just stand and talk a bit. You'll just have a word or two.* Defying my own voice screaming, *"Don't go!"* I went briskly down the street.

Her face pale, my wife was standing by the road in front of the hardware store. Her legs were unchanged, and it only seemed as if her feet from the ankles down were buried in the earth. Expressionlessly, as if striving to see nothing, feel nothing, she stared steadily ahead. Compared with two days before, her cheeks seemed a bit hollow. Two passing factory workers pointed at her, made some vulgar joke, and passed on, guffawing uproariously. I went up to her and raised my voice.

"Michikoo!" I yelled right in her ear.

My wife looked at me, and blood rushed to her cheeks. She brushed one hand through her tangled hair.

"You've come again? Really, you mustn't."

"I can't help coming."

The hardware-store mistress, tending shop, saw me. With an air of feigned indifference, she averted her eyes and retired to the back of the store. Full of gratitude for her consideration, I

47

drew a few steps closer to Michiko and faced her.

"You've gotten pretty used to it?"

With all her might she formed a bright smile on her stiffened face. "Mmm. I'm used to it."

"Last night it rained a little."

Still gazing at me with large, dark eyes, she nodded lightly. "Please don't worry, I hardly feel anything."

"When I think about you, I can't sleep." I hung my head. "You're always standing out here. When I think that, I can't possibly sleep. Last night I even thought I should bring you an umbrella."

"Please don't do anything like that!" My wife frowned just a little. "It would be terrible if you did something like that."

A large truck drove past behind me. White dust thinly veiled my wife's hair and shoulders, but she didn't seem bothered.

"Standing isn't really all that bad." She spoke with deliberate lightness, working to keep me from worrying.

I perceived a subtle change in my wife's expressions and speech from two days before. It seemed that her words had lost a shade of delicacy, and the range of her emotions had become somewhat impoverished. *Watching from the sidelines like this, seeing her gradually grow more expressionless, it's all the more desolating for having known her as she was before—those keen responses, the bright vivacity, the rich, full expressions.*

"These people," I asked her, running my

eyes over the hardware store, "are they good to you?"

"Well, of course. They're kind at heart. Just once they told me to ask if there's anything I want done. But they still haven't done anything for me."

"Don't you get hungry?"

She shook her head.

"It's better not to eat."

So. Unable to endure being a manpillar, she was hoping to become a mantree even so much as a single day faster.

"So please don't bring me food." She stared at me. "Please forget about me. I think, certainly, even without making any particular effort, I'm going to forget about you. I'm happy that you come to see me, but then the sadness drags on that much longer. For both of us."

"Of course you're right, but—" Despising this self that could do nothing for his own wife, I hung my head again. "But I won't forget you." I nodded. The tears came. "I won't forget. Ever."

When I raised my head and looked at her again, she was gazing steadily at me with eyes that had lost a little of their luster, her whole face beaming in a faint smile like a carved image of Buddha. It was the first time I had ever seen her smile like that.

I felt I was having a nightmare. *No,* I told myself, *this isn't your wife anymore.*

The suit she had been wearing when she was arrested had become terribly dirty and filled with wrinkles. But of course I wouldn't be allowed to bring a change of clothes. My eyes rested on a dark stain on her skirt.

"Is that blood? What happened?"

"Oh, this," she spoke falteringly, looking down at her skirt with a confused air." Last night two drunks played a prank on me.

"The bastards!" I felt a furious rage at their inhumanity. If you put it to them, they would say that since my wife was no longer human, it didn't matter what they did.

"They can't do that kind of thing! It's against the law!"

"That's right. But I can hardly appeal."

And of course I couldn't go to the police and appeal, either. If I did, I'd be looked on as even more of a problem person.

"The bastards! What did they—" I bit my lip. My heart hurt enough to break. "Did it bleed a lot?"

"Mmm, a little."

"Does it hurt?"

"It doesn't hurt anymore."

Michiko, who had been so proud before, now showed just a little sadness in her face. I was shocked by the change in her. A group of young men and women, penetratingly comparing me and my wife, passed behind me.

"You'll be seen," my wife said anxiously. "I beg of you, don't throw yourself away."

"Don't worry," I smiled thinly for her in self-contempt. "I don't have the courage."

"You should go now."

"When you're a mantree," I said in parting,

50

"I'll petition. I'll get them to transplant you in our garden."

"Can you do that?"

"I should be able to." I nodded liberally. "I should be able to."

"I'd be happy if you could," my wife said expressionlessly.

"Well, see you later."

"It'd be better if you didn't come again," she said in a murmur, looking down.

"I know. That's my intention. But I'll probably come anyway."

For a few minutes we were silent.

Then my wife spoke abruptly.

"Goodbye."

"Umm."

I began walking.

When I looked back as I rounded the corner, Michiko was following me with her eyes, still smiling like a graven Buddha.

Embracing a heart that seemed ready to split apart, I walked. I noticed suddenly that I had come out in front of the station. Unconsciously, I had returned to my usual walking course.

Opposite the station is a small coffee shop I always go to called Punch. I went in and sat down in a corner booth. I ordered coffee, drinking it black. Until then I had always had it with sugar. The bitterness of sugarless, creamless coffee pierced my body, and I savored it masochistically. *From now on I'll always drink it black*. That was what I resolved.

Three students in the next booth were talking about a critic, who had just been arrested and made into a manpillar.

"I hear he was planted smack in the middle of the Ginza."

"He loved the country. He always lived in the country. That's why they set him up in place like that."

"Seems they gave him a lobotomy."

"And the students who tried to use force in the Diet, protesting his arrest—they've all been arrested and will be made into manpillars, too."

"Weren't there almost thirty of them? Where'll they plant them all?"

"They say they'll be planted in front of their own university, down both sides of a street called Students Road."

"They'll have to change the name now. Violence Grove, or something."

The three snickered.

"Hey, let's not talk about it. We don't want someone to hear."

The three shut up.

When I left the coffee shop and headed home, I realized that I had begun to feel as if I was already a manpillar myself. Murmuring the words of a popular song to myself, I walked on.

I am a wayside manpillar. You, too, are a wayside manpillar. What the hell, the two of us, in this world. Dried grasses that never flower.

ST. AMY'S TALE

By Orson Scott Card

Mother could kill with her hands. Father could fly. These are miracles. But they were not miracles then. Mother Elouise taught me that there were no miracles then.

I am the child of Wreckers, born while the angel was in them. This is why I am called Saint Amy, though I perceive nothing in me that should make me holier than any other old woman. Yet Mother Elouise denied the angel in her, too, and it was no less there.

Sift your fingers through the soil, all you who read my words. Take your spades of iron and your picks of stone. Dig deep. You will find no ancient works of man hidden there. For the Wreckers passed through the world, and all the vanity was consumed in fire; all the pride broke in pieces when it was smitten by God's shining hand.

* * *

Elouise leaned on the rim of the computer keyboard. All around her the machinery was alive, the screens displaying information. Elouise felt nothing but weariness. She was leaning because, for a moment, she had felt a frightening vertigo. As if the world underneath the airplane had dissolved and slipped away into a rapidly receding star and she would never be able to land.

True enough, she thought. *I'll never be able to land, not in the world I knew.*

"Getting sentimental about the old computers?"

Elouise, startled, turned in her chair and faced her husband, Charlie. At that moment the airplane lurched, but like sailors accustomed to the shifting of the sea, they adjusted unconsciously and did not notice the imbalance.

"Is it noon already?" she asked.

"It's the mortal equivalent of noon. I'm too tired to fly this thing anymore, and it's a good thing Bill's at the controls."

"Hungry?"

Charlie shook his head. "But Amy probably is," he said.

"Voyeur," said Elouise.

Charlie liked to watch Elouise nurse their daughter. But despite her accusation, Elouise knew there was nothing sexual in it. Charlie liked the idea of Elouise being Amy's mother. He liked the way Amy's sucking resembled the sucking of a calf or a lamb or a puppy. He had said, "It's the best thing we kept from the

54

animals. The best thing we didn't throw away.''

"Better than sex?'' Elouise had asked. And Charlie had only smiled.

Amy was playing with a rag doll in the only large clear space in the airplane, near the exit door. "Mommy Mommy Mamommy Mommy-o,'' Amy said. The child stood and reached to be picked up. Then she saw Charlie. "Daddy Addy Addy.''

"Hi,'' Charlie said.

"Hi,'' Amy answered. "Ha-ee.'' She had only just learned to close the diphthong, and she exaggerated it. Amy played with the buttons on Elouise's shirt, trying to undo them.

"Greedy,'' Elouise said, laughing.

Charlie unbuttoned the shirt for her, and Amy seized on the nipple after only one false grab. She sucked noisily, tapping her hand gently against Elouise's breast as she ate.

"I'm glad we're so near finished,'' Elouise said. "She's too old to be nursing now.''

"That's right. Throw the little bird out of the nest.''

"Go to bed,'' Elouise said.

Amy recognized the phrase. She pulled away. "La-lo,'' she said.

"That's right. Daddy's going to sleep,'' Elouise said.

Elouise watched as Charlie stripped off most of his clothing and lay down on the pad. He smiled once, then turned over, and was immediately asleep. He was in tune with his body. Elouise knew that he would awaken in exactly six hours, when it was time for him to take the controls again.

Amy's sucking was a subtle pleasure now, though it had been agonizing the first few months, and painful again when Amy's first teeth had come in and she had learned to her delight that by nipping she could make her mother scream. But better to nurse her than ever have her eat the predigested pap that was served as food on the airplane. Elouise thought wryly that it was even worse than the microwaved veal cordon bleu that they used to inflict on commercial passengers. Only eight years ago. And they had calibrated their fuel so exactly that when they took the last draft of fuel from the last of their storage tanks, the tank registered empty; they would burn the last of the processed petroleum, instead of putting it back into the earth. All their caches were gone now, and they would be at the tender mercies of the world that they themselves had created.

Still, there was work to do; the final work, in the final checks. Elouise held Amy with one arm while she used her free hand slowly to key in the last program that her role as commander required her to use. Elouise Private, she typed. Teacher teacher I declare I see someone's underwear, she typed. On the screen appeared the warning she had put there: "You may think you're lucky finding this program, but unless you know the magic words, an alarm is going to go off all over this airplane and you'll be had. No way out of it, sucker. Love, Elouise."

Elouise, of course, knew the magic words. Einstein sucks, she typed. The screen went blank, and the alarm did not go off.

Malfunction? she queried. "None," answered the computer.

Tamper? she queried, and the computer answered, "None."

Nonreport? she queried, and the computer flashed, "AFscanP7bb55."

Elouise had not really been dozing. But still she was startled, and she lurched forward, disturbing Amy, who really had fallen asleep. "No no no," said Amy, and Elouise forced herself to be patient; she soothed her daughter back to sleep before pursuing whatever it was that her guardian program had caught. Whatever it was? Oh, she knew what it was. It was treachery. The one thing she had been sure *her* group, *her* airplane would never have. Other groups of Rectifiers—wreckers, they called themselves, having adopted their enemies' name for them — other groups had had their spies or their fainthearts, but not Bill or Heather or Ugly-Bugly.

Specify, she typed.

The computer was specific.

Over northern Virginia, as the airplane followed its careful route to find and destroy everything made of metal, glass, and plastic; somewhere over northern Virginia, the airplanes path bent slightly to the south, and on the return, at the same place, the airplane's path bent slightly to the north, so that a strip of northern Virginia two kilometers long and a few dozen meters wide could contain some nonbiodegradable artifact, hidden from the airplane, and if Elouise had not queried this program, she would never have known it.

But she should have known it. When the plane's course bent, alarms should have sounded. Someone had penetrated the first line of defense. But Bill could not have done that, nor could Heather, really—they didn't have the sophistication to break up a bubble program. Ugly-Bugly?

She knew it wasn't faithful old Ugly-Bugly. No, not her.

The computer voluntarily flashed, "Override M577b, commandmo4, intwis CtTttT." It was an apology. Someone aboard ship had found the alarm override program and the overrides for the alarm overrides. Not my fault, the computer was saying.

Elouise hesitated for a moment. She looked down at her daughter and moved a curl of red hair away from Amy's eye. Elouise's hand trembled. But she was a woman of ice, yes, all frozen where compassion made other women warm. She prided herself on that, on having frozen the last warm places in her—frozen so goddamn rigid that it was only a moment's hesitation. And then she reached out and asked for the access code used to perform the treachery, asked for the name of the traitor.

The computer was even less compassionate than Elouise. It hesitated not at all.

The computer did not underline; the letters on the screen were no larger than normal. Yet Elouise felt the words as a shout, and she answered them silently with a scream.

Charles Evan Hardy, b24ag61-richlandWA.

It was Charlie who was the traitor—Charlie, her sweet, soft, hard-bodied husband, Charlie who secretly was trying to undo the end of the world.

God has destroyed the world before. Once in a flood, when Noah rode it out in the Ark. And once the tower of the world's pride was destroyed in the confusion of tongues. The other times, if there were any other times, those times are all forgotten.

The world will probably be destroyed again, unless we repent. And don't think you can hide from the angels. They start out as ordinary people, and you never know which ones. Suddenly God puts the power of destruction in their hands, and they destroy. And just as suddenly, when all the destruction is done, the angel leaves them, and they're ordinary people. Just my mother and my father.

I can't remember Father Charlie's face. I was too young.

Mother Elouise told me often about Father Charlie. He was born far to the west in a land where water only comes to the crops in ditches, almost never from the sky. It was a land unblessed by God. Men lived there, they believed, only by the strength of their own hands. Men made their ditches and forgot about God and became scientists. Father Charlie became a scientist. He worked on tiny animals, breaking their heart of hearts and combining it in new ways. Hearts were broken too often where he worked, and one of the little animals escaped and killed people until they lay in great heaps like fish in the ship's hold.

But this was not the destruction of the world.

Oh, they were giants in those days, and they forgot the Lord, but when their people lay in piles of moldering flesh and brittling bone, they remembered they were weak.

Mother Elouise said, "Charlie came weeping." This is how Father Charlie became an angel. He saw what the giants had done, by thinking they were greater than God. At first he sinned in his grief. Once he cut his own throat. They put Mother Elouise's blood in him to save his life. This is how they met: In the forest where he had gone to die privately, Father Charlie woke up from a sleep he thought would be forever to see a woman lying next to him in the tent and a doctor bending over them both. When he saw that this woman gave her blood to him whole and unstintingly, he forgot his wish to die. He loved her forever. Mother Elouise said he loved her right up to the day she killed him.

When they were finished, they had a sort of ceremony, a sort of party. "A benediction," said Bill, solemnly sipping at the gin. "Amen and amen."

"My shift," Charlie said, stepping into the cockpit. Then he noticed that everyone was there and that they were drinking the last of the gin, the bottle that had been saved for the end. "Well, happy us," Charlie said, smiling.

Bill got up from the controls of the 787. "Any preferences on where we set down?" he asked. Charlie took his place.

The others looked at one another. Ugly-Bugly shrugged. "God, who ever thought about it?"

"Come on, we're all futurists," Heather said. "You must know where you want to live."

"Two thousand years from now," Ugly-Bugly said. "I want to live in the world the way it'll be two thousand years from now."

"Ugly-Bugly opts for resurrection," Bill said. "I, however, long for the bosom of Abraham."

"Virginia," said Elouise. They turned to face her. Heather laughed.

"Resurrection," Bill intoned, "the bosom of Abraham, and Virginia. You have no poetry, Elouise."

"I've written down the coordinates of the place where we are supposed to land," Elouise said. She handed them to Charlie. He did not avoid her gaze. She watched him read the paper. He showed no sign of recognition. For a moment she hoped that it had all been a mistake, but no. She would not let herself be misled by her desires.

"Why Virginia?" Heather asked.

Charlie looked up. "It's central."

"It's east coast," Heather said.

"It's central in the high survival area. There isn't much of a living to be had in the western mountains or on the plains. It's not so far south as to be in hunter-gatherer country and not so far north as to be unsurvivable for a high proportion of the people. Barring a hard winter."

"All very good reasons," Elouise said. "Fly us there, Charlie."

Did his hands tremble as he touched the controls? Elouise watched very carefully, but he did not tremble. Indeed, he was the only one who did not. Ugly-Bugly suddenly began to cry, tears coming from her good eye and streaming down her good cheek. *Thank God she doesn't cry out of the other side,* Elouise thought; then she was angry at herself, for she had thought Ugly-Bugly's deformed face didn't bother her anymore. Elouise was angry at herself, but it only made her cold inside, determined that there would be no failure. Her mission would be complete. No allowances made for personal cost.

Elouise suddenly started out of her contemplative mood to find that the two other women had left the cockpit—their sleep shift, though it was doubtful they would sleep. Charlie silently flew the plane, while Bill sat in the copilot's seat, pouring himself the last drop from the bottle. He was looking at Elouise.

"Cheers," Elouise said to him.

He smiled sadly back at her. "Amen," he said. Then he leaned back and sang softly:

Praise God, from whom all blessings flow.
Praise him, ye creatures here below.
Praise him, who slew the wicked host.
Praise Father, Son, and Holy Ghost.

Then he reached for Elouise's hand. She was surprised, but let him take it. He bent to her and kissed her palm tenderly. "For many have entertained angels unaware," he said to her.

62

A few moments later he was asleep. Charlie and Elouise sat in silence. The plane flew on south as darkness overtook them from the east. At first their silence was almost affectionate. But as Elouise sat and sat, saying nothing, she felt the silence grow cold and terrible, and for the first time she realized that when the airplane landed, Charlie would be her—Charlie, who had been half her life for these last few years, whom she had never lied to and who had never lied to her—would be her enemy.

I have watched the little children do a dance called Charlie-El. They sing a little song to it, and if I remember the words, it goes like this:

I am made of bones and glass.
Let me pass, let me pass.
I am made of brick and steel.
Take my heel, take my heel.
I was killed just yesterday.
Kneel and pray, kneel and pray.
Dig a hole where I can sleep.
Dig it deep, dig it deep.
Will I go to heaven or hell?
Charlie-El. Charlie-El.

I think they are already nonsense words to the children. But the poem first got passed word of mouth around Richmond when I was little, and living in Father Michael's house. The children do not try to answer their song. They just sing it and do a very clever little dance while they sing. They always end the song with all the children falling down on the ground,

laughing. That is the best way for the song to
end.

Charlie brought the airplane straight down
into a field, great hot winds pushing against the
ground as if to shove it back from the plane.
The field caught fire, but when the plane had
settled upon its three wheels, foam streaked out
from the belly of the machine and overtook the
flames. Elouise watched from the cockpit,
thinking, *Wherever the foam has touched,
nothing will grow for years.* It seemed symmetrical to her. Even in the last moments of the
last machine, it must poison the earth. Elouise
held Amy on her lap and thought of trying to
explain it to the child. But Elouise knew Amy
would not understand or remember.

"Last one dressed is a sissy-wissy," said
Ugly-Bugly in her husky, ancient-sounding
voice. They had dressed and undressed in front
of each other for years now, but today as the
old plastic-polluted clothing came off and the
homespun went on, they felt and acted like
school kids on their first day in coed gym. Amy
caught the spirit of it and kept yelling at the top
of her lungs. No one thought to quiet her.
There was no need. This was a celebration.

But Elouise, long accustomed to self-
examination, forced herself to realize that there
was a strain to her frolicking. She did not
believe it, not really. Today was not a happy
day, and it was not just from knowing the
confrontation that lay ahead. There was something so final about the death of the last of the

engines of mankind. Surely something could be—but she forced the thought from her, forced the coldness in her to overtake that sentiment. Surely she could not be seduced by the beauty of the airplane. Surely she must remember that it was not the machines but what they inevitably did to mankind that was evil.

They looked and felt a little awkward, almost silly, as they left the plane and stood around in the blackened field. They had not yet lost their feel for stylish clothing, and the homespun was so lumpy and awkward and rough. It didn't look right on any of them.

Amy clung to her doll, awed by the strange scenery. In her life she had been out of the airplane only once, and that was when she was an infant. She watched as the trees moved unpredictably. She winced at the wind in her eyes. She touched her cheek, where her hair moved back and forth in the breeze, and hunted through her vocabulary for a word to name the strange invisible touch of her skin. "Mommy," she said. "Uh! Uh! Uh!"

Elouise understood. "Wind," she said. The sounds were still too hard for Amy, and the child did not attempt to say the word. *Wind,* thought Elouise, and immediately thought of Charlie. Her best memory of Charlie was in the wind. It was during his death-wish time, not long after his suicide. He had insisted on climbing a mountain, and she knew that he meant to fall. So she had climbed with him, even though there was a storm coming up. Charlie was angry all the way. She remembered a terrible hour clinging to the face of a cliff, held only by small bits of metal forced into cracks in the rock. She had insisted on remaining tied to Charlie. "If one of us fell, it would only drag the other down, too," he kept saying. "I know," she kept answering. And so Charlie had not fallen, and they made love for the first time in a shallow cave, with the wind howling outside and occasional sprays of rain coming in to dampen them. They refused to be dampened. Wind. Damn.

And Elouise felt herself go cold and unemotional, and they stood on the edge of the field in the shade of the first trees. Elouise had left the Rectifier near the plane, set on 360 degrees. In a few minutes the Rectifier would go off, and they had to watch, to witness the end of their work.

Suddenly Bill shouted, laughed, held up his wrist. "My watch!" he cried.

"Hurry," Charlie said. "There's time."

Bill unbuckled his watch and ran toward the Rectifier. He tossed the watch. It landed within a few meters of the small machine. Then Bill returned to the group, jogging and shaking his head. "Jesus, what a moron! Three years wiping out everything east of the Mississippi, and I almost save a digital chronograph."

"Dixie Instruments?" Heather asked.

"Yeah."

"That's not high technology," she said, and they all laughed. Then they fell silent, and Elouise wondered whether they were all thinking the same thing: that jokes about brand names would be dead within a generation, if they were not already dead. They watched the Rectifier in silence, waiting for the timer to finish its delay. Suddenly there was a shining in the air, a dazzling not-light that made them squint. They had seen this many times before, from the air and from the ground, but this was the last time, and so they saw it as if it were the first.

The airplane corroded as if a thousand years were passing in seconds. But it wasn't a true corrosion. There was no rust—only dissolution as molecules separated and seeped down into the loosened earth. Glass became sand; plastic corrupted to oil; the metal also drifted down into the ground and came to rest in a vein at the bottom of the Rectifier field. Whatever else the metal might look like to a future geologist, it wouldn't look like an artifact. It would look like iron. And with so many similar pockets of iron and copper and aluminum and tin spread all over the once-civilized world, it was not likely that they would suspect human interference. Elouise was amused, thinking of the treatises that would someday be written, about the two states of workable metals—the ore state and the pure-metal vein. She hoped it would retard their progress a little.

The airplane shivered into nothing, and the Rectifier also died in the field. A few minutes after the Rectifier disappeared, the field also faded.

"Amen and amen," said Bill, maudlin again.

"All clean now."

Elouise only smiled. She said nothing of the other Rectifier, which was in her knapsack. Let the others think all the work was done.

Amy poked her finger in Charlie's eye. Charlie swore and set her down. Amy started to cry, and Charlie knelt by her and hugged her. Amy's arms went tightly around his neck. "Give Daddy a kiss," Elouise said.

"Well, time to go," Ugly-Bugly's voice rasped. "Why the hell did you pick this particular spot?"

Elouise cocked her head. "Ask Charlie."

Charlie flushed. Elouise watched him grimly. "Elouise and I once came here," he said. "Before Rectification began. Nostalgia, you know." He smiled shyly, and the others laughed. Except Elouise. She was helping Amy to urinate. She felt the weight of the small Rectifier in her knapsack and did not tell anyone the truth: that she had never been in Virginia before in her life.

"Good a spot as any," Heather said. "Well, bye."

Well, bye. That was all, that was the end of it, and Heather walked away to the west, toward the Shenandoah Valley.

"See ya," Bill said.

"Like hell," Ugly-Bugly added.

Impulsively Ugly-Bugly hugged Elouise, and Bill cried, and then they took off northeast, toward the Potomac, where they would doubtlessly find a community growing up along the clean and fish-filled river.

Just Charlie, Amy, and Elouise left in the empty, blackened field where the airplane had died. Elouise tried to feel some great pain at the separation from the others, but she could not. They had been together every day for years now, going from supply dump to supply dump, wrecking cities and towns, destroying and using up the artificial world. But had they been friends? If it had not been for their task, they would never have been friends. They were not the same kind of people.

And then Elouise was ashamed of her feelings. Not her kind of people? Because Heather liked what grass did to her and had never owned a car or had a driver's license in her life? Because Ugly-Bugly had a face hideously deformed by cancer surgery? Because Bill always worked Jesus into the conversation, even though half the time he was an atheist? Because they just weren't in the same social circles? There were no social circles now. Just people trying to survive in a bitter world they weren't bred for. There were only two classes now: those who would make it and those who wouldn't.

Which class am I? thought Elouise.

"Where should we go?" Charlie asked.

Elouise picked Amy up and handed her to Charlie. "Where's the capsule, Charlie?"

Charlie took Amy and said, "Hey, Amy, baby, I'll bet we find some farming community between here and the Rappahannock."

"Doesn't matter if you tell me, Charlie. The instruments found it before we landed. You did

a damn good job on the computer program.''
She didn't have to say, Not good enough.

Charlie only smiled crookedly. "Here I was
hoping you were forgetful." He reached out to
touch her knapsack. She pulled abruptly away.
He lost his smile. "Don't you know me?" he
asked softly.

He would never try to take the Rectifier from
her by force. But still. This was the last of the
artifacts they were talking about. Was anyone
really predictable at such a time? Elouise was
not sure. She had thought she knew him well
before, yet the time capsule existed to prove
that her understanding of Charlie was far from
complete.

"I know you, Charlie," she said, "but not as
well as I thought. Does it matter? Don't try to
stop me."

"I hope you're not too angry," he said.

Elouise couldn't think of anything to say to
that. *Anyone could be fooled by a traitor, but
only I am fool enough to marry one.* She turned
from him and walked into the forest. He took
Amy and followed.

All the way through the underbrush Elouise
kept expecting him to say something. A threat,
for instance: You'll have to kill me to destroy
that time capsule. Or a plea: You have to leave
it, Elouise, please, please. Or reason, or
argument, or anger, or something.

But instead it was just his silent footfalls
behind her. Just his occasional playtalk with
Amy. Just his singing as he put Amy to sleep on
his shoulder.

The capsule had been hidden well. There was no surface sign that men had ever been here. Yet, from the Rectifier's emphatic response, it was obvious that the time capsule was quite large. There must have been heavy, earth-moving equipment. Or was it all done by hand?

"When did you ever find the time?" Elouise asked when they reached the spot.

"Long lunch hours," he said.

She set down her knapsack and then stood there, looking at him.

Like a condemned man who insists on keeping his composure, Charlie smiled wryly and said, "Get on with it, please."

After Father Charlie died, Mother Elouise brought me here to Richmond. She didn't tell anyone that she was a Wrecker. The angel had already left her, and she wanted to blend into the town, be an ordinary person in the world she and her fellow angels had created.

Yet she was incapable of blending in. Once the angel touches you, you cannot go back, even when the angel's work is done. She first attracted attention by talking against the stockade. There was once a stockade around the town of Richmond, when there were only a thousand people here. The reason was simple: People still weren't used to the hard way life was without the old machines. They had not yet learned to depend on the miracle of Christ. They still trusted in their hands, yet their hands could work no more magic. So there were tribes in the winter that didn't know how to find game, that had no reserves of grain, that had no shelter adequate to hold the head of a fire.

"Bring them all in," said Mother Elouise. "There's room for all. There's food for all. Teach them how to build ships and make tools and sail and farm, and we'll all be richer for it."

But Father Michael and Uncle Avram knew more than Mother Elouise. Father Michael had been a Catholic priest before the destruction, and Uncle Avram had been a professor at a university. They had been nobody. But when the angels of destruction finished their work, the angels of life began to work in the hearts of men. Father Michael threw off his old allegiance to Rome and taught Christ simple, from his memory of the Holy Book. Uncle Avram plunged into his memory of ancient metallurgy and taught the people who gathered at Richmond how to make iron hard enough to use for tools. And weapons.

Father Michael forbade the making of guns and forbade that anyone teach children what guns were. But for hunting there had to be arrows, and what will kill a deer will also kill a man.

Many people agreed with Mother Elouise about the stockade. But then in the worst of winter a tribe came from the mountains and threw fire against the stockade and against the ships that kept trade alive along the whole coast. The archers of Richmond killed most of them, and people said to Mother Elouise, "Now you must agree we need the stockade."

Mother Elouise said, "Would they have come with fire if there had been no wall?"

How can anyone judge the greatest need? Just as the angel of death had come to plant the seeds of a better life, so that angle of life had to be hard and endure death so the many could live. Father Michael and Uncle Avram held to the laws of Christ simple, for did not the Holy Book say, "Love your enemies, and smite them only when they attack you; chase them not out into the forest, but let them live as long as they leave you alone"?

I remember that winter. I remember watching while they buried the dead tribesmen. Their bodies had stiffened quickly, but Mother Elouise brought me to see them and said, "This is death, remember it, remember it." What did Mother Elouise know? Death is our passage from flesh into the living wind, until Christ brings us forth into flesh again. Mother Elouise will find Father Charlie again, and every wound will be made whole.

Elouise knelt by the Rectifier and carefully set it to go off in half an hour, destroying itself and the time capsule buried thirty meters under the ground. Charlie stood near her, watching, his face nearly expressionless; only a faint smile broke his perfect repose. Amy was in his arms, laughing and trying to reach up to pinch his nose.

"This Rectifier responds only to me," Elouise said quietly. "Alive. If you try to move it, it will go off early and kill us all."

"I won't move it," Charlie said.

And Elouise was finished. She stood up and reached for Amy. Amy reached back, holding out her arms to her mother. "Mommy," she said.

Because I couldn't remember Father Charlie's face, Mother Elouise thought I had forgotten everything about him, but that is not true. I remember very clearly one picture of him, but he is not in the picture.

This is very hard for me to explain. I see a small clearing in the trees, with Mother Elouise standing in front of me. I see her at my eye level, which tells me that I am being held. I cannot see Father Charlie, but I know that he is holding me. I can feel his arms around me, but I cannot see his face.

This vision has come to me often. It is not like other dreams. It is very clear, and I am always very afraid, and I don't know why. They are talking, but I do not understand their words. Mother Elouise reaches for me, but Father Charlie will not let me go. I feel afraid that Father Charlie will not let me go with Mother Elouise. But why should I be afraid? I love Father Charlie, and I never want to leave him. Still I reach out, reach out, reach out, and still the arms hold me and I cannot go.

Mother Elouise is crying. I see her face twisted in pain. I want to comfort her. "Mommy is hurt," I say again and again.

And then, suddenly, at the end of this vision I am in my mother's arms and we are running, running up a hill, into the trees. I am looking back over her shoulder. I see Father Charlie then. I see him, but I do not see him. I know exactly where he is, in my vision. I could tell you his height. I could tell you where his left foot is and where his right foot is, but still I can't see him. He has no face, no color; he is just a man-shaped emptiness in the clearing, and then the trees are in the way and he is gone.

Elouise stopped only a little way into the woods. She turned around, as if to go back to Charlie. But she would not go back. If she returned to him, it would be to disconnect the Rectifier. There would be no other reason to do it.

"Charlie, you son of a bitch!" she shouted.

There was no answer. She stood, waiting. Surely he could come to her. He would see that she would never go back, never turn off the machine. Once he realized it was inevitable, he would come running from the machine, into the forest, back to the clearing where the 787 had landed. Why would he want to give his life so meaninglessly? What was in the time capsule, after all? Just history—that's what he said, wasn't it? Just history, just films and metal plates engraved with words and microdots and other ways of preserving the story of mankind. "How can they learn from our mistakes, unless we tell them what they were?" Charlie had asked.

Sweet, simple, naive Charlie. It is one thing to preserve a hatred for the killing machines and the soul-destroying machines and the garbage-making machines. It was another to leave behind detailed, accurate, unquestionable descriptions. History was not a way of preventing the repetition of mistakes. It was a way of guaranteeing them. Wasn't it?

She turned and walked on, not very quickly, out of the range of the Rectifier, carrying Amy and listening, all the way, for the sound of Charlie running after her.

What was Mother Elouise like? She was a woman of contradictions. Even with me, she would work for hours teaching me to read, helping me make tablets out of river clay and write on them with a shaped stick. And then, when I had written the words she taught me, she would weep and say, "Lies, all lies," Sometimes she would break the tablets I had made. But whenever part of her words was broken, she would make me write it again.

She called the collection of words The Book of the Golden Age. I have named it The Book of the Lies of the Angel Elouise, for it is important for us to know that the greatest truths we have seem like lies to those who have been touched by the angel.

She told many stories to me, and often I asked her why they must be written down. "For Father Charlie," she would always say.

"Is he coming back, then?" I would ask.

But she shook her head, and finally one time she said, "It is not for Father Charlie to read. It is because Father Charlie wanted it written."

"Then why didn't he write it himself?" I asked.

And Mother Elouise grew very cold with me, and all she would say was, "Father Charlie bought these stories. He paid more for them than I am willing to pay to have them left unwritten." I wondered then whether Father Charlie was rich, but other things she said told me that he wasn't. So I do not understand except that Mother Elouise did not want to tell the stories, and Father Charlie, though he was not there, constrained her to tell them.

There are many of Mother Elouise's lies that I love, but I will say now which of them she said were most important:

1. In the Golden Age for ten times a thousand years men lived in peace and love and joy, and no one did evil one to another. They shared all things in common, and no man was hungry while another was full, and no man had a home while another stood in the rain, and no wife wept for her husband, killed before his time.

2. The great serpent seems to come with great power. He has many names: Satan, Hitler, Lucifer, Nimrod, Napoleon. He seems to be beautiful, and he promises power to his friends and death to his enemies. He says he will right all wrongs. But really he is weak, until people believe in him and give him the power of their bodies. If you refuse to believe in the serpent, if no one serves him, he will go away.

3. There are many cycles of the world. In every cycle the great serpent has arisen and the world has been destroyed to make way for the

return of the Golden Age. Christ comes again in every cycle, also. One day when He comes men will believe in Christ and doubt the great serpent, and that time the Golden Age will never end, and God will dwell among men forever. And all the angels will say. "Come not to heaven but to Earth, for Earth is heaven now."

These are the most important lies of Mother Elouise. Believe them all, and remember them, for they are true.

All the way to the airplane clearing, Elouise deliberately broke branches and let them dangle so that Charlie would have no trouble finding a straight path out of the range of the Rectifier, even if he left his flight to the last second. She was sure Charlie would follow her. Charlie would bend to her as he had always bent, resilient and accommodating. He loved Elouise, and Amy he loved even more. What was in the metal under his feet that would weigh in the balance against his love for them?

So Elouise broke the last branch and stepped into the clearing and then sat down and let Amy play in the unburnt grass at the edge while she waited. *It is Charlie who will bend,* she said to herself, *for I will never bend on this. Later I will make it up to him, but he must know that on this I will never bend.*

The cold place in her grew larger and colder until she burned inside, waiting for the sound of feet crashing through the underbrush. The damnable birds kept singing, so that she could not hear the footsteps.

Mother Elouise never hit me, or anyone else so far as I knew. She fought only with her words and silent acts, though she could have killed easily with her hands. I saw her physical power only once. We were in the forest, to gather firewood. We stumbled upon a wild hog. Apparently it felt cornered, though we were weaponless; perhaps it was just mean. I have not studied the ways of wild hogs. It charged, not Mother Elouise, but me. I was five at the time, and terrified, I ran to Mother Elouise, tried to cling to her, but she threw me out of the way and went into a crouch. I was screaming. She paid no attention to me. The hog continued rushing, but seeing I was down and Mother Elouise erect, it changed its path. When it came near, she leaped to the side. It was not nimble enough to turn to face her. As it lumbered past, Mother Elouise kicked it just behind the head. The kick broke the hog's neck so violently that its head dropped and the hog rolled over and over, and when it was through rolling, it was already dead.

Mother Elouise did not have to die.

She died in the winter when I was seven. I should tell you how life was then, in Richmond. We were only two thousand souls by then, not the large city of ten thousand we are now. We had only six finished ships trading the coast, and they had not yet gone so far north as Manhattan, though we had run one voyage all the way to Savannah in the south. Richmond already ruled and protected from the Potomac to Dismal Swamp. But it was a very hard winter, and the town's leaders insisted on hoarding all the stored grain and fruits and vegetables and meat for our protected towns, and let the distant tribes trade or travel where they would, they would get no food from Richmond.

It was then that my mother, who claimed she did not believe in God, and Uncle Avram, who was a Jew, and Father Michael, who was a priest, all argued the same side of the question. It's better to feed them than to kill them, they all said. But when the tribes from west of the mountains and north of the Potomac came into Richmond lands, pleading for help, the leaders of Richmond turned them away and closed the gates of the towns. An army marched then, to put the fear of God, as they said, into the hearts of the tribesmen. They did not know which side God was on.

Father Michael argued and Uncle Avram stormed and fumed, but Mother Elouise silently went to the gate at moonrise one night and alone overpowered the guards. Silently she gagged them and bound them and opened the gates to the hungry tribesmen. They came through weaponless, as she had insisted. They quietly went to the storehouses and carried off as much food as they could. They were found only as the last few fled. No one was killed.

But there was an uproar, a cry of treason, a trial, and an execution. They decided on beheading, because they thought it would be quick and merciful. They had never seen a beheading.

It was Jack Woods who used the ax. He practiced all afternoon with pumpkins. Pumpkins have no bones.

In the evening they all gathered to watch, some because they hated Mother Elouise, some because they loved her, and the rest because they could not stay away. I went also, and Father Michael held my head and would not let me see. But I heard.

Father Michael prayed for Mother Elouise. Mother Elouise damned his and everyone else's soul to hell. She said, "If you kill me for bringing life, you will only bring death on your own heads."

"That's true," said the men around her. "We will all die. But you will die first."

"Then I'm the luckier," said Mother Elouise. It was the last of her lies, for she was telling the truth, and yet she did not believe it herself, for I heard her weep. With her last breaths she wept and cried out, "Charlie! Charlie!" There are those who claim she saw a vision of Charlie waiting for her on the right hand of God, but I doubt it. She would have said so. I think she only wished to see him. Or wished for his forgiveness. It doesn't matter. The angel had long since left her, and she was alone.

Jack swung the ax and it fell, more with a smack than a thud. He had missed her neck and struck deep in her back and shoulder. She screamed. He struck again and this time silenced her. But he did not break through her spine until the third blow. Then he turned away splattered with blood, and vomited and wept and pleaded with Father Michael to forgive him.

Amy stood a few meters away from Elouise, who sat on the grass of the clearing, looking toward a broken branch on the nearest tree. Amy called, "Mommy! Mommy!" Then she bounced up and down, bending and unbending her knees. "Da! Da!" she cried. "La la la la la." She was dancing and wanted her mother to dance and sing, too. But Elouise only looked toward the tree, waiting for Charlie to appear. *Any minute,* she thought. *He will be angry. He will be ashamed,* she thought. *But he will be alive.*

In the distance, however, the air all at once was shining. Elouise could see it clearing because they were not far from the edge of the Rectifier field. It shimmered in the trees, where it caused no harm to plants. Any vertebrates within the field, any animals that lived by electricity passing along nerves, were instantly dead, their brains stilled. Birds dropped from tree limbs. Only insects droned on.

The Rectifier field lasted only minutes.

Amy watched the shining air. It was as if the empty sky itself were dancing with her. She was transfixed. She would soon forget the airplane, and already her father's face was disappearing from her memories. But she would remember the shining. She would see it forever in her dreams, a vast thickening of the air, dancing and vibrating up and down, up and down. In her dreams it would always be the same, a terrible shining light that would grow and grow and grow and press against her in her bed. And always with it would come the sound of a voice she loved, saying, "Jesus. Jesus. Jesus." This dream would come so clearly when she was twelve that she would tell it to her adopted father, the priest named Michael. He told her that it was the voice of an angel, speaking the name of the source of all light. "You must not fear the light," he said. "You must embrace it." It satisfied her.

But at the moment she first heard the voice, in fact and not in dream, she had no trouble recognizing it, it was the voice of her mother, Elouise, saying, "Jesus." It was full of grief that only a child could fail to understand. Amy did not understand. She only tried to repeat the word, "Deeah-zah."

"God," said Elouise, rocking back and forth, her face turned up toward a heaven she was sure was unoccupied.

"Dog," Amy repeated, "Dog dog doggie." In vain she looked around for the four-footed beast.

"Charlie!" Elouise screamed as the Rectifier field faded.

"Daddy," Amy cried, and because of her mother's tears she also wept. Elouise took her daughter in her arms and held her, rocking back and forth. Elouise discovered that there were some things that could not be frozen in her.

Some things that must burn: Sunlight. And lightning. And everlasting, inextinguishable regret.

My mother, Mother Elouise, often told me about my father. She described Father Charlie in detail, so I would not forget. She refused to let me forget anything. "It's what Father Charlie died for," she told me, over and over. "He died so you would remember. You cannot forget."

So I still remember, even today, every word she told me about him. His hair was red, as mine was. His body was lean and hard. His smile was quick, like mine, and he had gentle hands. When his hair was long or sweaty, it kinked tightly at his forehead, ears, and neck. His touch was so delicate he could cut in half an animal so tiny it could not be seen without a machine; so sensitive that he could fly—an art that Mother Elouise said was a not a miracle, since it could be done by many giants of the Golden Age, and they took with them many others who could not fly alone. This was Charlie's gift. Mother Elouise said. She also told me that I loved him dearly.

But for all the words that she taught me, I still have no picture of my father in my mind. It is as if the words drove out the vision, as so often happens.

Yet I still hold that one memory of my father, so deeply hidden that I can neither lose it nor fully find it again. Sometimes I wake up weeping. Sometimes I wake up with my arms in the air, curved just so, and I remember that I was dreaming of embracing that large man who loved me. My arms remember how it feels to hold Father Charlie tight around the neck and cling to him as he carries his child. And when I cannot sleep, and the pillow seems to be always the wrong shape, it is because I am hunting for the shape of Father Charlie's shoulder, which my heart remembers, though my mind cannot.

God put angels into Mother Elouise and Father Charlie, and they destroyed the world, for the cup of God's indignation was full, and all the works of men become dust, but out of dust God makes men, and out of men and women, angels.

THE LAST JERRY FAGIN SHOW

By John Morressy

The other networks were wiped out, and they knew it. After this there would be no more "Big Three." There would be only a single network, and Jerry Fagin would rule it like a king.

The others tried to put up a fight, of course. There are no good losers in this business. One network threw together a nude musical version of the *Kama Sutra*. Another did a live eight-hour report on torture and execution of political prisoners around the world. The PBS stations had the best solution: They reran the Fischer-Spassky match.

But only the Jerry Fagin show could offer a real live honest-to-H. G. Wells alien from outer space as a guest. The projected audience was 99.3 percent of all potential viewers. It was figured that 0.4 percent would tune in to the other networks purely out of habit, and the remaining 0.3 percent would be watching their own canned reruns of *The Lawrence Welk Show*.

Given Jerry's personality and the nature of the television industry, the wipeout was inevitable. A cage of tigers can be pretty impressive, but if you drop a gigantic dinosaur into the cage, the tigers all of a sudden turn into pussycats. And Jerry Fagin was looking like a very big tyrannosaurus rex. He had been one all along, but he kept the fact hidden. Most people thought he was a pussycat. Those of us who knew better said nothing—and kept our jobs.

Jerry Fagin was a funny man, as everybody knows. He had half a dozen foolproof comic characters, but he didn't really need any of them. He could stand in front of a camera deadpan, hands in his pockets, looking up at the ceiling, and reel off a monologue that had everybody helpless with laughter. He was born with pure comic instinct. At a party I've seen him zero in on the one person out of, maybe, two hundred total strangers who could feed him perfect straight lines.

Jerry was probably the funniest man I ever worked for, and I've worked for them all. Along with all the funny he had a streak of pure killer. But Jerry had talent, and, more important, he had luck; so the killer side hardly ever showed. He always seemed to be on the scene at the right time or to know just the right person and have something on him.

So he wound up, at twenty-nine, hosting *Late Night Live*. At thirty, he was the hottest thing in the industry. The *Late Night Live* title was forgotten. Everybody called it *The Jerry Fagin Show*.

Jerry could play an audience like Horowitz playing the fiddle, or the piano, or whatever the hell Horowitz plays. You know what I mean. He took small-town talent-show winners and made them into stars of their own. Just by holding up a book, he could turn a piece of schlock by an unknown hack into a best-seller. He could take a clubhouse errand boy and make him into a political figure. And he did. And they always paid.

The payoff was never money. By this time Jerry wasn't worried about money. He wanted other things. He just hung in there and smiled and played kindly Uncle Jerry until he needed a favor. He never had to ask twice. Everybody knew that what Jerry Fagin had built up overnight he could tear down just as fast.

When the alien ship landed in Washington, Jerry counted up his I.O.U.'s and decided that it was pay-up time. He must have called in every one he had to get that thing on his show, but he succeeded. At the personal request of the President, no less.

The alien was called Twelve. He came from a planet with a name that sounded like cowflop being tossed into a mudhole. Some White House speech writer tagged it Brother Earth, and that was the name that stuck, over the protests of the enraged feminists.

Twelve looked like a human being designed

by a committee and built by nursery-school dropouts. He seemed to have started out to be symmetrical, but missed. Two arms and two legs, like us, but they were of different lengths and thicknesses and set just a bit off center. Body lumpy as a potato, with a smaller potato for a head. Two eyes, a nose, and a mouth, but they moved around like the features of a melting snowman. Above one eye was a shiny spot. Twelve called it the weiox and tried to explain its function. No one understood a damned thing he said about it. They figured it was some kind of ear and let it go at that.

Aside from his weiox and a few other small details, mostly internal, Twelve made himself pretty clear right from the start. It turned out that he had been orbiting Earth for the last sixty-three hailumes, which was somewhere around twenty-seven of our years. All that time he was monitoring our broadcasts. And since most of his source material was supplied by television and radio, he had picked up a peculiar view of humanity.

For one thing, I think Twelve never really grasped the fact that there's a difference—most of the time, anyway—between a sitcom rerun and the *Eleven O'Clock News,* or an old Cagney movie and a junk-food commercial. They were all new to him, and all equally real. Or unreal. Or whatever.

Twelve's civilization had no word for *entertainment*. The concept simply did not exist for them. They did have some kind of music, but it wasn't an art form; it was a part of their digestive process. And that was all. They had no drama, no literature of any kind, no art, and absolutely no sense of humor.

They didn't have wars, either, and Twelve didn't seem to know what weapons were for. So everyone breathed a lot easier.

Now, it was clear to me that if you're going to interview something like Twelve on television, live—before the biggest audience in history—you go get Sevareid out of retirement, or you hunt up a Lippmann or a Cronkite or somebody serious like that. You want the kind of people who cover elections and moon landings. You don't want Jerry Fagin.

But nobody asked me. Jerry Fagin landed the alien and scheduled him for a Friday night show. Then he sat back, read the headlines, listened to his telephones ring, and gloated.

I watched the show by myself that night, and I certainly didn't gloat. I had been alone most of the past month, ever since Jerry dropped me from his staff, loudly and publicly. In this business there is nobody as untouchable as a loser, and an out-of-work comedy writer is a loser of the *Hindenburg* class.

So I settled in, hoping to see Jerry screw up and blow his big moment and knowing all the time that no matter how big a son of a bitch Jerry Fagin might be, he was a pro and this would be the show of his career. But I could hope.

At the same time I didn't want to see Jerry completely wrecked, just badly damaged and requiring some repairs. Humiliation and disgrace were fine, but I didn't want him ruined. He was still my best potential source of income, and I was starting to feel the pinch. Trouble tonight, and Jerry would be calling me back, asking me to polish up some of the failure-proof routines that had helped put him where he was. And I'd be there. I was not about to turn down the best-paying job in the business just because Jerry had made me look like a fool in public and closed every studio door to me. I mean, I have my pride, but I have my bills, too.

I started watching early, so I could savor the full hype. Spot announcements every fifteen minutes. On the *Seven O'Clock News,* a special five-minute report on the universe. At eight, ninety minutes of interviews with astronauts, starlets, clergymen, science-fiction writers, senators, a rock group, and the president of the Descendants of Prehistoric Alien Visitors. During the nine-thirty commercial interlude—toothpaste, deodorants, and detergents hawked in skits starring, respectively, teen-agers and aliens, secretaries and aliens, and housewives and aliens—I started drinking. I could tell it was going to be better than a one-bottle night, and I wanted to start early and avoid having to rush things later on.

After the barrage of commercials came a special one-hour feature on alien visitors as depicted by Hollywood. Sixty minutes of blobs, globs, bugs, slugs, crawling eyes, brain-eaters, body-snatchers, mind-stealers, worms, germs, robots, and androids, and every ten minutes a screaming reminder of tonight's once-in-a-lifetime *Jerry Fagin Show.*

What kind of impression all this was supposed to make on Twelve, I could not imagine. Maybe they made sure he was nowhere near a television set.

At ten-thirty, a longer, louder announcement. Then, after the mature-viewer commercials—wine, tampons, and laxatives peddled, respectively, by diplomats and aliens, female skydivers and aliens, and grandmothers and aliens—a half-hour special to remind the viewer who might have forgotten that there are nine planets in the solar system, that we are but a grain of sand on the shore of the great ocean of infinity, and so on. Very profound stuff, delivered like *Sermonette* or an insurance commercial. I kept on drinking.

Eleven o'clock brought the traditional mix of news, commercials, and station ID, and then, at eleven-thirty, came *The Jerry Fagin Show.* It was presented like the Second Coming.

The familiar Jerry Fagin theme was gone, and so was the studio orchestra. In their place was a selection from the *The Planets,* performed by the Hollywood Symphony and the Mormon Tabernacle Choir. Billy Bragg. Jerry's apple-cheeked, white-haired butterball of an announcer, did no clowning on this sacred night. He marched on camera with the step of a man in a college commencement procession. He was in white-tie and tails. I took another big drink.

* * *

As I should have anticipated, Jerry was playing with his audience. After the solemn buildup, the show opened with a young comic. Billy appealed for a big hand for the kid in his first TV appearance, and the poor jerk—his name was Frankie Mars, for God's sake—came on an did a monologue about aliens landing in Brooklyn. It was the thirty-first one I'd heard since Twelve's arrival. There were alien-and-Puerto Rican jokes, alien-and-cop jokes, Jewish mother-and-alien jokes. I found it all very cozy and familiar. I had stolen a lot of those very same gags for my early sketches.

The comic died, and he was followed by a singer who did a new number written in honor of Twelve. The only lines I can remember are "The whole room rocks, and I shake in my socks, when you jiggle your eyes and wink your weiox." The rest was a lot worse.

The singer gave it all she had, but she went down like the *Titanic,* same as Frankie Mars. Scattered applause from three relatives in the studio audience, silence from everybody else. The entire home audience was either in the bathroom or at the refrigerator. Comics and singers they could get anytime. What they wanted was Jerry and his guest.

That was a distinct Jerry Fagin touch. Subtle and deadly. I could picture him setting it up: the Uncle Jerry smile and "This will be the biggest audience in history, and I'm going to give some new talent a chance." And it's not until they're on camera that the new talent realize that they couldn't hold this audience if they stripped naked and sacrifice themselves to a trash compactor. I wondered why Jerry had picked this particular comic and this particular singer to destroy. Probably an interesting story there if I could dig it out. I drank to their memory.

Jerry sauntered on camera, white-tie and all, and was greeted with five solid minutes of uproar. He stood with his hands in his pockets, looking humble and saintly, and when the noise died down, he made a little speech in which he used the words *honor* nine times and *privilege* eight. *Grateful* came up eleven times in just over a minute.

Then Twelve appeared at last. I turned the welcoming ovation low and took a good look. He moved smoothly for something as lopsided as he appeared to be. The lumpy, grayish-brown plastic sack that covered his pale body didn't help his looks much. He looked like something that stepped off the cover of a cereal box, and those wacky, wandering, off-center features were halfway between a nightmare monster and an idiot mask.

I turned up the sound. The people in the audience were still applauding wildly, and Jerry let them go on. But when someone whistled. Jerry held up his hands for quiet. Twelve's eyes and nose moved around a little and then were still.

"Our guest has requested one courtesy," Jerry said. "Whistling sets up a painful feedback in his communication apparatus; so I must insist that no one whistle during the show."

"Thank you, Mr. Jerry Fagin," said Twelve. His voice rolled out in a deep, gluey flow, like gravel being tumbled around in syrup.

"Thank you for consenting to appear on our show, Mr. Ambassador. It's a great honor." Jerry said.

Once Jerry got started thanking he couldn't stop himself. He thanked the President, Congress, the armed forces, the American people, the audience, the network, his friends, his sponsors—individually, by name—his parents, and his current wife, then went on to thank the rulers of Twelve's planet, the spaceship industry there, and everyone else—right down to Newton, Galileo, and Einstein—who might possibly have had a bearing on Twelve's appearance here. The only name he didn't drop was God's. Maybe he should have thrown that in.

Finally, after all the preliminaries and all the back-patting, Twelve got his chance to speak. This was the big moment, the message to humankind from outer space, the voice from the stars. Everyone listened in absolute silence.

And Twelve was boring as hell.

It's ridiculous to think that someone who has actually crossed interstellar space with word from another world could be dull, but that's what Twelve was. He may have been dynamite on his own world, but on Earth he was a dud. It wasn't entirely his fault. In his monitoring he had picked up every cliche in the English language, and he was using all of them. That burbly voice didn't help, either.

By the time Twelve had assured everyone that he looked upon his mission as a great and historic challenge, that he came in hopes of establishing a lasting friendship between our two great peoples, that a new era in the history of the galaxy was dawning and he was proud and humbled to be given the chance to serve and so on and so on—it sounded as if he had memorized every campaign handout of the past forty years—Jerry could smell trouble. The studio audience was fidgeting noisily. People were coughing and shuffling their feet.

I caught the quick flickering of the eyes, the giveaway that Jerry was getting edgy. I could almost hear his brain going. Here was Jerry on the biggest night of his career, the biggest night in television history, and his guest was bombing. He could picture that audience of a hundred ninety-two million American viewers scratching their bellies and saying. "Hey, Honey, what do you say we switch over to the naked dancers on Channel 8?"

So Jerry made his move. If Twelve couldn't carry his weight as a guest, he'd just have to pay his passage any way he could.

Twelve was gurgling on, ending a long speech about interplanetary solidarity. I returned my attention to him. ". . . With shared hope for the future and with a deep and abiding faith in the basic decency and fundamental goodwill of the fine people of Earth that encourages me to predict a new age of brotherhood and justice in which races will ask not what the galaxy will do for their planet but rather what their planet can do for the galaxy,'' he said.

There was polite applause. Twelve looked pleased, but he wasn't in the business. The applause was the kind that sounds in every performer's ears like a death rattle.

"Gee, that's just the way my daddy used to put it," Jerry said, turning to the audience.

That drew the first laugh of the evening. Everyone recognized the tag line of one of Jerry's oldest characters, Dummy Lummox the Clumsy Cop. It gave the audience something safe and familiar to deal with. They knew how to react now.

"But in a higher sense, this night represents only the beginning of what I venture to call the Galactic Age," Twelve went on, "for there is much to be done before we march together with arms linked in friendship and trust to meet the challenge of the future."

"That sounds mighty good, but we do it different back home," Jerry said.

The audience caught that one, too, and gladdened my heart. It was the tag line of my very own character, Elmo Klunk the Shitkicker Aboard. Elmo was one of Jerry's dependables, sure to make an appearance at least once very two weeks. The audience loosened up and laughed a bit louder, and longer.

I poured another drink, a bigger one, and edged forward on my chair. It isn't every night that you get to see an alien visitor turned into a stooge.

"We're honored by your tribute, Mr.

Ambassador,'' Jerry said, ''but I'm sure you understand our audience's curiosity about your planet and its customs. For instance, I'm told that you have no comedy on your world.''

''It is correct, we have no comedy.''

Jerry nodded sympathetically. ''I've run into the same problem. You must need new writers.''

I felt that one right between the shoulders. Welcome to Pearl Harbor, this is your host. Jerry Fagin. If my glass hadn't been nearly full. I would have thrown it at the screen.

Twelve, after a pause, burbled, ''It is correct, we have no writers.''

''I'll let you have mine. You still won't have any comedy, but you'll be getting a great bowling team.''

Again Twelve paused amid the laughter to evaluate Jerry's line and said, ''I know this bowling that is the work of your Saturdays in the regressing hailumes. We have no bowling.''

''No comedy, no writers, no bowling. Tell me, Mr. Ambassador, what do your people do for entertainment?''

''It is correct, we have no entertainment. I do not grasp the concept.''

''It's simple. Entertainment is what you do when you're not working.''

Twelve was silent for a longer time. Clearly he was having trouble with Jerry's lines, which weren't saying what they appeared to be saying. The audience tittered with anticipation. Finally, in a gurgle that already sounded to me to be a bit defensive. Twelve said, ''When we are not working, we sleep.''

"Like all those people who used to watch the other networks. I see. But seriously, Mr. Ambassador . . .'' And Jerry went on, a little faster now, confident, feeling the audience with him. They were laughing in the right places, waiting for the lines they knew he was going to feed his stooge from outer space.

Jerry jumped from topic to topic, always balancing the serious question with the quick punch line or asking a dumb question and then going statesmanlike, until the audience was helpless and Twelve didn't know what the hell was going on. Those syrupy responses came slower and slower. Each pause was longer than the one before. Finally, when Jerry got on the subject of reproduction, Twelve gave up completely and sat very still. Except for his eyes and nose and mouth. They were crawling around his face like flies trapped in vanilla pudding.

By now Jerry was sailing. The biggest audience in TV history was watching him, and he was showing them that nobody and nothing, not even a creature from another world, could top Jerry Fagin on his own show. I caught the wild, piercing gleam of ego in Jerry's eyes as he stood up, tousled his hair, and boomed out, "Well, I'll tell you the whole story, citizen, but you'll have to promise not to interrupt me. If there's one thing I can't stand, citizen, it's an interrupter.''

He was slipping into a favorite character. Senator Wynn Baggs, the filibuster champion of Washington. The audience applauded and howled with delighted recognition as Jerry ranted on.

All this time Twelve sat like a statue, watching every move that Jerry made. He didn't look angry or insulted. At least, nothing on that Silly Putty face suggested irritation. As far as I could read him, Twelve was fascinated. It was as if he had Jerry under a microscope and couldn't believe what he was seeing. And Jerry ate up the attention like a kid with a hot fudge sundae.

Then Twelve threw up both his arms in a "Eureka!" gesture. I could almost see an old-fashioned light bulb go on over his head. For the first time that night his features stayed put. The audience got very quiet all of a sudden.

"This is a tohei-meiox!" Twelve announced suddenly, as if that explained everything.

Instinctively Jerry topped him. "If it is, you'll wipe it up. But I ought to warn you—the producer's wife loves it."

Twelved worked his face around into something like an untidy smile. "Now it becomes clear what is my role in this ritual," he said. His voice sounded a little less gooey.

When Twelve began to get up, Jerry had the first whiff of trouble ahead. He bounced to his feet while Twelve was still halfway up, and with a big smile at his guest he said, "Thank you, Mr. Ambassador, for honoring us by consenting to appear on *The Jerry Fagin Show*. It's been a great pleasure and an exciting experience for all of us, and we're sorry you have to rush off, but we know how crowded your schedule is." Stepping to the forestage, Jerry began to clap. "And now let's have a big hand for the ambassador," he said to the delighted audience.

That didn't stop Twelve, who was acting like a kid who has just learned the facts of life. "In my ignorance I assumed that this was to be a hoeimeius encounter. I employed my fourth voice. Had I known that it was to be a toheimeiox, I would have spoken thirdishly. Please forgive me, Mr. Jerry Fagin."

On the last few words, as Twelve took his place at Jerry's side, his voice had changed completely. It was really weird. I wondered whether Jerry had somehow shocked the alien into instant puberty. In seconds Twelve had gone from that sumpy gurgle to a flat, staccato, nowhere-in-particular accent not a hell of a lot different from Jerry's.

"Please take my wife," he said.

Nobody made a sound. They probably all thought Twelve was going out of his head. So did I, for just an instant, and then I recognized that line and had my first clue of what Twelve was up to.

I didn't believe it. It was too crazy. But when Twelve wobbled his face a little—just a little, very nervously—it all became clear: He was mugging for a laugh. This crazy-looking thing from outer space that couldn't even get a four-word one-liner straight was trying to be a stand-up comic. I felt kind of sorry for the poor blob. Imagine coming all that way and bombing on your very first appearance.

What I didn't know at the time was that Twelve learned fast.

"Thanks again, Mr. Ambassador," Jerry said, edging away. "You've been a wonderful guest, and we hope you'll visit us again whenever your demanding schedule permits."

"It's a pleasure to be here, Jerry," Twelve said, stepping in front of his host, talking directly to the audience. "I would have been here earlier, but there was a holdup in traffic. I stopped for a light, and two men held me up." He did a quick jerk of his features—eyes left, nose right. The audience laughed. They were cautious about it, but they laughed.

"We're all sorry to hear that, Mr. Ambassador. And now our next guest, the well-known—" Jerry started to say, but Twelve went right on.

"The producer took me to dinner at this place on Fifty-fourth. The salad wasn't bad, but I didn't like the little men in loincloths who kept dipping their arrows into the Russian dressing."

"—Well-known star of stage and screen who for the past three seasons has been delighting viewers with her portrayal—" Jerry tried again, louder, pushing in front of the alien.

Twelve rolled his eyes in opposite directions and blinked his weiox. "I asked the waiter if the lobster Newburg was any good. He said, 'Where did you see that on the menu?' I said, 'I didn't see it on the menu. I saw it on your tie.' " The audience laughed harder and longer this time. They liked him.

Shoving Twelve aside, Jerry snarled, "This lovely and talented lady who has won the hearts of millions of viewers with her portrayal of the zany, lovable Mrs. Pregnowski in—"

Twelve reeled, staggered back, waved his arms, did a flying leap into the air, and came down in a classic pratfall with a noise like a bagpipe assaulting a whoopee cushion. The audience went wild, applauding and cheering, drowning Jerry out completely. When Twelve climbed to his feet, his nose doing a back-and-forth crawl like a slow pendulum, he had to signal for quiet before he could be heard.

"The producer said, 'I hate to eat and run, but the way I tip, it's absolutely necessary,' " he said, spinning both forearms around like propellers.

The material was lousy, sure, but I could see that Twelve had a great natural delivery. With a good writer, he could go places. A show of his own, maybe.

What happened next, I will never believe was an accident. The camera cut to Jerry, purple-faced, restrained by four elderly security guards and a weeping producer. It held on the group. One hundred ninety-two million viewers heard Jerry scream, "Get that mush-faced intersteller son of a bitch off my stage! Shoot him! Drop a light on him! He's killing us!"

Which was an exaggeration. Twelve was doing wonders for the show. He was only killing Jerry.

We call the show *Twelve at Twelve* now,

even though it still comes on half an hour before midnight. The producer felt that *Twelve at Eleven-thirty* would only confuse people.

But Twelve is a great guy to work for. It's a nostalgia trip just talking to him. During those years he was monitoring, he heard all the great ones—Berle, Gleason, Caesar, Groucho, Carson, you name them—and memorized every gag, every shtick, every bit of business. He just didn't know what the hell to do with his material until he saw Jerry putting it all together. Now Twelve is like a guy who's found his true calling. I think he's going to stay right here on Earth, and in the business, for good.

Twelve is also a very hard worker. He drops in every afternoon to run through the monologue for that night's show. We've already come up with some lines that everyone in the world recognizes. I've seen "Well, wink my weiox" on everything from kids' lunch boxes to bikinis, and a day doesn't pass without my hearing someone say, "Please take my wife," and then seeing him collapse in hysterics. Even Henny Youngman used it when Twelve had him on the show as a guest.

We have a good running gag going on Twelve's dumb friend from home. Old Thirty-one. And if a line goes flat, all he has to do is jiggle his features and the audience breaks up.

He's even developing into a good impressionist. Some of his impressions are weird—he's the only one I know who does all the members of the Politburo while simultaneously trying to get a stuffed elk into a Honda—but his Jack

Benny is nearly perfect.

What convinces me that Twelve is in the business to stay is that he's learned to be sincere. Two nights ago he graciously had Jerry back as a special guest to celebrate Jerry's new afternoon quiz show. They were hugging like a couple of high-school sweethearts.

Twelve was beautiful. A real pro. He ended the show by wiping his eyes, putting an arm around Jerry, and saying. "This crazy guy is my dearest friend on your whole wonderful planet. Everything I have, I owe to Jerry Fagin."

I could tell from Jerry's expression that he'd love to collect.

But my money is on Twelve.

GOD IS AN IRON

By Spider Robinson

I smelled her before I saw her. Even so, the first sight of her was shocking. She was sitting in a tan plastic-surfaced armchair, the kind where the front comes up as the back goes down. It was back as far as it would go. It was placed beside the large living-room window, whose curtains were drawn. A plastic block table next to it held a digital clock, a dozen unopened packages of Peter Jackson cigarettes, a glass jar full of packs of matches, an empty ashtray, a full vial of cocaine, and a lamp with a bulb of at least 150 watts. It illuminated her with brutal clarity.

She was naked. Her skin was the color of vanilla pudding. Her hair was in rats, her nails unpainted and untended, some overlong and some broken. There was dust on her. She sat in a ghastly sludge of feces and urine. Dried vomit was caked on her chin and between her breasts and down her ribs to the chair.

These were only part of what I had smelled. The predominant odor was of freshbaked bread. It is the smell of a person who is starving to death. The combined effluvia had prepared me to find a senior citizen, paralyzed by a stroke or some such crisis.

I judged her to be about twenty-five years old.

I moved to where she could see me, and she did not see me. That was probably just as well, because I had just seen the two most horrible things. The first was the smile. They say that when the bomb went off at Hiroshima, some people's shadows were baked onto walls by it. I think that smile got baked on the surface of my brain in much the same way. I don't want to talk about that smile.

The second most horrible thing was the one that explained all the rest. From where I now stood I could see a triple socket in the wall beneath the window. Into it were plugged the lamp, the clock, and her.

I knew about wireheading, of course—I had lost a couple of acquaintances and one friend to the juice. But I had never seen a wirehead. It is by definition a solitary vice, and all the public usually gets to see is a sheeted figure being carried out to the wagon.

The transformer lay on the floor beside the chair where it had been dropped. The switch was on, and the timer had been jiggered so that instead of providing one five- or ten- or fifteen-second jolt per hour it allowed continuous flow. That timer is required by law on all juice rigs sold, and you need special tools to defeat it. Say, a nail file. The input cord was long, fell in crazy coils from the wall socket. The output cord disappeared beneath the chair, but I knew where it ended. It ended in the tangled snarl of her hair, at the crown of her head, ended in a miniplug. The plug was snapped into a jack surgically implanted in her skull, and from the jack tiny wires snaked their way through the wet jelly to the hypothalamus, to the specific place in the medial forebrain bundle where the major pleasure center of her brain was located. She had sat there in total transcendent ecstasy for at least five days.

I moved, finally. I moved closer, which surprised me. She saw me now, and impossibly the smile became a bit wider. I was marvelous. I was captivating. I was her perfect lover. I could not look at the smile; a small plastic tube ran from one corner of the smile and my eyes followed it gratefully. It was held in place by small bits of surgical tape at her jaw, neck, and shoulder, and from there it ran in a lazy curve to the big fifty-liter water-cooler bottle on the floor. She had plainly meant her suicide to last: She had arranged to die of hunger rather than thirst, which would have been quicker. She could take a drink when she happened to think of it; and if she forgot, what the hell.

My intention must have showed on my face, and I think she even understood it—the smile began to fade. That decided me. I moved before she could force her neglected body to react, whipped the plug out of the wall and stepped back warily.

Her body did not go rigid as if galvanized. It had already been so for many days. What it did was the exact opposite, and the effect was just as striking. She seemed to shrink. Her eyes slammed shut. She slumped. *Well,* I thought, *it'll be a long day and night before she can move a voluntary muscle again,* and then she hit me before I knew she had left the chair, breaking my nose with the heel of one fist and bouncing the other off the side of my head. We cannoned off each other and I managed to keep on my feet; she whirled and grabbed the lamp. Its cord was stapled to the floor and would not yield, so she set her feet and yanked and it snapped off clean at the base. In near-total darkness she raised the lamp on high and came to me, and I lunged inside the arc of her swing and punched her in the solar plexus. She said guff! and went down.

I staggered to a couch and sat down and felt my nose and fainted.

I don't think I was out very long. The blood tasted fresh. I woke with a sense of terrible urgency. It took me a while to work out why. When someone has been simultaneously starved and unceasingly stimulated for days on end, it is not the best idea in the world to depress that someone's respiratory center. I lurched to my feet.

It was not completely dark; there was a moon somewhere out there. She lay on her back, arms

at her side, perfectly relaxed. Her ribs rose and
fell in great slow swells. A pulse showed
strongly at her throat. As I knelt beside her she
began to snore, deeply and rhythmically.

I had time for second thoughts, now. It
seemed incredible that my impulsive action had
not killed her. Perhaps that had been my sub-
conscious intent. Five days of wireheading
alone should have killed her, let alone sudden
cold turkey.

I probed in the tangle of hair, found the
empty jack. The hair around it was dry. If she
hadn't torn the skin in yanking herself loose, it
was unlikely that she had sustained any more
serious damage within. I continued probing,
found no soft places on the skull. Her forehead
felt cool and sticky to my hand. The fecal smell
was overpowering the baking bread now, sourly
fresh.

There was no pain in my nose yet, but it felt
immense and pulsing. I did not want to touch
it, or to think about it. My shirt was soaked
with blood; I tossed it into a corner. It took
everything I had to lift her. She was unreason-
ably heavy, and I have carried drunks and
corpses. There was a hall off the living room,
and all halls lead to a bathroom. I headed that
way in a clumsy staggering trot, and just as I
reached the deeper darkness, with my pulse at
its maximum, my nose woke up and began
screaming. I nearly dropped her then and
clapped my hands to my face; the temptation
was overwhelming. Instead I whimpered like a
dog and kept going. Childhood feeling: runny

nose you can't wipe. At each door I came to teetered on one leg and kicked it open, and the third one gave the right small-room, acoustic-tile echo. The light switch was where they almost always are; I rubbed it on with my shoulder and the room flooded with light.

Large aquamarine tub. Styrofoam recliner pillow at the head end, nonslip bottom. Aquamarine sink with ornate handles, cluttered with toiletries and cigarette butts and broken shards of mirror from the medicine cabinet above. Aquamarine commode, lid up and seat down. Brown throw rug, expensive. Scale shoved back in a corner. I made a massive effort and managed to set her reasonably gently in the tub. I adjusted her head, fixed the chin-strap. I held both feet away from the faucet until I had the water adjusted, and then left with one hand on my nose and the other beating against my hip, in search of her liquor.

There was plenty to choose from. I found some Metaxa in the kitchen. I took great care not to bring it near my nose, sneaking it up on my mouth from below. It tasted like burning lighter fluid and made sweat spring out on my forehead. I found a roll of paper towels, and on my way back to the bathroom I used a great wad of them to swab most of the sludge off the chair and rug. There was a growing pool of water siphoning from the plastic tube, and I stopped that. When I got back to the bathroom the water was lapping over her bloated belly, and horrible tendrils were weaving up from beneath her. It took three rinses before I was satisfied with the body. I found a hose-and-spray under the sink that mated with the tub's faucet, and that made the hair easy.

I had to dry her there in the tub. There was only one towel, none too clean. I found a first-aid spray that incorporated a good topical anesthetic, and I put it on the sores on her back and butt. I had located her bedroom on the way to the Metaxa. Wet hair slapped my arm as I carried her there. She seemed even heavier, as though she had become waterlogged. I eased the door shut behind me and tried the light-switch trick again, and it wasn't there. I moved forward into a footlocker and lost her and went down amid multiple crashes, putting all my attention into guarding my nose. She made no sound at all, not even a grunt.

The light switch turned out to be a pull chain over the bed. She was on her side, still breathing slow and deep. I wanted to punt her up onto the bed. My nose was a blossom of pain. I nearly couldn't lift her the third time. I was moaning with frustration by the time I had her on her left side on the king-size mattress. It was a big brass four-poster bed, with satin sheets and pillow-cases, all dirty. The blankets were shoved to the bottom. I checked her skull and pulse again, peeled up each eyelid and found uniform pupils. Her forehead and cheek still felt cool, so I covered her. Then I kicked the footlocker clear into the corner, turned out the light, and left her snoring like a chainsaw.

Her vital papers and documents were in her

study, locked in a strongbox on the closet shelf. It was an expensive box, quite sturdy and proof against anything short of nuclear explosion. It had a combination lock with all of twenty-seven possible combinations. It was stuffed with papers. I laid her life out on her desk like a losing hand of solitaire and studied it with a growing frustration.

Her name was Karen Shavitski, and she used the name Karyn Shaw, which I thought phony. She was twenty-two. Divorced her parents at fourteen, uncontested no-fault. Since then she had been, at various times, waitress, secretary to a lamp salesman, painter, free-lance typist, motorcycle mechanic, library assistant, and unlicensed masseuse. The most recent paycheck stub was from The Hard Corps, a massage parlor with a cut-rate reputation. It was dated eight months ago. Her bank balance combined with paraphernalia I'd found in the closet to tell me that she was currently self-employed as a tootlegger, a cocaine dealer. The richness of the apartment and furnishings told me that she was a foolish one; even if the narcs missed her, very shortly the IRS was going to come down on her like a ton of bricks. Perhaps subconsciously she had not expected to be around.

Nothing there; I kept digging. She had attended community college for one semester, as an art major, and dropped out failing. She had defaulted on a lease three years ago. She had wrecked a car once and been shafted by her insurance company. Trivia. Only one major trauma in recent years: A year and a half ago

she had contracted out as host-mother to a
couple named Lombard/Smyth. It was a pretty
good fee—she had good hips and the right rare
blood type—but six months into the pregnancy
they had caught her using tobacco and canceled
the contract. She fought, but they had photographs. And better lawyers, naturally. She had
to repay the advance, and pay for the abortion,
of course, and got socked for court costs
besides.

It didn't make sense. To show clean lungs at
the physical, she had to have been off cigarettes
for at least three to six months. Why backslide,
with so much at stake? Like the minor traumas,
it felt more like an effect than a cause. Self-
destructive behavior. I kept looking.

Near the bottom I found something that
looked promising. Both her parents had been
killed in a car smash when she was eighteen.
Their obituary was paper-clipped to her father's
will. It was one of the most extraordinary
documents I've ever read. I could understand
an angry father cutting off his only daughter
without a dime. But what he had done was
worse. Much worse.

Dammit, it didn't work either. So-there
suicides don't wait four years. And they don't
use such a garish method either. It devalues the
tragedy. I decided it had to be either a very big
and dangerous coke deal gone bad, or a very
reptilian lover. No, not a coke deal. They'd
never have left her in her own apartment to die
the way she wanted to. It could not be murder:
Even the most unscrupulous wire surgeon needs

an awake, consenting subject to place the wire correctly.

A lover, then. I realized, pleased with my sagacity, and irritated as hell. I didn't know why. I chalked it up to my nose. It felt as though a large shark with rubber teeth was rhythmically biting it as hard as he could. I shoveled the papers back into the box, locked and replaced it, and went to the bathroom.

Her medicine cabinet would have impressed a pharmacist. She had lots of allergies. It took me five minutes to find aspirin. I took four. I picked the largest shard of mirror out of the sink, propped it on the septic tank, and sat down backward on the toilet. My nose was visibly displaced to the right, and the swelling was just hitting its stride. There was a box of kleenex on the floor. I ripped it apart, took out all the tissues, and stuffed them into my mouth. Then I grabbed my nose with my right hand and tugged out and to the left, flushing the toilet simultaneously with my left hand. The flushing coincided with the scream, and my front teeth met through the kleenex. When I could see again the nose looked straight and my breathing was unimpaired. I gingerly washed my face, and then hands, and left. A moment later I returned; something had caught my eye. It was the glass-and-toothbrush holder. There was only one toothbrush in it. I looked through the medicine chest again and noticed this time that there was no shaving cream, no razor either manual or electric, no masculine toiletries of any kind. All the prescriptions were in her name and seemed perfectly legitimate.

I went thoughtfully to the kitchen, mixed myself a Preacher's Downfall by moonlight, and took it to her bedroom. The bedside clock said five. I lit a match, moved the footlocker in front of an armchair, sat down, and put my feet up. I sipped my drink and listened to her snore and watched her breathe in the feeble light of the clock. I decided to run through all the possibilities, and as I was formulating the first one day-light smacked me hard in the nose.

My hands went up reflexively, and I poured my drink on my head and hurt my nose more. I wake up hard in the best of times. She was still snoring. I nearly threw the empty glass at her.

It was just past noon now; light came strongly through the heavy curtains, illuminating so much mess and disorder that I could not decide whether she had thrashed her bedroom herself or it had been tossed by a pro. I finally settled on the former: The armchair I'd slept on was intact. Or had the pro found what he wanted before he'd gotten that far?

I gave it up and went to make myself breakfast.

It took me an hour or two to clean up and air out the living room. The cord and transformer went down the oubliette, along with most of the perished items from the fridge. The dishes took three full cycles for each load, a couple of hours all told. I passed the time vacuuming and dusting and snooping, learning nothing more of significance. I was making up a shopping list about fifteen minutes later when I heard her moan. I reached her bedroom door in seconds, waited in the doorway with both hands in sight, and said slowly and clearly, "My name is Joseph Templeton, Karen. I am a friend. You are all right now."

Her eyes were those of a small tormented animal.

"Please don't try to get up. Your muscles won't work properly and you may hurt yourself."

No answer.

"Karen, are you hungry?"

"Your voice is ugly," she said despairingly, and her own voice was so hoarse I winced. *"My* voice is ugly." She sobbed gently. "It's *all* ugly." She screwed her eyes shut.

She was clearly incapable of movement. I told her I would be right back and went to the kitchen. I made up a tray of clear strong broth, unbuttered toast, tea with too much sugar, and saltine crackers. She was staring at the ceiling when I got back. I put the tray down, lifted her, and made a backrest of pillows.

"I want a drink."

"After you eat," I said agreeably.

"Who're you?"

"Mother Templeton. Eat."

"The soup, maybe. Not the toast." She got about half of it down, accepted some tea. I didn't want to overfill her. "My drink."

"Sure thing." I took the tray back to the kitchen, finished my shopping list, put away the last of the dishes, and put a frozen steak into the oven for my lunch. When I got back she was fast asleep.

Emaciation was near total; except for breasts and bloated belly she was all bone and taut skin. Her pulse was steady. At her best she would not have been very attractive by conventional standards. Passable. Too much waist, not enough neck, upper legs a bit too thick for the rest of her. It's hard to evaluate a starved and unconscious face, but her jaw was a bit too square, her nose a trifle hooked, her blue eyes just the least little bit too far apart. Animated, the face might have been beautiful—any set of features can support beauty—but even a superb makeup job could not have made her pretty. There was an old bruise on her chin. Her hair was sandy blond, long and thin; it had dried in snarls that would take an hour to comb out. Her breasts were magnificent, and that saddened me. In this world, a woman whose breasts are her best feature is in for a rough time.

I was putting together a picture of a life that would have depressed anyone with the sensitivity of a rhino. Back when I had first seen her, when her features were alive, she had looked sensitive. Or had that been a trick of the juice? Impossible to say now.

But damn it all to hell, I could find nothing to really explain the socket in her skull. You can hear worse life stories in any bar, on any street corner. I was prepared to match her scar for scar myself. Wireheads are usually addictive personalities, who decide at last to skip the small shit. There were no tracks on her anywhere, no nasal damage, no sign that she used any of the coke she sold. Her work history, pitiful and fragmented as it was, was too steady for any kind of serious jones; she had undeniably been hitting the sauce hard lately, but only lately. Tobacco seemed to be her only serious addiction.

That left the hypothetical bastard lover. I worried at that for a while to see if I could make it fit. Assume a really creatively sadistic son of a bitch had gutted her like a trout, for the pure fun of it. You can't do that to some- one as a visitor or even a guest; you have to live with them. So he did a world-class job of crippling a lady who by her history is a tough little cookie, and when he had broken her he vanished. Leaving not even so much as empty space in drawers, closets, or medicine chest. Unlikely. So perhaps after he was gone *she* scrubbed all traces of him out of the apartment—and then discovered that there is only one really good way to scrub memories. No, I couldn't picture such a sloppy house- keeper being so efficient.

Then I thought of my earlier feeling that the bedroom might have been tossed by a pro, and my blood turned to ice water. Suppose she wasn't a sloppy housekeeper? The jolly sadist returns unexpectedly for one last nibble. And finds her in the living room, just as I did. And leaves her there.

After five minutes' thought I relaxed. That didn't parse either. True, this luxury co-op did inexplicably lack security cameras in the halls—but for that very reason its rich tenants would be sure to take notice of comings and goings. If he had lived here for any time at all, his spoor was too diffuse to erase—so he would not have tried. Besides, a monster of that unique and rare kind thrives on the corruption of innocence. Tough little Karen was simply not toothsome enough.

At that point I went to the bathroom, and that settled it. When I lifted the seat to urinate I found written on the underside with felt-tip pen: "It's so nice to have a man around the house!" The handwriting was hers. She had lived alone.

I was relieved, because I hadn't relished thinking about my hypothetical monster or the necessity of tracking and killing him. But I was irritated as hell again.

I wanted to *understand*.

For something to do I took my steak and a mug of coffee to the study and heated up her terminal. I tried all the typical access codes, her birthdate and her name in numbers and such, but none of them would unlock it. Then on a hunch I tried the date of her parents' death, and that did it. I ordered the groceries she needed, instructed the lobby door to accept delivery, and tried everything I could think of to get a diary or a journal out of the damned thing, without success. So I punched up the public library and asked the catalog for *Britannica* on wireheading. It referred me to brain-reward, autostimulus of. I skipped over the history, from discovery by Olds and others in 1956 to emergence as a social problem in the late '80s when surgery got simple; declined the offered diagrams, graphs, and technical specs; finally found a brief section on motivations.

There was indeed one type of typical user I had overlooked. The terminally ill.

Could that really be? At her age? I went to the bathroom and checked the prescriptions. Nothing for heavy pain, nothing indicating anything more serious than allergies. Back before telephones had cameras I might have conned something out of her personal physician, but it would have been a chancy thing even then. There was no way to test the hypothesis.

It was possible, even plausible—but it just wasn't *likely* enough to satisfy the thing inside me that demanded an explanation. I dialed a game of four-wall squash, and made sure the computer would let me win. I was almost enjoying myself when she screamed.

It wasn't much of a scream; her throat was shot. But it fetched me at once. I saw the problem as I cleared the door. The topical anesthesia had worn off the large "bedsores" on her back and buttocks, and the pain had waked her. Now that I thought about it, it should have happened earlier; that spray was only supposed to be good for a few hours. I decided that her pleasure-pain system was weakened by overload.

The sores were bad; she would have scars. I resprayed them, and her moans stopped nearly at once. I could devise no means of securing her on her belly that would not be nightmare-inducing, and decided it was unnecessary. I thought she was out again and started to leave. Her voice, muffled by pillows, stopped me in my tracks.

"I don't know you. Maybe you're not even real. I can tell you."

"Save your energy. Karen. You—"

"Shut up. You wanted the karma, you got it."

I shut up.

Her voice was flat, dead. "All my friends were dating at twelve. *He* made me wait until fourteen. Said I couldn't be trusted. Tommy came to take me to the dance, and he gave Tommy a hard time. I was so embarrassed. The dance was nice for a couple of hours. Then Tommy started chasing after Jo Tompkins. He just left me and went off with her. I went in the ladies' room and cried for a long time. A couple of girls got the story out of me, and one of them had a bottle of vodka in her purse. I never drank before. When I started tearing up cars in the parking lot, one of the girls got ahold of Tommy. She gave him shit and made him take me home. I don't remember it, I found out later."

Her throat gave out and I got water. She accepted it without meeting my eyes, turned her face away and continued.

"Tommy got me in the door somehow. I was out cold by then. He must have been too scared to try and get me upstairs. He left me on the couch and my underpants on the rug and went home. The next thing I knew I was on the floor and my face hurt. *He* was standing over me. Whore he said. I got up and tried to explain and he hit me a couple of times. I ran for the door but he hit me hard in the back. I went into the stairs and banged my head real hard."

Feeling began to come into her voice for the first time. The feeling was fear. I dared not move.

"When I woke up it was day. Mama must have bandaged my head and put me to bed. My head hurt a lot. When I came out of the bathroom I heard him call me. He and Mama were in bed. He started in on me. He wouldn't let me talk, and kept getting madder and madder. Finally I hollered back at him. He got up off the bed and started in hitting me again. My robe came off. He kept hitting me in the belly and tits, and his fists were like hammers. Slut, he kept saying. Whore. I thought he was going to kill me, so I grabbed one arm and bit. He roared like a dragon and threw me across the room. Onto the bed; Mama jumped up. Then he pulled down his underpants and it was big and purple. I screamed and screamed and tore at his back and Mama just stood there. Her eyes were big and round, just like in cartoons. I screamed and screamed and—"

She broke off short and her shoulders knotted. When she continued her voice was stone dead again. "I woke up in my own bed again. I took a real long shower and went downstairs. Mama was making pancakes. I sat down and she gave me one and I ate it, and then I threw it up right there on the table and ran out the door. She never said a word, never called me back. After school that day I found a Sanctuary and started the divorce proceedings. I never saw either of them again. I never told this to anybody before."

The pause was so long I thought she had fallen asleep. "Since that time I've tried it with men and women and boys and girls, in the dark and in the desert sun, with people I cared for and people I didn't give a damn about, and I have never understood the pleasure in it. The best it's ever been for me is not uncomfortable. God, how I've wondered . . . now I know." She was starting to drift. "Only thing my whole life turned out *better*'n cracked up to be." She snorted sleepily. "Even alone."

I sat there for a long time without moving. My legs trembled when I got up, and my hands trembled while I made supper.

That was the last time she was lucid for nearly forty-eight hours. I plied her with successively stronger soups every time she woke up, and once I got some tea-soggy toast into her. Sometimes she called me others' names, and sometimes she didn't know I was there, and everything she said was disjointed. I listened to her tapes, watched some of her video, charged some books and games to her computer. I took a lot of her aspirin. And drank surprisingly little of her booze.

It was a time of frustration for me. I still

couldn't make it all fit together, still could not quite understand. There was a large piece missing. The animal who sired and raised her had planted the charge, of course, and I perceived that it was big enough to blow her apart. But why had it taken eight years to go off? If his death four years ago had not triggered it, what had? I could not leave until I knew. I did not know why not. I prowled her apartment like a caged bear, looking everywhere for something else to think about.

Midway through the second day her plumbing started working again; I had to change the sheets. The next morning a noise woke me and I found her on the bathroom floor on her knees in a pool of urine. I got her clean and back to bed and just as I thought she was going to drift off again she started yelling at me. "Lousy son of a bitch, it could have been over! I'll never have the guts again now! How could you *do* that, you *bastard,* it was so *nice!*" She turned violently away from me and curled up. I had to make a hard choice then, and I gambled on what I knew of loneliness and sat on the edge of the bed and stroked her hair as gently and impersonally as I knew how. It was a good guess. She began to cry, in great racking heaves first, then the steady wail of total heartbreak. I had been praying for this and did not begrudge the strength it cost her.

She cried for so long that every muscle in my body ached from sitting still by the time she fell off the edge into sleep. She never felt me get up, stiff and clumsy as I was. There was something different about her sleeping face now. It was not slack but relaxed. I limped out in the closest thing to peace I had felt since I arrived, and as I was passing the living room on the way to the liquor I heard the phone.

Silently, I looked over the caller. The picture was undercontrasted and snowy; it was a pay phone. He looked like an immigrant construction worker, massive and florid and neckless, almost brutish. And, at the moment, under great stress. He was crushing a hat in his hands; mortally embarrassed.

"Sharon, don't hang up," he was saying. "I *gotta* find out what this is all about."

Nothing could have made me hang up.

"Sharon? Sharon, I know you're there. Terry says you ain't there, she says she called you every day for a week and banged on your door a few times. But I know you're there, now anyway. I walked past your place an hour ago and I seen your bathroom light go on and off. Sharon, will you please tell me what the hell's going on? Are you listening to me? I know you're listening to me. Look, you gotta understand, I thought it was all set, see? I mean I thought it was *set*. Arranged. I put it to Terry, cause she's my regular, and she says not *me,* lover, but I know a gal. Look, was she lying to me or what? She told me for another bill you play them kind of games."

Regular $200 bank deposits plus a cardboard box full of scales, vials, bags, and milk powder makes her a coke dealer, right, Travis McGee? Don't be misled by the fact that the box was shoved in a corner, sealed with tape, and covered with dust. After all, the only other illicit profession that pays regular sums at regular intervals is hooker, and $200 is too much for square-jawed, hook-nosed, wide-eyed little Karen, breasts or no breasts.

For a garden-variety hooker . . .

"Dammit, she told me she *called* you and set it up, she gave me your *apartment* number." He shook his head violently. "I can't make sense of this. Dammit, she *couldn't* be lying to me. It don't figure. You let me in, didn't even turn the camera on first, it was all arranged. Then you screamed and . . . and I done like we arranged, and I thought you was maybe overdoin' it a bit but Terry *said* you was a terrific actress. I was real careful not to really hurt you, I know I was. Then I put on my pants and I'm putting the envelope on the dresser and you bust that chair on me and come at me with that knife and I hadda bust you one. It just don't make no sense, will you *goddammit say something to me?* I'm twisted up inside going on two weeks now. I can't even eat."

I went to shut off the phone, and my hand was shaking so bad I missed, spinning the volume knob to minimum. "Sharon, you gotta believe me," he hollered from far far away. "I'm into rape fantasy. I'm not into rape!" And then I had found the right switch and he was gone.

I got up very slowly and toddled off to the liquor cabinet, and I stood in front of it taking pulls from different bottles at random until I could no longer see his face, his earnest, baffled, half-ashamed face hanging before me.

Because his hair was thin sandy blond, and his jaw was a bit too square, and his nose was a trifle hooked, and his blue eyes were just the least little bit too far apart. They say everyone has a double somewhere. And Fate is such a witty little motherfucker, isn't he?

I don't remember how I got to bed.

I woke later that night with the feeling that I would have to bang my head on the floor a couple of times to get my heart started again. I was on my makeshift doss of pillows and blankets beside her bed, and when I finally peeled my eyes open she was sitting up in bed staring at me. She had fixed her hair somehow, and her nails were trimmed. We looked at each other for a long moment. Her color was returning somewhat, and the edge was off her bones.

"What did Jo Ann say when you told her?"

I said nothing.

"Come on, Jo Ann's got the only other key to this place, and she wouldn't give it to you if you weren't a friend. So what did she say?"

I got painfully up out of the tangle and walked to the window. A phallic church steeple rose above the low-rises, a couple of blocks away.

"God is an iron," I said. "Did you know that?"

I turned to look at her, and she was staring. She laughed experimentally, stopped when I failed to join in. "And I'm a pair of pants with a hole scorched through the ass?"

"If a person who indulges in gluttony is a

glutton, and a person who commits a felony is a felon, then God is an iron. Or else He's the dumbest designer that ever lived.''

Of a thousand possible snap reactions she picked the most flattering and hence most irritating. She kept silent, kept looking at me, and thought about what I had said. At last she said, ''I agree. What particular design fuckup did you have in mind?''

''The one that nearly left you dead in a pile of your own shit,'' I said harshly. ''Everybody talks about the new menace, wireheading, fifth most common cause of death in only a decade. Wireheading's not new—it's just a technical refinement.''

''I don't follow.''

''Are you familiar with the old cliche 'Everything I like in the world is either illegal, immoral, or fattening'?''

''Sure.''

''Didn't that ever strike you as damned odd? What's the most nutritionally useless and physiologically dangerous 'food' substance in the world? Sugar. And it seems to be beyond the power of the human nervous system to resist it. They put it in virtually all the processed food there is, which is next to all the food there is, because *nobody can resist it.* And so we poison ourselves and whipsaw our dipositions and rot our teeth. Isn't that odd? There is a primitive programming in our skulls that rewards us, literally overwhelmingly, every time we do something damned silly. Like smoke a poison, or eat or drink or snort or shoot a poison. Or *over*eat *good* foods. Or engage in complicated sexual behavior without procreative intent, which if it were not for the pleasure would be pointless and insane. And which, when pursued for the pleasure alone, quickly becomes pointless and insane anyway. A suicidal brain-reward system is built into us."

"But the reward system is for survival."

"So how the hell did ours get wired up so that survival-threatening behavior gets rewarded best of all? Even the pro-survival pleasure stimuli are wired so that a dangerous *overload* produces the maximum pleasure. On a purely biological level Man is programmed to strive hugely for more than he needs, more than he can profitably use.

"The error doesn't show up as glaringly in other animals. Even surrounded by plenty, a stupid animal has to work hard simply to meet his needs. But add in intelligence and everything goes to hell. Man is capable of outgrowing any ecological niche you put him in—he survives at all because he is the animal that *moves*. Given half a chance he kills himself of surfeit."

My knees were trembling so badly I had to sit down. I felt feverish and somehow larger than myself, and I knew I was talking much too fast. She had nothing whatever to say, with voice, face, or body.

"Given Man's gregarious nature," I went on, fingering my aching nose, "it's obvious that kindness is more pro-survival than cruelty. But which *feels* better? Which provides more pleasure? Poll any hundred people at random and you'll find at least twenty or thirty who

131

know all there is to know about psychological torture and psychic castration—and maybe two that know how to give a terrific back rub. That business of your father leaving all his money to the Church and leaving you a hundred dollars, the going rate—that was *artistry*. I can't imagine a way to make you feel as good as that made you feel rotten. That's why sadism and masochism are the last refuge of the jaded, the most enduring of the perversions; their piquancy is—"

"Maybe the Puritans were right," she said. "Maybe pleasure is the root of all evil. But God! life is bleak without it."

"One of my most precious possessions," I said, "is a button that my friend Slinky John used to hand-paint and sell below cost. He was the only practicing anarchist I ever met. The button reads: 'GO, LEMMINGS, GO!' A lemming surely feels intense pleasure as he gallops to the sea. His self-destruction is programmed by nature, a part of the very small life force that insisted on being conceived and born in the first place. If it feels good, do it." I laughed, and she flinched. "So it seems to me that God is either an iron, or a colossal jackass. I don't quite know whether to be admiring or contemptuous."

All at once I was out of words, and out of strength. I yanked my gaze away from hers and stared at my knees for a long time. I felt vaguely ashamed, as befits one who has thrown a tantrum in a sickroom.

After a time she said. "You talk good on your feet."

I kept looking at my knees. "I was an economics teacher for a year once."

"Will you tell me something?"

"If I can."

"What was the pleasure in putting me back together again?"

I jumped.

"Look at me. There. I've got a half-ass idea of what shape I was in when you met me, and I can guess what it's been like since. I don't know if I'd have done as much for Jo Ann, and she's my best friend. You don't look like a guy whose favorite kick is sick fems, and you sure as *hell* don't look like you're so rich you got time on your hands. So what's been your pleasure, these last few days?"

"Trying to understand," I snapped. "I'm nosy."

"And do you understand?"

"Yeah. I put it together."

"So you'll be going now?"

"Not yet." I said automatically. "You're not—"

And caught myself.

"There's something else besides pleasure," she said. "Another system of reward, only I don't think it has much to do with the one I got wired up to my scalp here. Not brain-reward. Call it mind-reward. Call it joy—the thing like pleasure that you feel when you've done a good thing or passed up a real tempting chance to do a bad thing. Or when the unfolding of the

133

Universe just seems especially apt. It's nowhere near as flashy and intense as pleasure can be. *Believe* me. But it's got *some*thing going for it. Something that can make you do without pleasure or even accept a lot of pain to get it.

"That thing you're thinking about, that's there, that's true. What's messing us up is the animal nervous system and instincts we inherited. But you said yourself, Man is the animal that outgrows and moves. Ever since the first brain grew a mind we've been trying to outgrow our instincts, grow new ones. By Jesus, we will yet. Evolution works pretty slow, is all. Couple of hundred million years to develop a thinking ape, and you want a smart one in a lousy few hundred thou? That lemming drive is there—but there's another kind of drive, another kind of force, that's working against it. Or else there wouldn't still be any people and there wouldn't be the words to have this conversation and—" She looked down at herself. "And I wouldn't be here to say them."

"That was just random chance."

She snorted. "What isn't?"

"Well, that's *fine,*" I shouted. "That's *fine*. Since the world is saved and you've got it under control I'll just be going along."

I've got a lot of voice when I yell. She ignored it utterly, continued speaking as if nothing had happened. "Now I can say that I have sampled the spectrum of the pleasure system at both ends—none and all there is—and I think the rest of my life I will dedicate myself to the middle of the road and see how that works out. Starting

with the very weak tea and toast I'm going to ask
you to bring me in another ten minutes or so.
But as for this other stuff, this joy thing, that I
would like to begin exploring, in as much
intensity as possible. I don't really know a
goddamn thing about it, but I understand it has
something to do with sharing and caring, and
what did you say your name was?"

"It doesn't matter!" I yelled.

"All right. What can *I* do for *you?*"

"Nothing!"

"What did you come here for?"

I was angry enough to be honest. "To burgle
your fucking apartment!"

Her eyes opened wide, and then she slumped
back against the pillows and laughed until the
tears came, and I tried and could not help myself
and laughed too, and we shared laughter for a
long time, as long as we had shared her tears the
night before.

And then straightfaced she said. "You'll have
to wait a week or two; you're gonna need help
with those stereo speakers. Butter on the toast."

COUNT THE CLOCK
THAT TELLS THE TIME

By Harlan Ellison

When I do count the clock that tells the time,
And see the brave day sunk in hideous night;
When I behold the violet past prime,
And sable curls all silver'd o'er with white;
When lofty trees I see barren of leaves
Which erst from heat did canopy the herd,
And summer's green all girded up in sheaves
Borne on the bier with white and bristly beard;
Then of the beauty do I question make,
That thou among the wastes of time must go . . .
>   William Shakespeare,
>   *The XIIth Sonnet*

Waking in the cool and cloudy absolute dead middle of a Saturday afternoon one day, Ian Ross felt lost and vaguely frightened. Lying there in his bed, he was disoriented, and it took

him a moment to remember when it was and
where he was. Where he was: in the bed where
he had awakened every day of his 35-year-old
life. When it was: the Saturday he had resolved
to spend *doing* something. But as he lay there
he realized he had come to life in the early
hours just after dawn, it had looked as though
it would rain, the sky seen through the high
French windows, and he had turned over and
gone back to sleep. Now the clock-radio on the
bedside table told him it was the absolute dead
middle of the afternoon; and the world outside
his windows was cool and cloudy. "Where does
the time go?" he said.

He was alone, as always: there was no one to
hear him or to answer. So he continued lying
there, wasting time, feeling vaguely frightened.
As though something important were passing
him by.

A fly buzzed him, circled, buzzed him again.
It had been annoying him for some time. He
tried to ignore the intruder and stared off across
Loch Tummel to the amazing flesh tones of the
October trees, preparing themselves for
Winter's disingenuous attentions and the utter
absence of tourism. The silver birches were
already a blazing gold, the larches and ash trees
still blending off from green to rust; in a few
weeks the Norway spruces and the other
conifers would darken until they seemed mere
shadows against the slate sky.

Perthshire was most beautiful at this time of
year. He had taken the time to learn to pro-
nounce the names—Schiehallion, Killiecrankie,

Pitlochry, Aberfeldy—and had come here to sit.
The dream. The one he had always held: silent,
close to him, unspoken, in his idle thoughts.
The dream of going to Scotland. For what
reason he could not say. But this was the place
that had always called, and he had come.

For the first time in his life, Ian Ross had
done something. Thirty-seven years old, rooted
to a tiny apartment in Chicago, virtually friend-
less, working five days a week at a drafting
table in a firm of industrial designers, watching
television till sign-off, tidying the two and a half
rooms till every picture hung from the walls in
perfect true with the junctures of walls and
ceiling, entering each checkbook notation in the
little ledger with a fine-point ink pen, unable to
remember what had happened last Thursday
that made it different from last Wednesday,
seeing himself reflected in the window of the
cafeteria slowly eating the $2.95 Christmas
Dinner Special, a solitary man, somehow never
making the change of the seasons save to understand only by his skin that it was warmer or
colder, never tasting joy because he could never
remember having been told what it was, reading
books about *things* and *subject matter,* topics
not people, because he knew so few people and
knew none of them, drawing straight lines,
feeling deserted but never knowing where to put
his hands to relieve that feeling: a transient
man, passing down the same streets every day
and perceiving only dimly that there were streets
beyond those streets, drinking water and apple

juice, and water, replying when he was addressed directly, looking around sometimes when he was addressed to see if it was, in fact, himself to whom the speaker was speaking, buying gray socks and white undershorts, staring out the windows of his apartment at the Chicago snow, staring for hours at the invisible sky, feeling the demon wind off Lake Michigan rattling the window glass in its frame and thinking this year he would reputty and this year failing to reputty, combing his hair as he always had, cooking his own meals, alone with the memories of his mother and father who had died within a year of each other and both from cancer, never having been able to speak more than a few awkward sentences to any woman but his mother . . . Ian Ross had lived his life like the dust that lay in a film across the unseen top of the tall wardrobe cabinet in his bedroom; colorless, unnoticed, inarticulate, neither giving nor taking.

Until one day he had said. "Were does the time go?" And in the months following those words he had come to realize he had not, in any remotely valuable manner, *lived* his life. He had wasted it. Months after the first words came, unbidden and tremulous, he admitted to himself that he had wasted his life.

He resolved to actualize at least the one dream. To go to Scotland. Perhaps to live. To rent or even buy a crofter's cottage on the edge of a moor or overlooking one of the lochs he had dreamed about. He had all the insurance money still put by; he hadn't touched a cent of it. And there, in that far, chill place in the north he would live . . . walking the hills with a dog by his side, smoking a pipe that trailed a fragrant pennant of blue-white smoke, hands thrust deep into the pocket of a fleece-lined jacket. He would *live* there. That was the dream.

And from King's Cross Station he had taken the 2130 sleeper to Edinburgh, and he had walked the Royal Mile and gazed in wonder at Edinburgh Castle high on the bluff overlooking that bountiful city, and finally he had rented a car and had driven north out the Queensferry Road, across the bridge that spanned the Firth of Forth, on up the A-90 till he reached Pitlochry. Then a left, a random left, but not so random that he did not know it would come out overlooking the Queens View, said to be the most beautiful view in the world, certainly in Scotland; and he had driven the twisting, narrow road till he was deep in the hills of Perth.

And there he had pulled off the road, gotten out of the car, leaving the door open, and walked away down the October hills to finally sit staring at the Loch, green and blue and silent as the mirror of his memory.

Where only the buzzing fly reminded him of the past.

He had been 35 when he said. "Where does the time go?" And he was 37 as he sat on the hill.

And it was there that the dream died.

He stared at the hills, at the valley that ran

off to left and right, at the sparkling water of
the Loch, and knew he had wasted his time
again. He had resolved to *do* something; but he
had done nothing. Again.

There was no place for him here.

He was out of phase with all around him. He
was an alien object. A beer can thrown into the
grass. A broken wall untended and falling back
into the earth from which it had been wrenched
stone by stone.

He felt lonely, starved, incapable of clenching
his hands or clearing his throat. A ruin from
another world, set down in foreign soil,
drinking air that was not his to drink. There
were no tears, no pains in his body, no deep and
trembling sighs. In a moment, with a fly
buzzing, the dream died for him. He had not
been saved; had, in fact, come in an instant to
understand that he had been a child to think it
could ever change. What do you want to be
when you grow up? Nothing. As I have always
been nothing.

The sky began to bleach out.

The achingly beautiful golds and oranges and
yellows began to drift toward sepia. The blue of
the loch slid softly toward chalkiness, like an
ineptly prepared painting left too long in direct
sunlight. The sounds of birds and forest
creatures and insects faded, the gain turned
down slowly. The sun gradually cooled for Ian
Ross. The sky began to bleach out toward a
gray-white newsprint colorlessness. The fly was
gone. It was cold now; very cold now.

Shadows began to superimpose themselves over the dusty mezzotint of the bloodless day:

A city of towers and minarets, as seen through shallow, disturbed water; a mountain range of glaciers with snow untracked and endless as an ocean; an ocean, with massive, serpent-necked creatures gliding through the jade deeps; a parade of ragged children bearing crosses hewn from tree branches; a great walled fortress in the middle of a parched wasteland, the yellow earth split like strokes of lightning all around the structure; a motorway with hundreds of cars speeding past so quickly they seemed to be stroboscopic lines of colored light: a battlefield with men in flowing robes and riding great-chested stallions, the sunlight dancing off curved swords and helmets; a tornado careening through a small town of slat-back stores and houses, lifting entire buildings from their foundations and flinging them into the sky; a river of lava burst through a fissure in the ground and boiled toward a shadowy indication of an amusement park, with throngs of holiday tourists moving in clots from one attraction to another.

Ian Ross sat, frozen, on the hillside. The world was dying around him. No . . . it was vanishing, fading out, dematerializing. As if all the sand had run out of the hourglass around him; as if he were the only permanent, fixed, and immutable object in a metamorphosing universe suddenly cut loose from its time-anchor.

The world faded out around Ian Ross: the shadows boiled and seethed and slithered past him, caught in a cyclonic wind-tunnel and swept away past him, leaving him in darkness.

He sat now, still, quiet, too isolated to be frightened.

He thought perhaps clouds had covered the sun.

There was no sun.

He thought perhaps it had been an eclipse, that his deep concentration of his hopeless state had kept him from noticing.

There was no sun.

No sky. The ground beneath him was gone. He sat, merely sat, but on nothing, surrounded by nothing, seeing and feeling nothing save a vague chill. It was cold now, very cold now.

After a long time he decided to stand and *did* stand: there was nothing beneath or above him. He stood in darkness.

He could remember everything that had ever happened to him in his life. Every moment of it, with absolute clarity. It was something he had never experienced before. His memory had been no better or worse than anyone else's, but he had forgotten all the details, many years in which nothing had happened, during which he had wasted time—almost as a mute witness at the dull rendition of his life.

But now, as he walked through the limbo that was all he had been left of the world, he recalled everything perfectly. The look of terror on his mother's face when he had sliced through the tendons of his left hand with the lid from the tin can of pink lemonade: he had been four years old. The feel of his new Thom McAn shoes that had always been too tight from the moment they had been bought but that he had been forced to wear to school every day, even though they rubbed him raw at the back of his heels: he had been seven years old. The Four Freshmen standing and singing for the graduation dance. He had been alone. He had bought one ticket to support the school event. He had been 16. The taste of egg roll at Choy's, the first time. He had been 24. The woman he had met at the library, in the section where they kept the books on animals. She had used a white lace handkerchief to dry her temples. It had smelled of perfume. He had been 30. He remembered all the sharp edges of every moment from his past. It was remarkable. In this nowhere.

And he walked through gray spaces, with the shadows of other times and other places swirling past. The sound of rushing wind, as though the emptiness through which he moved was being constantly filled and emptied, endlessly, without measure or substance.

Had he known what emotions to call on for release, he would have done so. But he was numb in his skin. Not merely chilled, as this empty place was chilled, but somehow inured to feeling from the edge of his perceptions to the center of his soul. Sharp, clear, drawn back from the absolute past, he remembered a day when he had been 11, when his mother had suggested that for his birthday they make a small party to which he would invite a few friends. And so (he remembered with diamond-bright perfection), he had invited six boys and girls. They had never come. He sat alone in the house that Saturday, all his comic books laid out in case the cake and party favors and pin-the-tail-on-the-donkey did not hold their attention sufficiently. Never came. It grew dark. He sat alone, with his mother occasionally walking through the living room to make some consoling remark. But he was alone, and he knew there was only one reason for it: they had all forgotten. It was simply that he was a waste of time of those actually living their lives. Invisible, by token of being unimportant. A thing unnoticed: on a street, who notices the mailbox, the fire hydrant, the crosswalk lines? He was an invisible, useless thing.

He had never permitted another party to be thrown for him.

He remembered that Saturday now. And found the emotion, 26 years late, to react to this terrible vanishment of the world. He began to tremble uncontrollably, and he sat down where there was nothing to sit down on, and he rubbed his hands together, feeling the tremors in his knuckles and the ends of his fingers. Then he felt the constriction in his throat, he turned his head this way and that, looking for a nameless exit from self-pity and loneliness; and then he cried. Lightly, softly, because he had no experience at it.

A crippled old woman came out of the gray

mist of nowhere and stood watching him. His eyes were closed, or he would have seen her coming.

After a while, he snuffled, opened his eyes, and saw her standing in front of him. He stared at her. She was standing. At a level somewhat below him, as though the invisible ground of this nonexistent place was on a lower plane than that on which he sat.

"That won't help much," she said. She wasn't surly, but neither was there much succor in her tone.

He looked at her and immediately stopped crying.

"Probably just got sucked in here," she said. It was not quite a question, though it had something of query in it. She knew and was going carefully.

He continued to look at her, hoping she could tell him what had happened to him. And to her? She was here, too.

"Could be worse," she said, crossing her arms and shifting her weight off her twisted left leg. "I could've been a Saracen or a ribbon clerk or even one of those hairy pre-humans." He didn't respond. He didn't know what she was talking about. She smiled wryly, remembering. "First person I met was some kind of a retard, little boy about 15 or so. Must have spent what there'd been of his life in some padded cell or a hospital bed, something like that. He just sat there and stared at me, drooled a little, couldn't tell me a thing. I was scared out of my mind, ran around like a chicken with

its head cut off. Wasn't till a long time after
that before I met someone who spoke English."

He tried to speak and found his throat was
dry. His voice came out in a croak. He
swallowed and wet his lips. "Are there many
other, uh, other people . . . we're not all
alone . . . ?"

"Lots of others. Hundreds, thousands. God
only knows; maybe whole countries full of
people here. No animals, though. They don't
waste it the way we do."

"Waste it? What?"

"Time, son. Precious, lovely time. That's all
there is, just time. Sweet, flowing time. Animals
don't know about time."

As she spoke, a slipping shadow of some wild
scene whirled past and through them. It was a
great city in flames. It seemed more substantial
than the vagrant wisps of countryside or sea
scenes that had been ribboning past them as
they spoke. The wooden buildings and city
towers seemed almost solid enough to crush
anything in their path. Flames leaped toward
the gray, dead-skin sky; enormous tongues of
crackling flame that ate the city's gut and
chewed the phantom image, leaving ash. (But
even the dead ashes had more life than the grayness through which the vision swirled.)

Ian Ross ducked, frightened. Then it was
gone.

"Don't worry about it, son," the old woman
said. "Looked a lot like London during the Big
Fire. First the Plague, then the Fire. I've seen its

148

like before. Can't hurt you. None of it can hurt you."

He tried to stand, found himself still weak. "But what *is* it?"

She shrugged. "No one's ever been able to tell me for sure. Bet there's some around in here who can, though. One day I'll run into one of them. If I find out and we ever meet again I'll be sure to let you know. Bound to happen." But her face grew infinitely sad and there was desolation in her expression. "Maybe. Maybe we'll meet again. Never happens, but it might. Never saw that retarded boy again. But it might happen."

She started to walk away, hobbling awkwardly. Ian got to his feet with difficulty, but as quickly as he could. "Hey wait! Where are you going? Please, lady don't leave me here all alone. I'm scared to be here all alone. I'm scared to be here by myself."

She stopped and turned, tilting oddly on her bad leg. "Got to keep moving. Keep going, you know? If you stay in one place, you don't get anywhere: there's a way out . . . you've just got to keep moving till you find it." She started again, saying, over her shoulder, "I guess I won't be seeing you again: I don't think it's likely."

He ran after her and grabbed her arm. She seemed very startled. As if no one had ever touched her in this place during all the time she had been here.

"Listen, you've got to tell me some things, whatever you know. I'm awfully scared, don't

149

you understand? You have to have some understanding."

She looked at him carefully. "All right, as much as I can, then you'll let me go?"

He nodded.

"I don't know what happened to me . . . or to you. Did it all fade away and just disappear, and everything that was left was this, just this gray nothing?"

He nodded.

She sighed. "How old are you, son?"

"I'm 37. My name is Ian—"

She waved his name away with an impatient gesture. "That doesn't matter. I can see you don't know any better than I do. So I don't have the time to waste on you. You'll learn that, too. Just keep walking, just keep looking for a way out."

He made fists. "That doesn't tell me *anything!* What was that burning city, what are these shadows that go past all the time?" As if to mark his question a vagrant filmy phantom caravan of cassowary-like animals drifted through them.

She shrugged and sighed. "I think it's history. I'm not sure . . . I'm guessing, you understand. But I *think* it's all the bits and pieces of the past, going through on its way somewhere."

He waited. She shrugged again, and her silence indicated—with a kind of helpless appeal to be let go—that she could tell him nothing further.

He nodded resignedly. "All right. Thank you."

She turned with her bad leg trembling: she had stood with her weight on it for too long. And she started to walk off into the gray limbo. When she was almost out of sight, he found himself able to speak again, and he said . . . too softly to reach her . . . "Goodbye, lady. Thank you."

He wondered how old she was. How long she had been here. If he would one time far from now be like her. If it was all over and if he would wander in shadows forever.

He wondered if people died here.

Before he met Catherine, a long time before he met her, he met the lunatic who told him where he was, what had happened to him, and why it had happened.

They saw each other standing on opposite sides of a particularly vivid phantom of the Battle of Waterloo. The battle raged past them, and through the clash and slaughter of Napoleon's and Wellington's forces they waved to each other.

When the sliding vision had rushed by, leaving emptiness between them, the lunatic rushed forward, clapping his hands as if preparing himself for a long, arduous, but pleasurable chore. He was of indeterminate age but clearly past his middle years. His hair was long and wild, he wore a pair of rimless antique spectacles, and his suit was turn-of-the-eighteenth-century. "Well, well, well," he called, across the narrowing space between them, "so good to see you, sir!"

Ian Ross was startled. In the timeless time he had wandered through this limbo, he had encountered coolies and Berbers and Thracian traders and silent Goths . . . an endless stream of hurrying humanity that would neither speak nor stop. This man was something different. Immediately, Ian knew he was insane. But he wanted to *talk!*

The older man reached Ian and extended his hand. "Cowper, sir. Justinian Cowper. Alchemist, metaphysician, consultant to the forces of time and space, ah yes, *time!* Do I perceive in you, sir, one only recently come to our little Valhalla, one in need of illumination? Certainly! Definitely. I can see that is the case."

Ian began to say something, almost anything, in response, but the wildly gesticulating old man pressed on without drawing a breath. "This most recent manifestation, the one we were both privileged to witness was, I'm certain you're aware, the pivotal moment at Waterloo in which the Little Corporal had his fat chewed good and proper. Fascinating piece of recent history, wouldn't you say?"

Recent history? Ian started to ask him how long he had been in this gray place, but the old man barely paused before a fresh torrent of words spilled out.

"Stunningly reminiscent of that marvelous scene in Stendahl's *Charterhouse of Parma* in which Fabrizio, young, innocent, fresh to that environ, found himself walking across a large

152

meadow on which men were running in all directions, noise, shouts, confusion . . . and he knew not what was happening, and not till several chapters later do we learn—ah, marvelous!—that it was, in fact, the Battle of Waterloo through which he moved, totally unaware of history in the shaping all around him. He was there, while *not* there. Precisely *our* situation, wouldn't you say?"

He had run out of breath. He stopped, and Ian plunged into the gap. "That's what I'd like to know, Mr. Cowper: What's happened to me? I've lost *everything,* but I can *remember* everything, too. I know I should be going crazy or frightened, and I *am* scared, but not out of my mind with it . . . I seem to *accept* this, whatever it is. I-I don't know how to take it, but I know I'm not feeling it yet. And I've been here a long time!"

The old man slipped his arm around Ian's back and began walking with him, two gentlemen strolling in confidence on a summer afternoon by the edge of a cool park. "Quite correct, sir, quite correct. Dissociative behavior; mark of the man unable to accept his destiny. Accept it, sir. I urge you; and fascination follows. Perhaps even obsession, but we must run that risk, mustn't we?"

Ian wrenched away from him, turned to face him. "Look, mister, I don't want to hear all that crazinesss! I want to know where I am and how I get out of here. And if you can't tell me, then leave me alone!"

"Nothing easier, my good man. Explanation

is the least of it. Observation of phenomena, ah, *that's* the key. You can follow? Well, then: we are victims of the law of conservation of time. Precisely and exactly linked to the law of the conservation of matter; matter, which can neither be created nor destroyed. Time exists without end. But there is an ineluctable entropic balance, absolutely necessary to maintain order in the universe. Keeps events discrete, you see. As matter approaches universal distribution, there is a counterbalancing, how shall I put it, a counterbalancing 'leaching out' of time. Unused time is not wasted in places where nothing happens. *It goes somewhere.* It goes here, to be precise. In measurable units—which I've decided, after considerable thought, to call 'chronons'."

He paused, perhaps hoping Ian would compliment him on his choice of nomenclature. Ian put a hand to his forehead: his brain was swimming.

"That's insane. It doesn't make sense."

"Makes perfectly *good* sense. I assure you. I was a top savant in my time; what I've told you is the only theory that fits the facts. Time unused is not wasted; it is leached out, drained through the normal space-time continuum and recycled. All this history you see shooting past us is that part of the time-flow that was wasted. Entropic balance. I assure you."

"But what am *I* doing here?"

"You force me to hurt your feelings, sir."

"What am I doing here?!"

"You wasted your life. Wasted time. All

around you, throughout your life, unused chronons were being leached out, drawn away from the contiguous universe, until their pull on you was irresistible. Then you went on through, pulled loose like a piece of wood in a rushing torrent, a bit of chaff whirled away on the wind. Like Fabrizio, you were never really *there*. You wandered through, never seeing, never participating and so there was nothing to moor you solidly in your own time."

"But how long will I stay here?"

The old man looked sad and spoke kindly for the first time: "Forever. You never used your time, so you have nothing to rely on as anchorage in normal space."

"But everyone here thinks there's a way out. I know it! They keep walking, trying to find an exit."

"Fools. There is no way back."

"But you don't seem to be the sort of person who wasted his life. Some of the others I've seen, yes. I can seen that; but *you?*"

The old man's eyes grew misty. He spoke with difficulty. "Yes, I belong here . . ."

Then he turned and, like one in a dream, lost, wandered away. Lunatic, observing phenomena. And then gone in the grayness of time-gorged limbo. Part of a glacial period slid past Ian Ross and he resumed his walk without destination.

And after a long, long time that was timeless but filled with an abundance of time, he met Catherine.

* * *

He saw her as a spot of darkness against the gray limbo. She was quite a distance away, and he walked on for a while, watching the dark blotch against gray, and then decided to change direction. It didn't matter. Nothing mattered: he was alone with his memories, replaying again and again.

The sinking of the *Titanic* wafted through him.

She did not move, even though he was approaching on a direct line.

When he was quite close he could see that she was sitting cross-legged on nothingness; she was asleep. Her head was propped in one hand, the bracing arm supported by her knee. Asleep.

He came right up to her and stood there simply watching. He smiled. She was like a bird, he thought, with her head tucked under her wing. Not really, but that was how he saw her. Though her cupped hand covered half her face he could make out a sweet face, very pale skin, a mole on her throat; her hair was brown, cut quite short. Her eyes were closed; he decided they would be blue.

The Greek Senate, the Age of Pericles, men in a crowd—property owners—screaming at Lycurgus's exhortations in behalf of socialism. The shadow of it sailed past not very far away.

Ian stood staring, and after a while he sat down opposite her. He leaned back on his arms and watched. He hummed an old tune the name of which he did not know.

Finally, she opened her brown eyes and stared at him.

At first momentary terror, startlement, chagrin, curiosity. Then she took umbrage. "How long have *you* been there?"

"My name is Ian Ross." he said.

"I don't care what your name is!" she said angrily. "I asked you how long you've been sitting there watching me."

"I don't know. A while."

"I don't like being watched; you're being very rude."

He got to his feet without answering and began walking away. Oh well.

She ran after him. "Hey, wait!"

He kept walking. He didn't have to be bothered like that. She caught up with him and ran around to stand in front of him. "I suppose you just think you can walk off like that!"

"Yes. I can. I'm sorry I bothered you. Please get out of my way if you don't want me around."

"I didn't say that."

"You said I was being rude. I am *never* rude; I'm a very well-mannered person, and you were just being insulting."

He walked around her. She ran after him.

"All right, okay, maybe I was a little out of sorts. I *was* asleep, after all."

He stopped. She stood in front of him. Now it was her move. "My name is Catherine Molnar. How do you do?"

"Not too well, that's how."

"Have you been here long?"

"Longer than I wanted to be here, *that's* for sure."

157

"Can you explain what's happened to me?"

He thought about it. Walking *with* someone would be a nice change. "Let me ask you something." Ian Ross said, beginning to stroll off toward the phantom image of the Hanging Gardens of Babylon wafting past them. "Did you waste a lot of time, sitting around, not doing much, maybe watching television a lot?"

They were lying down side by side because they were tired. Nothing more than that. The Battle of Ardennes, First World War, was all around them. Not a sound. Just movement. Mist, fog, turretless tanks, shattered trees all around them. Some corpses left lying in the middle of no-man's land. They had been together for a space of time . . . it was three hours, it was six weeks, it was a month of Sundays, it was a year to remember, it was the best of times, it was the worst of times: who could measure it? There were no signposts, no town criers, no grandfather clocks, no change of seasons, who could measure it?

They had begun to talk freely. He told her again that his name was Ian Ross, and she said Catherine. Catherine Molnar again. She confirmed his guess that her life had been empty. "Plain," she said. "I was plain. I *am* plain. No, don't bother to say you think I have nice cheekbones or a trim figure; it won't change a thing. If you want plain, I've got it."

He didn't say she had nice cheekbones or a trim figure. But he didn't think she was plain.

The Battle of the Ardennes was swirling away now.

She suggested they make love.

Ian Ross got to his feet quickly and walked away.

She watched him for a while, keeping him in sight. Then she got up, dusted off her hands though there was nothing on them, an act of memory, and followed him. Quite a long time later, after trailing him but not trying to catch up to him, she ran to match his pace and finally, gasping for breath, reached him.

"I'm sorry," she said.

"Nothing to be sorry about."

"I offended you."

"No, you didn't. I just felt like walking."

"Stop it, Ian. I did. I offended you."

He stopped and spun on her. "Do you think I'm a virgin? I'm not a virgin."

His vehemence pulled her back from the edge of boldness. "No, of course you're not. I never thought such a thing." Then she said. "Well . . . I am."

"Sorry," he said, because he didn't know the right thing to say, if there *was* a right thing.

"Not your fault," she said. Which *was* the right thing to say.

From nothing *to* nothing. Thirty-four years old, the properly desperate age for unmarried, unmotherhooded, unloved, Catherine Molnar. Janesville, Wisconsin. Straightening the trinkets in her jewelry box, ironing her clothes, removing and refolding the sweaters in her drawers, hanging the slacks with the slacks, skirts with the skirts, blouses with the blouses, coats with the coats, all in order in the closet, reading every word in *Time* and *Reader's Digest*, learning seven new words every day, never using seven new words every day, mopping the floors in the three-room apartment, putting aside one full evening to pay the bills and spelling out Wisconsin completely, never the WI abbreviation on the return envelopes, listening to talk-radio, calling for the correct time to set the clocks, spooning out the droppings from the kitty box, repasting photos in the album of scenes with round-faced people, pinching back the buds on the coleus, calling Aunt Beatrice every Tuesday at seven o'clock, talking brightly to the waitress in the orange-and-blue uniform at the chicken pie shoppe, repainting fingernails carefully so the moon on each nail is showing, heating morning water for herself alone for the cup of herbal tea, setting the table with a cloth napkin and a placemat, doing dishes, going to the office and straightening the bills of lading precisely. *From* nothing *to* nothing. Thirty-four.

They lay side by side but they were not tired. There was more to it than that.

"I hate men who can't think past the pillow," she said, touching his hair.

"What's that?"

"Oh, it's just something I practiced, to say after the first time I slept with a man. I always felt there should be something original to say, instead of all the things I read in novels.''

"I think it's a very clever phrase.'' Even now, he found it hard to touch her. He lay with hands at his sides.

She changed the subject. "I was never able to get very far playing the piano. I have absolutely *no* give between the thumb and first finger. And that's essential, you know. You have to have a long reach, a good spread, I think they call it, to play Chopin. A tenth: that's two notes over an octave. A *full* octave, a *perfect* octave, those are just technical terms. Octave is good enough. I don't have that.''

"I like piano playing,'' he said, realizing how silly and dull he must sound and frightened (very suddenly) that she would find him so, that she would leave him. Then he remembered where they were and he smiled. Where could she go? Where could *he* go?

"I always hated the fellows at parties who could play the piano . . . all the girls clustered around those people. Except these days it's not so much piano; not too many people have pianos in their homes anymore. The kids grow up and go away and nobody takes lessons and the kids don't buy pianos. They get those electric guitars.''

"Acoustical guitars.''

"Yes, those. I don't think it would be much better for fellows like me who don't play, even if it's acoustical guitars.''

They got up and walked again.

Once they discussed how they had wasted

their lives, how they had sat there with hands folded as time filled space around them, swept through, was drained off, and their own "chronons" (he had told her about the lunatic; she said it sounded like Benjamin Franklin; he said the man hadn't looked like Benjamin Franklin, but maybe, it might have been) had been leached of all potency.

Once they discussed the guillotine executions in the Paris of the Revolution, because it was keeping pace with them. Once they chased the Devonian and almost caught it. Once they were privileged to enjoy themselves in the center of an Arctic snowstorm that held around them for a measure of measureless time. Once they saw nothing for an eternity but were truly chilled—unlike the Arctic snowstorm that had had no effect on them—by the winds that blew past them. And once he turned to her and said, "I love you, Catherine."

But when she looked at him with a gentle smile, he noticed for the first time that her eyes seemed to be getting gray and pale.

Then, not too soon after, she said she loved him, too.

But she could see mist through the flesh of his hands when he reached out to touch her face.

They walked with their arms around each other, having found each other. They said many times, and agreed it was so, that they were in love and being together was the most important thing in that endless world of gray spaces, even if they never found their way back.

And they began to *use* their time together, setting small goals for each "day" upon awakening. We will walk *that* far; we will play word games in which *you* have to begin the name of a female movie star from the last letter of a male movie star's name that *I* have to begin off the last letter of a female movie star; we will exchange shirt and blouse and see how it feels for a while; we will sing every camp song we can remember. They began to *enjoy* their time together. They began to live.

And sometimes his voice faded out, and she could see him moving his lips but there was no sound.

And sometimes when the mist cleared she was invisible from the ankles down and her body moved as through thick soup.

And as they used their time, they became alien in that place where wasted time had gone to rest.

And they began to fade. As the world had leached out for Ian Ross in Scotland, and for Catherine Molnar in Wisconsin, *they* began to vanish from limbo. Matter could neither be created nor destroyed, but it could be disassembled and sent where it was needed for entropic balance.

He saw her pale skin become transparent.

She saw his hands as clear as glass.

And they thought: *too late. It comes too late*.

Invisible motes of their selves were drawn off and were sent away from that gray place. Were sent where needed to maintain balance. One and one and one, separated on the wind and blown to the farthest corners of the tapestry that was time and space. And could never be recalled. And could never be rejoined.

So they touched, there in that vast limbo of wasted time, for the last time, and shadows existed for an instant, and then were gone; he first, leaving her behind for the merest instant of terrible loneliness and loss, and then she, without shadow, pulled apart and scattered, followed. Separation without hope of return.

There was the faintest keening whine of matter fleeing.

There was the soundless echo of a diminishing moan.

The universe was poised to accept restored order.

And then balance was regained; as if they had never been.

Great events hushed in mist swirled past. Ptolemy crowned King of Egypt, the Battle of Teutoburger Forest, Jesus crucified, the founding of Constantinople, the Vandals plundering Rome, the massacre of the Omayyad family, the Court of the Fujiwaras in Japan. Jerusalem falling to Saladin . . . and on and on . . . great events . . . empty time . . . and the timeless population trudged past endlessly . . . unaware that finally, at last, hopelessly and too late . . . two of their nameless order had found the way out.

PETRA

By Greg Bear

"God is dead, God is dead.
. . . Perdition! When God dies, you'll know it."
—Confessions of St. Argentine

As near as I can discover, Mortdieu occurred seventy-seven years ago. Learned sons of pure flesh deny that magic was set loose, or even that the Alternate had gained supreme power. But few people could deny that God, as such, had died.

All the hinges of our once-great universe fell apart, the axis tilted, cosmic doors swung shut, and the rules of existence lost their foundations. I have heard wise men speak of the slow decline, have heard them speculate on the reasons, the process. Where human thought was strong, reality's sudden quaking was reduced to a tremor. Where human thought was weak, reality disappeared completely, swallowed by chaos.

With the passing of God's watchful gaze,
humankind had to reach out and grab hold of
the unraveling fabric of the world. Those conscious beings left alive—those who had had the
wits to keep their bodies from falling apart with
the end of the useful constants—became the
only cohesive force in the chaos. Imagine that
time, if you will:

When every delusion became as real as solid
matter. Blinding pain, flaming blood, bones
breaking, flesh powdering, steel flowing like
liquid, the sky raining amber. Crowds in the
shifting streets, gathering at intersections, not
knowing what to do, trapped by their own
ignorance. Their weak minds could not grab
hold. And where human thought gave way,
gradually the ancient order of nature returned,
with its own logic, its own way of adapting.
People watched, horrified, as city blocks
became forests. When they tried to stop the
metamorphosis, their unorganized mentality
only confused things further. With the first
faint suspicion that they had all gone mad, the
first crack in their all-too-weak reserves of will,
they projected their nightmares. Prodigal crows
perched atop the trees that had once been
buildings. Pigs ran through the streets on their
hind legs, pavement rushing to become soil
behind them. The forest prevailed over most of
the city.

Legend has it that it was the archexistentialist
Jansard—crucifier of the beloved St.
Argentine—who, realizing his error, discovered
that mind and thought could calm the foaming
sea of reality.

Most humans were entirely too irrational to begin with. Whole nations vanished or were turned into incomprehensible whirlpools of misery and depravity.

It is said that certain universities, libraries, and museums survived, but to this day we have little contact with them.

Our Cathedral survived. Rationality in this neighborhood, however, had weakened some centuries before Mortdieu, replaced only by a kind of rote. The Cathedral suffered. Survivors—clergy and staff, worshipers seeking sanctuary—had wretched visions, dreamed wretched dreams. They saw the stone ornaments of the great church come alive. With someone to see and believe, in a universe lacking any other foundation, my ancestors shook off stone and became flesh. Centuries of rock celibacy weighed upon them. Forty-nine nuns who had sought shelter in the Cathedral were discovered and were not entirely loath, for (so the coarser versions of the tale go) Mortdieu had had a surprising aphrodisiacal effect on the faithful. Conjugation took place. No definite gestation period has been established, because at that time the great stone wheel had not been set twisting back and forth to count the days. Nor had Kronos been appointed to the chair, to watch over the wheel and provide a baseline for everyday activities. But flesh did not reject stone, and there came into being the sons and daughters of flesh and stone, including me. Those who had fornicated with the gargoyles and animals were cast out to raise their monstrous young in the highest hidden recesses. Those who had accepted the embraces of the stone saints and other human figures were less abused but were still banished to the upper reaches. A wooden scaffold was erected, dividing the great nave into two levels. A canvas drop cloth was fastened over the scaffold, to prevent offal from raining down, and on the second level of the Cathedral the more human sons of stone and flesh set about creating a new life.

I'm an ugly son of stone and flesh; there's no denying it. I don't remember my mother. It's possible she abandoned me shortly after my birth. More than likely she is dead. My father—ugly, beaked, half-winged thing, if he resembles his son—I have never seen.

The moment my memory was born is very clear to me. It was about thirty years ago, by the swinging of the wheel, though I'm sure I lived many years before that—years lost to me. I squatted behind thick, dusty curtains in a vestibule and listened to a priest intoning Scripture to a gaggle of flesh children. That was on the ground floor, and I was in great danger; the people of pure flesh looked upon my kind as abominations. But it was worth taking the risk. In time I was able to steal a Psalter and learn to read. The other books I stole defined my own world by comparing it with others. At first I couldn't believe the others existed, only the Cathedral. I still have my doubts. I can look out a tiny round window on one side of my room and see the great forest and the river that surround the Cathedral, but I can see nothing else. So my experience with other worlds is far from direct.

No matter, I read, but I'm no scholar. What concerns me is recent history.

I am small—barely three English feet tall—and I can run quickly through most of the hidden passageways. This lets me observe without attracting attention. I may be the only objective historian in this whole structure.

Like any historian, however, I have my favorite subjects within the greater whole. Naturally enough, they are events in which I played an important role. If you prefer history in which the historian is not involved, then look to the records of larger communities.

At the time my history begins, the children of stone and flesh were still searching for the stone of Christ. Those of us born of the union of the stone saints and gargoyles with the bereaved nuns thought our salvation lay in the great stone Celibate, who came to life, as all the other statues had.

Of smaller import were the secret assignations between the Bishop's daughter and a young man of stone and flesh. Such assignations were forbidden even between those of pure flesh; because they were, of course, unmarried, their double sin was interesting to me.

Her name was Constantia, and she was fourteen, slender of limb, brown of hair, mature of bosom. Her eyes carried the stupid sort of divine life common in girls of that age. His name was Corvus, and he was fifteen. I don't recall his precise features, but he was handsome enough and dexterous. He could climb through the scaffolding almost as quickly as I. I first spied them talking when I made one of my frequent raids on the repository to steal another book. They were in shadow, but my eyes are keen. They spoke softly, hesitantly. My heart ached to see them and to think of their tragedy, for I knew right away that Corvus was not pure flesh. And Constantia was the daughter of the Bishop himself. I envisioned the old tyrant handing out the usual punishment to Corvus for such breaches of level and morality—castration. But in their talk was a sweetness that almost blanketed the powerful stench of the lower nave.

"Have you ever kissed a man before?"

"Yes."

"Who?"

"My brother." She laughed.

"And?" His voice was sharper, he might kill her brother, he intimated.

"A friend named Jules."

"Where is he?"

"Oh, he vanished on a wood-gathering expedition."

"Oh." And he kissed her again. I'm a historian, not a voyeur; so I discreetly hide the flowering of their passion. If Corvus had had any sense, he would have reveled in his conquest and never returned. But he was snared and continued to see her despite the risk. This was loyalty, love, faithfulness, and it was rare.

It fascinated me.

I have just been taking in sun, a nice day, and looking out over the buttresses. The Cathedral is like a low-bellied lizard, and the buttresses are its legs. There are little houses at the base of each buttress, where rainspouters with dragon faces used to lean out over the trees (or city or whatever was once down below). Now people live there. It wasn't always that way—the sun was once forbidden. From childhood, Corvus and Constantia were denied its light, and so even in their youthful prime they were pale and dirty with the smoke of candles and tallow lamps. The most sun anyone received in those days was obtained on wood-gathering expeditions.

After spying on one of the clandestine meetings of the young lovers, I mused in a dark corner for an hour, then went to see the copper giant Apostle Thomas. He was the only human form to live so high in the Cathedral. He carried a ruler on which was engraved his real name—he had been modeled after the Cathedral's restorer in times past, the architect Viollet-le-Duc. He knew the Cathedral better than anyone else, and I admired him greatly. Most of the monsters left him alone—out of fear, if nothing else. He was huge, black as night, but flaked with pale green, his face creased in eternal thought. He was sitting in his usual wooden compartment near the base of the spire, not twenty feet from where I write now, thinking about times the rest of us never knew:

of joy and past love, some say; of the burden
that rested on him now that the Cathedral was
the center of this chaotic world, others say.

It was the Giant who selected me from the
ugly hordes when he saw me with a Psalter. He
encouraged me in my efforts to read. "Your
eyes are bright," he told me. "You move as if
your brain were quick, and you keep yourself
dry and clean. You aren't hollow like the rainspouters. You have substance. For all our
sakes, put it to use and learn the ways of the
Cathedral."

And so I did.

He looked up as I came in. I sat on a box
near his feet and said, "A daughter of flesh is
seeing a son of stone and flesh."

He shrugged his massive shoulders. "So it
shall be, in time."

"Is it not a sin?"

"It is something so monstrous it is past sin
and become necessity," he said. "It will happen
more as time passes."

"They're in love, I think, or will be."

He nodded. "I—and one other—were the
only ones to abstain from fornication on the
night of Mortdieu," he said. "I am—except for
the other—alone fit to judge."

I waited for him to judge, but he sighed and
patted me on the shoulder. "And I never judge,
do I, ugly friend?"

"Never," I said.

"So leave me alone to be sad." He winked.
"And more power to them."

The Bishop of the Cathedral was an old, old

man. It was said he hadn't been Bishop before
Mortdieu but had been a wanderer who came
in during the chaos, before the forest had
replaced the city. He had set himself up as
titular head of this section of God's former
domain by saying it had been willed to him.

He was short, stout, with huge, hairy arms
like the clamps of a vise. He once killed a
spouter with a single squeeze of his fist, and
spouters are tough things, since they have no
guts like you (I suppose) and I. The hair
surrounding his bald pate was white, thick, and
unruly, and his eyebrows leaned over his nose
with marvelous flexibility. He rutted like a pig,
ate hugely, and shat liquidly (I know all). A
man for this time, if ever there was one.

It was his decree that all those not of pure
flesh be banned and that those not of human
form be killed on sight.

When I returned from the Giant's chamber, I
saw that the lower nave was in an uproar. They
had seen someone clambering about in the
scaffold, and troops had been sent to shoot him
down. Of course it was Corvus. I was a quicker
climber than he and knew the beams better; so
when he found himself trapped in an apparent
cul-de-sac, it was I who gestured from the
shadows and pointed to a hole large enough for
him to escape through. He took it without a
breath of thanks, but etiquette has never been
important to me. I entered the stone wall
through a nook a spare hand's width across and
wormed my way to the bottom to see what else
was happening. Excitement was rare.

A rumor was passing that the figure had been seen with a young girl, but the crowds didn't know who the girl was. The men and women who mingled in the smoky light, between the rows of open-roofed hovels, were chattering gaily. Castrations and executions were among the few moments of joy for us then; I relished them, too, but I had a stake in the potential victims now, and I was worried.

My worry and my interest got the better of me. I slid through an unrepaired gap and fell to one side of the alley between the outer wall and the hovels. A group of dirty adolescents spotted me. "There he is!" they screeched.

The Bishop's masked troops can travel freely on all levels. I was almost cornered by them, and when I tried one escape route, they waited at a crucial spot in the stairs—which I had to cross to complete the next leg—and I was forced back. I prided myself on knowing the Cathedral from top to bottom, but as I scrambled madly, I came upon a tunnel I had never noticed before. It led deep into a broad stone foundation wall. I was safe for the moment but afraid that they might find my caches of food and then poison my casks of rainwater. Still, there was nothing I could do until they had gone; so I decided to spend the anxious hours by exploring the tunnel.

The Cathedral is a constant surprise. I realize now I didn't know half of what it offered. There are always new ways to get from here to there (some, I suspect, are actually created while no one is looking) and, sometimes, even

new theres to be discovered. While troops
snuffled about the hole above, near the
stairs—where only a child of two or three could
have passed—I followed a flight of crude steps
deep into the stone. Water and slime made the
footing and handing difficult. For a moment I
was in a darkness deeper than any I had experienced before—a gloom more profound than
mere lack of light could explain. Then below me
I saw a faint yellow gleam. More cautious, I
slowed and progressed silently. Behind a
rusting, scabrous metal gate, I set foot into the
lighted room. There was the smell of crumbling
stone, a tang of mineral water, slime—and the
stench of a dead spouter. The beast lay on the
floor of the narrow chamber, several months
gone but still fragrant. I have mentioned that
spouters are very hard to kill, and this one had
been murdered. Three candles stood freshly
placed in nooks around the chamber, flickering
in a faint draft from above. Despite my fears, I
walked across the stone floor, took a candle,
and peered into the next section of tunnel.

It sloped down for several dozen feet, ending
at another metal gate. It was here that I de-
tected an odor I have never come across
before—the scent of the purest of stones, as of
rare jade or virgin marble. Such a feeling of
lightheadedness passed over me that I almost
laughed, but I was too wary for that. I pushed
aside the gate and was greeted by a rush of the
coldest, sweetest air, like a draft from the tomb
of a saint whose body does not corrupt but,
rather, pushes corruption away and expels it

miraculously into the nether pits. My beak dropped open. The candlelight fell across the darkness onto a figure I at first thought to be an infant. But I quickly disagreed with myself. The figure was several ages at once. As I blinked, it became a man of about thirty, well formed, with a high forehead and elegant hands, pale as ice. His eyes stared at the wall behind me. I bowed down on scaled knee and touched my forehead as best I could to the cold stone, shivering to my vestigial wingtips. "Forgive me, Joy of Man's Desiring," I said. "Forgive me." I had stumbled upon the hiding place of the stone Christ.

"You are forgiven," He said wearily. "You had to come sooner or later. Better now than later when . . . " His voice trailed away, and He shook His head. He was very thin, wrapped in a gray robe that still bore the scars of centuries of weathering. "Why did you come?"

"To escape the Bishop's troops," I said. He nodded.

"Yes. The Bishop. How long have I been here?"

"Since before I was born, Lord. Sixty or seventy years." He was thin, almost ephemeral, this figure I had imagined as a husky carpenter. I lowered my voice and besought, "What may I do for you, Lord?"

"Go away," He said.

"I could not live with such a secret," I said. "You are salvation. You can overthrow the Bishop and bring all the levels together."

"I am not a general or a soldier. Please go

away and tell no—"

I felt a breath behind me, then the whisper of a weapon. I leaped aside, and my hackles rose as a stone sword came down and shattered on the floor beside me. The Christ figure raised His hand. In shock, I stared at a beast much like myself. It stared back, face black with rage, stayed by the power of His hand. I should have been more careful—something had to have killed the spouter and kept the candles fresh.

"But, Lord," the great beast rumbled, "he will tell all."

"No," the Christ said. "He'll tell nobody." He looked half at me, half through me, and said, "Go, go."

Up the tunnels, into the orange dark of the Cathedral, crying, I crawled and slithered. I could not even go to the Giant. I had been silenced as effectively as if my throat had been cut.

The next morning I watched from a shadowy corner of the scaffold as a crowd gathered around a lone man in a dirty sackcloth robe, I had seen him before; his name was Psalo, and he was left alone as an example of the Bishop's largess. It was a token gesture; most of the people regarded him as barely half-sane.

Yet this time I listened and, in my confusion, found his words striking responsive chords in me. He was exhorting the Bishop and his forces to allow light into the Cathedral again, by dropping the canvas tarps that covered the windows. He had talked about this before, and the Bishop had responded with his usual statement—that with the light would come more chaos, for the human mind was now a pesthole of delusions. Any stimulus would drive away whatever security the inhabitants of the Cathedral had.

At this time it gave me no pleasure to watch the love of Constantia and Corvus grow. They were becoming more careless. Their talk was bolder:

"We shall soon announce a marriage," Corvus said.

"They will never allow it. They'll cut you."

"I'm nimble. They'll never catch me. The church needs leaders, brave revolutionaries. If no one breaks with tradition, everyone will suffer."

"I fear for your life—and mine. My father would push me from the flock like a diseased lamb."

"Your father is no shepherd."

"He is my father," Constantia said, eyes wide, mouth drawn tight.

I sat with beak in paws, eyes half-lidded, able to mimic each statement before it was uttered. Undying love . . . hope for a bleak future . . . shite and onions! I had read it all before, a cache of romance novels in the trash of a dead nun. As soon as I made the connection and realized the timeless banality—and the futility—of what I was seeing, and when I compared their prattle with the infinite sadness of the stone Christ, I went from innocent to cynic. The transition dizzied me, leaving little backwaters of noble emotion, but the future seemed clear. Corvus would be caught and executed; if it hadn't been for me, he would already have been gelded, if not killed. Constantia would weep, poison herself; the singers would sing of it (those selfsame warble-throats who cheered the death of her lover); perhaps I would write of it (I was planning this chronicle even then), and afterward, perhaps, I would follow them both—having succumbed to the sin of boredom.

With nightfall, things become less certain. It was easy to stare at a dark wall and let dreams become manifest. At one time, I've deduced from books, dreams couldn't take shape beyond sleep or brief fantasy. All too often I've had to fight things generated in my dreams, flowing from the walls, suddenly independent and hungry. People often die in the night. It was—is—a hard world we live in.

That night, falling to sleep with visions of the stone Christ in my head, I dreamed of holy men, angels, and saints. I came awake abruptly, by training, and one had stayed behind. The others I saw, vaguely, flitting outside the round window, where they whispered and made plans for flying off to heaven. The wraith who remained was a dark shape in one corner. His breathing was harsh. "I am Peter," he said, "also called Simon. I am the Rock of the Church, and popes are told that they are heir to my task."

"I'm rock, too." I said. "At least in part."

"So be it. You are heir to my task. Go forth

and be pope. Do not fear or even reverence the stone Christ, for a Christ is only as good as He does, and if He does nothing, there is no salvation in Him.''

The shadow reached out to pat my head, and I saw his eyes grow wide as he made out my form. He muttered some formula for banishing devils and oozed out the window to join his fellows.

I imagined that if such a thing were actually brought before the council, it would be decided that the benison of a dream person is not binding. I did not care. This was better advice than any I'd had since the Giant told me to read and learn.

But to be pope, one must have a hierarchy of servants to carry out one's orders. The biggest of rocks does not move by itself. So, swelled with power, I decided to appear in the upper nave and announce myself to the people.

It took a great deal of courage to appear in daylight, without cloak, and to walk across the scaffold's surface, on the second level, through crowds of vendors setting up the market for the day. Some reacted with typical bigotry and sought to kick or deride me. My beak discouraged them. I clambered to the top of a prominent stall and stood in a murky lamp's circle, clearing my throat to announce myself. Under a hail of rotten pomegranates and limp vegetables, I told the throng who I was, and I told them about my vision. Jeweled with beads of offal, I jumped down in a few minutes and fled to a tunnel entrance too small for most men. Some of the boys followed me, and one lost a finger, trying to slice me with a bit of colored glass.

I recognized that the tactic of open revelation was worthless. There are numerous levels of bigotry, and I was at the very bottom of any list.

My next strategy was to find some way to disrupt the Cathedral from top to bottom. Even bigots, when reduced to a mob, can be swayed by the presence of one obviously ordained and capable. I spent two days skulking through the walls. There had to be a basic flaw in so fragile a structure as the church, and, although I wasn't contemplating total destruction, I wanted something spectacular, unavoidable.

While I thought, hanging from the bottom of the second scaffold, above the community of pure flesh, the Bishop's deep gravelly voice roared over the noise of the crowd. I opened my eyes and looked down. The masked troops were holding a bowed figure, and the Bishop was intoning over its head, "Know all who hear me now, this young bastard of flesh and stone—"

Corvus, I told myself. *Finally caught.* I shut one eye, but the other refused to close out the scene.

"—has violated all we hold sacred and shall atone for his crimes on this spot, tomorrow at this time. Kronos! Mark the wheel's progress." The elected Kronos, a spindly old man with dirty gray hair down to his buttocks, took a piece of charcoal and marked an X on the huge bulkhead chart, behind which the wheel groaned and sighed in its circuit.

The crowd was enthusiastic. I saw Psalo pushing through the people.

"What crime?" he called out.

"Violation of the lower level!" the head of the masked troops declared.

"That merits a whipping and an escort upstairs." Psalo said. "I detect a more sinister crime here. What is it?"

The Bishop looked Psalo down coldly. "He tried to rape my daughter, Constantia."

Psalo could say nothing to that. The penalty was castration and death. All the pure humans accepted such laws. There was no other recourse.

I mused, watching Corvus being led to the dungeons. The future that I desired at that moment startled me with its clarity. I wanted that part of my heritage that had been denied to me—to be at peace with myself, to be surrounded by those who accepted me, by those no better than I. In time that would happen, as the Giant had said. But would I ever see it? What Corvus, in his own lusty way, was trying to do was equalize the levels, to bring stone into flesh until no one could define the divisions.

Well, my plans beyond that point were very hazy. They were less plans than glowing feelings, imaginings of happiness and children playing in the forest and fields beyond the island, as the world knitted itself together under the gaze of God's heir. My children, playing in the forest. A touch of truth came to me. I had

182

wished to be Corvus when he tupped
Constantia.

So I now had two tasks that could be merged,
if I was clever. I had to distract the Bishop and
his troops, and I had to rescue Corvus, fellow
revolutionary.

I spent that night in feverish misery in my
room. At dawn I went to the Giant and asked
his advice. He looked me over coldly and said,
"We waste our time if we try to knock sense
into them. But we have no better calling than to
waste our time, do we?"

"What shall I do?"

"Enlighten them."

I stomped my claw on the floor. "They are
bricks! Try enlightening bricks!"

He smiled his sad, narrow smile. "Enlighten
them," he said.

I left the Giant's chamber in a rage. I did not
have access to the great wheel's board of time;
so I couldn't know exactly when the execution
would take place. But I guessed—from
memories of a grumbling stomach—that it
would be in the early afternoon. I traveled from
one end of the nave to the other and, likewise,
the transepts. I nearly exhausted myself. Then,
crossing an empty aisle, I picked up a piece of
colored glass and examined it, puzzled. Many
of the boys on all levels carried these shards
with them, and the girls used them as
jewelry—against the wishes of their elders, who
held that bright objects bred more beasts in the
mind. Where did they get them?

In one of the books I had perused years

before, I had seen brightly colored pictures of the Cathedral windows. "Enlighten them," the Giant had said.

Psalo's request to let light into the Cathedral came to mind.

Along the peak of the nave, in a tunnel running its length, I found the ties that held the pulleys of the canvases over the windows. The best windows, I decided, would be the huge ones of the north and south transepts. Then I made a diagram in the dust, trying to decide what season it was and from which direction the sunlight would come: pure speculation, of course, but at this moment I was in a fever of brilliance. All the windows had to be clear. I could not decide which was best.

I was ready by early afternoon, just after sext prayers in the upper nave. I had cut the major ropes and weakened the clamps by prying them from the walls with a pick stolen from the armory. I walked along a ledge, took an almost vertical shaft through the wall to the lower floor, and waited.

Constantia was watching from a wooden balcony, the Bishop's special box for executions. She had a terrified, fascinated look on her face. And Corvus was on the dais across the nave, right in the center of the cross of the transepts. Torches illuminated him and his executioners, three men and one old woman.

I knew the procedure. The old woman would castrate him first; then the men would remove his head. He was dressed in the condemned's red robe, to hide any blood. Blood excitement among the impressionable was the last thing the Bishop wanted. Troops waited around the dais to sprinkle scented water in order to hide the loathsome smell.

I didn't have much time. It would take minutes, at the least, for the system of ropes and pulleys to clear and allow the canvases to fall. I went to my station and cut the remaining ties. Then, as the Cathedral filled with a hollow creaking sound, I followed the shaft back to my viewing post.

In three minutes the canvases were drooping. I saw Corvus look up, his eyes glazed. The Bishop was with his daughter in the box. He pulled her back into the shadows. In another two minutes the canvases fell onto the upper scaffold with a hideous crash. Their weight was too great for the ends of the structure, and it collapsed, allowing the canvas to cascade to the floor, many yards below. At first the illumination was dim and bluish, filtered perhaps by a passing cloud. Then, from one end of the Cathedral to the other, a burst of light threw my smoky world into clarity. The glory of thousands of pieces of colored glass, hidden for decades and hardly touched by childish vandals, fell upon upper and lower levels at once. A cry from the crowds nearly tossed me from my post. I slid quickly to the lower level and hid, afraid of what I had done. This was more than simple sunlight. Like the blossoming of flowers, the transept windows fixed all who saw them.

Eyes accustomed to orangey dark, to smoke and haze and shadow, cannot stare into such glory without drastic effect. I shielded my own face and tried to find a convenient exit.

But the population was increasing. As the light brightened and more faces rose to be locked, phototropic, the splendor unhinged some people. From their minds poured contents too wondrous to be accurately cataloged. The monsters thus released were not violent, however, and most of the visions were not monstrous.

The upper and lower naves shimmered with reflected glories, with dream figures and children clothed in baubles of light. Saints and prodigies dominated. A thousand newly created youngsters squatted on the bright floor and began to tell of marvels, of cities in the East, and of times as they had once been. Clowns dressed in fire entertained from the tops of the market stalls. Animals unknown to the Cathedral cavorted between the dwellings, giving friendly advice. Abstract things, glowing balls in nets of gold and ribbons of silk, sang and floated around the upper reaches. The Cathedral became a great vessel of all its citizens' bright dreams.

Slowly, from the lower nave, people of pure flesh climbed to the scaffold and walked the upper nave to see what they couldn't from below. From my hideaway I watched the masked troops of the Bishop carrying his litter up narrow stairs. Constantia walked behind, stumbling, her eyes shut in the new brightness.

All tried to cover their eyes, but none succeeded for long.

I wept. Almost blind with tears. I made my way still higher and looked down on the roiling crowds. I saw Corvus, his hands still wrapped in restraining ropes, being led by the old woman. Constantia saw him, too, and they regarded each other like strangers, then joined hands as best they could. She borrowed a knife from one of her father's soldiers and cut his ropes away. Around them the brightest dreams of all began to swirl, pure white and blood-red and sea-green, coalescing into visions of all the children they would innocently have.

I gave them a few hours to regain their senses—and to regain my own. Then I stood on the Bishop's abandoned podium and shouted over the heads of those on the lowest level.

"The time has come!" I cried. "We must all unite right now; we must unite—"

At first they ignored me. I was quite eloquent, but their excitement was still too great. So I waited some more, began to speak again, and was shouted down. Bits of fruit and vegetables arced up. "Freak!" they screamed, and drove me away.

I crept along the stone stairs, found the narrow crack, and hid in it, burying my beak in my paws, wondering what had gone wrong. It took a surprisingly long time for me to realize that, in my case, it was less the stigma of stone than the ugliness of my shape that doomed my quest for leadership. This knowledge was painful.

I had, however, paved the way for the stone Christ. *He will surely be able to take His place now,* I told myself. So I maneuvered along the crevice until I came to the hidden chamber and the yellow glow. All was quiet within. I met first the stone monster, who looked me over suspiciously with glazed gray eyes. "You're back," he said. Overcome by his wit, I leered, nodded, and asked that I be presented to the Christ.

"He's sleeping."

"Important tidings," I said.

"What?"

"I bring glad tidings."

"Then let me see them."

"His eyes only."

Out of the gloomy corner came the Christ, looking much older now, almost like a prophet. "What is it?" He asked.

"I have prepared the way for you," I said. "Simon called Peter and told me I was the heir to his legacy, that I should go before you—"

The stone Christ shook his head. "You believe I am the fount from which all blessings flow?"

I nodded, uncertain.

"What have you done out there?"

"Let in the light," I said.

He shook His head slowly. "You seem a wise enough creature. You know about Mortdieu."

"Yes."

"Then you should know that I barely have enough power to keep myself together, to heal myself, much less to minister to those out there." He gestured beyond the walls. "My own source has gone away." He said mournfully. "I'm operating on reserves, and those none too vast."

"He wants you to go away and stop bothering us," the monster explained.

"They have their light out there," the Christ said. "They'll play with that for a while, get tired of it, go back to what they had before. Is there room for you in that?"

I thought for a moment, then shook my head. "No room," I said. "I'm too ugly."

"You are too ugly, and I'm too famous." He said. "I'd have to come from their midst, anonymous, and that's clearly impossible. No, leave them alone for a while. They'll make me over again, perhaps, or, better still, forget about me. About us. We don't have any place there."

I was stunned. I sat down hard on the stone floor, and the Christ patted me on my head as He walked by. "Go back to your hiding place; live as well as you can," he said. "Our time is over."

I turned to go. When I reached the crevice, I heard His voice behind, saying, "Do you play bridge? If you do, find another. We need four to a table."

I clambered up the crack, through the walls, and along the arches over the revelry. Not only was I not going to be pope—after an appointment by St. Peter himself!—but I couldn't persuade someone much more qualified than I to take the leadership.

I returned to the copper Giant. He was lost in meditation. About his feet were scattered scraps

of paper with detailed drawings of parts of the
Cathedral. I waited patiently until he saw me.
He turned to me, chin in hand, and looked me
over.

"Why so sad?"

I shook my head. Only he could read my
features and recognize my moods.

"Did you take my advice below? I heard a
commotion."

"Mea maxima culpa," I said.

"And . . . ?"

I slowly, hesitantly, made my report, con-
cluding with the refusal of the stone Christ. The
Giant listened closely, without interrupting.
When I was done, he stood, towering over me,
and pointed with his ruler through an open
portal.

"Do you see that out there?" he asked. The
ruler swept over the forests beyond the island,
to the far, green horizon. I said that I did and
waited for him to continue. He seemed to be
lost in thought again.

"Once there was a city where trees now grow.
One of the finest cities in the world," he said.
"It was called Paris, and it was old even then. It
was famous for a peculiar kind of thought and
a peculiar kind of passion. Artists came by the
thousands, and whores, and philosophers, and
academics. And when God died, all the
academics and whores and artists couldn't hold
the fabric of the world together. How do you
expect us to succeed now?"

Us? "Expectations should not determine
whether one acts or not, should they?"

The Giant laughed and tapped my head with the ruler. "An age ago, before I was born or repaired the Cathedral, the Christ and what He represented stood tall in the city of thought, much as this spire rises over the forest. But everything grows old. Maybe we've been given a sign, and we just have to learn how to interpret it correctly." He shook his head.

I leered to show I was puzzled.

"Instead of God's death, we're faced with another process entirely. We have long bathed in God's milk, in His rules and creativity. Maybe Mortdieu is really a sign that we have been weaned. We must forage for ourselves, remake the world without help. What do you think of that?"

I was too tired to really judge the merits of what he was saying, but I had never known the Giant to be wrong before. "Okay. So?"

"The stone Christ indicates His charge is running down. If God weans us from the old ways, we can't expect His Son to replace the nipple, can we?"

"No . . ."

He hunkered next to me, his face bright. "I wondered who would really stand forth. It's obvious. He won't. So, little one, who's the next choice?"

"Me?" I asked, meekly. The giant looked me over almost pityingly.

"No," he said after a time. "I am the next. We're *weaned!*" He did a little dance, startling my beak up out of my paws. I blinked. He grabbed my vestigial wingtips and pulled me upright. "Tell me more."

"About what?"

"Tell me all that's going on below, and whatever else you know."

"I'm trying to figure out what you're saying," I protested, trembling a bit.

"Dense as stone!" Grinning, he bent over me. Then the grin went away and he tried to look stern. "It's a grave responsibility. We must remake the world ourselves now. We must coordinate our thoughts, our dreams. Chaos won't do. What an opportunity, to be the architect of an entire universe!" He waved the ruler at the ceiling. "To build the very skies! The last world was a training ground, full of harsh rules and strictures. Now we've been told we're ready to leave that behind, move on to something more mature. Did I teach you any of the rules of architecture? I mean, the aesthetics. The need for harmony, interaction, utility, beauty-within-science?"

"Some," I said.

"Good. I don't think making the universe anew will require any better rules. No doubt we'll need to experiment, and perhaps one or more of our great spires will topple. But now we work for ourselves, to our own glory, and the greater glory of the God who made us! No, ugly friend?"

Like many histories, mine must begin with the small, the tightly focused, and expand into the large. But, unlike most historians. I don't have the luxury of time. Indeed, my story isn't even concluded yet.

Soon the legions of Viollet-le-Duc will begin their campaigns. Most have been schooled pretty thoroughly. Kidnapped from below, brought up in the heights, taught as I was. We'll begin returning them, one by one.

I teach off and on, write off and on, observe all the time.

The next step will be the biggest. I haven't any idea how we're going to do it.

But, as the Giant puts it, "Long ago the roof fell in. Now we must push it up again, strengthen it, repair the beams." At this point he smiles to the pupils. "Not just repair them. Replace them! Now we are the beams. Flesh and stone become something much stronger."

Ah, but then some dolt will raise a hand and inquire, "What if our arms get tired holding up the sky?"

Our task will not soon be over.

SAM AND THE SUDDEN
BLIZZARD MACHINE

By Dean Ing

Sam's sudden blizzard is history now, and like all motor racing disasters its memory is rusting out in a junkyard of legends. Some claim Sam's design was faulty. Others say the fault was mine for listening to him. Smythe, our sports car club archivist, warns that we all orbit too closely around Sam, like moths around a rally car spotlight—but Smythe's a poly sci professor, so that's got to be wrong.

I blame it on the weather. The snow came a month early and all at once and froze out our plans for late fall competition.

"Tee-boned yer slalom event, did it?" Sam grunted happily as we slumped at his fireplace.

"Black-flagged us," I admitted. I sat watching flames as Sam arranged blazing chunks of hardwood. Now, anybody can poke at a fire with a Bugatti dipstick, but Sam was feeding his fire with old trophy bases. Pretty expensive way to heat a hangar, from the standpoint of effort expended. Actually, Sam only had to heat the living quarters in his surplus hangar, which is the only structure on his property. The rest of the place is crammed with machine tools, surplus aerospace materials, his vehicles, and his clean room, where he doesn't build racing cars. I mean, he doesn't anymore. That is, he does, but not as a business now. Sam was with Lockheed's "skunk works" until after the U-2 and SR-71 were public knowledge and then he turned to designing racing cars.

His series of fabled cars might have gone on forever had he not stolen computer time from Lockheed to make a study of racing trends. Sam took one hard scan at the printout and quit serious competition in mingled disgust and fear. In 1990, he predicts, go-carts will outgun Indy cars and dune buggies won't need wheels. Something to do with new power units, he says, with a glint in those gray granite eyes.

With all his engineering know-how and all his stolen hardware and both of his magician's hands in that hangar, Sam is roughly as important and predictable as the weather. His sudden blizzard was inevitable from the moment Sam softly rasped, as if to the fire, "You don't really have to hole up all winter, y'know."

I glared at him. "No, I could get me a sled and name it *Rosebud,*" I grumped. "Great sport."

"Sled; mm, yeah." Brief pregnant pause, then breech delivery: "You remember the old quarry course?"

I shivered, and not from the cold. The quarry racecourse had been outlawed after our first competition event there. We had had 73 entrants, and 21 didn't finish, and 52 canny dudes found excuses not to start. Any idiot could add that up. It was a week before we got the last car hauled out of there. I reminded Sam of this.

"Yup; and if you remember, I told you not to touch it with or without gloves," Sam countered. "But with a few, ah, *minor* changes I just might give it a try."

"This *winter*?"

He nodded.

"In thirty inches of *snow*?"

He hummed a snatch of "White Christmas."

"You're weird," I said. "We'd kill somebody."

"Quoth the craven," he said. "Shut up and let me think . . ."

I'm convinced now that Sam cheated; he must've been plotting the idea for a long time. He cupped his big stubby hands over one knee and smiled to himself. "Ever do any sledding?"

"Exactly once."

"Me, too. Never got used to the lack of power on the uphill straights."

"But what's that gottadowith . . ."

Sam raised a restraining hand. "Just listen," he soothed. "Take the old quarry course and run *down* it instead of *up*. Build your own frame. Use—heh, heh—any power plant you please, add steering, put a windscreen on, and be a hero at the quarry."

I gnawed my lip a moment. "Sounds simple," I hedged, "but if anybody goes off the edge—"

"He'll hit a nice cushy snowdrift instead of a bale of hay. I figure you hay raisers might find that a welcome change. Choice of power train is up to you. Wheels, chains, propeller, spikes, ducted fan, or a team of oxen if that's yer karma. Use any brake system that works at tech inspection. Sky's the limit."

Sam had something there. And it was catching; I tingled at the vision of sledding specials, specially built racers midwifed in our garages. It would be fun; hell, it could become a winter revolution: Speed Week in Springville! "Sam? Ah, would you—"

"Propose it to your club? I just did." Sam's smile seemed open, guileless. Maybe it was a leer. In any event, no pun intended, Sam's recommendation was as good as a direct order. Twenty-seven members of the club swore to build specials, and, oddly enough, many of us did. The rest, including me, gave help. I wanted to help Sam when he announced that he was building a surprise entry. I should've saved my breath.

The appointed Saturday dawned with a knifing chill in the clear sky. Snowballs flurried between early arrivals at the quarry. I checked off the conical pylons, fire extinguishers, doctor, and timing equipment, wishing we had attracted some racing journalists. The man from the local *Bugle* was worse than nothing; but him we had, like it or not. I fought the temptation to steal his hat for a pylon. It was already the right shape.

Scanning the entry list, I could see our first mistake was the lack of ground rules. Several guys used open propellers, one of 'em a front-mounted rig that nearly blew the driver off while it was idling. He got chilblains and became an instant spectator. Another theorist put six little tires across the rear axle to get more adhesion. It worked fine on firm snow, but at the technical inspection, he gunned it and his wheels hungrily chewed a hole two-feet deep. Of course, it dropped backward into the hole like a sounding whale and killed the engine and caught fire, with the usual result. We buried the hulk under a pile of slush and went on with tech inspection.

Sam's pickup eased up the access road with a towering, tarp-shrouded lump looming over its cab. Everything got very quiet. Sam had refused us even the slightest peek at his secretive entry. Small wonder.

With his usual stolid care, Sam flipped back the tarpaulin and revealed most of his special. One of the tech inspectors screamed, saving me the trouble.

To being with, the—thing—broke all the rules or, rather, the assumptions. Everybody but Sam used heavy frames, sandfilled tubes, bags of birdshot, or Corvette body parts to add weight. Sam had a gossamer birdcage frame of aluminum wrapped with quartz fiber tape. For a maniacal moment I wondered if he'd crocheted it.

Everybody with wheels used fat little studded tires, but Sam's wheel was two and a half meters high. Towering between a rear pair of ski runners was a single viciously cleated monstrosity of magnesium, like a kulak's ferris wheel a half a meter wide. It was mounted on an axle held by that spidery tubing frame.

Nearly everybody had cart engines mounted near the wheels. Sam used a turbine powered by a liquid that he handled with something very like terror—and Sam crimps dynamite caps with his teeth. The turbine wasn't near the wheel; it was inside! Sam had bolted it to the nonrotating axle within his hellish great wheel.

If I forgot the gear teeth around the inside of the wheel, forgive me. A simple drive gear transmitted the turbine's torque to the big wheel. Studying the gear ratio, I calculated that the monster wouldn't be very quick. To be competitive, the turbine would have to run at over 50,000 rpm. Later, Sam told me his little aerospace fugitive didn't run well at 50,000. It ran much better at 500.

Thousand. Which partly explains—but I'm getting ahead of myself.

The steering mechanism was a disappointment at first (and to me, a revelation at last): a forward pair of skis, pivoted from a box on the frame ahead of the driver's location. God only knows how any driver would dare to hunker down kneeling, his fanny up to tempt those cleats, and guide that flailing juggernaut over patches of glare ice on a twisty trail near sheer drops at the quarry. To any sane driver that rig was a case of shove at first sight.

A murmur from the crowd drew me back to

the course. High on the trail, a propeller-driven sled had just started when its brakes failed. Worse, the driver was a first-timer, our only woman entrant, wife of an inept mechanic, darling daughter of a city councilman. She had never learned to drive and thought it entertaining to start with something little and cute. I exchanged nervous tics with our club treasurer, Bernie Feinbaum, but everything was fine until Turn One. It always is.

When I first spotted it, the sled was spitting snow, slowly rotating down a short straight until it was directly bass-ackwards and aimed off the cliff face. That's when Bernie crossed himself.

And down she came, idling the prop on downslopes to build up speed. A surge of backward thrust nearly stopped her at each bend. She paddled around the course in just over seven minutes.

Three more stalwarts made their runs. The converted garden tractor managed to convert a patch of ice into hot water halfway down and did not finish. My money was on a twin-tread rig until its driver saw the short straight beyond Turn Two and tromped on it. The thing did a tread-stand just long enough to barf him out, crashed down, ruptured an oil line that made weewee under one tread, and hi-hoed away overland as a free and driverless spirit until it bisected a chickenhouse a kilometer away.

The guy on skis, sporting five little bitty model engines with propellers on each ski, was protested, but he tried anyhow. In deference to Sam, the printed rules stated, "The sky's the limit"—prophetically—and the sitzmark artist was judged within his rights. He made his mark, all right, just past Turn Four.

During all this, Sam completed tech inspection and only once was seen actually drivng his special. He had to fire it up for his braking test, and by the time the crowd leaped around to see what the ruckus was, it was over. The great thing accelerated for 60 meters on a thimbleful of fuel, with the wail of a lost soul in a sausage grinder, then reversed power in a geyser of snow. But it stopped like a Christmas tachymeter.

Sam suggested that the course be walked again, to be sure it was still open. Very few people could testify one way or the other. He also asked if he could make the tour afoot, and some fool said he could. After all, Sam wasn't competing for a trophy. His was to be a demonstration run, like a dragster at the soapbox derby. One more advantage wouldn't matter. So we thought.

Sam spent a few minutes dallying with a black box that evidently plugged into his special. Finally content, he ambled up the gentle black slope of the hill, carrying the little box. I followed at a distance.

Striding away from the start line, Sam pushed something on the box and tucked it under his arm. I watched him pace down the course, "absently" positioning himself for a fast approach to the first turn, and then I got involved with the *Bugle* reporter.

The scribbler is the sort who sniffs a story with gore potential from any distance and will end up manufacting most of the story if he feels like it. "I got a list of entrants," he mused, "but durn if I recognize anybody important."

"You might as well go home," I urged. "This is just a local fun-type event; no big prizes."

"Yeah?" He gloomed after Sam, jerked his head in Sam's direction. "Who's the tough old curmudgeon walking down The Last Mile?"

I told him about the former rocket man.

Pause. "Waitaminnit. Don't I know that name from someplace?"

I was casual. "Possibly. Indy, Atlanta 500, Le Mans—but Sam doesn't crave publicity these days."

"He's public property," the pencil pusher snorted. "But he musta turned chicken in his old age; he's registered as the owner of that Rube Goldberg waterwheel, but the driver's some lunatic named Botts."

While I fought myself to keep from feeding this guy a few knuckles, a nagging doubt clung to me. Why *wasn't* Sam driving? Had he finally lost his nerve on a measly small-time event?

The reporter wheedled more information. He had faucet charm and turned it on and off as it suited him. "You a good ol' friend of good ol' Sam?"

"That pleasure is mine," I said.

"Maybe you can gimme some details on his, uh, whatchamacallit. The *Bugle* prides itself on accuracy.'' His look dared me to disbelieve it.

"Sure. Kinda hard to know where to start," I hedged, wondering if I could get away with wild inaccuracies. I invented quickly. "You could mention the desmodromic valves," I began.

"I intended to. Uh, how d'you spell it?"

"Like the inventor," I lied, warming to the game. "Herr Desmond Droemik." I spelled it out. "And you'll notice the hydrodynamic spoilers."

He was writing like mad. "Come again?"

"To spoil the hydrodynamics," I frowned, with a wisp of scorn. "And the outer-space frame, obviously. With unlimited-slip differential and . . . and a chromed roll center."

When physicists learn to chrome plate the equator, or any other imaginary line, then Sam will be able to put chrome on a roll center, which is also an imaginary line. My twinge of guilt evaporated in a warm rush of fresh fantasy. "And of course it has computer-designed steering," I concluded, reaching wildly enough to grasp a great truth by the tail. But how could I know? I shrugged. "Otherwise, Sam's rig is pretty ordinary."

He cranked his spigot on for me. "Hey, you were lotsa help, fella. Maybe I could mention your name. Immortality in print!"

"Gaston Martin," I perjured, and shook his hand. Then I sloped off down the hill, whistling an innocent medley.

Sam had finished his trek before I reached bottom and was fiddling with something under his tarp. The word was spreading that Sam had lost his nerve. Nobody could locate Botts, his driver. Sam drove up the hill by the easy back way and parked near the start line. The start official was in brief conversation with him, and we watched them wrestle a ramp from the pickup to the ice. Presently, the last serious entrant made his run; it was a conventional go-cart and expired conventionally in a deep snowdrift. By the time the driver was exhumed from his own personal avalanche, Sam had his vehicle fueled and waiting at the start line. Sure enough, Sam wasn't driving.

A chubby stranger in a sleek black coverall was strapped in place, inhumanly calm under the circumstances. During his last-minute checks, Sam was in a lively dialogue with the official. I was heartbroken that Sam could accept another driver in his place, and through my misting eyes it seemed that Sam and the official were actually arguing. I heard the muted buzz around me; everybody had a theory because nobody knew anything.

The P.A. system crackled. "THE SAM-BOTT SPECIAL," it boomed; "DRIVER, R.O. BOTTS." Then, like everybody else, it fell silent.

High above us, the tiny figure of Sam made an adjustment at his power unit. A spurt of steam billowed like an omen in the frosty air. A moment later its harsh tooth-loosening wail reached us, and Sam was fooling around near the steering. I could swear the little black box was nestled there.

Sam knelt clear of the great machine, intent

on the steering. The official, stamping and yelling with hands over his ears, slipped on the ice and caught himself on the controls. And engaged the drive gear and was flung into Sam, and Botts didn't bother to hit the reverse. As a matter of cold fact, Botts had no brakes.

In an instant, Sam was on his feet, running after the special; an exercise in pure loserism. The machine keened its air-raid siren song, the big wheel churning down the slope, a roostertail of snow lofting up, up, and away behind. The gasp from the crowd must've lowered ambient air pressure by five pounds; we all expected a god-awful smash at Turn One.

But the special simply laid over at an angle and disappeared around the bend. When it reappeared near Turn Tree, a cheer went up and Sam went down, having blindly run through the roostertail into banked snow. Next came a twisty uphill stretch, and judging by the noise, the turbine was revving harder than ever. Sam abandoned his direct chase and half-clambered, half-fell straight down the embankment. It was a maneuver that would bring him to the course just past the last turn, before the timer at the finish line. I wondered if he intended to trip the damned thing, intimidate Botts, or signal him—assuming they both survived that long.

The special was surviving, but only by inches. Turn Six was a fiendish righthander of decreasing radius, bounded by the bluff on the outside and thin air on the inside. Botts would *have* to shut down his power long before he reached it: but Botts was not shutting down at all. Before our bulging eyes, the machine angled toward the outside and, running flat-out, swept up the side of the bluff that followed the curve of the course. Like a trick cyclist at a carnival, Botts and the machine shrieked around the curving wall while absolutely horizontal, then shot out of the curve onto the course again.

Still accelerating.

The scream of the turbine grew nearer, higher-pitched, impossibly abrasive on the ears. Sam scrambled to his feet just as the special slued around the last turn. Now there was nothing ahead of it but a straight path and a gaggle of timing people flanking the finish line. This group got one glimpse of the thundering wheel, saw it gaining speed and trailing a seven-story roostertail of snow, and abandoned ship like cats on polished linoleum. All, that is, except for the girl at the timer who had ear-muffs on and wasn't looking and will always describe the passage of Sam's special as the Sudden Blizzard of Seventy-Nine.

Sam had his windbreaker off as the thing howled past him, and in one deft swoop he threw it into the blur of the great wheel. It was, he told me later, his only hope of jamming something because there was lots more fuel to be burned and he did not own an antitank gun.

The wadded cloth was effective in its way. For an instant the wheel skipped a beat, digested the offering, then belched shreds of nylon in all directions. Something, probably a sleeve, caught in a cleat and started to beat Botts rhythmically. The special accelerated

down the straight at something over 160 kilometers an hour. Sam wiped slush from his eyes
and watched, now helpless. The pounding was
too much for Botts and suddenly the driver was
ejected.

The Botts trajectory was simply unbelievable
if you didn't know what you were watching.
From the driving position of a praying Moslem,
Botts rose majestically toward heaven and
began to pirouette in the air to one side. Tiring
of this, Botts jerked, seemed to shrug, then fell
in a series of falling leaf aerobatics before
hitting flat in the snow. Flatter than we knew.

The special was bumping hard now. Every
bump caused a higher bounce, and as it headed
toward our parked cars the wheel steadied a few
inches above the surface. Then the errant sleeve
sailed away, carrying the cleat with it, and the
big machine arrowed upward. It was airborne,
and more so every second. The course physician
sprinted after Botts, aspirin jouncing from his
open bag.

The rest of us gaped at the special, daring and
swooping above us in a pattern that seemed
vaguely familiar. Half a minute later it rocketed
away again, still higher, and began the same
routine. It was then that Sam reached us.

The doctor returned flinty-eyed, holding up a
rubber suit. "Where'd you hide the body;" he
accused.

Sam nodded at the suit. "That's him. I just
took an old scuba suit, sealed it, stuck a helmet
on it, and pumped it up. I'll give it two hot
patches and call you in the morning."

"You can't run a race without a driver," someone said.

"That's what the start official kept hollering," Sam responded, "and I kept explaining that my driver was really in the programming box." He squinted toward the sky. "But I wasn't finished programming it when the idiot hit the controls. The box was set to go where I had taken it before, but I didn't get a chance to program a stop."

The facts interlocked in my head. "Sam! Your driver was a robot?"

"Welcome to the machine age," Sam said drily. "I didn't figure on my driver springing a leak, though; thought I had ol' Botts strapped in pretty well."

The reporter huffed up, looking grimly pleased. "What about that—that thing up there?" He pointed on high, where a contrail of steam followed a flashing silver streak. At that height it sounded like a sex-crazed mosquito. "Who's to say that iron windmill won't chew up a satellite or something?"

"I am," Sam said quietly. "I knew there'd be a low-pressure area over the wheel, but that piece of nylon created a higher differential when it bent the cleats. More lift. Now the special will go as high as thin air will let it, and then it'll run out of peroxide, and it'll keep running the same damn course I programmed until then—only skewed upwards."

The doctor, a nice guy but a bit out of his element now, shambled off, dragging the punctured scuba suit and muttering about an autopsy with Cousteau. A group of rescuers dug out the girl at the finish line. She was still at her post and only a little stunned under her mound of powder snow. She swore that Sam's machine had clocked the course in 27 seconds, roughly a 112-kilometer-an-hour average. That figured.

The reporter, still trying to promote fireworks, drew a crowd with the old citizen's arrest gambit. "You stand accused of reckless driving," he began.

"Only I wasn't driving," Sam reminded him.

"Unauthorized flying of unlicensed aircraft," he ployed. God knows, that much was true.

"If you can prove it," Sam murmured, glancing up.

"I'll impound it when it comes down. Ah, it *will* come down." It was a statement, but it was a question too.

"How very right you are," Sam said, glancing at his chronometer. "And it should be out of fuel shortly."

"Good." The reporter folded his arms, Fletcher Christian on the *Bounty*'s deck, and glared into the sky. "And you should be jailed for improper construction. I know a few things, mister."

"Front page news," Sam replied. "Name one."

"You can embrittle something if you don't put the chrome on right. I read it somewhere. Right?"

Sam chewed an ebony cuticle reflectively. "It happens," he conceded.

"I thought so," snarled the reporter. "And you went and embrittled your roll center!"

Sam blinked, shook his head as if to clear it. I drew him aside and whispered how I'd had some sport with the *Bugle*boy, who didn't know an imaginary reference line from a breadline. Sam tried to hide the smile that was growing as he listened.

Then he called to the reporter. "You were right. Guess you'll have to write me up for that." Course workers stopped to listen. "And one other thing: the special is your impounded property, but barring wind drift, I'd say you have a problem." Sam headed for his pickup truck, cheerily shouting. "When it comes down, it will be doing roughly Mach two. Your problem is not being anywhere near *where* it hits, *when* it hits." He made a quick one-fingered obeisance from his pickup. "Wear it in good health."

The quarry was innocent of human life in two minutes flat.

Sam never recovered the special, though we found a new sinkhole near the quarry later. It was too cold to dig, and anyway Sam and I were too busy. The *Bugle*'s coverage was everything we'd hoped, and the writer of the best sarcastic letter to the editor won a place on Sam's pit crew. True to his resolve against serious competition, Sam was preparing his old Nash Metropolitan for that race where—but everybody's heard about that.

BURNING CHROME

By William Gibson

It was hot the night we burned Chrome. Out in the malls and plazas moths were batting themselves to death against the neon, but in Bobby's loft the only light came from a monitor screen and the green and red LEDs on the face of the matrix simulator. I knew every chip in Bobby's simulator by heart; it looked like your workaday Ono-Sendai VII, the "Cyberspace Seven," but I'd rebuilt it so many times that you'd have had a hard time finding a square millimeter of factory circuitry in all that silicon.

We waited side by side in front of the simulator console, watching the time-display in the screen's lower left corner.

"Go for it," I said, when it was time, but Bobby was already there, leaning forward to drive the Russian program into its slot with the heel of his hand. He did it with the tight grace of a kid slamming change into an arcade game, sure of winning and ready to pull down a string of free games.

A silver tide of phosphenes boiled across my field of vision as the matrix began to unfold in my head, a 3-D chessboard, infinite and perfectly transparent. The Russian program seemed to lurch as we entered the grid. If anyone else had been jacked into that part of the matrix, he might have seen a surf of flickering shadow roll out of the little yellow pyramid that represented our computer. The program was a mimetic weapon, designed to absorb local color and present itself as a crash-priority override in whatever context it encountered.

"Congratulations," I heard Bobby say. "We just became an Eastern Seaboard Fission Authority inspection probe . . ." That meant we were clearing fiberoptic lines with the cybernetic equivalent of a fire siren, but in the simulation matrix we seemed to rush straight for Chrome's data base. I couldn't see it yet, but I already knew those walls were waiting. Walls of shadow, walls of ice.

Chrome: her pretty childface smooth as steel, with eyes that would have been at home on the bottom of some deep Atlantic trench, cold gray eyes that lived under terrific pressure. They said she cooked her own cancers for people who crossed her, rococo custom variations that took years to kill you. They said a lot of things about Chrome, none of them at all reassuring.

So I blotted her out with a picture of Rikki. Rikki kneeling in a shaft of dusty sunlight that slanted into the loft through a grid of steel and glass: her faded camouflage fatigues, her translucent rose sandals, the good line of her bare

214

back as she rummaged through a nylon gear bag. She looks up, and a half-bound curl falls to tickle her nose. Smiling, buttoning an old shirt of Bobby's, frayed khaki cotton drawn across her breasts.

She smiles.

"Son of a bitch," said Bobby, "we just told Chrome we're an IRS audit and three Supreme Court subpoenas . . . Hang on to your ass, Jack . . ."

So long, Rikki. Maybe now I see you never.

And so dark, in the halls of Chrome's ice.

Bobby was a cowboy and ice was the nature of his game, *ice* from ICE, Intrusion Countermeasures Electronics. The matrix is an abstract representation of the relationships between data systems. Legitimate programmers jack into their employers' sector of the matrix and find themselves surrounded by bright geometries representing the corporate data.

Towers and fields of it ranged in the colorless nonspace of the simulation matrix, the electronic consensus hallucination that facilitates the handling and exchange of massive quantities of data. Legitimate programmers never see the walls of ice they work behind, the walls of shadow that screen their operations from others, from industrial espionage artists and hustlers like Bobby Quine.

Bobby was a cowboy. Bobby was a cracksman, a burglar, casing mankind's extended electronic nervous system, rustling data and credit in the crowded matrix, monochrome nonspace where the only stars are dense concentrations of information, and high above it all burn corporate galaxies and the cold spiral arms of military systems.

Bobby was another one of those young-old faces you see drinking in the Gentleman Loser, the chic bar for computer cowboys, rustlers, cybernetic second-story men. We were partners.

Bobby Quine and Automatic Jack. Bobby's the thin pale dude with the dark glasses, and Jack's the mean-looking guy with the myoelectric arm. Bobby's software and Jack's hard; Bobby punches console and Jack runs down all the little things that can give you an edge. Or, anyway, that's what the scene watchers in the Gentleman Loser would've told you, before Bobby decided to burn Chrome. But they also might've told you that Bobby was losing his edge, slowing down. He was twenty-eight, Bobby, and that's old for a console cowboy.

Both of us were good at what we did, but somehow that one big score just wouldn't come down for us. I knew where to go for the right gear, and Bobby had all his licks down pat. He'd sit back with a white terry sweatband across his forehead and whip moves on those keyboards faster than you could follow, punching his way through some of the fanciest ice in the business, but that was when something happened that managed to get him totally wired, and that didn't happen often. Not highly motivated, Bobby, and I was the kind of guy who's happy to have the rent covered and a clean shirt to wear.

But Bobby had this thing for girls, like they were his private Tarot or something, the way he'd get himself moving. We never talked about it, but when it started to look like he was losing his touch that summer he started to spend more time in the Gentleman Loser. He'd sit at a table by the open doors and watch the crowd slide by, nights when the bugs were at the neon and the air smelled of perfume and fast food. You could see his sunglasses scanning those faces as they passed, and he must have decided that Rikki's was the one he was waiting for, the wild card and the luck changer. The new one.

I went to New York to check out the market, to see what was available in hot software.

The Finn's place has a defective hologram in the window, METRO HOLOGRAFIX, over a display of dead flies wearing fur coats of gray dust. The scrap's waist-high, inside, drifts of it rising to meet walls that are barely visible behind nameless junk, behind sagging pressboard shelves stacked with old skin magazines and yellow-spined years of *National Geographics*.

"You need a gun," said the Finn. He looks like a recombo DNA project aimed at tailoring people for high-speed burrowing. "You're in luck. I got the new Smith and Wesson, the four-oh-eight Tactical. Got this xenon projector slung under the barrel, see, batteries in the grip, throw you a twelve-inch high-noon circle in the pitch dark at fifty yards. The light source is so narrow, it's almost impossible to spot. It's just like voodoo in a nightfight."

I let my arm clunk down on the table and started the fingers drumming; the servos in the hand began whining like overworked mosquitoes. I knew that the Finn really hated the sound.

"You looking to pawn that?" He prodded the duralumin wrist joint with the chewed shaft of a felt-tip pen. "Maybe get yourself something a little quieter?"

I kept it up. "I don't need any guns, Finn."

"Okay," he said, "okay," and I quit drumming. "I only got this one item, and I don't even know what it is." He looked unhappy. "I got it off these bridge-and-tunnel kids from Jersey last week."

"So when'd you ever buy anything you didn't know what it was, Finn?"

"Wise ass." And he passed me a transparent mailer with something in it that looked like an audio cassette through the bubble padding. "They had a passport," he said. "They had credit cards and a watch. And that."

"They had the contents of somebody's pockets, you mean."

He nodded. "The passport was Belgian. It was also bogus, looked to me: so I put in the furnace. Put the cards in with it. The watch was okay, a Porsche, nice watch."

It was obviously some kind of plug-in military program. Out of the mailer, it looked like the magazine of a small assault rifle, coated with nonreflective black plastic. The edges and corners showed bright metal; it had been knocking around for a while.

"I'll give you a bargain on it, Jack. For old time's sake."

I had to smile at that. Getting a bargain from the Finn was like God repeating the law of gravity when you have to carry a heavy suitcase down ten blocks of airport corridor.

"Looks Russian to me," I said. "Probably the emergency sewage controls for some Leningrad suburb. Just what I need."

"You know," said the Finn. "I got a pair of shoes older than you are. Sometimes I think you got about as much class as those yahoos from Jersey. What do you want me to tell you, it's the keys to the Kremlin? You figure out what the goddamn thing is. Me, I just sell the stuff."

I bought it.

Bodiless, we swerve into Chrome's castle of ice. And we're fast, fast. It feels like we're surfing the crest of the invading program, hanging ten above the seething glitch systems as they mutate. We're sentient patches of oil swept along down corridors of shadow.

Somewhere we have bodies, very far away, in a crowded loft roofed with steel and glass. Somewhere we have microseconds, maybe time left to pull out.

We've crashed her gates disguised as an audit and three subpoenas, but her defenses are specifically geared to cope with that kind of official intrusion. Her most sophisticated ice is structured to fend off warrants, writs, subpoenas. When we breached the first gate, the bulk of her data vanished behind core-command ice, these walls we see as leagues of corridor, mazes of shadow. Five separate landlines spurted May Day signals to law firms, but the virus had already taken over the parameter ice. The glitch systems gobble the distress calls as our mimetic subprograms scan anything that hasn't been blanked by core command.

The Russian program lifts a Tokyo number from the unscreened data, choosing it for frequency of calls, average length of calls, the speed with which Chrome returned those calls.

"Okay," says Bobby, "we're an incoming scrambler call from a pal of hers in Japan. That should help."

Ride 'em cowboy.

Bobby read his future in women; his girls were omens, changes in the weather, and he'd sit all night in the Gentleman Loser, waiting for the season to lay a new face down in front of him like a card.

I was working late in the loft one night, shaving down a chip, my arm off and the little waldo jacked straight into the stump.

Bobby came in with a girl I hadn't seen before, and usually I feel a little funny if a stranger sees me working that way, with those leads clipped to the hard carbon studs that stick out of my stump. She came right over and looked at the magnified image on the screen, then saw the waldo moving under its vacuum-sealed dustcover. She didn't say anything, just watched. Right away I had a good feeling about her; it's like that sometimes.

"Automatic Jack, Rikki. My associate."

He laughed, put his arm around her waist, something in his tone letting me know that I'd be spending the night in a dingy room in a hotel.

"Hi," she said. Tall, nineteen or maybe twenty, and she definitely had the goods. With just those few freckles across the bridge of her nose, and eyes somewhere between dark amber and French coffee. Tight black jeans rolled to mid-calf and narrow plastic belt that matched the rose-colored sandals.

But now when I see her sometimes when I'm trying to sleep, I see her somewhere out on the edge of all this sprawl of cities and smoke, and it's like she's a hologram stuck behind my eyes, in a bright dress she must've worn once, when I knew her, something that doesn't quite reach her knees. Bare legs long and straight. Brown hair, streaked with blond, hoods her face, blown in a wind from somewhere, and I see her wave good-bye.

Bobby was making a show of rooting through a stack of audio cassettes. "I'm on my way, cowboy," I said, unclipping the waldo. She watched attentively as I put my arm back on.

"Can you fix things?" she asked.

"Anything, anything you want, Automatic Jack'll fix it." I snapped my duralumin fingers for her.

She took a little simstim deck from her belt and showed me the broken hinge on the cassette cover.

"Tomorrow," I said, "no problem."

And my oh my, I said to myself, sleep pulling me down the six flights to the street, *what'll Bobby's luck be like with a fortune cookie like that? If his system worked, we'd be striking it rich any night now.* In the street I grinned and yawned and waved for a cab.

Chrome's castle is dissolving, sheets of ice shadow flickering and fading, eaten by the glitch systems that spin out from the Russian program, tumbling away from our central logic thrust and infecting the fabric of the ice itself. The glitch systems are cybernetic virus analogs, self-replicating and voracious. They mutate constantly, in unison, subverting and absorbing Chrome's defenses.

Have we already paralyzed her, or is a bell ringing somewhere, a red light blinking? Does she know?

Rikki Wildside, Bobby called her, and for those first few weeks it must have seemed to her that she had it all, the whole teeming show spread out for her, sharp and bright under the neon. She was new to the scene, and she had all the miles of malls and plazas to prowl, all the shops and clubs, and Bobby to explain the wild side, the tricky wiring on the dark underside of things, all the players and their names and their games. He made her feel at home.

"What happened to your arm?" she asked me one night in the Gentleman Loser, the three of us drinking at a small table in a corner.

"Hang-gliding," I said, "accident."

"Hang-gliding over a wheatfield," said Bobby, "place called Kiev. Our Jack's just hanging there in the dark, under a Nightwing parafoil, with fifty kilos of radar jammer between his legs, and some Russian asshole accidentally burns his arm off with a laser."

I don't remember how I changed the subject, but I did.

I was still telling myself that it wasn't Rikki who was getting to me, but what Bobby was doing with her. I'd known him for a long time, since the end of the war, and I knew he used women as counters in a game. Bobby Quine versus fortune, versus time and the night of cities. And Rikki had turned up just when he needed something to get him going, something to aim for. So he'd set her up as a symbol for everything he wanted and couldn't have, everything he'd had and couldn't keep.

I didn't like having to listen to him tell me how much he loved her, and knowing he believed it only made it worse. He was a past master at the hard fall and the rapid recovery, and I'd seen it happen a dozen times before. He might as well have had NEXT printed across his sunglasses in green dayglo capitals, ready to flash out at the first interesting face that flowed past the tables in the Gentleman Loser.

I knew what he did to them. He turned them into emblems, sigils on the map of his hustler's life, navigation beacons he could follow through a sea of bars and neon. What else did he have to steer by? He didn't love money, in and of itself, not enough to follow its light. He wouldn't work for power over other people; he hated the responsibility it brings. He had some basic pride in his skill, but that was never enough to keep him pushing.

So he made do with women.

When Rikki showed up, he needed one in the worst way. He was fading fast, and smart money was already whispering that the edge was off his game. He needed that one big score, and soon, because he didn't know any other kind of life, and all his clocks were set for hustler's time, calibrated in risk and adrenaline and that supernal dawn calm that comes when every move's proved right and a sweet lump of someone else's credit clicks into your own account.

It was time for him to make his bundle and get out; so Rikki got set up higher and farther away than any of the others ever had, even though—and I felt like screaming it at him—she was right there, alive, totally real, human, hungry, resilient, bored, beautiful, excited, all the things she was . . .

Then he went out one afternoon, about a week before I made the trip to New York to see the Finn. Went out and left us there in the loft, waiting for a thunderstorm. Half the skylight was shadowed by a dome they'd never finished, and the other half showed sky, black and blue with clouds. I was standing by the bench, looking up at that sky, stupid with the hot afternoon, the humidity, and she touched me, touched my shoulder, the half-inch border of taut pink scar that the arm doesn't cover. Anybody else ever touched me there, they went on to the shoulder, the neck . . .

But she didn't do that. Her nails were lacquered black, not pointed, but tapered oblongs, the lacquer only a shade darker than the carbon-fiber laminate that sheathes my arm. And her hand went down the arm, black nails tracing a weld in the laminate, down to the black anodized elbow joint, out to the wrist, her hand soft-knuckled as a child's, fingers spreading to lock over mine, her palm against the perforated duralumin.

Her other palm came up to brush across the feedback pads, and it rained all afternoon, raindrops drumming on the steel and soot-stained glass above Bobby's bed.

Ice walls flick away like supersonic butterflies made of shade. Beyond them, the matrix's illusion of infinite space. It's like watching a tape of a prefab building going up; only the tape's reversed and run at high speed, and these walls are torn wings.

Trying to remind myself that this place and the gulfs beyond are only representations, that we aren't "in" Chrome's computer, but interfaced with it, while the matrix simulator in Bobby's loft generates this illusion . . . The core data begin to emerge, exposed, vulnerable . . . This is the far side of ice, the view of the matrix I've never seen before, the view that fifteen million legitimate console operators see daily and take for granted.

The core data tower around us like vertical

freight trains, color-coded for access. Bright primaries, impossibly bright in that transparent void, linked by countless horizontals in nursery blues and pinks.

But ice still shadows something at the center of it all; the heart of all Chrome's expensive darkness, the very heart . . .

It was late afternoon when I got back from my shopping expedition to New York. Not much sun through the skylight, but an ice pattern glowed on Bobby's monitor screen, a 2-D graphic representation of someone's computer defenses, lines of neon woven like an Art Deco prayer rug. I turned the console off, and the screen went completely dark.

Rikki's things were spread across my workbench, nylon bags spilling clothes and makeup, a pair of bright red cowboy boots, audio cassettes, glossy Japanese magazines about simstim stars. I stacked it all under the bench and then took my arm off, forgetting that the program I'd bought from the Finn was in the righthand pocket of my jacket, so that I had to fumble it out lefthanded and then get it into the padded jaws of the jeweler's vise.

The waldo looks like an old audio turntable, the kind that played disc records, with the vise set up under a transparent dustcover. The arm itself is just over a centimeter long, swinging out on what would've been the tone arm on one of those turntables. But I don't look at that when I've clipped the leads to my stump; I look at the scope, because that's my arm there in black and white, magnification 40 ×.

I ran a tool check and picked up the laser. It felt a little heavy; so I scaled my weight-sensor input down to a quarter kilo per gram and got to work. At 40 × the side of the program looked like a trailer-truck.

It took eight hours to crack; three hours with the waldo and the laser and four dozen taps, two hours on the phone to a contact in Colorado, and three hours to run down a lexicon disc that could translate eight-year-old technical Russian.

Then Cyrillic alphanumerics started reeling down the monitor, twisting themselves into English halfway down. There were a lot of gaps, where the lexicon ran up against specialized military acronyms in the readout I'd bought from my man in Colorado, but it did give me some idea of what I'd bought from the Finn.

I felt like a punk who'd gone out to buy a switchblade and come home with a small neutron bomb.

Screwed again, I thought. *What good's a neutron bomb in a streetfight?* The thing under the dustcover was right out of my league. I didn't even know where to unload it, where to look for a buyer. Someone had, but he was dead, someone with a Porsche watch and a fake Belgian passport, but I'd never tried to move in those circles. The Finn's muggers from the 'burbs had knocked over someone who had some highly arcane connections.

The program in the jeweler's vise was a

Russian military icebreaker, a killer-virus program.

It was dawn when Bobby came in alone. I'd fallen asleep with a bag of take-out sandwiches in my lap.

"You want to eat?" I asked him, not really awake, holding out my sandwiches. I'd been dreaming of the program, of its waves of hungry glitch systems and mimetic subprograms; in the dream it was an animal of some kind, shapeless and flowing.

He brushed the bag aside on his way to the console, punched a function key. The screen lit with the intricate pattern I'd seen there that afternoon. I rubbed sleep from my eyes with my left hand, one thing I can't do with my right. I'd fallen asleep trying to decide whether to tell him about the program. Maybe I should try to sell it alone, keep the money, go somewhere new, ask Rikki to go with me.

"Whose is it?" I asked.

He stood there in a black cotton jumpsuit, an old leather jacket thrown over his shoulder like a cape. He hadn't shaved for a few days, and his face looked thinner than usual.

"It's Chrome's," he said.

My arm convulsed, started clicking, fear translated to the myoelectrics through the carbon studs. I spilled the sandwiches, limp sprouts, and bright yellow dairy-product slices on the unswept wooden floor.

"You're stone-crazy," I said.

"No," he said, "you think she rumbled it? No way. We'd be dead already. I locked onto her through a triple-blind rental system in Mombasa and an Algerian commsat. She knew somebody was having a look-see, but she couldn't trace it.''

If Chrome had traced the pass Bobby had made at her ice, we were good as dead. But he was probably right, or she'd have had me blown away on my way back from New York. "Why her, Bobby? Just give me one reason . . ."

Chrome: I'd seen her maybe half a dozen times in the Gentleman Loser. Maybe she was slumming, or checking out the human condition, a condition she didn't exactly aspire to. A sweet little heartshaped face framing the nastiest pair of eyes you ever saw. She'd looked fourteen for as long as anyone could remember, hyped out of anything like a normal metabolism on some massive program of serums and hormones. She was as ugly a customer as the street ever produced, but she didn't belong to the street anymore. She was one of the Boys, Chrome, a member in good standing of the local Mob subsidiary. Word was, she'd gotten started as a dealer, back when synthetic pituitary hormones were still proscribed. But she hadn't had to move hormones for a long time. Now she owned the House of Blue Lights.

"You're flat-out crazy, Quine. You give me one sane reason for having that stuff on your screen. You ought to dump it, and I mean *now* . . ."

"Talk in the Loser," he said, shrugging out of the leather jacket. "Black Myron and Crow Jane. Jane, she's up on all the sex lines, claims she knows where the money goes. So she's arguing with Myron that Chrome's the controlling interest in the Blue Lights, not just some figurehead for the Boys.''

" 'The Boys,' Bobby,'' I said. ''That's the operative word there. You still capable of seeing that? We don't mess with the Boys, remember? That's why we're still walking around.''

''That's why we're still poor, partner.'' He settled back into the swivel chair in front of the console, unzipped his jumpsuit, and scratched his skinny white chest. ''But maybe not for much longer.''

''I think maybe this partnership just got itself permanently dissolved.''

Then he grinned at me. That grin was truly crazy, feral and focused, and I knew that right then he really didn't give a shit about dying.

''Look,'' I said, ''I've got some money left, you know? Why don't you take it and get the tube to Miami, catch a hopper to Montego Bay. You need a rest, man. You've got to get your act together.''

''My act, jack,'' he said, punching something on the keyboard, ''never has been this together before.'' The neon prayer rug on the screen shivered and woke as an animation program cut in, ice lines waving with hypnotic frequency, a living mandala. Bobby kept punching, and the movement slowed; the pattern resolved itself, grew slightly less complex, became an alternation between two distinct configurations. A first-class piece of work, and I hadn't thought he was still that good. ''Now,'' he said, "there, see it? Wait. There. There again. And there. Easy to miss. That's it. Cuts in every hour and twenty minutes with a squirt transmission to their commsat. We could live for a year on what she pays them weekly in negative interest."

"Whose commsat?"

"Zurich. Her bankers. That's her bankbook, Jack. That's where the money goes. Crow Jane was right."

I just stood there. My arm forgot to click.

"So how'd you do in New York, partner? You get anything that'll help me cut ice? We're going to need whatever we can get."

I kept my eyes on his, forced myself not to look in the direction of the waldo, the jeweler's vise. The Russian program was there, under the dustcover.

Wild cards, luck changers.

"Where's Rikki?" I asked him, crossing to the console, pretending to study the alternating patterns on the screen.

"Friends of hers," he shrugged, "kids, they're all into simstim." He smiled absently. "I'm going to do it for her, man."

"I'm going out to think about this, Bobby. You want me to come back, you keep your hands off the board."

"I'm doing it for her," he said as the door closed behind me. "You know I am."

And down now, down, the program a roller coaster through this fraying maze of shadow walls, gray cathedral spaces between the bright towers. Headlong speed.

Black ice. Don't think about it. Black ice.

Too many stories in the Gentleman Loser; black ice is a part of the mythology. Ice that kills. Illegal, but then aren't we all? Some kind of neural-feedback weapon, and you connect with it only once. Like some hideous Word that eats the mind from the inside out. Like an epileptic spasm that goes on and on until there's nothing left at all . . .

And we're diving for the floor of Chrome's shadow castle.

Trying to brace myself for the sudden stopping of breath, a sickness and final slackening of the nerves. Fear of that cold Word waiting, down there in the dark.

I went out and looked for Rikki, found her in a cafe with a boy with Sendai eyes, half-healed suture lines radiating from his bruised sockets. She had a glossy brochure spread open on the table. Tally Isham smiling up from a dozen photographs, the Girl with the Zeiss Ikon Eyes.

Her little simstim deck was one of the things I'd stacked under my bench the night before, the one I'd fixed for her the day after I'd first seen her. She spent hours jacked into that unit, the contact band across her forehead like a gray plastic tiara. Tally Isham was her favorite, and with the contact band on, she was gone, off somewhere in the recorded sensorium of simstim's biggest star. Stimulated stimuli: the world—all the interesting parts, anyway—as perceived by Tally Isham. Tally raced a black

Fokker ground-effect plane across Arizona mesa tops. Tally dived the Truk Island preserves. Tally partied with the superrich on private Greek islands, heartbreaking purity of those tiny white seaports at dawn.

Actually she looked a lot like Tally, same coloring and cheekbones. I thought Rikki's mouth was stronger. More sass. She didn't want to *be* Tally Isham, but she coveted the job. That was her ambition, to be in simstim. Bobby just laughed it off. She talked to me about it, though. "How'd I look with a pair of these?" she'd ask, holding a full-page headshot, Tally Isham's blue Zeiss Ikons lined up with her own amber-brown. She'd had her corneas done twice, but she still wasn't twenty-twenty; so she wanted Ikons. Brand of the stars. Very expensive.

"You still window-shopping for eyes?" I asked as I sat down.

"Tiger just got some," she said. She looked tired, I thought.

Tiger was so pleased with his Sendais that he couldn't help smiling, but I doubted whether he'd have smiled otherwise. He had the kind of uniform good looks you get after your seventh trip to the surgical boutique; he'd probably spend the rest of his life looking vaguely like each new season's media frontrunner; not too obvious a copy, but nothing too original, either.

"Sendai, right?" I smiled back.

He nodded. I watched as he tried to take me in with his idea of a professional simstim glance. He was pretending that he was recording. I thought he spent too long on my arm. "They'll be great on peripherals when the muscles heal," he said, and I saw how carefully he reached for his double espresso. Sendai eyes are notorious for depth-perception defects and warranty hassles, among other things.

"Tiger's leaving for Hollywood tomorrow."

"Then maybe Chiba City, right?" I smiled at him. He didn't smile back. "Got an offer, Tiger? Know an agent?"

"Just checking it out," he said quietly. Then he got up and left. He said a quick good-bye to Rikki, but not to me.

"That kid's optic nerves may start to deteriorate inside six months. You know that, Rikki? Those Sendais are illegal in England, Denmark, lots of places. You can't replace nerves."

"Hey, Jack, no lectures." She stole one of my croissants and nibbled at the tip of one of its horns.

"I thought I was your adviser, kid."

"Yeah. Well, Tiger's not too swift, but everybody knows about Sendais. They're all he can afford. So he's taking a chance. If he gets work, he can replace them."

"With these?" I tapped the Zeiss Ikon brochure. "Lots of money, Rikki. You know better than to take a gamble like that?"

She nodded. "I want Ikons."

"If you're going up to Bobby's, tell him to sit tight until he hears from me."

"Sure. It's business?"

"Business," I said. But it was craziness.

I drank my coffee, and she ate both my

croissants. Then I walked her down to Bobby's. I made fifteen calls, each one from a different pay phone.

Business. Bad craziness.

All in all, it took us six weeks to set the burn up, six weeks of Bobby telling me how much he loved her. I worked even harder, trying to get away from that.

Most of it was phone calls. My fifteen initial and very oblique inquiries each seemed to breed fifteen more. I was looking for a certain service Bobby and I both imagined as a requisite part of the world's clandestine economy, but which probably never had more than five customers at a time. It would be one that never advertised.

We were looking for the world's heaviest fence, for a nonaligned money laundry capable of drycleaning a megabuck on-line cash transfer and then forgetting about it.

All those calls were a waste, finally, because it was the Finn who put me on to what we needed. I'd gone up to New York to buy a new blackbox rig, because we were going broke paying for all those calls.

I put the problem to him as hypothetically as possible.

"Macao," he said.

"Macao?"

"The Long Hum family. Stockbrokers."

He even had the number. You want a fence, ask another fence.

The Long Hum people were so oblique that they made my idea of a subtle approach look like a tactical nuke-out. Bobby had to make two shuttle runs to Hong Kong to get the deal straight. We were running out of capital, and fast. I still don't know why I decided to go along with it in the first place; I was scared of Chrome, and I'd never been all that hot to get rich.

I tried telling myself that it was a good idea to burn the House of Blue Lights because the place was a creep joint, but I just couldn't buy it. I didn't like the Blue Lights, because I'd spent a supremely depressing evening there once, but that was no excuse for going after Chrome. Actually I halfway assumed we were going to die in the attempt. Even with that killer program, the odds weren't exactly in our favor.

Bobby was lost in writing the set of commands we were going to plug into the dead center of Chrome's computer. That was going to be my job, because Bobby was going to have his hands full, trying to keep the Russian program from going straight for the kill. It was too complex for us to rewrite, and so he was going to try to hold it back for the two seconds I needed.

I made a deal with a streetfighter named Miles. He was going to follow Rikki, the night of the burn, keep her in sight, and phone me at a certain time. If I wasn't there, or didn't answer in just a certain way, I'd told him to grab her and put her on the first tube out. I gave him an envelope to give her, money and a note.

Bobby really hadn't thought about that, much, how things would go for her if we blew it. He just kept telling me he loved her, where they were going to go together, how they'd spend the money.

"Buy her a pair of Ikons first, man. That's what she wants. She's serious about that simstim scene."

"Hey," he said, looking up from the keyboard, "she won't need to work. We're going to make it, Jack. She's my luck. She won't ever have to work again."

"Your luck," I said. I wasn't happy. I couldn't remember when I had been happy. "You seen your luck around lately?"

He hadn't, but neither had I. We'd both been too busy.

I missed her. Missing her reminded me of my one night in the House of Blue Lights, because I'd gone there out of missing someone else. I'd gotten drunk to begin with, then I'd started hitting vasopressin inhalers. If your main squeeze has just decided to walk out on you, booze and vasopressin are the ultimate in masochistic pharmacology; the juice makes you maudlin and the vasopressin makes you remember, I mean really remember. Clinically they use the stuff to counter senile amnesia, but the street finds its own uses for things. So I'd bought myself an ultra-intense replay of a bad affair; trouble is, you get the bad with the good. Go gunning for transports of animal ecstasy and you get what you said, too, and what she said to that, how she walked away and never looked back.

I don't remember deciding to go to the Blue

Lights, or how I got there, hushed corridors and this really tacky decorative waterfall trickling somewhere, or maybe just a hologram of one. I had a lot of money that night; somebody had given Bobby a big roll for opening a three-second window in someone else's ice.

I don't think the crew on the door liked my looks, but I guess my money was okay.

I had more to drink there when I'd done what I went there for. Then I made some crack to the barman about closet necrophiliacs, and that didn't go down too well. Then this very large character insisted on calling me War Hero, which I didn't like. I think I showed him some tricks with the arm, before the lights went out, and I woke up two days later in a basic sleeping module somewhere else. A cheap place, not even room to hang yourself. And I sat there on that narrow foam slab and cried.

Some things are worse than being alone. But the thing they sell in the House of Blue Lights is so popular that it's almost legal.

At the heart of darkness, the still center, the glitch systems shred the dark with whirlwinds of light, translucent razors spinning away from us; we hang in the center of a silent slow-motion explosion, ice fragments falling away forever, and Bobby's voice comes in across light-years of electronic void illusion—

"Burn the bitch down. I can't hold the thing back—"

The Russian program, rising through towers of data, blotting out the playroom colors. And

I plug Bobby's homemade command package into the center of Chrome's cold heart. The squirt transmission cuts in, a pulse of condensed information that shoots straight up, past the thickening tower of darkness, the Russian program, while Bobby struggles to control that crucial second. An unformed arm of shadow twitches from the towering dark, too late.

We've done it.

The matrix folds itself around me like an origami trick.

And the loft smells of sweat and burning circuitry.

I thought I heard Chrome scream, a raw metal sound, but I couldn't have.

Bobby was laughing, tears in his eyes. The elapsed-time figure in the corner of the monitor read 07:24:05. The burn had taken a little under eight minutes.

And I saw that the Russian program had melted in its slot.

We'd given the bulk of Chrome's Zurich account to a dozen world charities. There was too much there to move, and we knew we had to break her, burn her straight down, or she might come after us. We took less than ten percent for ourselves and shot it through the Long Hum setup in Macao. They took sixty percent of that for themselves and kicked what was left back to us through the most convoluted sector of the Hong Kong exchange. It took an hour before our money started to reach the two accounts we'd opened in Zurich.

I watched zeros pile up behind a meaningless figure on the monitor. I was rich.

Then the phone rang. It was Miles. I almost blew the code phrase.

"Hey, Jack, man, I dunno—What's it all about, with this girl of yours? Kinda funny thing here . . ."

"What? Tell me."

"I been on her, like you said, tight but out of sight. She goes to the Loser, hangs out, then she gets a tube. Goes to the House of Blue Lights—"

"She what?"

"Side door. *Employees* only. No way I could get past their security."

"Is she there now?"

"No, man, I just lost her. It's insane down here, like the Blue Lights just shut down, looks like for good, seven kinds of alarms going off, everybody running, the heat out in riot gear . . . Now there's all this stuff going on, insurance guys, real estate types, vans with municipal plates . . ."

"Miles, where'd she go?"

"Lost her, Jack."

"Look, Miles, you keep the money in the envelope, right?"

"You serious? Hey, I'm real sorry. I—"

I hung up.

"Wait'll we tell her," Bobby was saying, rubbing a towel across his bare chest.

"You tell her yourself, cowboy, I'm going for a walk."

So I went out into the night and the neon and let the crowd pull me along, walking blind, willing myself to be just a segment of that mass organism, just one more drifting chip of consciousness under the geodesics. I didn't think, just put one foot in front of another, but after a while I did think, and it all made sense. She'd needed the money.

I thought about Chrome, too. That we'd killed her, murdered her, as surely as if we'd slit her throat. The night that carried me along through the malls and plazas would be hunting her now, and she had nowhere to go. How many enemies would she have in this crowd alone? How many would move, now they weren't held back by fear of her money? We'd taken her for everything she had. She was back on the street again. I doubted she'd live till dawn.

Finally I remembered the cafe, the one where I'd met Tiger.

Her sunglasses told the whole story, huge black shades with a telltale smudge of fleshtone painstick in the corner of one lens. "Hi, Rikki," I said, and I was ready when she took them off.

Blue. Tally Isham blue. The clear trademark blue they're famous for, ZEISS IKON ringing each iris in tiny capitals, the letters suspended there like flecks of gold.

"They're beautiful," I said. Painstick covered the bruising. No scars with work that good. "You made some money."

"Yeah. I did." Then she shivered. "But I

won't make any more, not that way."

"I think that place is out of business."

"Oh." Nothing moved in her face then. The new blue eyes were still and very deep.

"It doesn't matter. Bobby's waiting for you. We just pulled down a big score."

"No. I've got to go. I guess he won't understand, but I've got to go."

I nodded, watching the arm swing up to take her hand; it didn't seem to be part of me at all, but she held on to it like it was.

"I've got a one-way ticket to Hollywood. Tiger knows some people I can stay with. Maybe I'll even get to Chiba City."

She was right about Bobby. I went back with her. He didn't understand. But she'd already served her purpose, for Bobby, and I wanted to tell her not to hurt for him, because I could see that she did. He wouldn't even come out into the hallway after she had packed her bags. I put the bags down and kissed her and messed up the paintstick, and something came up inside me the way the killer program had risen above Chrome's data. A sudden stopping of the breath, in a place where no word is. But she had a plane to catch.

Bobby was slumped in the swivel chair in front of his monitor, looking at his string of zeros. He had his shades on, and I knew he'd be in the Gentlemen Loser by nightfall, checking out the weather, anxious for a sign, someone to tell him what his new life would be like. I couldn't see it being very different. More comfortable, but he'd always be waiting for that next card to fall.

I tried not to imagine her in the House of Blue Lights, working three-hour shifts in an approximation of REM sleep, while her body and bundle of conditional reflexes took care of business. The customers never got to complain that she was faking it, because those were real orgasms. But she felt them, if she felt them at all, as faint silver flares somewhere out on the edge of sleep. Yeah, it's so popular, it's almost legal. The customers are torn between needing someone and wanting to be alone at the same time, which has probably always been the name of that particular game, even before we had the neuroelectronics to enable them to have it both ways.

I picked up the phone and punched the number for her airline. I gave them her real name, her flight number. "She's changing that," I said, "to Chiba City. That's right. Japan." I thumbed my credit card into the slot and punched my ID code. "First class." Distant hum as they scanned my credit records. "Make that a return ticket."

But I guess she cashed the return fare, or else she didn't need it, because she hasn't come back. And sometimes late at night I'll pass a window with posters of simstim stars, all those beautiful, identical eyes staring back at me out of faces that are nearly as identical, and sometimes the eyes are hers, but none of the faces are, none of them ever are, and I see her far out on the edge of all this sprawl of night and cities, and then she waves good-bye.

IKE AT THE MIKE

By Howard Waldrop

Ambassador Pratt leaned over toward Senator Presley. "My mother's ancestors don't like to admit it," he said, "but they all came to the island from the Carpathians two centuries ago. Their name then was something like Karloff." He laughed through his silver mustache.

"Hell," said Presley, with the tinge of the drawl that came to his speech when he was excited, as he was tonight. "My folks been dirt farmers all the way back to Adam. They don't even remember coming from anywhere. But that don't mean they ain't wonderful folks. Good people all the same."

"Of course not," said Pratt. "My father was a shopkeeper. He worked to send all my older brothers into the Foreign Service. But when my time came, I thought I had another choice. I wanted to run off to Canada or Australia, perhaps try my hand at acting. I was in several local dramatic clubs, you know. My father took me aside before my service exams. The day before—I remember quite distinctly—he said, 'William'—he was the only member of the family who used my full name—'William,' he said, 'actors do not get paid the last workday of each and every month.' Well, I thought about it awhile, and next day passed my exams with absolute top grades.''

Pratt smiled his ingratiating smile once more. There was something a little scary about it, Presley thought, sort of like Raymond Massey's smile in *Arsenic and Old Lace*. But the smile had seen Pratt through sixty years of government service. It had been a smile that made the leaders of small countries smile back as King Georges, number after number, took yet more of their lands. It was a good smile; it made everyone remember his grandfather. Even Presley.

"Folks is funny," said Presley. "God knows, I used to get up at barn dances and sing myself silly. I was just a kid then, playing around.''

"My childhood is so far behind me," said Ambassador Pratt. "I hardly remember it. I was small. Then I had the talk with my father, and went to service school, then found myself in Turkey, which at that time owned a large portion of the globe. The Sick Man of Europe, it was called. You know I met Lawrence of Arabia, don't you? Before the Great War. He was an archaeologist then. Came to us to get the Ottomans to give him permission to dig up Petra. They thought him to be a fool. Wanted the standard ninety percent share of everything, just the same.''

"You've seen a lot of the world change," said Senator E. Aaron Presley. He took a sip of wine. "I've had trouble enough keeping up with it since I was elected congressman six years ago. I almost lost touch during my senatorial campaign, and I'll be damned if everything hadn't changed again by the time I got back here."

Pratt laughed. He was eighty years old, far past retirement age, but still bouncing around like a man of sixty. He had alternately quit and had every British P.M. since Churchill call him out of retirement to patch up relations with this or that nation.

Presley was thirty-three, the youngest senator in the country for a long time. The United States was in bad shape, and he was one of the symbols of the new hope. There was talk of revolution, several cities had been burned, there was a war on in South America (again). Social change, life-style readjustment, call it what they would. The people of Mississippi had elected Presley senator after he had served five years as a representative. It was a sign of renewed hope. At the same time they had passed a tough new wiretap act and had turned out for massive Christian revivalist meetings.

1968 looked to be the toughest year yet for America.

But there were still things that made it all worth living. Nights like tonight. A huge appreciation dinner, with the absolute cream of Washington society turned out in its gaudiness. Most of Congress, President Kennedy, Vice-

President Shriver. Plus the usual hangers-on.

Presley watched them. Old Dick Nixon, once a senator from California. He came back to Washington to be near the action, though he'd lost his last election in Fifty-eight.

The President was there, of course, looking as young as he had when he was reelected in 1964, the first two-term president since Huey "Kingfish" Long, blessed of Southern memory. *Say whatever else you could of Joe Kennedy, Jr.,* Presley thought, *he was a hell of a good man in his Yankee way.* His three young brothers were in the audience somewhere, representatives from two states.

Waiters hustled in and out of the huge banquet room. Presley watched the sequined gowns and the feathers on the women; the spectacular pumpkin-blaze of a neon orange suit of some hotshot Washington lawyer. The lady across the table had engaged Pratt in conversation about Wales. The ambassador was explaining that he had seen Wales once, back in 1923 on holiday, but that he didn't think it had changed much since then.

E. Aaron studied the table where the guests of honor sat—the President and First Lady, the Veep and his wife, and Armstrong and Eisenhower, with their spouses.

Armstrong and Eisenhower. Two of the finest citizens in the land. Armstrong, the younger, in his sixty-eighth year, getting a little jowly. *Born with the century,* Presley thought. *Symbol of his race and of his time. A man deserving of honor and respect.*

248

But Eisenhower was Presley's man. The senator had read all the biographies, re-read all the old newspaper files, listened to him every chance he got.

If Presley had an ideal, it was Eisenhower. As both a leader and a person. A little too liberal, perhaps, in his personal opinions, but that was the only fault the man had. When it came time for action, Eisenhower, the "Ike" of the popular press, came through.

Senator Presley tried to catch his eye. He was only three tables away and could see Ike through the hazy pall of smoke from after-dinner cigarettes and pipes. It was no use, though. Ike was busy.

Eisenhower looked worried, distracted. He wasn't used to testimonials. He'd come out of semiretirement to attend, only because Armstrong had persuaded him to do it. They were both getting presidential medals.

But it wasn't for the awards that all the other people were here, or the speeches that would follow; it . . .

Pratt turned to him.

"I've noticed his preoccupation, too," he said.

Presley was a little taken aback. But Pratt was a sharp old cookie, and he'd been around God knows how many people through wars, floods, conference tables. He'd probably drunk enough tea in his life to float the battleship *Kropotkin*.

"Quite a man," said Presley, afraid to let his true, misty-eyed feelings show. "Pretty much the man of the century, far as I'm concerned.''

"I've been with Churchill, and Lenin, and Chiang," said Ambassador Pratt, "but they were just cagey politicians, movers of men and materiel, as far as I'm concerned. I saw him once before, early on, must have been Thirty-eight, Thirty-nine. Nineteen Thirty-eight. I was very, very impressed then. Time has done nothing to change that.''

"He's just not used to this kind of thing," said Presley.

"Perhaps it was that Patton fellow."

"Wild George? That who you mean?"

"Oh, didn't you hear?" Pratt asked, eyes all concern.

"I was in committee most of the week. If it wasn't about the new drug bill, I didn't hear about it.''

"Oh, of course. This Patton fellow died a few days ago. Circumstances rather sad, I think. Eisenhower and Mr. Armstrong just returned from his funeral this afternoon.''

"Gee, that's too bad. You know they worked together, Patton and Ike, for thirty years or so—''

The toastmaster, one of those boisterous, bald-headed, abrasive California types, rose. People began to stub out their cigarettes and applaud. Waiters disappeared as if a magic wand had been waved.

Well, thought Presley, as he and Pratt applauded, *an hour of pure boredom coming up.* Some jokes, the President, the awarding of the medals, the obligatory standing ovation. Then the entertainment.

Ah, thought Presley. *The thing everybody has come for.*

After the ceremony, they were going to bring out the band, Armstrong's band. Not just the one he toured with, but what was left of the old guys, *the* Armstrong Band, and they were going to rip the joint.

But also, also . . .

For the first time in twenty years, since Presley had been a boy, a kid in his teens . . . Eisenhower was going to break his vow. Eisenhower was going to dust off that clarinet.

For two hours Ike was going to play with Armstrong, just like in the good old days.

"Cheer up," said gravelly-voiced Pops while the President was making his way to the rostrum. Armstrong smiled at Eisenhower. "You're gonna blow 'em right outta the grooves."

"All reet," said Ike.

The thunderous applause was dying down. Backstage, Ike handed the box with the Presidential Medal to his wife of twenty years, Helen Forrest, the singer. "Here goes, honey," he said. "Come out when you feel like it."

They were in the outer hall, behind the head tables. Some group of young folksingers, very nervous but very good, were out there killing time while Armstrong's band set up.

"Hey, hey," said Pops. He'd pinned the Presidential Medal, ribbon and all, to the front of his jacket through the boutonniere hole. "Wouldn't old Jelly Roll like to have seen me now?"

251

"Hey, hey," yelled some of the band right back at him.

"Quiet, quiet!" yelled Pops. "Let them kids out there sing. They're good. Listen to 'em. Reminds me of me when I was young."

Ike had been concentrating on licking his reed and doing tongue exercises. "You never were young, Pops," he said. "You were born older than me."

"That's a lie!" said Pops. "You could be my father."

"Maybe he is!" yelled Perkins, the guitar man, fiddling with the knobs on his amp.

Ike nearly swallowed his mouthpiece. The drummer did a paradiddle.

"Hush, hush, you clowns!" yelled Pops.

Ike smiled and looked up at the drummer, a young kid. But he'd been with Pops's new band for a couple of years. So he must be all right.

Eisenhower heaved a sigh when no one was looking. He had to get the tightness out of his chest. It had started at George S.'s funeral, a pain crying did not relieve. No one but he and Helen knew that he had had two mild heart attacks in the last six years. *Hell,* he thought, *I'm almost eighty years old. I'm entitled to a few heart attacks. But not here, not tonight.*

They dimmed the work lights. Pops had run into the back kitchen and blown a few screaming notes, which they heard through two concrete walls. He was ready.

"When you gonna quit playing, Pops?" asked Ike.

"Man, I ain't ever gonna quit. They're gonna

have to dig me up three weeks after I die and break this horn to stop the noise comin' outta the ground.'' He looked at the lights. ''Ease on off to the left there, Ike. Let us get them all ready for you. Come in on the chorus of the third song.''

''Which one's that?'' asked Ike, looking for his play sheet.

''You'll know it when you hear it,'' said Pops. He took out his handkerchief. ''You taught it to me.''

Ike went into the wings and waited.

The crowd was tasteful, expectant.

The band hit the music hard, from the opening, and Armstrong led off with ''The King Porter Stomp.'' His horn was flashing sparks, and the medal on his jacket front caught the spotlight like a big golden eye.

Then they launched into ''Basin Street Blues,'' the horn sweet and slow and mellow, the band doing nothing but carrying a light line behind. Armstrong was totally absorbed in his music, staring not at the audience but down at his horn.

He had come a long way since he used to hawk coal from the back of a wagon; since he was thrown into the Colored Waifs Home in New Orleans for firing off a pistol on New Year's Eve, 1912. One noise more or less shouldn't have mattered on that night, but it did, and the cops caught him. It was those music lessons at the home that started him on his way, through New Orleans and Memphis and Chicago to the world beyond.

Armstrong might have been a criminal, he might have been a bum, he might have been killed unknown and unmourned in some war somewhere. But he wasn't. He was born to play that music. It wouldn't have mattered what world he had been born into. As soon as his fingers closed around that cornet, music was changed forever.

The audience applauded wildly, but they weren't there just to hear Armstrong. They were waiting.

The band hit up something that began nondescriptly—a slow blues, beginning with the drummer heavy on his brushes.

The tune began to change, and as it changed, a pure sweet clarinet began to play above the other instruments, and Ike walked onstage, playing his theme song. "Don't You Know What It Means to Miss New Orleans?"

His clarinet soared above the audience. Presley wasn't the only one who got chill bumps all the way down the backs of his ankles.

Ike and Armstrong traded off slow pure verses of the song; Ike's the sweet music of a craftsman, Armstrong's the heartfelt remembrance of things as they were. Ike never saw Storyville; Armstrong had to leave it when the Navy closed it down.

Together they built to a moving finale and descended into a silence like the dimming of lights, with Ike's clarinet the last one to wink out.

The cream of Washington betrayed their origins with their applause.

And before they knew what had happened, a new tune started up with the opening screech of "Mississippi Mud."

Ike and Armstrong traded licks, running on and off the melody. Pops wiped his face with his handkerchief, his face seemed all teeth and sweat, Ike's bald head shone, the freckles standing out above the wisps of white hair on his temples.

This wasn't like the old days. It was as if they'd never quit playing together at all. This was *now,* and Ike and Pops were hot.

They played and played.

Ike's boyhood had been on the flat pan of Kansas, smalltown-church America at the turn of the century. A town full of laborers and businessmen, barbershops, milliners, and ice-cream parlors.

He had done all the usual things, swimming naked in the creek, running through town and finding things to build up or tear down. He had hunted and fished and gone to services on Sunday; he had camped out overnight or for days at a time with his brothers, made fun of his girl cousins, stolen watermelons.

He first heard recorded music on an old Edison cylinder machine at the age of eight, long-hair music and opera his aunt collected.

There was a firehouse band that played each Wednesday night in the park across the street from the station. There were real band concerts on the courthouse lawn on Sunday, mostly military music, marches, and the instrumental parts of ballads.

Eisenhower heard it all. Music was part of his background, and he didn't think much of it.

So Ike grew up in Kansas, where the music was as flat as the land.

Louis Daniel Armstrong was rared back, tooting out some wild lines of "Night and Day." In the old days it didn't matter how well you played; it was the angle of your back and tilt of your horn. The band was really tight; they were playing for their lives.

The trombone player came out of his seat, jumped down onto the stage on his knees, and matched Armstrong for a few bars.

The audience yelled.

Eisenhower tapped his foot and smiled, watching Armstrong and the trombone man cook.

The drummer was giving a lot of rim shots. The whole ballroom sounded like the overtaxed heart of a bird ready to fly away to meet Jesus.

Ike took off his coat and loosened his tie down to the first button.

The crowd went wild.

Late August, 1908.

The train was late. Young Dwight David Eisenhower hurried across the endless street grid of the Kansas City railyards. He was catching the train to New York City. There he would board another bound for West Point.

He carried his admission papers, a congratulatory letter from his congressman (gotten after some complicated negotiations—for a while it looked like he would be Midshipman Eisenhower), his train ticket, and twenty-one dollars in emergency money in his jacket.

He'd asked the porter for the track number. It was next to the station proper. A spur track confused him. He looked down the tracks, couldn't see a number. Trains waited all around, ready to hurl themselves toward distant cities. He went to the station entrance.

Four black men, ragged of dress, were smiling and playing near the door. What they played, young David had never heard before; it was syncopated music, but not like a rag, not a march, something in between, something like nothing else. He had never heard polyrhythms like them before. They stopped him dead.

The four had a banjo, a cornet, a violin, and a clarinet. They played, smiled, danced a little for the two or three people watching them. A hat lay on the ground before them. In it were a few dimes, some pennies, and a single new half-dime.

They finished the song. A couple of people said. "Very nice, very nice," and added a few cents to the hat.

The four men started to talk among themselves.

"What was that song?" young David asked.

The man with the cornet looked at him through large horn-rimmed spectacles. "That song was called 'Struttin' with Some Barbecue,' young sir," he replied.

Dwight David reached into his pocket and took out a shiny dollar gold piece.

"Play it again," he said.

They nearly killed themselves this time, running through it. It was great art, it was on the street, and they were getting a whole dollar for it. David watched them, especially the clarinet player, who made his instrument soar above the others. They finished the number, and all tipped theirs hats to him.

"Is that hard to learn to play?" he asked the man with the clarinet.

"For some it is," he answered.

"Could you teach me?" Davis asked.

The black man looked at the others, who looked away; they were no help at all. "Let me see your fingers," he said.

Eisenhower held out his hands, wrists up, then down.

"I could probably teach you to play in six weeks," he said. "I don't know if I could teach you to play like that. You've got to feel that music." He was trying not to say that Eisenhower was white.

"Wait right here," said Ike.

He went inside the depot and cashed in his ticket. He sent two telegrams, one home and one to the Army. He was back outside in fifteen minutes, with thirty-three dollars in his pocket.

"Let's go find me a clarinet," he said to the black man.

He knew he would not sleep well that night, and neither would anybody back on the farm. He probably wouldn't sleep well for weeks. But he sure as heck knew what he wanted.

* * *

Armstrong smiled, wiped his face, and blew the opening notes of "When It's Sleepy Time Down South." Ike joined in.

They went into "Just a Closer Walk with Thee," quiet, restrained, the horn and clarinet becoming one instrument for a while. Then Ike bent his notes around Armstrong's, then Pops lifted Eisenhower up, then the instruments walked arm in arm toward Heaven.

Ike listened to the drummer as he played. He sure missed Wild George.

The first time they had met, Ike was the new kid in town, just another guy with a clarinet. Some gangster had hired him to fill in with a band, sometime in 1911.

Ike didn't say much. He was working his way south from K.C., toward Memphis, toward New Orleans (which he would never see until after New Orleans didn't mean the same anymore).

Ike could cook anyone with his clarinet— horn player, banjo man, even drummers. They might make more noise, but when they ran out of things to do, Ike was just starting.

He'd begun at the saloon, filling in, but the bandleader soon had sense enough to put him out front. They took breaks, leaving just him and the drummer up there, and the crowds never noticed. Ike was hot before there was hot music.

Till one night a guy came in—a new drummer. He was a crazy man. "My name is

Wild George S. Patton,'' he said before the first set.

"What's the S. stand for?" asked Ike.

"Shitkicker!" said the drummer.

Ike didn't say anything.

That night they tried to cut each other, chop each other off the stage. Patton was doing two-hand cymbal shots, paradiddles, and flails. His bass foot never stopped. Ike wasn't a show-off, but this guy drove him to it. He blew notes that killed mice for three square blocks. Patton ended up by kicking a hole through the bass drum and ramming his sticks through his snare like he was opening a can of beans with them.

The bandleader fired Patton on the spot and threatened to call the cops. The crowd nearly lynched the manager for it.

As soon as the hubbub died down, Patton said to Ike, "The S. stands for Smith." And he shook his hand.

He and Ike took off that night to start up their own band.

And were together for almost thirty years.

Armstrong blew "Dry Bones."

Ike did "St. Louis Blues."

They had never done either better. This Washington audience loved them.

So had another, long ago.

The first time he and Armstrong met was in Washington, too. It was a hot, bleak July day in 1932.

The Bonus Army had come to the Capitol,

asking their congressmen and their nation for some relief in the third year of the Depression. President Al Smith was virtually powerless; he had a Republican Congress under him, led by Senator Nye.

The bill granting the veterans of the Great War their bonus, due in 1945, had been passed back in the Twenties. The vets wanted it to be paid immediately. It had been sitting in the treasury, gaining interest, and was already part of the budget. The vote was coming up soon.

Thousands, dubbed the B.E.F., had poured into Washington, camping on Anacostia Flats, in tin boxes, towns of shanties dubbed Smithvilles, or under the rain and stars.

Homeless men who had slogged through the mud of Europe, had been gassed and shelled, and had lived with rats in the trenches while fighting for democracy; now they found themselves back in the mud again.

This time they were out of money, out of work, out of luck.

The faces of the men were tired. Soup kitchens had been set up. They tried to keep their humor. It was all they had left. May dragged by, then June, then July. The vote was taken in Congress on the twelfth.

Congress said no.

They accused the Bonus Marchers of being Reds. They said they were an armed rabble. Rumors ran wild. Such financial largess, Congress said, could not be afforded.

Twenty thousand of the thirty thousand men tried to find some way back home, out of the city, back to No Place, U.S.A.

Ten thousand stayed, hoping for something to happen. Anything.

Ike went down to play for them. So did Armstrong. They ran into each other in town, got their bands and equipment together. They set up a stage in the middle of the Smithville, now a forlorn-looking bunch of mud-straw shacks.

About five thousand of the jobless men came to hear them play. They were in a holiday mood. They sat on the ground, in the mud. They didn't much care anymore.

Armstrong and Ike had begun to play that day. Half the band, including Wild George, had hangovers. They had drunk with the Bonus Marchers the night before and well into the morning before the noon concert.

They played great jazz that day anyway. Just before the music began, a cloud of smoke had risen up from some of the abandoned warehouses the veterans had been living in. There was some commotion over toward the Potomac. The band just played louder and wilder.

The marchers clapped along. Wild George smiled a bleary-eyed smile toward the crowd. They were doing half his job.

Automatic rifle fire rang out, causing heads to turn.

The Army was coming. Sons and nephews of some of the Bonus Marchers there were coming toward them on orders from Douglas MacArthur, the Chief of Staff. He had orders to clear them out.

The men came to their feet, picking up rocks and bottles.

Marching lines of soldiers came into view, bayonets fixed. Small two-man tanks, armed with machine guns, rolled between the soldiers. The lines stopped. The soldiers put on gas masks.

The Bonus Marchers, who remembered phosgene and the trenches, drew back.

"Keep playing!" said Ike.

"Keep goin'. Let it roll!" said Armstrong.

Tear-gas grenades flew toward the Bonus Marchers. Rocks and bottles sailed toward the masked soldiers. There was an explosion a block away.

The troops came on.

The gas rolled toward the marchers. Some who picked up the spewing canisters to throw them back fell coughing to the ground, overcome.

The tanks and bayonets came forward in a solid line.

The marchers broke and ran.

Their shacks and tents were set afire by Chemical Corpsmen behind the tanks.

"Let it roll! Let it roll!" said Armstrong, and they played "Didn't He Ramble?" The gas cloud hit them, and the music died in chokes and vomiting.

That night the Bonus Marchers were loaded on Army trucks, taken fifty miles due west, and let out on the sides of the roads.

Ike and Louis went up before the Washington magistrate, paid a ten-dollar fine each, and took a train to New York City.

* * *

The last time he had seen Wild George alive was two years ago. Patton had been found by somebody who'd know him in the old days.

He'd been in four bad marriages, his only kid had died in the taking of the Japanese Home Islands in early Forty-seven, and he'd lost one of his arms in a car wreck in Fifty-five. He was found in a flophouse. They'd put him in a nursing home and paid the bills.

Ike had gone to visit. The last time they had seen each other in those intervening twenty-odd years had been the day of the fistfight in Forty-three, just before the Second World War broke out. Patton had joined the Miller Band for a while but was too much for them. He'd gone from band to band and marriage to marriage to oblivion.

He was old, old. Wild George was only five years older than Ike. He looked a hundred. One eye was almost gone. He had no teeth. He was drying out in the nursing home, turning brittle as last winter's leaves.

"Hello, George," said Ike, shaking his only hand.

"I knew you'd come first," said Patton.

"You should have let somebody know."

"What's to know? One old musician lives, another one dies."

"George, I'm sorry. The way things have turned out."

"I've been thinking it over, about that fight we had," Patton stopped to cough up some bloody spittle into a basin Ike held for him. George's eyes watered.

"God. Oh, jeez. If I could only have a drink." He stared into Ike's eyes. Then he said, "About that fight. You were still wrong."

Then he coughed some more.

Ike was crying as they went into the final number. He stepped forward to the mike Helen had used when she came out to sing with them for the last three numbers.

"This song is for the memory of George Smith Patton," he said.

They played "The Old, Rugged Cross." No one had ever played it like that before.

Ike broke down halfway through. He waved to the crowd, took his mouthpiece off, and walked into the wings.

Pops kept playing. He tried to motion Ike back. Helen was hugging him. He waved and brushed the tears away.

Armstrong finished the song.

The audience tore the place apart. They were on their feet and stamping, screaming, applauding.

Presley sat in his chair.

He was crying, too, but quickly stood up and cheered.

The whole thing was over.

At home, later, in Georgetown, Senator Presley was lying in bed beside his wife, Muffy. They had made love. They had both been excited. It had been terrific.

Now Muffy was asleep.

Presley got up and went to the kitchen,

poured himself a scotch, and stood with his naked butt against the countertop.

It was a cold night. Through the half-curtains on the window he saw stars over the city. If you could call this seventeenth-century jumble a city.

He went into the den. The servants would be asleep.

He turned the power on the stereo, took down four or five of his Eisenhower records, looked through them. He put on *Ike at the Mike,* a four-record set made for RCA in 1947, toward the end of the last war.

Ike was playing "No Love, No Nothing," a song his wife had made famous three years before. She wasn't on this record, though. This was all Ike and his band.

Presley got the bottle from the kitchen, sat back down, poured himself another drink. There were more hearings tomorrow. And the day after.

Someday, he thought, *someday E. Aaron Presley will be President of these here United States. Serves them right.*

Ike was playing "All God's Chillun Got Shoes."

I didn't even get to shake his hand, thought Presley.

I'd give it all away to be like him, he thought.

He went to sleep sitting up.

THE PALACE AT MIDNIGHT

By Robert Silverberg

The foreign minister of the Empire of San Francisco was trying to sleep late. Last night had been a long one, a wild if not particularly gratifying party at the Baths, too much to drink, too much to smoke, and he had seen the dawn come up like thunder out of Oakland 'crost the Bay. Now the telephone was ringing. He integrated the first couple of rings nicely into his dream, but the next one began to undermine his slumber, and the one after that woke him up. He groped for the receiver and, eyes still closed, managed to croak, "Christensen here."

"Tom, are you awake? You don't sound awake. It's Morty, Tom. Wake up."

The undersecretary for external affairs. Christensen sat up, rubbed his eyes, ran his tongue around his lips. Daylight was streaming into the room. His cats were glaring at him from the doorway. The little Siamese pawed daintily at her empty bowl and looked up expectantly. The fat Persian just sat.

"Tom?"

"I'm up! I'm up! What is it, Morty?"

"I didn't mean to wake you. How was I supposed to know, one in the afternoon—"

"*What is it,* Morty?"

"We got a call from Monterey. There's an ambassador on the way up, and you've got to meet with her."

The foreign minister worked hard at clearing the fog from his brain. He was thirty-nine years old, and all-night parties took more out of him than they once had.

"You do it, Morty."

"You know I would, Tom. But I can't. You've got to handle this one yourself. It's prime."

"Prime? What kind of prime? You mean, like a great dope deal? Or are they declaring war on us?"

"How would I know the details? The call came in, and they said it was prime. Ms. Sawyer must confer with Mr. Christensen. It wouldn't involve dope, Tom. And it can't be war, either. Shit, why would Monterey want to make war on us? They've only got ten soldiers, I bet, unless they're drafting the Chicanos out of the Salinas *calabozo,* and besides—"

"All right." Christensen's head was buzzing. "Go easy on the chatter. Okay? Where am I supposed to meet her?"

"In Berkeley."

"You're kidding."

"She won't come into the city. She thinks it's too dangerous over here."

"What do we do, kill ambassadors and

barbecue them? She'll be safe here, and she knows it."

"Look. I talked to her. She thinks the city is too crazy. She'll come as far as Berkeley, but that's it."

"Tell her to go to hell."

"Tom, Tom—"

Christensen sighed. "Where in Berkeley will she be?"

"The Claremont, at half past four."

"Jesus," Christensen said. "How did you get me into this? All the way across to the East Bay to meet a lousy ambassador from Monterey! Let her come to San Francisco. This is the Empire, isn't it? They're only a stinking republic. Am I supposed to swim over to Oakland every time an envoy shows up and wiggles a finger? Some bozo from Fresno says boo, and I have to haul my ass out to the Valley, eh? Where does it stop? What kind of clout do I have, anyway?"

"Tom—"

"I'm sorry, Morty. I don't feel like a goddamned diplomat this morning."

"It isn't morning anymore, Tom. But I'd do it for you if I could."

"All right. All right. I didn't mean to yell at you. You make the ferry arrangements."

"Ferry leaves at three-thirty. Chauffeur will pick you up at your place at three, okay?"

"Okay," Christensen said. "See if you can find out any more about all this, and have somebody call me back in an hour with a briefing, will you?"

He fed the cats, showered, shaved, took a couple of pills, and brewed some coffee. At half past two the ministry called. Nobody had any idea what the ambassador might want. Relations between San Francisco and the Republic of Monterey were cordial just now. Ms. Sawyer lived in Pacific Grove and was a member of the Monterey Senate; that was all that was known about her. *Some briefing,* Christensen thought.

He went downstairs to wait for his chauffeur. It was a late autumn day, bright and clear and cool. The rains hadn't begun yet, and the streets looked dusty. The foreign minister lived on Frederick Street, just off Cole, in an old white Victorian with a small front porch. He settled in on the steps, feeling wide awake but surly, and a few minutes before three his car came putt-putting up, a venerable gray Chevrolet with the arms of imperial San Francisco on its doors. The driver was Vietnamese, or maybe Thai. Christensen got in without a word, and off they went at an imperial velocity through the virtually empty streets, down to Haight, eastward for a while, then onto Oak, up Van Ness, past the palace, where at this moment the Emperor Norton VII was probably taking his imperial nap, and along Post and then Market to the ferry slip.

The stump of the Bay Bridge glittered magically against the sharp blue sky. A small power cruiser was waiting for him. Christensen was silent during the slow, dull voyage. A chill wind cut through the Golden Gate and made him huddle into himself. He stared broodingly at the low, rounded East Bay hills, dry and brown from a long summer of drought, and thought about the permutations of fate that had transformed an adequate architect into the barely competent foreign minister of this barely competent little nation. The Empire of San Francisco, one of the early emperors had said, is the only country in history that was decadent from the day it was founded.

At the Berkeley marina Christensen told the ferry skipper, "I don't know what time I'll be coming back. So no sense waiting. I'll phone in when I'm ready to go."

Another imperial car took him up the hillside to the sprawling nineteenth-century splendor of the Claremont Hotel, that vast, antiquated survivor of all the cataclysms. It was seedy now, the grounds a jungle, ivy almost to the tops of the palm trees, and yet it still looked fit to be a palace, with hundreds of rooms and magnificent banquet halls. Christensen wondered how often it had guests. There wasn't much tourism these days.

In the parking plaza outside the entrance was a single car, a black-and-white California Highway Patrol job that had been decorated with the insignia of the Republic of Monterey, a contorted cypress tree and a sea otter. A uniformed driver lounged against it, looking bored. "I'm Christensen," he told the man.

"You the foreign minister?"

"I'm not the Emperor Norton."

"Come on. She's waiting in the bar."

Ms. Sawyer stood up as he entered—a slender, dark-haired woman of about thirty, with cool, green eyes—and he flashed her a quick, professionally cordial smile, which she returned just as professionally. He did not feel at all cordial.

"Senator Sawyer," he said. "I'm Tom Christensen."

"Glad to know you." She pivoted and gestured toward the huge picture window that ran the length of the bar. "I just got here. I've been admiring the view. It's been years since I've been in the Bay Area."

He nodded. From the cocktail lounge one could see the slopes of Berkeley, the bay, the ruined bridges, the still-imposing San Francisco skyline. Very nice. They took seats by the window, and he beckoned to a waiter, who brought them drinks.

"How was your drive up?" Christensen asked.

"No problems. We got stopped for speeding in San Jose, but I got out of it. They could see it was an official car, but they stopped us anyway."

"The lousy bastards. They love to look important."

"Things haven't been good between Monterey and San Jose all year. They're spoiling for touble."

"I hadn't heard," Christensen said.

"We think they want to annex Santa Cruz. Naturally we can't put up with that. Santa Cruz is our buffer."

He asked sharply. "Is that what you came here for, to ask our help against San Jose?"

She stared at him in surprise. "Are you in a hurry, Mr. Christensen?"

"Not particularly."

"You sound awfully impatient. We're still making preliminary conversation, having a drink, two diplomats playing the diplomatic game. Isn't that so?"

"Well?"

"I was telling you what happened to me on the way north. In response to your question. Then I was filling you in on current political developments. I didn't expect you to snap at me like that."

"Did I snap?"

"It certainly sounded like snapping to me," she said, with some annoyance.

Christensen took a deep pull of his bourbon-and-water and gave her a long, steady look. She met his gaze imperturbably. She looked composed, amused, and very, very tough. After a time, when some of the red haze of irrational anger and fatigue had cleared from his mind, he said quietly, "I had about four hours' sleep last night, and I wasn't expecting an envoy from Monterey today. I'm tired and edgy, and if I sounded impatient or harsh or snappish, I'm sorry."

"It's all right. I understand."

"Another bourbon or two and I'll be properly unwound." He held his empty glass toward the hovering waiter. "A refill for you, too?" he asked her.

"Yes. Please." In a formal tone she said, "Is the Emperor in good health?"

"Not bad. He hasn't really been well for a couple of years, but he's holding his own. And President Morgan?"

"Fine," she said. "Hunting wild boar in Big Sur this week."

"A nice life it must be, President of Monterey. I've always liked Monterey. So much quieter and cleaner and more sensible down there than in San Francisco."

"Too quiet sometimes. I envy you the excitement here."

"Yes, of course. The rapes, the muggings, the arson, the mass meetings, the race wars, the—"

"Please," she said gently.

He realized he had begun to rant. There was a throbbing behind his eyes. He worked to gain control of himself.

"Did my voice get too loud?"

"You must be terribly tired. Look, we can confer in the morning, if you'd prefer. It isn't *that* urgent. Suppose we have dinner and not talk politics at all, and get rooms here, and tomorrow after breakfast we can—"

"No," Christensen said. "My nerves are a little ragged, that's all. But I'll try to be more civil. And I'd rather not wait until tomorrow to find out what this is all about. Suppose you give me a précis of it now, and if it sounds too complicated, I'll sleep on it and we can discuss it in detail tomorrow. Yes?"

"All right." She put her drink down and sat

quite still, as if arranging her thoughts. At length she said, "The Republic of Monterey maintains close ties with the Free State of Mendocino. I understand that Mendocino and the Empire broke off relations a little while back."

"A fishing dispute, nothing major."

"But you have no direct contact with them right now. Therefore this should come as news to you. The Mendocino people have learned, and have communicated to our representative there, that an invasion of San Francisco is imminent."

Christensen blinked twice. "By whom?"

"The Realm of Wicca," she said.

"Flying down from Oregon on their broomsticks?"

"Please. I'm being serious."

"Unless things have changed up there," Christensen said, "the Realm of Wicca is nonviolent, like all the neopagan states. As I understand it, they tend their farms and practice their little pagan rituals and do a lot of dancing around the Maypole and chanting and screwing. You expect me to believe that a bunch of gentle, goofy witches are going to make war on the Empire?"

She said, "Not war. An invasion."

"Explain."

"One of their high priests has proclaimed San Francisco a holy place and has instructed them to come down here and build a Stonehenge in Golden Gate Park in time for proper celebration of the winter solstice. There are at least a quarter of a million neopagans in the Willamette Valley, and more than half of them are expected to take part. According to our Mendocino man, the migration has already begun and thousands of Wiccans are spread out between Mount Shasta and Ukiah right now. The solstice is only seven weeks away. The Wiccans may be gentle, but you're going to have a hundred fifty thousand of them in San Francisco by the end of the month, pitching tents all over town.''

"Holy Jesus," Christensen muttered.

"Can you feed that many strangers? Can you find room for them? Will San Franciscans meet them with open arms? Do you think it'll be a love festival?"

"It'll be a fucking massacre," Christensen said tonelessly.

"Yes. The witches may be nonviolent, but they know how to practice self-defense. Once they're attacked, there'll be rivers of blood, and it won't all be Wiccan blood."

Christensen's head was pounding again. She was absolutely right: chaos, strife, bloodshed. And a merry Christmas to all. He rubbed his aching forehead, turned away from her, and stared out at the deepening twilight and the sparkling lights of the city on the other side of the bay. A bleak, bitter depression was taking hold of his spirit. He signaled for another round of drinks. Then he said slowly, "They can't be allowed to enter the city. We'll need to close the imperial frontier and turn them back before they get as far as Santa Rosa. Let them build their goddamned Stonehenge in Sacramento if they like.'' His eyes flickered. He started to assemble ideas. "The Empire might just have enough troops to contain the Wiccans by itself, but I think this is best handled as a regional problem. We'll call in forces from our allies as far out as Petaluma and Napa and Palo Alto. I don't imagine we can expect much help from the Free State or from San Jose. And of course Monterey isn't much of a military power, but still—''

"We are willing to help,'' Ms. Sawyer said.

"To what extent?''

"We aren't set up for much actual warfare, but we have access to our own alliances from Salinas down to Paso Robles, and we could call up, say, five thousand troops all told. Would that help?''

"That would help,'' Christensen said.

"It shouldn't be necessary for there to be any combat. With the imperial border sealed and troops posted along the line from Guerneville to Sacramento, the Wiccans won't force the issue. They'll revise their revelation and celebrate the solstice somewhere else.''

"Yes,'' he said. "I think you're right." He leaned toward her and asked, "Why is Monterey willing to help us?''

"We have problems of our own brewing—with San Jose. If we are seen making a conspicuous gesture of solidarity with the Empire, it might discourage San Jose from proceeding with its notion of annexing Santa Cruz. That amounts to an act of war against us.

Surely San Jose isn't interested in making any moves that will bring the Empire down on its back.''

She wasn't subtle, but she was effective. *Quid pro quo, we help you keep the witches out, you help us keep San Jose in line, and all remains well without a shot being fired. These goddamned little nations,* he thought, *these absurd jerkwater sovereignties, with their wars and alliances and shifting confederations.* It was like a game, like playground politics. Except that it was real. What had fallen apart was not going to be put back together, not for a long while, and this miniaturized *Weltpolitik* was the realest reality there was just now. At least things were saner in Northern California than they were down south, where Los Angeles was gobbling everything and there were rumors that Pasadena had the Bomb. Nobody had to contend with that up here.

Christensen said, "I'll have to propose all this to the Defense Ministry, of course. And get the Emperor's approval. But basically I'm in agreement with your thinking.''

"I'm so pleased.''

"And I'm very glad that you took the trouble to travel up from Monterey to make these matters clear to us.''

"Merely a case of enlightened self-interest,'' Ms. Sawyer said.

"Mmm. Yes.'' He found himself studying the sharp planes of her cheekbones, the delicate arch of her eyebrows. Not only was she cool and competent, Christensen thought, but now that the business part of their meeting was over, he was coming to notice that she was a very attractive woman and that he was not as tired as he had thought he was. Did international politics allow room for a little recreational hanky-panky? Metternich hadn't jumped into bed with Talleyrand, nor Kissinger with Indira Gandhi, but times had changed, after all, and—no. *No.* He choked off that entire line of thought. In these shabby days they might all be children playing at being grown-ups, but nevertheless international politics still had its code, and this was a meeting of diplomats, not a blind date or a singles-bar pickup. *You will sleep in your own bed tonight,* he told himself, *and you will sleep alone.*

All the same he said, "It's past six o'clock. Shall we have dinner together before I go back to the city?"

"I'd love to."

"I don't know much about Berkeley restaurants. We're probably better off eating right here."

"I think that's best," she said.

They were the only ones in the hotel's enormous dining room. A staff of three waited on them as if they were the most important people who had ever dined there. And dinner turned out to be quite decent, he thought— calamari and abalone and sand dabs and grilled thresher shark, washed down with a dazzling bottle of Napa Chardonnay. Even though the world had ended, it remained possible to eat very well in the Bay Area, and the breakdown

279

of society had not only reduced maritime pollution but also made local seafood much more readily available for local consumption. There wasn't much of an export trade possible with eleven heavily guarded national boundaries and eleven sets of customs barriers between San Francisco and Los Angeles.

Dinner conversation was light, relaxed—diplomatic chitchat, gossip about events in remote territories, reports about the Voodoo principality, expanding out of New Orleans and the Sioux conquests in Wyoming and the Prohibition War now going on in what used to be Kentucky. There was a bison herd again on the Great Plains, she said, close to a million head. He told her what he had heard about the Suicide People, who ruled between San Diego and Tijuana, and about King Barnum & Bailey III, who governed in northern Florida with the aid of a court of circus freaks. She smiled and said, "How can they tell the freaks from the ordinary people? The whole world's a circus now, isn't it?"

He shook his head and replied. "No, a zoo," and he beckoned the waiter for more wine. He did not ask her about internal matters in Monterey, and she tactfully stayed away from the domestic problems of the Empire of San Francisco. He was feeling easy, buoyant, a little drunk, more than a little drunk; to have to answer questions now about the little rebellion that had been suppressed in Sausalito or the secessionist thing in Walnut Creek would be a bringdown, and bad for the digestion.

About half past eight he said, "You aren't going back to Monterey tonight, are you?"

"God, no! It's a five-hour drive, assuming no more troubles with the San Jose Highway Patrol. And the road's so bad below Watsonville that only a lunatic would drive it at night. I'll stay here at the Claremont."

"Good. Let me put it on the imperial account."

"That isn't necessary. We—"

"The hotel is always glad to oblige the government and its guests."

Ms. Sawyer shrugged. "Very well. We'll reciprocate when you come to Monterey."

"Fine."

And then her manner suddenly changed. She shifted in her seat and fidgeted and played with her silverware, looking awkward and ill at ease. Some new and big topic was obviously about to be introduced, and Christensen guessed that she was going to ask him to spend the night with her. In a fraction of a second he ran through all the possible merits and de-merits of that, and came out on the plus side, and had his answer ready when she said, "Tom, can I ask a big favor?"

Which threw him completely off balance. Whatever was coming, it certainly wasn't what he was expecting.

"I'll do my best."

"I'd like an audience with the Emperor."

"What?"

"Not on official business. I know the Emperor talks business only with his ministers

281

and privy councillors. But I want to see him, that's all." Color came to her cheeks. "Doesn't it sound silly? But it's something I've always dreamed of, a kind of adolescent fantasy. To be in San Francisco, to be shown into the imperial throne room, to kiss his ring, all the pomp and circumstance. I want it, Tom. Just to *be* there, to see him. Do you think you could manage that?"

He was astounded. The facade of cool, tough competence had dropped away from her, revealing unanticipated absurdity. He did not know what to answer.

She said, "Monterey's such a poky little place. It's just a *town*. We call ourselves a republic, but we aren't much of anything. And I call myself a senator and a diplomat, but I've never really been anywhere. San Francisco two or three times when I was a girl, San Jose a few times. My mother was in Los Angeles once, but I haven't been anywhere. And to go home saying that I had seen the Emperor—" Her eyes sparkled. "You're really taken aback, aren't you? You thought I was all ice and microprocessors, and instead I'm only a hick, right? But you're being very nice. You aren't even laughing at me. Will you get me an audience with the Emperor for tomorrow?"

"I thought you were afraid to go into San Francisco."

She looked abashed. "That was just a ploy. To make you come over here, to get you to take me seriously and put yourself out a little. Diplomatic wiles. I'm sorry about that. The word was that you were snotty, that you had to be met with strength or you'd be impossible to deal with. But you aren't like that at all. Tom, I want to see the Emperor. He does give audiences, doesn't he?"

"In a manner of speaking. I suppose it could be done."

"Oh, would you? Tomorrow?"

"Why wait for tomorrow?"

"Are you being sarcastic?"

"Not at all," Christensen said. "This is San Francisco. The Emperor keeps weird hours just like the rest of us. I'll phone over there and see if we can be received." He hesitated. "I'm afraid it won't be what you're expecting."

"What do you mean? In what way?"

"The pomp, the circumstance. You're going to be disappointed. You may be better off not meeting him, actually. Stick to your fantasy of imperial majesty. Seriously, I'll get you an audience if you insist, but I don't think it's a great idea."

"Can you be more specific?"

"No."

"I still want to see him. Regardless."

He left the dining room and, with misgivings, began arranging things. The telephone system was working sluggishly that evening, and it took him fifteen minutes to set the whole thing up, but there were no serious obstacles. He returned to her and said, "The ferry will pick us up at the marina in about an hour. There'll be a car waiting on the San Francisco side. The Emperor will be available for viewing around midnight. I tell you that you're not going to enjoy this. The Emperor is old, and he's been sick; he isn't a very interesting person to meet.''

"All the same,'' she said. "The one thing I wanted, when I volunteered to be the envoy, was an imperial audience. Please don't discourage me.''

"As you wish. Shall we have another drink?''

"How about these?'' She produced an enameled cigarette case. "Humboldt County's finest. Gift of the Free State.''

He smiled and nodded and took the joint from her. It was elegantly manufactured, fine cockleshell paper, gold monogram, igniter cap, even a filter. *Everything else has come apart,* he thought, *but the technology of marijuana is at its highest point in history*. He flicked the cap, took a deep drag, passed it to her. The effect was instantaneous, a new high cutting through the wooze of bourbon and wine and brandy already in his brain, clearing it, expanding his limp and sagging soul. When they were finished with it, they floated out of the hotel. His driver and hers were still waiting in the parking lot. Christensen dismissed his, and they took the Republic of Monterey car down the slopes of Berkeley to the marina. The boat from San Francisco was late. They stood around shivering at the ferry slip for twenty minutes, peering bleakly across at the glittering lights of the far-off city. Neither of them was dressed for the nighttime chill, and he was tempted to pull her close and hold her in his arms, but he did not. There was a boundary he was not yet willing to cross. *Hell,* he thought, *I don't even know her first name*.

It was nearly eleven by the time they reached San Francisco.

An official car was parked at the pier. The driver hopped out, saluting, bustling about—one of those preposterous little civil-service types, doubtless keenly honored to be taxiing bigwigs around late at night. He wore the red-and-gold uniform of the imperial dragoons, a little frayed at one elbow. The car coughed and sputtered and reluctantly lurched into life, up Market Street to Van Ness and then north to the palace. Ms. Sawyer's eyes were wide, and she stared at the ancient high-rises along Van Ness as if they were cathedrals.

When they came to the Civic Center area, she gasped, obviously overwhelmed by the majesty of everything, the shattered hulk of the Symphony Hall, the Museum of Modern Art, the great dome of City Hall, and the Imperial Palace itself, awesome, imposing, a splendid, many-columned building that long ago had been the War Memorial Opera House. With the envoy from the Republic of Monterey at his elbow, Christensen marched up the steps of the palace and through the center doors into the lobby, where a great many of the ranking ministers and plenipotentiaries of the Empire were assembled. "How absolutely marvelous," Ms. Sawyer murmured. Smiling graciously, bowing, nodding, Christensen pointed out the notables, the defense minister, the minister of finance, the minister of suburban affairs, the chief justice, the minister of transportation.

Precisely at midnight there was a grand
flourish of trumpets and the door to the throne
room opened. Christensen offered Ms. Sawyer
his arm; together they made the long journey
down the center aisle and up the ramp to the
stage, where the imperial throne, a resplendent
thing of rhinestones and foil, glittered
brilliantly under the spotlights. Ms. Sawyer was
wonderstruck. She pointed toward the six
gigantic portraits suspended high over the stage
and whispered a question, and Christensen
replied, "The first six emperors. And here
comes the seventh one."

"Oh," she gasped. But was it awe, surprise,
or disgust?

He was in his full regalia, the scarlet robe, the
bright green tunic with ermine trim, the gold
chains. But he was wobbly and tottering, a
clumsy, staggering figure, gray-faced and
feeble, supported on one side by Mike Schiff,
the Imperial Chamberlain, and on the other by
the Grand Sergeant-at-Arms, Terry Coleman.
He was not so much leaning on them as being
dragged by them. Bringing up the rear of the
procession were two sleek, pretty boys, one
black and one Chinese, carrying the orb, the
scepter, and the massive crown. Ms. Sawyer's
fingers tightened on Christensen's forearm, and
he heard her catch her breath as the Emperor,
in the process of being lowered into his throne,
went boneless and nearly spilled to the floor.
Somehow the Imperial Chamberlain and the
Grand Sergeant-at-Arms settled him properly in

place, balanced the crown on his head, and stuffed the orb and sceptor into his trembling hands. "His Imperial Majesty, Norton the Seventh of San Francisco!" cried Mike Schiff in a magnificent voice that went booming up to the highest balcony. The Emperor giggled.

"Come on," Christensen whispered and led her forward.

The old man was really in terrible shape. It was weeks since Christensen had last seen him, and by now he looked like something dragged from the crypt, slack-jawed, drooling, vacant-eyed, utterly burned out. The envoy from Monterey seemed to draw back, tense and rigid, repelled, unable or unwilling to go closer, but Christensen persisted, urging her onward until she was no more than a dozen feet from the throne. A sickly-sweet, vaguely familiar odor emanated from the old man.

"What do I do?" she asked, panicking.

"When I introduce you, go forward, curtsey if you know how, touch the orb. Then step back. That's all."

She nodded.

Christensen said, "Your Majesty, the ambassador from the Republic of Monterey, Senator Sawyer, to pay her respects."

Trembling, she went to him, curtseyed, touched the orb. As she backed away, she nearly fell, but Christensen came smoothly forward and steadied her. The Emperor giggled again, a shrill, horrific cackle. Slowly, carefully, Christensen guided the shaken Ms. Sawyer from the stage.

"How long has he been like that?"

"Two years, three, maybe more. Completely senile. Not even housebroken anymore. You could probably tell. I'm sorry. I told you you'd be better off skipping this. I'm enormously sorry. Ms.—Ms.—what's your first name, anyway?"

"Elaine."

"Let's get out of here, Elaine. Yes?"

"Yes. Please."

She was shivering. He walked her up the side aisle. A few of the courtiers were clambering up onto the stage now, one with a guitar, one with juggler's clubs. The imperial giggle pierced the air again and again, becoming rasping and wild. The imperial levee would go on half the night. Emperor Norton VII was one of San Francisco's most popular amusements.

"Now you know," Christensen said.

"How does the Empire function, if the Emperor is crazy?"

"We manage. We do our best without him. The Romans managed it with Caligula. Norton's not half as bad as Caligula. Not a tenth. Will you tell everyone in Monterey?"

"I think not. We believe in the power of the Empire and in the grandeur of the Emperor. Best not to disturb that faith."

"Quite right," said Chistensen.

They emerged into the clear, cold night.

Christensen said, "I'll ride back to the ferry slip with you before I go home."

"Where do you live?"

"In the other direction. Out near Golden Gate Park."

She looked up at him and moistened her lips. "I don't want to ride across the bay in the dark, alone, at this hour of the night. Is it all right if I go home with you?"

"Sure," he said.

She managed a jaunty smile. "You're straight, aren't you?"

"Sure. Most of the time, anyway."

"I thought you were. Good."

They got into the car. "Frederick Street," he told the driver, "between Clayton and Cole."

The trip took twenty minutes. Neither of them spoke. He knew what she was thinking about: the senile Emperor, dribbling and babbling under the bright spotlights. The mighty Norton VII, ruler of everything from San Rafael to San Mateo, from Half Moon Bay to Walnut Creek. Such is pomp and circumstance in imperial San Francisco in these latter days of Western civilization. Christensen sent the driver away, and they went upstairs. The cats were hungry again.

"It's a lovely apartment," she told him.

"Three rooms, bath, hot and cold running water. Not bad for a mere foreign minister. Some of the boys have suites at the palace, but I like it better here." He opened the door to the deck and stepped outside. Somehow, now that he was home, the night was not so cold. He thought about the Realm of Wicca, far off up there in green, happy Oregon, sending a hundred fifty thousand kindly goddess-worshiping neopagans down here to celebrate the rebirth of the sun. A nuisance, a mess, a head-

289

ache. Tomorrow he'd have to call a meeting of the Cabinet, when everybody had sobered up, and start the wheels turning, and probably he'd have to make trips to places like Petaluma and Palo Alto to get the alliance flanged together. Damn. But it was his job. Someone had to carry the load.

He slipped his arm around the slender woman from Monterey.

"The poor Emperor," she said softly.

"Yes," he agreed. "The poor Emperor. Poor everybody."

He looked toward the east. In a few hours the sun would be coming up over that hill, out of the place that used to be the United States of America and now was a thousand, thousand crazy, fractured, fragmented entities. Christensen shook his head. The Grand Duchy of Chicago, he thought. The Holy Carolina Confederation. The Three Kingdoms of New York. The Empire of San Francisco. No use getting upset—much too late for getting upset. You played the hand that was dealt you, and you did your best, and you carved little islands of safety out of the night. Turning to her, he said, "I'm glad you came home with me tonight." He brushed his lips lightly against hers. "Come. Let's go inside."

THE ANGEL'S GIFT

By Oxford Williams

He stood at his bedroom window, gazing happily out at the well-kept grounds and manicured park beyond them. The evening was warm and lovely. Dinner with the guests from overseas had been perfect; the deal was going smoothly, and he would get all the credit for it. As well as the benefits.

He was at the top of the world now, master of it all, king of the hill. The old dark days of fear and failure were far behind him now. Everything was going his way at last. He loved it.

His wife swept into the bedroom, just slightly tipsy from the champagne.

Beaming at him, she said, "You were magnificent tonight, darling."

He turned from the window, surprised beyond words. Praise from her was so rare that he treasured it, savored it like expensive wine, just as he had always felt a special glow within his breast on those extraordinary occasions when his mother had vouchsafed him a kind word.

"Uh. . .thank you," he said.

"Magnificent, darling," she repeated. "I am so proud of you!"

His face went red with embarrassed happiness.

"And these people are so much nicer than those Latin types," she added.

"You . . . you know, you were . . . you *are* . . . the most beautiful woman in this city," he stammered. He meant it. In her gown of gold lamé and with her hair coiffed that way, she looked positively regal. His heart filled with joy.

She kissed him lightly on the cheek, whispering into his ear, "I shall be waiting for you in my boudoir, my prince."

The breath gushed out of him. She pirouetted daintily, then waltzed to the door that connected to her own bedroom. Opening the door, she turned back toward him and blew him a kiss.

As she closed the door behind her, he took a deep, sighing, shuddering breath. Brimming with excited expectation, he went directly to his closet, unbuttoning his tuxedo jacket as he strode purposefully across the thickly carpeted floor.

He yanked open the closet door. A man was standing there, directly under the light set into the ceiling.

"Wha. . . ?"

Smiling, the man made a slight bow. "Please

do not be alarmed, sir. And don't bother to call for your security guards. They won't hear you.''

Still fumbling with his jacket buttons, he staggered back from the closet door, a thousand wild thoughts racing through his mind. An assassin. A kidnapper. A newspaper columnist!

The stranger stepped as far as the closet door. ''May I enter your room, sir? Am I to take your silence for assent? In that case, thank you very much.''

The stranger was tall but quite slender. He was perfectly tailored in a sky blue Brooks Brothers three-piece suit. He had the youthful, innocent, golden-curled look of a European terrorist. His smile revealed perfect, dazzling teeth. Yet his blue eyes seemed infinitely sad, as though filled with knowledge of all human failings. They pierced right through the man in the tuxedo.

''Wh . . . what do you want? Who are you?''

''I'm terribly sorry to intrude this way. I realize it must be a considerable shock to you. But you're always so busy. It's difficult to fit an appointment into your schedule.'' His voice was a sweet, mild tenor, but the accent was strange: east coast, surely. Harvard, no doubt.

''How did you get in here? My security . . .''

The stranger gave a slightly guilty grin and hiked one thumb ceilingward. ''You might say I came in through the roof.''

''The roof? Impossible!''

''Not for me. You see, I am an angel.''

293

"A . . . angel?"

With a self-assured nod, the stranger replied, "Yes. One of the Heavenly Host. Your very own guardian angel, to be precise."

"I don't believe you."

"You don't believe in angels?" The stranger cocked a golden eyebrow at him. "Come now, I can see into your soul. You do believe."

"My church doesn't go in for that sort of thing," he said, trying to pull himself together.

"No matter. You do believe. And you do well to believe, because it is all true. Angels, devils, the entire system. It is as real and true as this fine house you live in." The angel heaved a small sigh. "You know, back in medieval times people had a much firmer grasp on the realities of life. Today. . ." He shook his head.

Eyes narrowing craftily, the man asked, "If you're an angel, where are your wings? Your halo? You don't look anything like a real angel."

"Oh!" The angel seemed genuinely alarmed. "Does that bother you? I thought it would be easier on your nervous system to see me in a form that you're accustomed to dealing with every day. But if you want. . ."

The room was flooded with blinding golden light. Heavenly voices sang. The stranger stood before the man robed in radiance, huge white wings outspread, filling the room.

The man sank to his knees and buried his face in the rug. "Have mercy on me! Have mercy on me!"

He felt strong yet gentle hands pull him

tenderly to his feet. The angel was back in his Brooks Brothers suit. The searing light and ethereal chorus were gone.

"It is not in my power to show you either mercy or justice," he said, his sweetly youthful face utterly grave. "Only the Creator can dispense such things."

"But why . . . who . . . how . . ." he babbled.

Calming him, the angel explained, "My duty as your guardian angel is to protect your soul from damnation. But you must cooperate, you know. I cannot *force* you to be saved."

"My soul is in danger?"

"In danger?" The angel rolled his eyes heavenward. "You've just about handed it over to the enemy, giftwrapped. Most of the millionaires you dined with tonight have a better chance to attain salvation than you have, at the moment. And you know how difficult it is for a rich man."

The man tottered to the wingback chair next to his king-sized bed and sank into it. He pulled the handkerchief from his breast pocket and mopped his sweaty face.

The angel knelt beside him and looked up into his face pleadingly. "I don't want to frighten you into a premature heart seizure, but your soul really is in mortal peril."

"But I haven't done anything wrong! I'm not a crook. I haven't killed anyone or stolen anything. I've been faithful to my wife."

The angel gave him a skeptical smile.

"Well. . ." he wiped perspiration from his

upper lip. "Nothing serious. I've always honored my mother and my father."

Gently, the angel asked, "You've never told a lie?"

"Uh, well. . .nothing big enough to. . ."

"You've never cheated anyone?"

"Um."

"What about that actor's wife in California? And the money you accepted to swing certain deals? And all the promises you've broken?"

"You mean things like that—they count?"

"Everything counts," the angel said firmly. "Don't you realize that the enemy has your soul almost in his very hands?"

"No, I never thought. . ."

"All those deals you've made. All the corners you've cut." The angel suddenly shot him a piercing glance. "You haven't signed any documents in blood, have you?"

"No!" His heart twitched. "Certainly not!"

"Well, that's something, at least."

"I'll behave," he promised. "I'll be good. I'll be a model of virtue."

"Not enough," the angel said, shaking his golden locks. "Not nearly enough. Things have already gone much too far."

His eyes widened with fear. He wanted to argue, to refute, to debate the point with his guardian angel, but the words simply would not force their way through his constricted throat.

"No, it is not enough merely to promise to reform," the angel repeated. "Much stronger action is needed."

"Such as . . . what?" he croaked.

The angel got to his feet, paced across the room a few steps, then turned back to face him. His youthful visage brightened. "Why not? If *they* can make a deal for a soul, why can't we?"

"What do you mean?"

"Hush!" The angel seemed to be listening to another voice, one that the man could not hear. Finally the angel nodded and smiled. "Yes. I see. Thank you."

"What?"

Turning back to the man, the angel said, "I've just been empowered to make you an offer for your soul. If you accept the terms, your salvation is assured."

The man instantly grew wary. "Oh no you don't. I've heard all about deals for souls. Some of my best friends. . ."

"But this is a deal to *save* your soul!"

"How do I know that?" the man demanded. "How do I know you're really what you say you are? The devil has power to assume pleasing shapes, doesn't he?"

The angel smiled joyfully. "Good for you! You remember some of your childhood teaching."

"Don't try to put me off. I've negotiated a few tricky deals in my day. How do I know you're really an angel, and you want to save my soul?"

"By their fruits ye shall know them," the angel replied.

"What are you talking about?"

Still smiling, the angel replied, "When the devil makes a deal for a soul, what does he promise? Temporal gifts, such as power, wealth, respect, women, fame.''

"I have all that," the man said. "I'm on top of the world, everyone knows that."

"Indeed."

"And I didn't sign any deals with the devil to get there, either," he added smugly.

"None that you know of," the angel warned. "A man in your position delegates many decisions to his staff, does he not?"

The man's face went gray. "Oh my God, you don't think. . ."

With a shrug, the angel said, "It doesn't matter. The deal that I offer guarantees your soul's salvation, if you meet its terms."

"How? What do I have to do?"

"You have power, respect, women, fame." The angel ticked each point off on his slender, graceful fingers.

"Yes, yes, I know."

"You must give them up."

The man lurched forward in the wingchair. "Huh?"

"Give them up."

"I can't!"

"You must, if you are to attain the Kingdom of Heaven."

"But you don't understand! I can't just drop everything! This world doesn't work that way. I can't just. . .walk away from all this!"

"That's the deal," the angel said. "Give it up. All of it. Or spend eternity in hell."

"But you can't expect me to. . ." He gaped. The angel was no longer in the room with him.

For several minutes he stared into the empty air. Then, knees shaking, he arose and walked to the closet. It too was empty of strange personages.

He looked down at his hands. They trembled.

"I must be going crazy," he muttered to himself. "Too much strain. Too much tension." But even as he said it, he made his way to the telephone on the bedside table. He hesitated a moment, then grabbed up the phone and punched a number he had memorized months earlier.

"Hello, Chuck? Yes, this is me. Yes, yes, everything went fine tonight. Up to a point."

He listened to his underling burbling flattery into the phone, wondering how many times he had given his power of attorney to this weakling and to equally venal deputies.

"Listen, Chuck," he said at last. "I have a job for you. And it's got to be done right, understand? Okay, here's the deal—" he winced inwardly at the word. But, taking a deep manly breath, he plunged ahead. "You know the Democrats are setting up their campaign quarters in that new apartment building— what's it called, Watergate? Yeah. Okay. Now I think it would serve our purposes very well if we bugged the place before the campaign really starts to warm up . . ."

There were tears in his eyes as he spoke. But from far, far away, he could hear a heavenly chorus singing.

THE HITMAKER

By Cynthia Morgan

The town was perfect, Jordan Barrett had
sensed it when he saw the spec films, and his
first visit to the town had confirmed his
feelings. Now a month later, standing beside the
network limousine parked across the center line
of the highway bisecting the town, he felt the
same certainty. There were none of the doubts
that sometimes cropped up after he'd made a
decision, irrevocably committing the network's
money and his own reputation. The town could
go public; it was perfect for a CV series.

He was glad he'd waited. He'd been looking
for over five months, the longest search ever for
a location for a continuous-viewing series.
There'd been some pressure from Carl
Martinson, ATN's programming chief, during
the fourth month, when the other networks
began to announce their CV locations for the
new year. But Barrett had ignored the memos,
the hints that he was setting his standards too
high, and after a few weeks they'd stopped.

Barrett had given ATN five successful CV series in a row; all Martinson could do, finally, was sit back and hope that the producer would deliver again.

He wandered away from the limousine, walking on the shoulder of the road to avoid a pickup truck that drove slowly past and turned down a side street. There'd been no other traffic in the past half hour; the barricades had gone up when construction began on the liason center two kilometers outside of town. Twenty meters down the highway, Jordan stopped and looked around indecisively. There wasn't much to the town: fewer than a hundred houses, one tiny general store. A service station stood at one end of town, a fast-food joint at the other, stapling the community to the two-lane strip of blacktop that linked it to the rest of the country. But he didn't have any idea where his director, Sharon Pettet, had gone for the interviews she'd scheduled this morning, and the town was too large for him to go door to door looking for her. He should have waited at the liaison center until she returned, but he'd felt useless, superfluous, at the liaison center. Once a location was selected and the locals' approval had been won, he had little to do but take care of administrative details. Things ran too smoothly now. The first years of CV broadcasting had been chaotic, but he'd been more involved then. Happier. Almost as happy as he'd been in film school, two years earlier.

"Hey! Hey, kid! Can you lend me a hand?"

He turned. The pickup truck was parked in a

driveway half a block away. A burly, middle-aged man stood beside it, watching him.

Jordan glanced back toward the limousine. The driver was standing outside, smoking; he'd overheard the request and was grinning. Jordan shrugged, laughed, and went to help the man.

There was a large console television in the back of the pickup. By the time they had it inside and set in a corner of the living room, the older man was sweating and red-faced. He stood leaning on the television while he caught his breath. Finally he looked up at Jordan.

"You're from the network, aren't you?"

Jordan nodded.

"Some of your colleagues gave me a hell of a lot of trouble about bringing this set home. Had to show them proof that I'd ordered it two months ago, before any of you people got here."

"They were only doing their job."

The man snorted. He pulled out a wallet and opened it. Jordan retreated, shaking his head.

"No? Well, can I get you a drink?"

"Thanks, but no. I can't stay."

The man looked disappointed. Jordan knew that in a moment that expression would change to one of hurt, then anger at the aloofness of network people. "Some other time."

"Sure." He followed Jordan as far as the door. "Hey, thanks for the help."

"Anytime."

The heat was brutal. By the time Jordan reached the highway, he was regretting not having accepted the drink. Sharon was still

nowhere in sight, but he spotted a soft-drink
machine, the squat, red shape tucked into a
corner of the service station. He started toward
it.

He could understand the man's anger at
being forced to prove when he'd ordered the
television, but Jordan's sympathies were with
his staff. Despite the contract stipulations that
no essential changes were to be made in life-
style or environment during the year of the
contract, locals were always trying to improve
their image. The early changes were usually
obvious—new furniture, home repairs,
painting—and easy to catch. Things got worse
after the locals began to take the vacations
guaranteed by the contract. They came back
with designer clothes, expensive cars, jewelry,
and other new luxuries that had to be
confiscated at the liaison center for safekeeping.
But what really gave the continuity people
headaches were the inappropriate mannerisms
they picked up, the expressions, the accents.
Jordan sometimes wished they could return to
contracts that restricted residents to location.
They'd had such contracts for the first two
years of CV, but during the second year there
had been two deaths in one town during the
contract period. It had been another network's
show, but the resulting brouhaha, over the
couple's never having enjoyed the financial
rewards they'd sacrificed their privacy to
obtain, had forced all the networks to guarantee
vacations, giving up a crucial degree of control.

Ten years from now, Jordan thought, the

locals would be running the show. But he wouldn't be doing television then. This was only a stepping-stone.

He fed a dollar into the machine. The can of pop that rolled out was warm; he set it on top of the machine without opening it. The light breeze didn't reach him here, but the shade gave some respite from the heat. He shoved his hands into his jeans pockets and looked around. A van bearing the ATN logo was parked two blocks away, where a technician was installing a camera beneath the eaves of a house. Jordan watched for a few minutes before he became aware of someone staring at him from inside the station.

It was a girl, eighteen or so. Long, dark hair. Tanned, but so lightly she seemed pale in comparison with the other natives. Pretty, in a way. Maybe a bit stocky. It was hard to tell, since she wore heavy coveralls.

He gave her his best smile while he ransacked his memory for her name.

By the time he found it, he realized there was nothing friendly about the way she was staring at him. He dropped the smile.

Marianne Fisher.

She'd been one of the five who'd voted against letting the town accept the network contract. Usually dissidents moved away after the contract was signed; it made things easier for all concerned. Sometimes, though, they couldn't leave—not if the town was to keep the contract, and the millions of dollars it meant. Certain key people, identified by the preliminary studies, had to stay, but surely that didn't apply to her. Of the general population, a certain percentage was free to leave. He wouldn't have thought that five people were too many, but the town was very small. He'd have to ask Sharon about this.

Her gaze hadn't wavered. He studied the tense, unyielding set of her shoulders and jaw and decided it would be a waste of time to try talking to her. He shook his head and went back to the limousine.

The driver had opened the door, and Jordan was ducking inside before he realized Sharon was already there, talking to someone on the phone. She said good-bye and hung up, then smiled at Jordan.

"I see you've changed your policy about mixing with the locals."

"Mixing?"

"I saw you come out of Joe Meyer's house."

"Oh. I was just helping him carry a TV inside."

She nodded, still smiling. Her amusement nettled him. He wondered again whether it had been such a good idea to let her supervise all dealings with the locals. He'd sensed resentment beneath her mockery before this; she'd come to regard the territory as her own. But he couldn't deny that she handled the area better than he ever could. It had been three years since he'd heard any *Wunderkind* remarks from industry people, success finally silencing the same comments it had inspired. But the locals didn't know his reputation. It didn't help that he looked younger than twenty-seven.

Sharon had no such image problems. She looked several years younger than her actual age, thirty-five, but her demeanor was so thoroughly professional that not even the oldest locals had ever been heard referring to her as a girl. She was treated with more respect than that. And she was liked. The most frequent comment was, "She understands us."

She should, Barrett reflected, thinking of her doctorate in psychology and six years' experience as a clinical psychologist. She'd never worked with actors, but that had not proved to be a handicap when it came to directing a CV series. Jordan's director for the first CV series, a man with more than twenty years' experience in television, had quit after a few months, leaving the producer working blind. He didn't delude himself about how much of that first year's success had been due to the novelty of continuous viewing. Matters had changed completely after Sharon arrived, with her ability to prepare a CV script, an in-depth study that delineated the locals' relationships and forecast their development. The other networks, entering the game later, had learned from his mistakes, and Sharon's four counterparts were also psychologists. Resident wizards, a rival producer had labeled them. Jordan suspected that the man, like himself, was often baffled by his director.

The limousine's engine came to life quietly. A minute put the town behind them. Jordan stared out at the drab west Texas landscape. There was something he'd meant to ask Sharon, but he couldn't remember it now.

"I'm sorry I kept you waiting," Sharon said.

"It's okay."

"The last interview was going so well, I hated to end it. It's the third marriage I've run across that's breaking up. Two of the couples don't know it yet, but the signs are there."

"You don't think that's too much?"

"It might be, if they all broke up at the same time, but they won't. The couple I interviewed this morning works the night shift."

"Good." Small towns were the most popular locales for CV, but they were the least likely to show the right twenty-four-hour profile of activity. Fortunately, there was a plant nearby that employed several of the locals on its evening and night shifts.

"Martinson thought so. That was him on the phone just now. He wants us back in L.A. tonight, for a party. He thinks we have reason to celebrate."

They celebrated again in late October, when it was apparent they'd won the ratings race. This time, instead of a dozen people at Martinson's Bel-Air home, there were several hundred, and the party was held atop the ATN Building in Los Angeles. The weather was so mild, the translucent panels that usually shielded the rooftop garden had been removed. The music was just loud enough to cover the din of traffic twenty stories below.

Jordan hated these parties, but he was

expected to attend. He'd made his obligatory speech and listened to the others. There'd been praise for him and for Sharon, and the usual bows toward Carl Martinson. No one had mentioned the main reason for their success this season, as in past years: The opposition had dealt themselves out of the game early. CBS had opted for scenery, a picture-postcard Vermont hamlet so dull that the sponsors had demanded its cancellation before three weeks were out; it was replaced by game shows and movies, until a new location could be found. ABC, with its choice of an urban neighborhood, had misjudged the importance of conflict in CV television; it was next to last. NTS, which had selected a Florida Gulf Coast village, had led the ratings for a few weeks. Then it was discovered that the eight beachcombers sharing a house that had been the site's main attraction were actors and actresses sent to the area two years earlier at network expense; they were gone now, and so was the threat that the series had posed. ATN had a forty-five share of the CV audience. NBC's Utah mining town ran a poor second, with a thirty share.

Jordan stayed as long as he thought was necessary, then began to make his way toward the elevator. He was neaarly there when Martinson stopped him.

"Jordan, you're not leaving already?"

Caught off guard, Barrett mumbled something about not feeling well, but Martinson remained standing in his path.

"I thought you looked tired," the programming chief said. "I'm amazed at the amount of work you and Sharon put into these series."

"The worst is over for the year. The script's done. There haven't been any problems. We can take it easier now."

"For the rest of the year."

Barrett nodded, suddenly wary.

"Then you have to start searching for a new location in January."

The producer shrugged. "So it goes."

"Have you thought about extending the series for another year?"

Jordan stared at him. NTS had tried it two years before. The show had sunk without a trace a week into the new season, not even retaining its old audience.

"It's been done before. It didn't work."

"You mean at NTS? But their show wasn't as popular as ours."

"I'm not sure that would make any difference, once it came up against fresh competition from the other networks."

"We won't know for certain unless we try."

"So you're going to ask for an extension of the contract?"

"Not if you're opposed to it, Jordan. It's your decision. But I hate to see you and Sharon putting so much time into the series each year. I'd like you to think about it at least."

And shoulder the responsibility for it if it fails, Jordan thought, but his anger was held in check by pity. Martinson, while superficially jovial, was a frightened man. He saw the viewing audience as a giant maw—a maw that had to be fed, and constantly. If it wasn't fed the right programs, people—even programming chiefs—might have to be sacrificed.

What held Jordan's pity in check was the knowledge that Martinson had overseen more than a few of those sacrifices himself.

"All right," he said reluctantly. "I'll think about it."

He started for the elevator again as soon as Martinson, looking pleased, ambled off. He was reaching for the button when a hand closed on his wrist.

"What did Martinson want?" Sharon asked in a low voice.

The location residents, who never saw her in anything other than the tailored suits she called her business uniforms, wouldn't have recognized her tonight. Dressed in clinging wisps of an iridescent fabric that revealed more than it concealed, her pale gold hair falling free to her waist, she looked more like a starlet than a director.

"He wants to extend the contract."

"And?"

"And what?"

"What's the official party line?"

"I told him I didn't think it was a good idea."

He watched her face for a reaction, but there was none. She'd released his wrist. He pressed the button, and the elevator doors opened.

"Going home already?"

He nodded. For a second he thought she was

going to offer to go home with him. For another second he thought of asking her. When she'd asked him about Martinson, she looked very young. Uncertain. Vulnerable. But the moment hadn't lasted. He was too much in awe of her ability to understand people better than they understood themselves. He'd been attracted to her as long as he'd known her, but five years ago the age difference had held him back. Now it was too late. How could you take a resident wizard to bed?

He said good-night. She was turning back to the party before the elevator doors closed.

Knowing that he would be free much of November and December, Jordan had begun mentioning, as early as August, that he'd be interested in producing a documentary. War had broken out between Chile and Bolivia; he'd let people know that he was following the situation. But he met with no response: The network apparently wasn't going to give the war anything more than the standard news coverage. He was disappointed, but he'd made other plans, just in case.

There was a vacation in Mexico, then three days in Chicago at a national conference of social scientists. He'd been delighted when he was asked to speak, not least because Sharon was jealous, convinced the invitation should have been extended to her. He spent Thanksgiving with relatives in Massachusetts. In early December he was back in Los Angeles. A friend was teaching at UCLA's film school, and

Jordan had promised to be a guest speaker. It didn't turn out the way he'd expected. The students weren't impressed by his title or salary. They wanted to talk about artistry, and they brushed aside everything he'd learn about the sociological merits of CV television in Chicago two weeks before. They hit him with the same questions he'd been asking himself at 3 a.m., the nights he couldn't sleep. He left for Aspen four days earlier than he had originally planned.

He was still there December 20, when Sharon called him.

"How's the skiing?"

"Terrific. We had two inches of powder last night, on a forty-inch base. But I thought you hated snow."

"I do. I'd still rather be there than here."

He looked more closely at the phone's tiny picture screen, examining the office behind her. She was at the liaison center. "What's the problem?"

"One of the locals isn't following the script."

There was a trace of indignation in her voice. It was hard not to smile. "Who is it?"

"Marianne Fisher. And she won't talk to me. She won't talk to anyone on my staff. She says she'll talk only to the person in charge."

Despite himself, he laughed. She frowned but said nothing.

"I'm sorry. It really isn't funny."

"No, it isn't."

"You could just pay her off and ask her to leave." There was a clause in the contract providing for such cases, though they'd never had to use it.

Sharon laughed. "She'd love that, after we told her that we couldn't offer the town the contract unless she stayed. No." She shook her head. "There are too few locals in her age bracket now. We'd risk losing viewer identification if she left. We'll have to think of something else." She hesitated, frowning again. "Should I tell her you're too busy to see her?"

He realized she was asking the question only as a formality; it was what she'd already planned to tell the girl.

"No, I'll talk to her. How soon can you have the plane here?"

"Sometime this afternoon, I suppose. I'll have to check. It will only cause trouble. Are you sure you want to talk to her?"

"Positive."

She nodded, looking unhappy. "It'll take a while to find out about the plane. I'm not even sure where it is right now."

"I'll wait."

It was dark when he finally reached the town after meeting with Sharon for an hour at the liaison center. The weather was cold, but there'd been only a little snow, already wind sorted into grimy drifts along the curb.

The girl's hours at the service station had changed; she worked until midnight now. As they drove down the highway, Jordan was conscious of the cameras mounted where they would observe the limousine's passage. The camera crew, advised of his plans, would be directing the viewers eyes away from him; he didn't exist in the world they saw. It was something he was always aware of, but tonight the thought depressed him. He must be tired.

There was only one car being served at the station, a small electric import, and it drove away as the limousine pulled in. Marianne was back inside already, at the cash register. She stood there watching him as he got out of the limousine and hurried inside.

"Hi." He'd tried to sound cheerful, but his voice rang hollow in his ears. It was ominously silent in the station, without the ever-present wailing of a radio that he'd come to associate with such places. "I heard you wanted to talk to me."

"Not really. It was your people who wanted to talk to me."

"Whichever."

He looked away. There was the usual service-station clutter. Cans of oil and transmission fluid, work gloves, batteries, miscellaneous junk food. He took a few steps away, rounding the edge of the counter. She turned to follow him with her eyes. He noticed a handgun lying on the shelf below the stacks of credit forms. There'd been a wave of station robberies in the area a few years ago. He thought of how clear a target she'd been from outside, standing here in her bright orange uniform. The thought angered him, until he realized the glass would be bulletproof.

"You're here about Bill Morrisey," she said.
He nodded. He'd never heard the name until

an hour before, but Sharon had told him all she'd thought he would need to know. The kid was a high-school football hero, mature for his age, very attractive to the high-school girls, but himself attracted to Marianne, who'd graduated the year before. There was an eight-month age difference. "Which makes her an older woman," Sharon had said, with a laugh.

"I heard you haven't been terribly friendly to him lately. You used to be close friends, before the contract was signed."

She shrugged. "So?"

"We need this relationship," Sharon had told him. "There aren't that many romantic relationships possible in a town this size. The boy really isn't the problem, since he's still in school. But there isn't anyone else for the girl. Not locally, anyway. And we want this particular relationship. The age difference makes it more interesting."

"Do you think you're being fair to Bill? After all, he didn't vote for the contract."

"That's not it."

"Isn't it? You're punishing him."

"You don't understand."

"I understand that you're hurting him. And yourself, too. If you care for him. If you weren't merely pretending to like him, until a few months ago."

"I wasn't pretending. It's just that the contract—the cameras—" She broke off, averting her gaze.

"I know you don't like the contract. But since you chose to stay"—he hesitated, seeing her mouth harden—"you have to live with it. It has almost ten months to run. Do you think you can treat Bill this way for ten months and then start over when the contract period ends? Assuming he's still here then."

He hated himself for playing that last card, but Sharon had told him to use it. "The boy will be graduating from high school in May. He'll be free to leave the town then. She knows that, but it won't hurt to remind her of it."

Whom wouldn't it hurt? The girl was on the verge of tears, and he didn't feel much better.

"I have to go back to the liaison center now," he said, "and I'll be leaving there tomorrow morning. But I'll tell my staff that they're to relay your calls to me from now on, without any delays. I want you call me if there are any other problems."

Her eyes turned toward him again. He waited for the angry response he felt he deserved, but she simply nodded.

He left without saying any more, knowing he'd said too much already. The wind was stronger now, and the night seemed colder than it had a few minutes before. He turned up the collar of his parka, then kicked at a sandwich wrapping that had blown down the highway into his path. He gazed silently at the bleak countryside on the way back to the liaison center, ignoring the driver's attempts at conversation.

Jordan returned to Aspen, and three days later Sharon called him again, this time from Los Angeles.

"Congratulations," she said. "Marianne's following the script again."

He said nothing. She regarded him for a few seconds, one eyebrow raised, then looked down at a piece of paper in her hand.

"There's a memo circulating that says you're willing to talk to her personally, whenever she calls. Is that wise?"

"It seemed like a good idea at the time."

"You've always limited your contract with the locals."

"I doubt she'll take advantage of it."

Sharon shrugged. "If you say so. I called because I thought you should know that Martinson had a survey done of three thousand of our viewers. More than ninety percent liked the idea of keeping this location more than one year."

"That's meaningless. It's too early in the season. August would be too early. The only findings that matter will be Nielsen's, when the new season begins."

"I know that."

"Did you tell Martinson?"

"He didn't ask for my opinion. He hasn't talked to me about it at all. I didn't even know he was doing the survey until the results were published in the newsletter this morning."

"Great."

"I thought so. You wouldn't believe the rumors flying around here."

"They'll die down."

"Sure. But I think you should cut your vacation short. It might help put an end to those rumors if we started the search this week."

"Before the holidays are over? We've never started this early before."

"I know. But you should see the studies my staff has prepared on next year's posibilities.

"That bad?"

She nodded and made a face.

"I promise I'll be there this afternoon."

"I'll have a drink ready. You'll need it."

Barrett saw more snowbound small towns that winter than he'd thought could exist. He came down with a mild case of influenza and suggested to Sharon that they confine their search to the Sun Belt until spring. She told him they couldn't afford the luxury. They couldn't afford the two weeks he spent in the hospital in March, either, recovering from the pneumonia that had developed from the flu, but his doctor didn't ask Sharon for a second opinion.

Martinson paid him a visit after he'd been in the hospital a week. The programming chief made small talk for a few minutes, then told Jordan the network had decided to do a three-part documentary on the war between Bolivia and Chile.

"We've decided to let Dave Youngberg produce it. I was wondering what you thought of him."

Youngberg. Barrett remembered him from film school; they'd graduated the same year. Unlike Jordan, who'd been blessed by the Academy with an Oscar for a student film, Youngberg had had to work his way up, from mailboy to story analyst to assistant producer.

He hadn't made producer until this year.

"He's competent," Jordan admitted. *Competent, but with no real creative flair.*

"I'm glad you think so. I'm really sorry that we can't use you on this project, but the team will be leaving for South America tomorrow. Besides, you're still looking for a new CV location."

He changed the subject then and rattled on cheerfully for some time, seemingly unaware that Jordan was unusually quiet. For a long while after Martinson had gone, Jordan lay staring at the television, not really seeing anything on the screen.

Youngberg.

Jordan received a get-well card from Marianne the next day. She'd called him several times during the past few months. There were no further problems, and she had nothing in particular to say; he sensed she was testing his promise. He didn't mind, though. The calls were a welcome break. He'd watched the series from time to time before his illness, and he had the set on almost constantly while he was in the hospital. She was usually smiling now. Bill Morrisey was happier, and so, Sharon told him, were the viewers. The only people unhappy with the relationship were Morrisey's parents, and their opinions couldn't count against those of thirty million viewers.

There had been only twenty-five million in December, but the CV option had been marketed last year as a Christmas gift. Martinson claimed he wasn't surprised by the jump in ratings. ATN gained five new affiliates the same month, four of them switchovers from other networks. In February the ATN newsletter had printed a note from one of the station owners, explaining that his switch had been motivated by the success of the CV series. The rumor mill ground even faster. But Martinson hadn't brought up the subject of contract extension again with either Jordan or Sharon. Barrett felt as if he was living in the eye of a stationary hurricane, and not even Sharon could forecast when it would move. He was almost reluctant to leave the hospital.

It was the worst spring Jordan could remember. Sharon quoted T.S. Eliot on the subject of April and disappeared into her office for days at a time, sifting through the preliminary studies her staff sent in for any sign that a site might work. Out of sheer desperation, they'd taken options on four towns, but Barrett didn't want to think how they'd do in the ratings. Two other networks announced their CV locations in April, and they seemed no better than those ATN had optioned, but Barrett found little comfort in that. It was beginning to look as if CV's success was limiting its life span; it had become impossible to find a town where the locals weren't already picturing themselves on television.

Youngberg's documentary aired in late April. Both the reviews and the ratings were good.

Barrett was in Louisiana in May, looking over a sleepy bayou fishing village, when the liaison center contacted him. Marianne wanted to see him in person. He would have welcomed any other excuse to leave; the village was another washout. But he had a pretty good idea why Marianne wanted to see him. He postponed leaving until after midnight, and when he finally reached the liaison center, he decided to try to get a few hours' sleep before driving into town.

She was standing outside the door of his suite at five o'clock that morning.

He was still half-asleep when he opened the door, groggily wondering who the hell had taken his memo so literally they'd given her directions to the suite.

"I didn't know you got up so early."

She glared at him, saying nothing. Then her gaze fell to the ATN monogram embroidered on his silk robe; she grimaced and stalked past him, stopping in the middle of the living room.

"Can I get you a cup of coffee?"

No answer.

"Do you mind if I get some for myself?"

She'd turned to stare at him again, but she still didn't speak. He had the eerie feeling that the past months had melted away, that they'd never spoken at all since that first time he'd seen her inside the service station.

He went into the kitchen and came back with a cup of coffee. Gesturing toward a chair, he invited her to sit down. She remained standing. He sighed and sat down on the couch.

"I know you broke up with Bill Morrisey." He also knew she'd been dropped for a girl three years younger, but he decided it was safer not to mention that.

"You knew it was going to happen, too," she said. "Well, didn't you? You knew in December." She was crying openly, not trying to hide her tears.

"Marianne, it was a possibility. It's always a possibility."

She stared down at him, her hands clenched into fists. He set the coffee aside and took her wrists, gently drawing her down to sit beside him.

He opened his mouth to speak, then shut it again. He was going to tell her that Morrisey was only a kid, that she'd get over him, that she'd find someone better, but the words were banal, and they didn't negate the truth she suspected. He had known in December that there was a good chance Morrisey would leave her after a few months. The only thing that had surprised Sharon was that the relationship had lasted so long.

"The contract period's over in a few months," he said at last. "You can leave then. You can afford to move anywhere, do anything you want. You'll be able to meet new people . . ."

She looked away. He turned her face back toward him and kissed her. Her lips tasted of salt.

Sometime later she pulled away, suddenly tense.

"What's wrong?"

"There are cameras here. Are they on?"

He hesitated a moment, then nodded. The system was semiautomatic, activated when the door was opened. He'd shut the cameras off last night, but Marianne's entry would have reactivated them.

"Please . . ."

He stood and crossed the room to the mirror concealing the controls. The system was designed to record meetings between locals and network staff. No one ever saw the films anyway; they were stored in case they might be needed in a contract dispute, but they never had been. He slid the mirror aside and touched the controls. The red indicator light went out.

When he turned back toward her, she was taking off the rest of her clothes.

The weather in early July was torrid. Barrett and most of his staff escaped Los Angeles over the Fourth, but they were back on Tuesday, irresistibly drawn back, like people converging on the scene of an accident.

It had been a depressing morning. He and Sharon had reviewed the search to date, ticking off the forty-three towns that had been studied closely, out of more than two hundred considered, reexamining the seven communities under option. Several minutes had passed since either of them had spoken. Sharon sat at her desk, shuffling papers. Jordan sat at the windows, his hands tucked in his pockets, his eyes half-closed against the glare of the sun-battered streets.

"Martinson called me this morning," he said

when he couldn't stand the silence any longer. "Publicity's after him. They want a firm decision on the new location. They're afraid they won't have time to get their campaign in gear."

"They're afraid . . .'' She laughed, but the sound was humorless.

A minute later she said, "I ran into Jim Orton the other day."

Barrett nodded. Orton was Sharon's counterpart at NTS.

"You wouldn't believe how jealous they are of us."

"Jealous?"

"The ratings."

"Oh." The ratings had been climbing, slowly but steadily, all year.

"He kept asking me about next year's series. They're worried that we'll come up with something better."

"They must know we're still searching."

"I had the impression they're not sure our search is genuine. Their own luck was bad—Orton was willing to admit that—but your reputation scares them. They're expecting you to perform another of your magic tricks at the last minute, pull another winner out of your hat—" She broke off, eyeing him while he shook his head. "Well?"

"Hmm?"

"Are you still in the magic business?"

He stared at her. The words had mocked him, but her tone had been almost pleading. The way she was looking at him both surprised

325

and worried him.

He shook his head again.

"I didn't think so." She glanced down at her desk. "Martinson has asked me to direct another series. It's only an hour a week, but it's prime time. A drama. I'd have to start working on it next week. I could still keep an eye on the current CV script, but I wouldn't be able to help you with the search or draw up a new script for you."

"Are you going to take it?"

"I'd like to. It's a transition I've been wanting to make. A lot of industry people still treat me as an outsider. Working in CV has done wonders for my bank account, but I still don't have any credibility as a director. There's no way I could go back to the clinic." She paused. Jordan watched silently as she toyed with a pen. "I don't know when I'll get another chance like this. If I don't—"

She stopped suddenly, but she didn't have to finish the sentence for him. If she stayed on, and the next CV series wasn't a hit, she might never get another chance as a director.

"You should take it."

"Alan could help you with the search."

"Sure." But Alan Stein, no matter how competent as Sharon's assistant, could never replace her. She knew it. And Martinson had certainly known it when he made her the offer.

He wished her luck with the new series. As soon as she'd left, he placed a call to Martinson.

"What can I do for you, Jordan?"

It wasn't like Martinson to be so brusque; his usual style was one of indirection. But the programming chief knew Barrett would call. He would have no other choice.

"I'd like to talk to you about extending the contract with the current CV location."

Martinson spared Jordan the trouble of securing the locals' approval of the extension by assigning that chore to someone else. He sent Jordan to South America, to produce another documentary on the war there. It was a top news story again, now that Peru had entered the conflict. Jordan was there most of the remainder of the summer. When he returned in late August, his secretary told him there'd been several calls from Marianne Fisher.

"Why didn't you relay them?"

"To Bolivia?"

There was no point in berating her. So he dropped the subject. In a way he was glad that Marianne hadn't reached him. Still, he should call her. Not for a day or two, though. The footage they'd shot for the documentary hadn't been edited yet, and there were a million other matters to attend to.

He was in his office the next afternoon, talking to Sharon on the phone, when he saw Marianne on television. The set was always on and tuned to the CV series, but he rarely paid any attention to it. Now he stared at the screen.

"I'll get back to you later, Sharon," he said abruptly and hung up.

Marianne was walking down the center of the

highway. Luckily, traffic was light; she seemed oblivious of the cars that went by. Jordan leaned forward, his eyes narrowing. The cameraman must have recognized that object in her hand at the same time as Jordan did, because he zoomed in suddenly, focusing on the pistol. She raised her arm then; the shot had been so tight that Jordan lost sight of the gun. He heard it fire, and the screen went dark.

A second later Marianne reappeared, seen from a different angle. The camerman tracked her relentlessly as she made her way down the road. He switched cameras from time to time as she hit yet another lens. Jordan thought the man had to be locked into the same detached fascination he'd recognized in himself a few minutes earlier, when he'd caught himself wondering where she'd learned to shoot so accurately.

Marianne stopped for a few seconds to put a fresh clip into the pistol. She had an audience in the town; white faces could be seen watching from windows and doorways. But none of them ventured out as she continued down the highway, taking out more cameras as she went. There was no one within fifty meters of her when she turned the gun on herself.

He was still facing the screen, too numbed to move, when Sharon came in a few minutes later. He didn't hear the door open. He didn't know she was there until she spoke.

"I've talked to our lawyers." Her face was pale, her voice low but shaky. "They say we aren't liable for this incident. If the girl's neighbors pressured her into signing the contract, the network can't be held responsible for that.''

He looked away, sickened.

"I know you met with her at the liaison center in May. You didn't say anything to her then about not extending the contract, did you? Jordan, please answer me. This is important.''

"I said something to her about the contract being over in a few months, that she'd be happier then . . .''

"That's all right. We didn't know then that we were going to extend the contract. But you're sure you didn't give her any guarantees? You didn't promise her that we wouldn't extend her contract?''

He shook his head.

"Good. Then with the film of your meeting to back us up, we shouldn't . . .'' Her voice trailed off as he turned to stare at her blindly.

"Oh, no, Jordan. You didn't—'' She whirled and ran out of the office.

He looked back at the screen. The ambulance finally arrived; it nudged slowly through the crowd that had gathered. Jordan watched as the body was placed on a stretcher and then lifted into an ambulance. The doors slammed shut, and the people scattered, clearing out of the way as the vehicle started moving.

His phone began to ring, the noise soft but insistent against the background of the wailing siren.

He let it ring. Finally it stopped, leaving only the sound of the siren, fading.

SANDKINGS

By George R.R. Martin

Simon Kress lived alone in a sprawling manor house among dry, rocky hills fifty kilometers from the city. So, when he was called away unexpectedly on business, he had no neighbors he could conveniently impose on to take his pets. The carrion hawk was no problem; it roosted in the unused belfry and customarily fed itself anyway. The shambler Kress simply shooed outside and left to fend for itself; the little monster would gorge on slugs and birds and rockjocks. But the fish tank, stocked with genuine earth piranha, posed a difficulty. Finally Kress just threw a haunch of beef into the huge tank. The piranha could always eat one another if he were detained longer than expected. They'd done it before. It amused him.

Unfortunately, he was detained *much* longer than expected this time. When he finally returned, all the fish were dead. So was the carrion hawk. The shambler had climbed up the belfry and eaten it. Kress was vexed.

The next day he flew his skimmer to Asgard, a journey of some two hundred kilometers. Asgard was Baldur's largest city and boasted the oldest and largest starport as well. Kress liked to impress his friends with animals that were unusual, entertaining, and expensive; Asgard was the place to buy them.

This time, though, he had poor luck. Xenopets had closed its doors, t'Etherane the Petseller tried to foist another carrion hawk off on him, and Strange Waters offered nothing more exotic than piranha, glowsharks, and spider squids. Kress had had all those; he wanted something new, something that would stand out.

Near dusk he found himself walking down Rainbow Boulevard, looking for places he had not patronized before. So close to the starport, the street was lined by importers' marts. The big corporate emporiums had impressive long windows, in which rare and costly alien artifacts reposed on felt cushions against dark drapes that made the interiors of the stores a mystery. Between them were the junk shops—narrow, nasty little places whose display areas were crammed with all manner of offworld bric-a-brac. Kress tried both kinds of shops, with equal dissatisfaction.

Then he came across a store that was different.

It was very near the port. Kress had never been there before. The shop occupied a small, single-story building of moderate size, set between a euphoria bar and a temple brothel of the Secret Sisterhood. Down this far, Rainbow Boulevard grew tacky. The shop itself was unusual. Arresting.

The windows were full of mist—now a pale red, now the gray of true fog, now sparkling and golden. The mist swirled and eddied and glowed faintly from within. Kress glimpsed objects in the window—machines, pieces of art, other things he could not recognize—but he could not get a good look at any of them. The mists flowed sensuously around them, displaying a bit of first one thing and then another, then cloaking all. It was intriguing.

As he watched, the mist began to form letters. One word at a time. Kress stood and read.

WO. AND. SHADE. IMPORTERS. ARTIFACTS. ART. LIFEFORMS. AND. MISC.

The letters stopped. Through the fog Kress saw something moving. That was enough for him, that and the LIFEFORMS in their advertisement. He swept his walking cloak over his shoulder and entered the store.

Inside, Kress felt disoriented. The interior seemed vast, much larger than he would have guessed from the relatively modest frontage. It was dimly lit, peaceful. The ceiling was a starscape, complete with spiral nebulas, very dark and realistic, very nice. All the counters shone faintly, to better display the merchandise within. The aisles were carpeted with ground fog. It came almost to his knees in places and swirled about his feet as he walked.

"Can I help you?"

She almost seemed to have risen from the fog. Tall and gaunt and pale, she wore a practical gray jumpsuit and a strange little cap that rested well back on her head.

"Are you Wo or Shade?" Kress asked. "Or only sales help?"

"Jala Wo, ready to serve you," she replied. "Shade does not see customers. We have no sales help."

"You have quite a large establishment," Kress said. "Odd that I have never heard of you before."

"We have only just opened this shop on Baldur," the woman said. "We have franchises on a number of other worlds, however. What can I sell you? Art, perhaps? You have the look of a collector. We have some fine Nor T'alush crystal carvings."

"No," Kress said. "I own all the crystal carvings I desire. I came to see about a pet."

"A lifeform?"

"Yes."

"Alien?"

"Of course."

"We have a mimic in stock. From Celia's World. A clever little simian. Not only will it learn to speak, but eventually it will mimic your voice, inflections, gestures, even facial expressions."

"Cute," said Kress. "And common. I have no use for either, Wo. I want something exotic. Unusual. And not cute. I detest cute animals. At the moment I own a shambler. Imported from Cotho, at no mean expense. From time to time I feed him a litter of unwanted kittens. That is what I think of *cute*. Do I make myself understood?''

Wo smiled enigmatically. ''Have you ever owned an animal that worshipped you?'' she asked.

Kress grinned. ''Oh, now and again. But I don't require worship, Wo. Just entertainment.''

''You misunderstand me,'' Wo said, still wearing her strange smile. ''I meant *worship* literally.''

''What are you talking about?''

''I think I have just the thing for you,'' Wo said. ''Follow me.''

She led him between the radiant counters and down a long, fog-shrouded aisle beneath false starlight. They passed through a wall of mist into another section of the store, then stopped in front of a large plastic tank. An aquarium, Kress thought.

Wo beckoned. He stepped closer and saw that he was wrong. It was a terrarium. Within lay a miniature desert about two meters square. Pale sand tinted scarlet by wan red light. Rocks: basalt and quartz and granite. In each corner of the tank stood a castle.

Kress blinked and peered and corrected himself; actually, there were only three castles standing. The fourth leaned, a crumbled, broken ruin. The three others were crude but intact, carved of stone and sand. Over their battlements and through their rounded porticoes tiny creatures climbed and scrambled. Kress pressed his face against the plastic.

"Insects?" he asked.

"No," Wo replied. "A much more complex lifeform. More intelligent as well. Smarter than your shambler by a considerable amount. They are called sandkings."

"Insects," Kress said, drawing back from the tank. "I don't care how complex they are." He frowned. "And kindly don't try to gull me with this talk of intelligence. These things are far too small to have anything but the most rudimentary brains."

"They share hiveminds," Wo said. "Castle minds, in this case. There are only three organisms in the tank, actually. The fourth died. You see how her castle has fallen."

Kress looked back at the tank. "Hiveminds, eh? Interesting." He frowned again. "Still, it is only an oversized ant farm. I'd hoped for something better."

"They fight wars."

"Wars? Hmmm." Kress looked again.

"Note the colors, if you will," Wo said. She pointed to the creatures that swarmed over the nearest castle. One was scrabbling at the tank wall. Kress studied it. To his eyes, it still looked like an insect. Barely as long as his fingernail, six-limbed, with six tiny eyes set all around its body. A wicked set of mandibles clacked visibly, while two long, fine antennae wove patterns in the air. Antennae, mandibles, eyes, and legs were sooty black, but the dominant color was the burnt orange of its armor plating. "It's an insect," Kress repeated.

"It is not an insect," Wo insisted calmly.

"The armored exoskeleton is shed when the sandkings grows larger. *If* it grows larger. In a tank this size, it won't." She took Kress by the elbow and led him around the tank to the next castle. "Look at the colors here."

He did. They were different. Here the sandkings had bright red armor; antennae, mandibles, eyes, and legs were yellow. Kress glanced across the tank. The denizens of the third live castle were off-white, with red trim. "Hmmm," he said.

"They war, as I said," Wo told him. "They even have truces and alliances. It was an alliance that destroyed the fourth castle in this tank. The blacks were becoming too numerous, and so the others joined forces to destroy them."

Kress remained unconvinced. "Amusing, no doubt. But insects fight wars, too."

"Insects do not worship," Wo said.

"Eh?"

Wo smiled and pointed at the castle. Kress stared. A face had been carved into the wall of the higher tower. He recognized it. It was Jala Wo's face. "How . . .?"

"I projected a hologram of my face into the tank, then kept it there for a few days. The face of god, you see? I feed them. I am always close. The sandkings have a rudimentary psionic sense. Proximity telepathy. They sense me and worship me by using my face to decorate their buildings. All the castles have them, see." They did.

On the castle, the face of Jala Wo was serene,

peaceful, and very lifelike. Kress marveled at the workmanship. "How do they do it?"

"The foremost legs double as arms. They even have fingers of a sort, three small, flexible tendrils. And they cooperate well, both in building and in battle. Remember, all the mobiles of one color share a single mind."

"Tell me more," Kress requested.

Wo smiled. "The maw lives in the castle. Maw is my name for her—a pun, if you will. The thing is mother and stomach both. Female, large as your fist, immobile. Actually, *sandking* is a bit of a misnomer. The mobiles are peasants and warriors. The real ruler is a queen. But that analogy is faulty as well. Considered as a whole, each castle is a single hermaphroditic creature."

"What do they eat?"

"The mobiles eat pap, predigested food obtained inside the castle. They get it from the maw after she has worked on it for several days. Their stomachs can't handle anything else. If the maw dies, they soon die as well. The maw . . . the maw eats anything. You'll have no special expense there. Table scraps will do excellently."

"Live food?" Kress asked.

Wo shrugged. "Each maw eats mobiles from the other castles, yes."

"I am intrigued," he admitted. "If only they weren't so small!"

"Yours can be larger. These sandkings are small because their tank is small. They seem to limit their growth to fit available space. If I moved these to a larger tank, they'd start growing again."

"Hmmm. My piranha tank is twice this size and vacant. It could be cleaned out, filled with sand . . ."

"Wo and Shade would take care of the installation. It would be our pleasure."

"Of course," Kress said, "I would expect four intact castles."

"Certainly," Wo said.

They began to haggle about the price.

Three days later Jala Wo arrived at Simon Kress's estate, with dormant sandkings and a work crew to take charge of the installation. Wo's assistants were aliens unlike any Kress was familiar with—squat, broad bipeds with four arms and bulging, multifaceted eyes. Their skin was thick and leathery and twisted into horns and spines and protrusions at odd places upon their bodies. But they were very strong, and good workers. Wo ordered them about in a musical tongue that Kress has never heard before.

In a day it was done. They moved his piranha tank to the center of his spacious living room, arranged couches on either side of it for better viewing, scrubbed it clean, and filled it two thirds of the way up with sand and rock. Then they installed a special lighting system, both to provide the dim red illumination the sandkings preferred and to project holographic images into the tank. On top they mounted a sturdy plastic cover, with a feeder mechanism built in. "This way you can feed your sandkings without removing the top of the tank," Wo explained.

"You would not want to take any chances on the mobiles escaping."

The cover also included climate-control devices, to condense just the right amount of moisture from the air. "You want it dry, but not too dry," Wo said.

Finally one of the four-armed workers climbed into the tank and dug deep pits in the four corners. One of his companions handed the dormant maws over to him, removing them, one by one, from their frosted cryonic traveling cases.

They were nothing to look at. Kress decided they resembled nothing so much as mottled, half-spoiled chunks of raw meat. Each with a mouth.

The alien buried them, one in each corner of the tank. Then the work party sealed it all up and took their leave.

"The heat will bring the maws out of dormancy," Wo said. "In less than a week mobiles will begin to hatch and burrow up to the surface. Be certain to give them plenty of food. They will need all their strength until they are well established. I would estimate that you will have castles rising in about three weeks."

"And my face? When will they carve my face?"

"Turn on the hologram after about a month," she advised him, "and be patient. If you have any questions, please call. Wo and Shade are at your service." She bowed and left.

Kress wandered back to the tank and lit a joy stick. The desert was still and empty. He drummed his fingers impatiently against the plastic and frowned.

On the fourth day Kress thought he glimpsed motion beneath the sand—subtle subterranean stirrings.

On the fifth day he saw his first mobile, a lone white.

On the sixth day he counted a dozen of them, whites and reds and blacks. The oranges were tardy. He cycled through a bowl of half-decayed table scraps. The mobiles sensed it at once, rushed to it, and began to drag pieces back to their respective corners. Each color group was highly organized. They did not fight. Kress was a bit disappointed, but he decided to give them time.

The oranges made their appearance on the eighth day. By then the other sandkings had begun carrying small stones and erecting crude fortifications. They still did not war. At the moment they were only half the size of those he had seen at Wo and Shade's, but Kress thought they were growing rapidly.

The castles began to rise midway through the second week. Organized battalions of mobiles dragged heavy chunks of sandstone and granite back to their corners, where other mobiles were pushing sand into place with mandibles and tendrils. Kress had purchased a pair of magnifying goggles so that he could watch them work wherever they might go in the tank. He wandered around and around the tall plastic walls, observing. It was fascinating.

The castles were a bit plainer than Kress would have liked, but he had an idea about that. The next day he cycled through some obsidian and flakes of colored glass along with the food. Within hours they had been incorporated into the castle walls.

The black castle was the first completed, followed by the white and red fortresses. The oranges were last, as usual. Kress took his meals into the living room and ate, seated on the couch so he could watch. He expected the first war to break out any hour now.

He was disappointed. Days passed, the castles grew taller and more grand, and Kress seldom left the tank except to attend to his sanitary needs and to answer critical business calls. But the sandkings did not war. He was getting upset.

Finally he stopped feeding them.

Two days after the table scraps had ceased to fall from their desert sky, four black mobiles surrounded an orange and dragged it back to their maw. They maimed it first, ripping off its mandibles and antennae and limbs, and carried it through the shadowed main gate of their miniature castle. It never emerged. Within an hour more than forty orange mobile marched across the sand and attacked the blacks' corner. They were outnumbered by the blacks that came rushing up from the depths. When the fighting was over, the attackers had been slaughtered. The dead and dying were taken down to feed the black maw.

Kress, delighted, congratulated himself on his genius.

When he put food into the tank the following day, a three-cornered battle broke out over its possession. The whites were the big winners.

After that, war followed war.

Almost a month to the day after Jala Wo had delivered the sandkings, Kress turned on the holographic projector, and his face materialized in the tank. It turned, slowly, around and around, so that his gaze fell on all four castles equally. Kress thought it rather a good likeness; it had his impish grin, wide mouth, full cheeks. His blue eyes sparkled, his gray hair was carefully arrayed in a fashionable sidesweep, his eyebrows were thin and sophisticated.

Soon enough the sandkings set to work. Kress fed them lavishly while his image beamed down at them from the sky. Temporarily the wars stopped. All activity was directed toward worship.

His face merged on the castle walls.

At first all four carvings looked alike to him, but as the work continued and Kress studied the reproductions, he began to detect subtle differences in technique and execution. The reds were the most creative, using tiny flakes of slate to put the gray in his hair. The white idol seemed young and mischievous to him, while the face shaped by the blacks—although virtually the same, line for line—struck him as wise and benevolent. The orange sandkings, as usual, were last and least. The wars had not gone well for them, and their castle was sad compared to those of the others. The image they carved was crude and cartoonish, and they seemed to intend to leave it this way. When they stopped work on the face, Kress grew quite piqued with them, but there really was nothing he could do.

When all of the sandkings had finished their Kress faces, he turned off the projector and decided that it was time to have a party. His friends would be impressed. He could even stage a war for them, he thought. Humming happily to himself, he began drawing up a guest list.

The party was a wild success.

Kress invited thirty people: a handful of close friends who shared his amusements, a few former lovers, and a collection of business and social rivals who could not afford to ignore his summons. He knew some of them would be discomfited and even offended by his sandkings. He counted on it. He customarily considered his parties a failure unless at least one guest walked out in high dudgeon.

On impulse he added Jala Wo's name to his list. "Bring Shade if you like," he added when he dictated the invitations to her.

Her acceptance surprised him just a bit: "Shade, alas, will be unable to attend. He does not go to social functions. As for myself, I look forward to the chance to see how your sandkings are doing."

Kress ordered a sumptuous meal. And when at last the conversation had died down and most of his guests had gotten silly on wine and joy sticks, he shocked them by personally scraping their table leavings into a large bowl. "Come, all of you," he commanded. "I want to introduce you to my newest pets." Carrying the bowl, he conducted them into his living room.

The sandkings lived up to his fondest expectations. He had starved them for two days in preparation, and they were in a fighting mood. While the guests ringed the tank, looking through the magnifying glasses that Kress had thoughtfully provided, the sandkings waged a glorious battle over the scraps. He counted almost sixty dead mobiles when the struggle was over. The reds and whites, which had recently formed an alliance, came off with most of the food.

"Kress, you're disgusting," Cath m'Lane told him. She had lived with him for a short time two years before, until her soppy sentimentality almost drove him mad. "I was a fool to come back here. I thought perhaps you'd changed and wanted to apologize." She had never forgiven him for the time his shambler had eaten an excessively cute puppy of which she had been fond. "Don't *ever* invite me here again, Simon." She strode out, accompanied by her current lover, to a chorus of laughter.

Kress's other guests were full of questions.

Where did the sandkings come from? they wanted to know. "From Wo and Shade, Importers," he replied, with a polite gesture toward Jala Wo, who had remained quiet and apart throughout most of the evening.

Why did they decorate their castles with his

likeness? "Because I am the source of all good things. Surely you know that?" This retort brought a round of chuckles.

Will they fight again? "Of course, but not tonight. Don't worry. There will be other parties."

Jad Rakkis, who was an amateur xenologist, began talking about other social insects and the wars they fought. "These sandkings are amusing, but nothing really. You ought to read about Terran soldier ants, for instance."

"Sandkings are not insects," Jala Wo said sharply, but Jad was off and running, and no one paid her the slightest attention. Kress smiled at her and shrugged.

Malada Blane suggested they have a betting pool the next time they got together to watch a war, and everyone was taken with the idea. An animated discussion about rules and odds ensued. It lasted for almost an hour. Finally the guests began to take their leave.

Jala Wo was the last to depart. "So," Kress said to her when they were alone, "it appears my sandkings are a hit."

"They are doing well," Wo said. "Already they are larger than my own."

"Yes," Kress said, "except for the oranges."

"I had noticed that," Wo replied. "They seem few in number, and their castle is shabby."

"Well, someone must lose," Kress said. "The oranges were late to emerge and get established. They have suffered for it."

"Pardon," said Wo, "but might I ask if you

are feeding your sandking sufficiently?"

Kress shrugged. "They diet from time to time. It makes them fiercer."

She frowned. "There is no need to starve them. Let them war in their own time, for their own reasons. It is their nature, and you will witness conflicts that are delightfully subtle and complex. The constant war brought on by hunger is artless and degrading."

Kress repaid Wo's frown with interest. "You are in my house, Wo, and here I am the judge of what is degrading. I fed the sandkings as you advised, and they did not fight."

"You must have patience."

"No," Kress said. "I am their master and their god, after all. Why should I wait on their impulses? They did not war often enough to suit me. I have corrected the situation."

"I see," said Wo. "I will discuss the matter with Shade."

"It is none of your concern, or his," Kress snapped.

"I must bid you good-night, then." Wo said with resignation. But as she slipped into her coat to leave, she fixed him with a final, disapproving stare. "Look to your faces, Simon Kress," she warned him. "Look to your faces." And she departed.

Puzzled, he wandered back to the tank and stared at the castles. His faces were still there, as ever. Except—he snatched up his magnifying goggles and slipped them on. He studied the faces for long moments. Even then exactly what it was, was hard to make out. But it seemed to him that the expression on the faces had changed slightly, that his smile was somehow twisted so that it seemed a touch malicious. But it was a very subtle change—if it was a change at all. Kress finally put it down to his suggestibility, and he resolved not to invite Jala Wo to any more of his gatherings.

Over the next few months Kress and about a dozen of his favorites got together weekly for what he liked to call his "war games." Now that his initial fascination with the sandkings was past, Kress spent less time around his tank and more on his business affairs and his social life, but he still enjoyed having a few friends over for a war or two. He kept the combinations sharp on a constant edge of hunger. It had severe effects on the orange sandkings, which dwindled visibly until Kress began to wonder whether their maw was dead. But the others did well enough.

Sometimes at night when he could not sleep, Kress would take a bottle of wine into the living room, where the red gloom of his miniature desert provided the only light. He would drink and watch for hours, alone. There was usually a fight going on somewhere; when there was not, he could easily start one by dropping some small morsel of food into the tank.

Kress's companions began betting on the weekly battles, as Malada Blane had suggested. Kress won a goodly amount by betting on the whites, which had become the most powerful and most numerous colony in the tank and which had the grandest castle. One week he slid the corner of the tank top aside, and he dropped the food close to the white castle instead of on the central battleground, where he usually let food fall. So the others had to attack the whites in their stronghold to get any food at all. They tried. The whites were brilliant in defense. Kress won a hundred standards from Jad Rakkis.

Rakkis, in fact, lost heavily on the sandkings almost every week. He pretended to a vast knowledge of them and their ways, claiming that he had studied them after the first party, but he had no luck when it came to placing his bets. Kress suspected that Jad's claims were empty boasting. He had tried to study the sandkings a bit himself, in a moment of idle curiosity, tying in to the library to find out what world his pets originally came from. But the library had no listing for sandkings. He wanted to get in touch with Wo and ask her about it, but he had other concerns, and the matter kept slipping his mind.

Finally, after a month in which his losses totaled more than a thousand standards, Rakkis arrived at the war games. He was carrying a small pastic case under his arm. Inside was a spiderlike thing covered with fine golden hair.

"A sand spider," Rakkis announced. "From Cathaday. I got it this afternoon from t'Etherane the Petseller. Usually they remove the poison sacs, but this one is intact. Are you game, Simon? I want my money back. I'll bet a thousand standards, sand spider against sand-kings."

349

Kress studied the spider in its plastic prison. His sandkings had grown—they were twice as large as Wo's, as she'd predicted—but they were still dwarfed by this thing. It was venomed, and they were not. Still, there were an awful lot of them. Besides, the endless sandking wars lately had begun to grow tiresome. The novelty of the match intrigued him.

"Done," Kress said. "Jad, you are a fool. The sandkings will just keep coming until this ugly creature of yours is dead."

"You are the fool, Simon," Rakkis replied, smiling. "The Cathadayan sand spider customarily feeds on burrowers that hide in nooks and crevices, and—well, watch—it will go straight into those castles and eat the maws."

Kress scowled amid general laughter. He hadn't counted on that. "Get on with it," he said irritably. Then he went to freshen his drink.

The spider was too large to be cycled conveniently through the food chamber. Two other guests helped Rakkis slide the tank top slightly to one side, and Malada Blane handed his case up to him. He shook the spider out. It landed lightly on a miniature dune in front of the red castle and stood confused for a moment, mouth working, legs twitching menacingly.

"Come on," Rakkis urged. They all gathered around the tank. Kress found his magnifies and slipped them on. If he was going to lose a thousand standards, at least he wanted a good view of the action.

The sandkings had seen the invader. All over the red castle activity had ceased. The small scarlet mobiles were frozen, watching.

The spider began to move toward the dark promise of the gate. From the tower above, Simon Kress's countenance stared down impassively.

At once there was a flurry of activity. The nearest red mobiles formed themselves into two wedges and streamed over the sand toward the spider. More warriors erupted from inside the castle and assembled in a triple line to guard where approach to the underground chamber where the maw lived. Scouts came scuttling over the dunes, recalled to fight.

Battle was joined.

The attacking sandkings washed over the spider. Mandibles snapped shut on legs and abdomen, and clung. Reds raced up the golden legs to the invader's back. They bit and tore. One of them found an eye and ripped it loose with tiny yellow tendrils. Kress smiled and pointed.

But they were *small*, and they had no venom, and the spider did not stop. Its legs flicked sandkings off to either side. Its dripping jaws found others and left them broken and stiffening. Already a dozen of the reds lay dying. The sand spider came on and on. It strode straight through the triple line of guardians before the castle. The lines closed around it, covered it, waging desperate battle. A team of sandkings had bitten off one of the spider's legs. Defenders leaped from atop the towers to land on the twitching, heavy mass.

Lost beneath the sandkings, the spider somehow lurched down into the darkness and vanished.

Rakkis let out a long breath. He looked pale. "Wonderful," someone else said. Malada Blane chuckled deep in her throat.

"Look," said Idi Noreddian, tugging Kress by the arm.

They had been so intent on the struggle in the corner that none of them had noticed the activity elsewhere in the tank. But now the castle was still, and the sands were empty save for dead red mobiles, and now they saw.

Three armies were drawn up before the red castle. They stood quite still, in perfect array, rank after rank of sandkings, orange and white and black—waiting to see what emerged from the depths.

Kress smiled. *"A cordon sanitaire,"* he said. "And glance at the other castles, if you will, Jad."

Rakkis did, and he swore. Teams of mobiles were sealing up the gates with sand and stone. If the spider somehow survived this encounter, it would find no easy entrance at the other castles. "I should have brought four spiders," Rakkis said. "Still I've won. My spider is down there right now, eating your damned maw."

Kress did not reply. He waited. There was motion in the shadows.

All at once red mobiles began pouring out of the gate. They took their positions on the castle and began repairing the damage that the spider had wrought. The other armies dissolved and began to retreat to their respective corners.

"Jad," Kress said, "I think you are a bit confused about who is eating whom."

The following week Rakkis brought four slim silver snakes. The sandkings dispatched them without much trouble.

Next he tried a large black bird. It ate more than thirty white mobiles, and its thrashing and blundering virtually destroyed that castle, but ultimately its wings grew tired, and the sandkings attacked in force wherever it landed.

After that it was a case of insects, armored beetles not too unlike the sandkings themselves. But stupid, stupid. An allied force of oranges and blacks broke their formation, divided them, and butchered them.

Rakkis began giving Kress promissory notes.

It was around that time that Kress met Cath m'Lane again, one evening when he was dining in Asgard at his favorite restaurant. He stopped at her table briefly and told her about the war games, inviting her to join them. She flushed, then regained control of herself and grew icy. "Someone has to put a stop to you, Simon. I guess it's going to be me," she said.

Kress shrugged and enjoyed a lovely meal and thought no more about her threat.

Until a week later, when a small, stout woman arrived at his door and showed him a police wristband. "We've had complaints," she said. "Do you keep a tank full of dangerous insects, Kress?"

"Not insects," he said, furious. "Come, I'll show you."

When she had seen the sandkings, she shook her head. "This will never do. What do you know about these creatures anyway? Do you know what world they're from? Have they been cleared by the Ecological Board? Do you have a license for these things? We have a report that they're carnivores and possibly dangerous. We also have a report that they are semisentient. Where did you get these creatures anyway?"

"From Wo and Shade," Kress replied.

"Never heard of them," the woman said. "Probably smuggled them in, knowing our ecologists would never approve them. No, Kress, this won't do. I'm going to confiscate this tank and have it destroyed. And you're going to have to expect a few fines as well."

Kress offered her a hundred standards to forget all about him and his sandkings.

She *tsked*. "Now I'll have to add attempted bribery to the charges against you."

Not until he raised the figure to two thousand standards was she willing to be persuaded. "It's not going to be easy, you know," she said. "There are forms to be altered, records to be wiped. And getting a forged license from the ecologists will be time-consuming. Not to mention dealing with the complainant. What if she calls again?"

"Leave her to me," Kress said. "Leave her to me."

He thought about it for a while. That night

he made some calls.

First he got t'Etherane the Petseller. "I want to buy a dog," he said. "A puppy."

The round-faced merchant gawked at him. "A puppy? That is not like you, Simon. Why don't you come in? I have a lovely choice."

"I want a very specific *kind* of puppy," Kress said. "Take notes. I'll describe to you what it must look like."

Afterwards he punched for Idi Noreddian. "Idi," he said, "I want you out here tonight with your holo equipment. I have a notion to record a sandking battle. A present for one of my friends."

The night after they made the recording, Kress stayed up late. He absorbed a controversial new drama in his sensorium, fixed himself a small snack, smoked a couple of joy sticks, and broke out a bottle of wine. Feeling very happy with himself, he wandered into the living room, glass in hand.

The lights were out. The red glow of the terrarium made the shadows look flushed and feverish. Kress walked over to survey his domain, curious as to how the blacks were doing in the repairs of their castle. The puppy had left it in ruins.

The restoration went well. But as Kress inspected the work through his magnifiers, he chanced to glance close at the face on the sandcastle wall. It startled him.

He drew back, blinked, took a healthy gulp of wine, and looked again.

The face on the wall was still his. But it was all wrong, all *twisted*. His cheeks were bloated and piggish; his smile was a crooked leer. He looked impossibly malevolent.

Uneasy, he moved around the tank to inspect the other castles. They were each a bit different, but ultimately all the same.

The oranges had left out most of the fine detail, but the result still seemed monstrous, crude; a brutal mouth and mindless eyes.

The reds gave him a satanic, twitching sort of smile. His mouth did odd, unlovely things at its corners.

The whites, his favorites, had carved a cruel idiot god.

Kress flung his wine across the room in rage. "You *dare*," he said under his breath. "Now you won't eat for a week, you damned . . ." His voice was shrill. "I'll teach you."

He had an idea. He strode out of the room, then returned a moment later with an antique iron throwing sword in his hand. It was a meter long, and the point was still sharp. Kress smiled, climbed up, and moved the tank cover aside just enough to give him working room, exposing one corner of the desert. He leaned down and jabbed the sword at the white castle below him. He waved it back and forth, smashing towers and ramparts and walls. Sand and stone collapsed, burying the scrambling mobiles. A flick of his wrist obliterated the features of the insolent, insulting caricature that the sandkings had made of his face. Then he poised the point of the sword above the dark mouth that opened down into the maw's chamber; he thrust with all his strength, meeting with resistance. He heard a soft, squishing sound. All the mobiles trembled and collapsed. Satisfied, Kress pulled back.

He watched for a moment, wondering whether he had killed the maw. The point of the throwing sword was wet and slimy. But finally the white sandkings began to move again—feebly, slowly—but they moved.

He was preparing to slide the cover back into place and move on to a second castle when he felt something crawling on his hand.

He screamed, dropping the sword, and brushed the sandking from his flesh. It fell to the carpet, and he ground it beneath his heel, crushing it thoroughly long after it was dead. It had crunched when he stepped on it. After that, trembling, he hurriedly sealed the tank up again. He rushed off to shower and inspected himself carefully. He boiled his clothing.

Later, after drinking several glasses of wine, he returned to the living room. He was a bit ashamed of the way he had been terrified by the sandking. But he was not about to open the tank again. From then on, the cover would stay sealed permanently. Still, he had to punish the others.

He decided to lubricate his mental processes with another glass of wine. As he finished it, an inspiration came to him. He went to the tank and made a few adjustments to the humidity controls.

By the time he fell asleep on the couch, his

wine glass still in his hand, the sand castles were melting in the rain.

Kress woke to angry pounding on his door.

He sat up, groggy, his head throbbing. Wine hangovers were always the worst, he thought. He lurched to the entry chanber.

Cath m'Lane was outside. "You monster," she said, her face swollen and puffy and streaked with tears. "I cried all night, damn you. But no more, Simon, no more."

"Easy," he said, holding his head. "I've got a hangover."

She swore and shoved him aside and pushed her way into his house. The shambler came peering round a corner to see what the noise was. She spat at it and stalked into the living room, Kress trailing ineffectually after her. "Hold on," he said, "where do you . . . you can't . . ." He stopped suddenly horror-struck. She was carrying a heavy sledgehammer in her left hand. "No," he said.

She went directly to the sandkings' tank. "You like the little charmers so much, Simon? Then you can live with them."

"Cath!" he shrieked.

Gripping the hammer with both hands, she swung as hard as she could against the side of the tank. The sound of the impact set Kress's head to screaming, and he made a low, blubbering sound of despair. But the plastic held.

She swung again. This time there was a *crack,* and a network of thin lines appeared in the wall of the tank.

Kress threw himself at her as she drew back her hammer to take a third swing. They went down flailing and rolled over. She lost her grip on the hammer and tried to throttle him, but Kress wrenched free and bit her on the arm, drawing blood. They both staggered to their feet, panting.

"You should see yourself, Simon," she said grimly. "Blood dripping from your mouth. You look like one of your pets. How do you like the taste?"

"Get out," he said. He saw the throwing sword where it had fallen the night before, and he snatched it up. "Get out," he repeated, waving the sword for emphasis. "Don't go near that tank again."

She laughed at him. "You wouldn't dare," she said. She bent to pick up the hammer.

Kress shrieked at her and lunged. Before he quite knew what was happening, the iron blade had gone clear through her abdomen. Cath m'Lane looked at him wonderingly and down at the sword. Kress fell back, whimpering. "I didn't mean . . . I only wanted . . ."

She was transfixed, bleeding, nearly dead, but somehow she did not fall. "You monster," she managed to say, though her mouth was full of blood. And she whirled, impossibly, the sword in her, and swung with her last strength, and Cath m'Lane was buried beneath an avalanche of plastic and sand and mud.

Kress made small hysterical noises and scrambled up onto the couch.

Sandkings were emerging from the muck on

his living-room floor. They were crawling across Cath's body. A few of them ventured tentatively out across the carpet. More followed.

He watched as a column took shape, a living, writhing square of sandkings, bearing something—something slimy and featureless, a piece of raw meat as big as a man's head. They began to carry it away from the tank. It pulsed.

That was when Kress broke and ran.

Before he found the courage to return home, he ran to his skimmer and flew to the nearest city, some fifty kilometers away, almost sick with fear. But, once safely away, he found a small restaurant, downed several mugs of coffee and two anti-hangover tabs, ate a full breakfast, and gradually regained his composure.

It had been a dreadful morning, but dwelling on that would solve nothing. He ordered more coffee and considered his situation with icy rationality.

Cath m'Lane was dead at his hand. Could he report it and plead that it had been an accident? Unlikely. He had run her through, after all, and he had already told that policer to leave her to him. He would have to get rid of the evidence and hope that Cath had not told anyone her plans for the day. It was very unlikely she had. She could only have gotten his gift late last night. She said that she had cried all night, and she was alone when she arrived. Very well, he had one body and one skimmer to dispose of.

That left the sandkings. They might prove more of a difficulty. No doubt they had all

escaped by now. The thought of them around
his house, in his bed and his clothes, infesting
his food—it made his flesh crawl. He shuddered
and overcame his revulsion. It really shouldn't
be too hard to kill them, he reminded himself.
He didn't have to account for every mobile.
Just the four maws, that was all. He could do
that. They were large, as he'd seen. He would
find them and kill them. He was their god; now
he would be their destroyer.

He went shopping before he flew back to his
home. He bought a set of skinthins that would
cover him from head to foot, several bags of
poison pellets for rockjock control, and a spray
canister containing an illegally strong pesticide.
He also bought a magnalock towing device.

When he landed late that afternoon, he went
about things methodically. First he hooked
Cath's skimmer to his own with the magnalock.
Searching it, he had his first piece of luck. The
crystal chip with Idi Noreddian's holo of the
sandking fight was on the front seat. He had
worried about that.

When the skimmers were ready, he slipped
into his skinthins and went inside to get Cath's
body.

It wasn't there.

He poked through the fast drying sand carefully, and there was no doubt of it, the body
was gone. Could she have dragged herself
away? Unlikely, but Kress searched. A cursory
inspection of his house turned up neither the
body nor any sign of the sandkings. He did not

have time for a more thorough investigation, not with the incriminating skimmer outside his front door. He resolved to try later.

Some seventy kilometers north of Kress's estate was a range of active volcanoes. He flew there, Cath's skimmer in tow. Above the glowering cone of the largest volcano he released the magnalock and watched the skimmer plummet down and vanish in the lava below.

It was dusk when he returned to his house. This gave him pause. Briefly he considered flying back to the city and spending the night there. He put the thought aside. There was work to do. He wasn't safe yet.

He scattered the poison pellets around the exterior of his house. No one would think this suspicious. He had always had a rockjock problem. When this task was completed, he primed the canister of pesticide and ventured back inside the house.

Kress went through the house, room by room, turning on lights everywhere he went until he was surrounded by a blaze of artificial illumination. He paused to clean up in the living room, shoveling sand and plastic fragments back into the broken tank. The sandkings were all gone, as he'd feared. The castles were shrunken and distorted, slagged by the watery bombardment Kress had visited upon them, and what little of them remained was crumbling as it dried.

He frowned and searched further, the canister of pest spray strapped across his shoulders.

Down in the wine cellar he could see Cath m'Lane's corpse.

It sprawled at the foot of a steep flight of stairs, the limbs twisted as if by a fall. White mobiles were swarming all over it, and as Kress watched, the body moved jerkily across the hard-packed dirt floor.

He laughed and twisted the illumination up to maximum. In the far corner a squat little earthen castle and a dark hole were visible between two wine racks. Kress could make out a rough outline of his face on the cellar wall.

The body shifted once again, moving a few centimeters toward the castle. Kress had a sudden vision of the white maw waiting hungrily. It might be able to get Cath's foot in its mouth, but no more. It was too absurd. He laughed again and stared down into the cellar, finger poised on the trigger of the hose that snaked down his right arm. The sandkings—hundreds of them moving as one—deserted the body and assumed battle formation, a field of white between him and their maw.

Suddenly Kress had another inspiration. He smiled and lowered his firing hand. "Cath was always hard to swallow," he said, delighted at his wit. "Especially for one your size. Here, let me give you some help. What are gods for, after all?"

He retreated upstairs, returning shortly with a cleaver. The sandkings, patient, waited and watched while Kress chopped Cath m'Lane into small, easily digestible pieces.

* * *

Kress slept in his skinthins that night, the pesticide close at hand, but he did not need it. The whites, sated, remained in the cellar, and he saw no sign of the others.

In the morning he finished the cleanup of the living room. When he was through, no trace of the struggle remained except for the broken tank.

He ate a light lunch and resumed his hunt for the missing sandkings. In full daylight it was not too difficult. The blacks had located in his rock garden, where they built a castle heavy with obsidian and quartz. The reds he found at the bottom of his long-disused swimming pool, which had partially filled with wind-blown sand over the years. He saw mobiles of both colors ranging about his grounds, many of them carrying poison pellets back to their maws. Kress felt like laughing. He decided his pesticide was unnecessary. No use risking a fight when he could just let the poison do its work. Both maws should be dead by evening.

That left only the burnt-orange sandkings unaccounted for. Kress circled his estate several times, in an ever-widening spiral, but he found no trace of them. When he began to sweat in his skinthings—it was a hot, dry day—he decided it was not important. If they were out here, they were probably eating the poison pellets, as the reds and blacks were.

He crunched several sandkings underfoot, with a certain degree of satisfaction, as he walked back to the house. Inside, he removed his skinthins, settled down to a delicious meal, and finally began to relax. Everything was under control. Two of the maws would soon be defunct, the third was safely located where he could dispose of it after it had served his purposes, and he had no doubt that he would find the fourth. As for Cath, every trace of her visit had been obliterated.

His reverie was interrupted when his view-screen began to blink at him. It was Jad Rakkis, calling to brag about some cannibal worms he would bring to the war games tonight.

Kress had forgotten about that, but he recovered quickly. "Oh, Jad, my pardons. I neglected to tell you. I grew bored with all that and got rid of the sandkings. Ugly little things. Sorry, but there'll be no party tonight."

Rakkis was indignant. "But what will I do with my worms?"

"Put them in a basket of fruit and send them to a loved one," Kress said, signing off. Quickly he began calling the others. He did not need anyone arriving at his doorstep now, with the sandkings alive and infesting the estate.

As he was calling Idi Noreddian, Kress became aware of an annoying oversight. The screen began to clear, indicating that someone had answered at the other end. Kress flicked off.

Idi arrived on schedule an hour later. She was surprised to find the party had been canceled but perfectly happy to share an evening alone with Kress. He delighted her with his story of Cath's reaction to the holo they had made together. While telling it, he managed to ascertain that she had not mentioned the prank to anyone. He nodded, satisfied, and refilled their wine glasses. Only a trickle was left. "I'll have to get a fresh bottle," he said. "Come with me to my wine cellar, and help me pick out a good vintage. You've always had a better palate than I."

She went along willingly enough but balked at the top of the stairs when Kress opened the door and gestured for her to precede him. "Where are the lights?" she asked. "And that smell—what's that peculiar smell, Simon?"

When he shoved her, she looked briefly startled. She screamed as she tumbled down the stairs. Kress closed the door and began to nail it shut with the boards and air hammer he had left for that purpose. As he was finishing, he heard Idi groan. "I'm hurt," she called. "Simon, what is this?" Suddenly she squealed, and shortly after that the screaming started.

It did not cease for hours. Kress went to his sensorium and dialed up a saucy comedy to blot it from his mind.

When he was sure she was dead, Kress flew her skimmer north to the volcanoes and discarded it. The magnalock was proving a good investment.

Odd scrabbling noises were coming from beyond the wine-cellar door the next morning when Kress went down to check things out. He listened for several uneasy moments, wondering whether Idi might possibly have survived and was scratching to get out. This seemed unlikely; it had to be the sandkings. Kress did not like the implications of this. He decided that he would keep the door sealed, at least for a while. He went outside with a shovel to bury the red and black maws in their own castles.

He found them very much alive.

The black castle was glittering with volcanic glass, and sandkings were all over it, repairing and improving. The higher tower was up to his waist, and on it was a hideous caricature of his face. When he approached, the blacks halted in their labors and formed up into two threatening phalanxes. Kress glanced behind him and saw others closing off his escape. Startled, he dropped his shovel and sprinted out of the trap, crushing several mobiles beneath his boots.

The red castle was creeping up the walls of the swimming pool. The maw was safely settled in a pit, surrounded by sand and concrete and battlements. The reds crept all over the bottom of the pool. Kress watched them carry a rock-jock and a large lizard into the castle. Horrified, he stepped back from the poolside and felt something crunch. Looking down, he saw three mobiles climbing up his leg. He brushed them off and stamped them to death, but others were approaching rapidly. they were larger than he remembered. Some were almost as big as his thumb.

He ran.

By the time he reached the safety of the house, his heart was racing and he was short of breath. He closed the door behind him and hurried to lock it. His house was supposed to be pestproof. He'd be safe in here.

A stiff drink steadied his nerves. So *poison doesn't faze them,* he thought. He should have known. Jala Wo had warned him that the maw could eat anything. He would have to use the pesticide. He took another drink for good measure, donned his skinthins, and strapped the canister to his back. He unlocked the door.

Outside, the sandkings were waiting.

Two armies confronted him, allied against the common threat. More than he could have guessed. The damned maws must be breeding like rockjocks. Mobiles were everywhere, a creeping sea of them.

Kress brought up the hose and flicked the trigger. A gray mist washed over the nearest rank of sandkings. He moved his hand from side to side.

Where the mist fell, the sandkings twitched violently and died in sudden spasms. Kress smiled. They were no match for him. He sprayed in a wide arc before him and stepped forward confidently over a litter of black and red bodies. The armies fell back. Kress advanced, intent on cutting through them to their maws.

All at once the retreat stopped. A thousand sandkings surged toward him.

Kress had been expecting the counterattack. He stood his ground, sweeping his misty sword before him in great looping strokes. They came at him and died. A few got through; he could not spray everywhere at once. He felt them climbing up his legs, then sensed their mandibles biting futilely at the reinforced plastic of his skinthins. He ignored them and kept spraying.

Then he began to feel the soft impacts on his head and shoulders.

Kress trembled and spun and looked up above him. The front of his house was alive with sandkings. Blacks and reds, hundreds of them. They were launching themselves into the air, raining down on him. They fell all around him. One landed on his faceplate, its mandibles scraping at his eyes for a terrible second before he plucked it away.

He swung up his hose and sprayed the air, sprayed the house, sprayed until the airborne sandkings were all dead or dying. The mist settled back on him, making him cough. But he kept spraying. Only when the front of the house was clean did Kress turn his attention back to the ground.

They were all around him, in him, dozens of them scurrying over his body, hundreds of others hurrying to join them. He turned the mist on them. The hose went dead. Kress heard a loud *hiss,* and the deadly fog rose in a great cloud from between his shoulders, cloaking him, choking him, making his eyes burn and blur. He felt for the hose, and his hand came away covered with dying sandkings. The hose was severed; they'd eaten it through. He was surrounded by a shroud of pesticide, blinded. He stumbled and screamed and began to run back to the house, pulling sandkings from his body as he went.

Inside, he sealed the door and collapsed on the carpet, rolling back and forth until he was sure he had crushed them all. The canister was empty by then, hissing feebly. Kress stripped off his skinthins and showered. The hot spray scalded him and left his skin reddened and sensitive, but it made his flesh stop crawling.

He dressed in his heaviest clothing, thick work plans and leathers, after shaking them out nervously. "Damn," he kept muttering, "damn." His throat was dry. After searching the entry hall thoroughly to make certain it was clean, he allowed himself to sit and pour a drink. "Damn," he repeated. His hand shook as he poured, slopping liquor on the carpet.

The alcohol settled him, but it did not wash away the fear. He had a second drink and went to the window furtively. Sandkings were moving across the thick plastic pane. He shuddered and retreated to his communications console. He had to get help, he thought wildly. He would punch through a call to the authorities, and policers would come out with flamethrowers, and . . .

Kress stopped in mid-call and groaned. He couldn't call in the police. He would have to tell them about the whites in his cellar, and they'd find the bodies there. Perhaps the maw might have finished Cath m'Lane by now, but certainly not Idi Noreddian. He hadn't even cut her up. Besides, there would be bones. No, the police could be called in only as a last resort.

He sat at the console, frowning. His communications equipment filled a whole wall. From here he could reach anyone on Baldur. He had plenty of money and his cunning; he had always prided himself on his cunning. He would handle this somehow.

Briefly he considered calling Wo, but he soon dismissed the idea. Wo knew too much, and she would ask questions, and he did not trust her. No, he needed someone who would do as he asked *without* questions.

His frown slowly turned into a smile. Kress had contacts. He put through a call to a number he had not used in a long time.

A woman's face took shape on his viewscreen—white-haired, blank of expression, with a long, hooked nose. Her voice was brisk and efficient. "Simon," she said. "How is business?"

"Business is fine, Lissandra," Kress replied. "I have a job for you."

"A removal? My price has gone up since last time. Simon. It has been ten years, after all."

"You will be well paid," Kress said. "You know I'm generous. I want you for a bit of pest control."

She smiled a thin smile. "No need to use euphemisms, Simon. The call is shielded."

"No, I'm serious. I have a pest problem. Dangerous pests. Take care of them for me. No questions. Understood?"

"Understood."

"Good. You'll need . . . oh, three to four operatives. Wear heat-resistant skinthins, and

equip them with flamethrowers, or lasers, something on that order. Come out to my place.
You'll see the problem. Bugs, lots and lots of
them. In my rock garden and the old swimming
pool you'll find castles. Destroy them, kill everything inside them. Then knock on the door, and
I'll show you what else needs to be done. Can
you get out here quickly?''

Her face remained impassive. ''We'll leave
within the hour.''

Lissandra was true to her word. She arrived
in a lean, black skimmer with three operatives.
Kress watched them from the safety of a
second-story window. They were all faceless in
dark plastic skinthins. Two of them wore
portable flamethrowers; a third carried
lasercannon and explosives. Lissandra carried
nothing; Kress recognized her by the way she
gave orders.

Their skimmer passed low overhead first,
checking out the situation. The sandkings went
mad. Scarlet and ebon mobiles ran everywhere,
frenetic. Kress could see the castle in the rock
garden from his vantage point. It sood tall as a
man. Its ramparts were crawling with black
defenders, and a steady stream of mobiles
flowed down into its depths.

Lissandra's skimmer came down next to
Kress's, and the operatives vaulted out and
unlimbered their weapons. They looked
inhuman, deadly.

The black army drew up between them and
the castle. The reds—Kress suddenly realized

that he could not see the reds. He blinked. Where had they gone?

Lissandra pointed and shouted, and her two flamethrowers spread out and opened up on the black sandkings. Their weapons coughed dully and began to roar, long tongues of blue-and-scarlet fire licking out before them. Sandkings crisped and shriveled and died. The operatives began to play the fire back and forth in an efficient, interlocking pattern. They advanced with careful, measured steps.

The black army burned and disintegrated, the mobiles fleeing in a thousand different directions, some back toward the castle, others toward the enemy. None reached the operatives with the flamethrowers. Lissandra's people were very professional.

Then one of them stumbled.

Or seemed to stumble. Kress looked again and saw that the ground had given way beneath the man. Tunnels, he thought with a tremor of fear; tunnels, pits, traps. The flamer was sunk in sand up to his waist, and suddenly the ground around him seemed to erupt, and he was covered with scarlet sandkings. He dropped the flamethrower and began to claw wildly at his own body. His screams were horrible to hear.

His companion hesitated, then swung and fired. A blast of flame swallowed human and sandkings both. The screaming stopped abruptly. Satisfied, the second flamer turned back to the castle, took another step forward, and recoiled as his foot broke through the ground and vanished up to the ankle. He tried to pull it back and retreat, and the sand all around him gave way. He lost his balance and stumbled, flailing, and the sandkings were everywhere, a boiling mass of them, covering him as he writhed and rolled. His flamethrower was useless and forgotten.

Kress pounded wildly on the window, shouting for attention. "The castle! Get the castle!"

Lissandra, standing back by her skimmer, heard and gestured. Her third operative sighted with the lasercannon and fired. The beam throbbed across the grounds and sliced off the top of the castle. He brought the cannon down sharply, hacking at the sand and stone parapets. Towers fell. Kress's face disintegrated. The laser bit into the ground, searching round and about. The castle crumbled. Now it was only a heap of sand. But the black mobiles continued to move. The maw was buried too deeply. The beams hadn't touched it.

Lissandra gave another order. Her operative discarded the laser, primed an explosive, and darted forward. He leaped over the smoking corpse of the first flamer, landed on solid ground within Kress's rock garden, and heaved. The explosive ball landed square atop the ruins of the black castle. White-hot light seared Kress's eyes, and there was a tremendous gout of sand and rock and mobiles. For a moment dust obscured everything. It was raining sandkings and pieces of sandkings.

Kress saw that the black mobiles were dead and unmoving.

"The pool!" he shouted down through the window. "Get the castle in the pool!"

Lissandra understood quickly; the ground was littered with motionless blacks, but the reds were pulling back hurriedly and re-forming. Her operative stood uncertain, then reached down and pulled out another explosive ball. He took one step forward, but Lissandra called him, and he sprinted back in her direction.

It was all so simple then. He reached the skimmer, and Lissandra took him aloft. Kress rushed to another window in another room to watch. They came swooping in just over the pool, and the operative pitched his bombs down at the red castle from the safety of the skimmer. After the fourth run, the castle was unrecognizable, and the sandkings stopped moving.

Lissandra was thorough. She had him bomb each castle several additional times. Then he used the lasercannon, crisscrossing methodically until it was certain that nothing living could remain intact beneath those small patches of ground.

Finally they came knocking at his door. Kress was grinning maniacally when he let them in. "Lovely," he said, "lovely."

Lissandra pulled off the mask of her skinthins. "This will cost you, Simon. Two operatives gone, not to mention the danger to my own life."

"Of course," Kress blurted. "You'll be well paid, Lissandra. Whatever you ask, just so you finish the job."

"What remains to be done?"

"You have to clean out my wine cellar," Kress said. "There's another castle down there. And you have to do it without explosives. I don't want my house coming down around me."

Lissandra motioned to her operative. "Go outside and get Rajk's flamethrower. It should be intact."

He returned armed, ready, silent. Kress led them to the wine cellar.

The heavy door was still nailed shut, as he had left it. But it bulged outward slightly, as if warped by some tremendous pressure. That made Kress uneasy, as did the silence that reigned about them. He stood well away from the door while Lissandra's operative removed his nails and planks. "Is that safe in here?" he found himself muttering, pointing at the flame-thrower. "I don't want a fire, either, you know."

"I have the laser," Lissandra said. "We'll use that for the kill. The flamethrower probably won't be needed. But I want it here just in case. There are worse things than fire, Simon."

He nodded.

The last plank came free of the cellar door. There was still no sound from below. Lissandra snapped an order, and her underling fell back, took up a position behind her, and leveled the flamethrower squarely at the door. She slipped her mask back on, hefted the laser, stepped forward, and pulled the door open.

No motion. No sound. It was dark down there.

"Is there a light?" Lissandra asked.

"Just inside the door," Kress said, "On the right-hand side. Mind the stairs. They're quite steep."

She stepped into the doorway, shifted the laser to her left hand, and reached up with her right, fumbling inside for the light panel. Nothing happened. "I feel it," Lissandra said, "but it doesn't seem to . . ."

Then she was screaming, and she stumbled backward. A great white sandking had clamped itself around her wrist. Blood welled through her skinthins where its mandibles had sunk in. It was fully as large as her hand.

Lissandra did a horrible little jig across the room and began to smash her hand against the nearest wall. Again and again and again. It landed with a heavy, meaty thud. Finally the sandking fell away. She whimpered and fell to her knees.

"I think my fingers are broken," she said softly. The blood was still flowing freely. She had dropped the laser near the cellar door.

"I'm not going down there," her operative announced in clear, firm tones.

Lissandra looked up at him. "No," she said. "Stand in the door and flame it all. Cinder it. Do you understand?"

He nodded.

Kress moaned. "My *house*," he said. His stomach churned. The white sandking had been so *large*. How many more were down there? "Don't," he continued. "Leave it alone. I've changed my mind."

Lissandra misunderstood. She held out her hand. It was covered with blood and greenish-black ichor. "Your little friend bit clean through my glove, and you saw what it took to get it off. I don't care about your house, Simon. Whatever is down there is going to die."

Kress hardly heard her. He thought he could see movement in the shadows beyond the cellar door. He imagined a white army bursting out, each soldier as big as the sandking that had attacked Lissandra. He saw himself being lifted by a hundred tiny arms and being dragged down into the darkness, where the maw waited hungrily. He was afraid. "Don't," he said.

They ignored him.

Kress darted forward, and his shoulder slammed into the back of Lissandra's operative just as the man was bracing to fire. The operative grunted, lost his balance, and pitched forward into the black. Kress listened to him fall down the stairs. Afterwards there were other noises—scuttlings and snaps and soft, squishing sounds.

Kress swung around to face Lissandra. He was drenched in cold sweat, but a sickly kind of excitement possessed him. It was almost sexual.

Lissandra's calm, cold eyes regarded him through her mask. "What are you doing?" she demanded as Kress picked up the laser she had dropped. *"Simon!"*

"Making a peace," he said, giggling. "They won't hurt god, no, not so long as god is good and generous. I was cruel. Starved them. I have to make up for it now, you see."

"You're insane," Lissandra said. It was the last thing she said. Kress burned a hole in her chest big enough to put his arm through. He drapped the body across the floor and rolled it down the cellar stairs. The noises were louder—chitinous clackings and scrapings and echoes that were thick and liquid. Kress nailed up the door once again.

As he fled, he was filled with a deep sense of contentment that coated his fear like a layer of syrup. He suspected it was not his own.

He planned to leave his home, to fly to the city and take a room for a night, or perhaps for a year. Instead he started drinking. He was not quite sure why. He drank steadily for hours and retched it all up violently on his living-room carpet. At some point he fell asleep. When he woke, it was pitch-dark in the house.

He cowered against the couch. He could hear *noises*. Things were moving in the walls. They were all around him. His hearing was extraordinarily acute. Every little creak was the footstep of a sandking. He closed his eyes and waited, expecting to feel their terrible touch, afraid to move lest he brush against one.

Kress sobbed and then was very still.

Time passed, but nothing happened.

He opened his eyes again. He trembled. Slowly the shadows began to soften and dissolve. Moonlight was filtering through the high windows. His eyes adjusted.

The living room was empty. Nothing there, nothing, nothing. Only his drunken fears.

Kress steeled himself and rose and went to a light.

Nothing there. The room was deserted.

He listened. Nothing. No sound. Nothing in the walls. It had all been his imagination, his fear.

The memories of Lissandra and the thing in the cellar returned to him unbidden. Shame and anger washed over him. Why had he done that? He could have helped her burn it out, kill it. *Why* . . . he knew why. The maw had done it to him, had put fear in him. Wo had said it was psionic, even when it was small. And now it was large, so large. It had feasted on Cath and Idi, and now it had two more bodies down there. It would keep growing. And it had learned to like the taste of human flesh, he thought.

He began to shake, but he took control of himself again and stopped. It wouldn't hurt him; he was god; the whites had always been his favorites.

He remembered how he had stabbed it with his throwing sword. That was before Cath came. Damn her, anyway.

He couldn't stay here. The maw would grow hungry again. Large as it was, it wouldn't take long. Its appetite would be terrible. What would it do then? He had to get away, back to the safety of the city while the maw was still contained in his wine cellar. It was only plaster and hard-packed earth down there, and the mobiles could dig and tunnel. When they got free . . . Kress didn't want to think about it.

He went to his bedroom and packed. He took three bags. Just a single change of clothing, that was all he needed; the rest of the space he filled with his valuables, with jewelry and art and other things he could not bear to lose. He did not expect to return to this place ever again.

His shambler followed him down the stairs, staring at him from its baleful, glowing eyes. It was gaunt. Kress realized that it had been ages since he had fed it. Normally it could take care of itself, but no doubt the pickings had grown lean of late. When it tried to clutch at his leg, he snarled at it and kicked it away, and it scurried off, obviously hurt and offended.

Carrying his bags awkwardly, Kress slipped outside and shut the door behind him.

For a moment he stood pressed against the house, his heart thudding in his chest. Only a few meters between him and his skimmer. He was afraid to take those few steps. The moonlight was bright, and the grounds in front of his house were a scene of carnage. The bodies of Lissandra's two flamers lay where they had fallen, one twisted and burned, the other swollen beneath a mass of dead sandkings. And the mobiles, the black and red mobiles, they were all around him. It took an effort to remember that they were dead. It was almost as if they were simply waiting, as they had waited so often before.

Nonsense, Kress told himself. More drunken fears. He had seen the castles blown apart. They were dead, and the white maw was trapped in his cellar. He took several deep and deliberate breaths and stepped forward onto the sandkings. They crunched. He ground them into the sand savagely. They did not move.

Kress smiled and walked slowly across the battleground, listening to the sounds, the sounds of safety.

Crunch, crackle, crunch.

He lowered his bags to the ground and opened the door to his skimmer.

Something moved from shadow into light. A pale shape on the seat of his skimmer. It was as long as his forearm. Its mandibles clacked together softly, and it looked up at him from six small eyes set all around its body.

Kress wet his pants and backed away slowly.

There was more motion from inside the skimmer. He had left the door open. The sandking emerged and came toward him, cautiously. Others followed. They had been hiding beneath his seats, burrowed into the unholstery. But now they emerged. They formed a ragged ring around the skimmer.

Kress licked his lips, turned, and moved quickly to Lissandra's skimmer.

He stopped before he was halfway there. Things were moving inside that one, too. Great maggoty things half-seen by the light of the moon.

Kress whimpered and retreated back toward the house. Near the front door, he looked up.

He counted a dozen long, white shapes, creeping back and forth across the walls of the building. Four of them were clustered close together near the top of the unused belfry, where the carrion hawk had once roosted. They were carving something. A face. A very recognizable face.

Kress shrieked and ran back inside. He headed for his liquor cabinet.

A sufficient quantity of drink brought him the easy oblivion he sought. But he woke. Despite everything, he woke. He had a terrific headache, and he stank, and he was hungry. Oh, so very hungry! He had never been so hungry.

Kress knew it was not his *own* stomach hurting.

A white sandking watched him from atop the dresser in his bedroom, its antennae moving faintly. It was as big as the one in the skimmer the night before. He tried not to shrink away. "I'll . . . I'll feed you," he said to it. "I'll feed you." His mouth was horribly dry, sandpaper-dry. He licked his lips and fled from the room.

The house was full of sandkings; he had to be

careful where he put his feet. They all seemed busy on errands of their own. They were making modifications in his house, burrowing into or out of his walls, carving things. Twice he saw his own likeness staring out at him from unexpected places. The faces were warped, twisted, livid with fear.

He went outside to get the bodies that had been rotting in the yard, hoping to appease the white maw's hunger. They were gone, both of them, Kress remembered how easily the mobiles could carry things many times their own weight.

It was terrible to think that the maw was *still* hungry after all of that.

When Kress reentered the house, a column of sandkings was wending its way down the stairs. Each carried a piece of his shambler. The head seemed to look at him reproachfully as it went by.

Kress emptied his freezers, his cabinets, everything, piling all the food in the house in the center of his kitchen floor. A dozen whites waited to take it away. They avoided the frozen food, leaving it to thaw in a great puddle, but carried off everything else.

When all the food was gone, Kress felt his own hunger pangs abate just a bit, though he had not eaten a thing. But he knew the respite would be short-lived. Soon the maw would be hungry again. He had to feed it.

Kress knew what to do. He went to his communicator. "Malada," he began casually when the first of his friends answered. "I'm having a small party tonight. I realize this is terribly short notice, but I hope you can make it. I really do.''

He called Jad Rakkis next, and then the others. By the time he had finished, five of them had accepted his invitation. Kress hoped that would be enough.

Kress met his guests outside—the mobiles had cleaned up remarkably quickly, and the grounds looked almost as they had before the battle—and walked them to his front door. He let them enter first. He did not follow.

When four of them had gone through, Kress finally worked up his courage. He closed the door behind his latest guest, ignoring the startled exclamations that soon turned into shrill gibbering, and sprinted for the skimmer the man had arrived in. He slid in safely, thumbed the startplate, and swore. It was programmed to lift only in response to its owner's thumbprint, of course.

Rakkis was the next to arrive. Kresser ran to his skimmer as it set down and seized Rakkis by the arm as he was climbing out. ''Get back in, quickly,'' he said, pushing. ''Take me to the city. Hurry, Jad. *Get out of here!*''

But Rakkis only stared at him and would not move. ''Why, what's wrong, Simon? I don't understand. What about your party?''

And then it was too late, because the loose sand all around them was stirring, and the red eyes were staring at them, and the mandibles were clacking. Rakkis made a choking sound and moved to get back in his skimmer, but a pair of mandibles snapped shut about his ankle, and suddenly he was on his knees. The sand seemed to boil with subterranean activity. Rakkis thrashed and cried terribly as they tore him apart. Kress could hardly bear to watch.

After that, he did not try to escape again. When it was all over, he cleaned out what remained in his liquor cabinet and got extremely drunk. It would be the last time he would enjoy that luxury, he knew. The only alcohol remaining in the house was stored down in the wine cellar.

Kress did not touch a bite of food the entire day, but he fell asleep feeling bloated, sated at last, the awful hunger vanquished. His last thoughts before the nightmares took him were about whom he could ask out tomorrow.

Morning was hot and dry. Kress opened his eyes to see the white sandking on his dresser again. He shut his eyes again quickly, hoping the dream would leave him. It did not, and he could not go back to sleep, and soon he found himself staring at the thing.

He stared for almost five minutes before the strangeness of it dawned on him; the sandking was not moving.

The mobiles could be preternaturally still, to be sure. He had seen them wait and watch a thousand times. But always there was some motion about them: The mandibles clacked, the legs twitched, the long, fine antennae stirred and swayed.

But the sandking on his dresser was completely still.

Kress rose, holding his breath, not daring to hope. Could it be dead? Could something have killed it? He walked across the room.

The eyes were glassy and black. The creature seemed swollen, somehow, as if it were soft and rotting inside, filling up with gas that pushed outward at the plates of white armor.

Kress reached out trembling hand and touched it.

It was warm; hot even, and growing hotter. But it did not move.

He pulled his hand back, and as he did, a segment of the sandking's white exoskeleton fell away from it. The flesh beneath was the same color, but soft-looking, swollen and feverish. And it almost seemed to throb.

Kress backed away and ran to the door.

Three more white mobiles lay in his hall. They were all like the one in his bedroom.

He ran down the stairs, jumping over sandkings. None of them moved. The house was full of them, all dead, dying, comatose, whatever. Kress did not care what was wrong with them. Just so they could not move.

He found four of them inside his skimmer. He picked them up, one by one, and threw them as far as he could. Damned monsters. He slid back in, on the ruined half-eaten seats, and thumbed the startplate.

Nothing happened.

Kress tried again and again. Nothing. It wasn't fair. This was *his* skimmer. It ought to start. Why wouldn't it lift? He didn't understand.

Finally he got out and checked, expecting the worst. He found it. The sandkings had torn apart his gravity grid. He was trapped. He was still trapped.

Grimly Kress marched back into the house. He went to his gallery and found the antique ax that had hung next to the throwing sword he had used on Cath m'Lane. He set to work. The sandkings did not stir even as he chopped them to pieces. But they splattered when he made the first cut, the bodies almost bursting. Inside was awful; strange half-formed organs, a viscous reddish ooze that looked almost like human blood, and the yellow ichor.

Kress destroyed twenty of them before he realized the futility of what he was doing. The mobiles were nothing, really. Besides, there were so *many* of them. He could work for a day and night and still not kill them all.

He had to go down into the wine cellar and use the ax on the maw.

Resolute, he started toward the cellar. He got within sight of the door, then stopped.

It was not a door anymore. The walls had been eaten away, so that the hole was twice the size it had been, and round. A pit, that was all.

There was no sign that there had ever been a door nailed shut over that black abyss.

A ghastly, choking, fetid odor seemed to come from below.

And the walls were wet and bloody and covered with patches of white fungus.

And worst, it was *breathing*.

Kress stood across the room and felt the warm wind wash over him as it exhaled, and he tried not to choke, and when the wind reversed direction, he fled.

Back in the living room he destroyed three more mobiles and collapsed. What was *happening?* He didn't understand.

Then he remembered the only person who might understand. Kress went to his communicator again, stepped on a sandking in his haste, and prayed fervently that the device still worked.

When Jala Wo answered, he broke down and told her everything.

She let him talk without interruption, no expression save for a slight frown on her gaunt, pale face. When Kress had finished, she said only, "I ought to leave you there."

Kress began to blubber. "You can't. Help me, I'll pay—"

"I ought to," Wo repeated, "but I won't."

"Thank you," Kress said. "Oh, thank—"

"Quiet," said Wo. "Listen to me. This is your own doing. Keep your sandkings well, and they are courtly ritual warriors. You turned yours into something else, with starvation and torture. You were their god. You made them what they are. That maw in your cellar is sick, still suffering from the wound you gave it. It is probably insane. Its behavior is . . . unusual.

"You have to get out of there quickly. The mobiles are not dead, Kress. They are dormant. I told you the exoskeleton falls off when they grow larger. Normally, in fact, it falls off much earlier. I have never heard of sandkings growing as large as yours while still in the insectoid stage. It is another result of crippling the white maw, I would say. That does not matter.

"What matters is the metamorphosis your sandkings are now undergoing. As the maw grows, you see, it gets progressively more intelligent. Its psionic powers strengthen, and its mind becomes more sophisticated, more ambitious. The armored mobiles are useful enough when the maw is tiny and only semisentient, but now it needs better servants, bodies with more capabilities. Do you understand? The mobiles are all going to give birth to a new breed of sandking. I can't say exactly what it will look like. Each maw designs its own, to fit its perceived needs and desires. But it will be biped, with four arms and opposable thumbs. It will be able to construct and operate advanced machinery. The individual sandkings will not be sentient. But the maw will be very sentient indeed."

Kress was gaping at Wo's image on the viewscreen. "Your workers," he said, with an effort. "The ones who came out here . . . who installed the tank . . ."

Wo managed a faint smile. "Shade," she said.

"Shade is a sandking," Kress repeated numbly. "And you sold me a tank of . . . of . . . infants, ah . . ."

"Do not be absurd," Wo said. "A first-stage sandking is more like a sperm than like an infant. The wars temper and control them in nature. Only one in a hundred reaches the second stage. Only one in a thousand achieves the third and final plateau and becomes like Shade. Adult sandkings are not sentimental about the small maws. There are too many of them, and their mobiles are pests." She sighed.

"And all this talk wastes time. That white sandking is going to waken to full sentience soon. It is not going to need you any longer, and it hates you, and it will be very hungry. The transformation is taxing. The maw must eat enormous amounts both before and after. So you have to get out of there. Do you understand?"

"I *can't,*" Kress said. "My skimmer is destroyed, and I can't get any of the others to start. I don't know how to reprogram them. Can you come out for me?"

"Yes," said Wo. "Shade and I will leave at once, but it is more than two hundred kilometers from Asgard to you, and there is equipment that we will need to deal with the deranged sandking you've created. You cannot wait there. You have two feet. Walk. Go due east, as near as you can determine, as quickly as you can. The land out there is pretty desolate. We can find you easily with an aerial search, and you'll be safely away from the sandkings. Do you understand?''

"Yes," Kress said. "Yes, oh yes."

They signed off, and he walked quickly toward the door. He was halfway there when he heard the noise, a sound halfway between a pop and a crack.

One of the sandkings had split open. Four tiny hands covered with pinkish-yellow blood came up out of the gap and began to push the dead skin aside.

Kress began to run.

He had not counted on the heat.

The hills were dry and rocky. Kress ran from the house as quickly as he could, ran until his ribs ached and his breath was coming in gasps. Then he walked, but as soon as he had recovered, he began to run again. For almost an hour he ran and walked, ran and walked, beneath the fierce, hot sun. He sweated, freely and wished that he had thought to bring some water, and he watched the sky in hopes of seeing Wo and Shade.

He was not made for this. It was too hot and too dry, and he was in no condition. But he kept himself going with the memory of the way the maw had breathed and the thought of the wriggling little things that by now were surely crawling all over his house. He hoped Wo and Shade would know how to deal with them.

He had his own plans for Wo and Shade. It was all their fault, Kress had decided, and they would suffer for it. Lissandra was dead, but he knew others in her profession. He would have his revenge. This he promised himself a hundred times as he struggled and sweated his way eastward.

At least he hoped it was east. He was not that good at directions, and he wasn't certain which way he had run in his initial panic, but since then he had made an effort to bear due east, as Wo had suggested.

When he had been running for several hours, with no sign of rescue, Kress began to grow certain that he had miscalculated his direction.

When several more hours passed, he began to grow afraid. What if Wo and Shade could not find him? He would die out here. He hadn't eaten in two days, he was weak and frightened, his throat was raw for want of water. He couldn't keep going. The sun was sinking now, and he'd be completely lost in the dark. What was wrong? Had the sandkings eaten Wo and Shade? The fear was on him again, filling him, and with it a great thirst and a terrible hunger. But Kress kept going. He stumbled now when he tried to run, and twice he fell. The second time he scraped his hand on a rock, and it came away bloody. He sucked at it as he walked, and he worried about infection.

The sun was on the horizon behind him. The ground grew a little cooler, for which Kress was grateful. He decided to walk until last light and settle down for the night. Surely he was far enough from the sandkings to be safe, and Wo and Shade would find him come morning.

When he topped the next rise, he saw the outline of a house in front of him.

It wasn't as big as his own house, but it was big enough. It was habitation, safety. Kress shouted and began to run toward it. Food and drink, he had to have nourishment, he could taste the meal already. He was aching with hunger. He ran down the hill toward the house, waving his arms and shouting to the inhabitants. The light was almost gone now, but he could still make out a half-dozen children playing in the twilight. "Hey there," he shouted. "Help, help."

They came running toward him.

Kress stopped suddenly. "No," he said, "oh, no. Oh, no." He backpedaled, slipping on the sand, got up, and tried to run again. They caught him easily. They were ghastly little things with bulging eyes and dusky orange skin. He struggled, but it was useless. Small as they were, each of them had four arms, and Kress had only two.

They carried him toward the house. It was a sad, shabby house, built of crumbling sand, but the door was quite large, and dark, and it breathed. That was terrible, but it was not the thing that set Simon Kress to screaming. He screamed because of the others, the little orange children who came crawling out of the castle, and watched impassively as he passed.

All of them had his face.

MORE EXCITING READING
IN THE ZEBRA/OMNI SERIES

ZEBRA BRINGS YOU EXCITING BESTSELLERS
by Lewis Orde

MUNICH 10   (1300, $3.95)

They've killed her lover, and they've kidnapped her son. Now the world-famous actress is swept into a maelstrom of international intrigue and bone-chilling suspense—and the only man who can help her pursue her enemies is a complete stranger. . . .

HERITAGE   (1100, $3.75)

Beautiful innocent Leah and her two brothers were forced by the holocaust to flee their parents' home. A courageous immigrant family, each battled for love, power and their very lifeline—their HERITAGE.

THE LION'S WAY   (900, $3.75)

An all-consuming saga that spans four generations in the life of troubled and talented David, who struggles to rise above his immigrant heritage and rise to a world of glamour, fame and success!

Available wherever paperbacks are sold, or order direct from the Publisher. Send cover price plus 50¢ per copy for mailing and handling to Zebra Books, 475 Park Avenue South, New York, N.Y. 10016. DO NOT SEND CASH.

THE SURVIVALIST SERIES
by Jerry Ahern

#1: TOTAL WAR (960, $2.50)

The first in the shocking series that follows the unrelenting search for ex-CIA covert operations officer John Thomas Rourke to locate his missing family—after the button is pressed, the missiles launched and the multimegaton bombs unleashed . . .

#2: THE NIGHTMARE BEGINS (810, $2.50)

After WW III, the United States is just a memory. But ex-CIA covert operations officer Rourke hasn't forgotten his family. While hiding from the Soviet forces, he adheres to his search!

#3: THE QUEST (851, $2.50)

Not even a deadly game of intrigue within the Soviet High Command, and a highly placed traitor in the U.S. government can deter Rourke from continuing his desperate search for his family.

#4: THE DOOMSAYER (893, $2.50)

The most massive earthquake in history is only hours away, and Communist-Cuban troops, Soviet-Cuban rivalry, and a traitor in the inner circle of U.S. II block Rourke's path.

#5: THE WEB (1145, $2.50)

Blizzards rage around Rourke as he picks up the trail of his family and is forced to take shelter in a strangely quiet Tennessee valley town. But the quiet isn't going to last for long!

#6: THE SAVAGE HORDE (1243, $2.50)

Rourke's search for his wife and family gets sidetracked when he's forced to help a military unit locate a cache of eighty megaton warhead missiles. But the weapons are hidden on the New West Coast—and the only way of getting to them is by submarine!

Available wherever paperbacks are sold, or order direct from the Publisher. Send cover price plus 50¢ per copy for mailing and handling to Zebra Books, 475 Park Avenue South, New York, N.Y. 10016. DO NOT SEND CASH.